QUALITY TIME

NORMA CURTIS was born in North Wales, but now lives in London with her family. Her first novel, *Living It Up, Living It Down*, was awarded the Romantic Novelists Association New Writing Award 1994 and selected for WHS Fresh Talent in 1995. *Quality Time* is her second novel, and she is currently at work on her third.

D1147644

ALSO BY NORMA CURTIS

Living It Up, Living It Down

Norma Curtis

QUALITY TIME

HarperCollins*Publishers*

HarperCollins *Publishers*
77–85 Fulham Palace Road,
Hammersmith, London W6 8JB

A paperback original 1996
1 3 5 7 9 8 6 4 2

ISBN 0 00 649025 5

Set in Postscript Galliard by
Rowland Phototypesetting Ltd,
Bury St Edmunds, Suffolk

Printed and bound in Great Britain by
Caledonian International Book Manufacturing Ltd,
Glasgow

To Elaine
And for Joe, with love

One's sorrow, two's mirth,
Three's a wedding, four's a birth
Five's a christening, six a dearth.
Seven's heaven, eight is hell,
And nine's the devil his ane sel'.

(Old Scots Rhyme)

PART ONE

One's Sorrow

1

In the egg a charred soldier leaned helplessly, dripping yolk.

Megan stood in the kitchen doorway with a white towel round her shoulders and her wet blonde hair plastered to her head, staring at the debris. She watched the small yellow globules pool on the tablecloth as she towel-dried her hair absently. On a Monday morning, faced with work or an eggy cloth, work won hands down.

'If the kitchen is the heart of the home,' she said, 'how come ours always looks as if it's suffering cardiac arrest?'

Ruth, the nanny, looked up from her egg and flicked her fair hair out of her eyes. Bill, almost four, looked up too, just for a moment, and then went back to playing with his banana skin.

Megan stared at him and adjusted the tie belt of her white bathrobe. Banana skins, she thought . . . it might be some sign of latent creativity . . . on the other hand, there was the oxidised banana on the tablecloth to consider. Who needed a creative child anyway? 'Bill – in the bin,' she said. 'Any coffee left, Ruth?'

Ruth sighed and Megan felt the full force of the nanny's reproachful dark eyes. Ruth had met the nanny of somebody from *The Bill* and didn't let them forget she could aspire to greater things. 'These eggs aren't free-range,' Ruth said, touching the toasted soldier gingerly. 'And there's a speck of blood in mine. It's a foetus.'

Megan was reaching out to feel the pot, and, distracted, she

3

burned her palm on the silver. She shook her hand violently and the pain made her irritable. Mornings made her irritable. Irrational people made her irritable. It was going to be a good day. 'What do you think eggs are? They're unborn chicks,' she said bluntly.

Ruth looked at her with eyes that had changed from hurt to incredulous. 'No, they're not. Not until they're fertilised. And this one is.'

Megan reached for a tea-towel and wrapped it around the handle of the coffee pot. It had a serious design flaw in that every time it was filled with hot liquid the handle became too hot to touch. 'Well they must be free-range,' she said. 'Otherwise how would a battery hen manage to find a partner? Or should I say a cock?' She was pleased with the pun. It was quite early in the day for the sense of humour to come into play. 'Get it?' she asked, glancing at Ruth as she poured herself a cup.

Ruth seemed not to have heard. She was delicately taking the soldier out of the egg and laying it on her blue striped plate. With her knife she pointed to a blob of mucus. 'Look. A potential life.'

Megan put the pot down and leaned over her. Sure enough, she could see a small speck of blood, about the size of a pin-head, embedded in the albumen on the toast. 'You're right,' she said, to show some solidarity, but as she looked at it she began to wonder if in fact it was nothing more than a burned crumb. 'Give me the knife,' she said. 'I didn't read James Herriot for nothing.'

Ruth looked at her suspiciously, very touchy about her York-shire roots. She handed it over and Megan touched the dark speck with the tip of the blade. It seemed to attach itself to the steel for a moment, stretching viscously between toast and knife-edge before snapping back into an opaque blob. Megan shook the knife, picked up the toast and flung it into the bin, disguising a shudder. 'There,' she said brightly. 'Shall I put another one on for you?'

'I'm never eating an egg ever again,' Ruth said with a fastidious shiver. She put her knife down. 'It's disgusting. The whole concept of eggs is disgusting.'

'You shouldn't look so closely at things,' Megan said. 'You said that eating factory farmed chicken will make boys grow breasts; well I've been eating chicken far longer than Bill and –' yes, well, she supposed there was no need to labour the point. She glanced at the clock. 'I'll take my coffee up with me – I'm going to dry my hair.' She picked up her cup and turned suddenly. 'Isn't Larry down yet?'

'He's outside, opening the roof of the car.'

The convertible was Larry's new toy, a company car that had come two months previously with his new job at the advertising agency of Burgess McLane. Larry had bought them all matching Raybans to wear in it. It made them look like a family firm of gangsters. Ruth always complained it was cold in the back and she and Bill fought over the travel rug.

Megan grinned; they never showed that in the commercials. 'It's not that warm, is it?' she asked, her blue cup rattling in its saucer as she opened the outside door. She was right, it wasn't that warm. The morning air was sharp and fresh, and the sky a faded, cloudless blue. She curled her bare feet on the cold step. She could just see Larry sitting in his car, stretching towards the passenger seat, feeling for his sunglasses in the glove compartment. He straightened up and when he saw Megan he put them on and grinned at her.

'What do you think?' he called.

Megan leaned against the doorframe and sipped her coffee, looking at him over the rim of the cup. In his suit and with his short dark hair still wet from the shower, he could have been anyone: a gangster or a film star or a tycoon or a thief. A man of many roles, was Larry.

5

She'd wondered why his parents had welcomed her with such enthusiasm – could have been, of course, her looks and wit, that sort of thing, but his mother had spilled the beans over a large gin and tonic one evening. 'Megàn,' – patting her knee – 'we love you because you're sensible.'

What a reference that was. Fortunately the gin and tonic hadn't been so strong that she'd said it in front of Larry. Still, Megan had never forgiven her for making her sound more like Larry's caretaker than his wife.

She put the cup back in the saucer, and didn't smile. 'What do I think?' she said, repeating his words. 'What do you think I think?'

She watched him grin, and she grinned back, suddenly amused, partly because he was so easily pleased with her non-committal answer and partly because she could tell from the angle of the rear-view mirror that Larry wasn't only practising his grin on her but on himself also. And really, he had reason to be vain. He was good-looking and he smiled a lot, a rare combination in a man. His only obvious flaw was a scar dissecting his eyebrow which he complained looked like morse code.

A small breeze gusted, chilling her damp hair and shaking the white blossom from the tree above the drive. She gave a shiver and watched the blossom fall in his hair and flutter on the dashboard and across the leather seats. A petal floated in the coffee that was left at the bottom of her cup.

'I'd better get dressed,' she said reluctantly and as she went inside she heard the car door slam and Larry came in after her.

Ruth didn't look up. She was now concentrating on the list of ingredients on the back of a packet of rice cakes.

'Any coffee left?' Larry asked her.

No reply.

'He needs it to warm his hands on,' Megan said, to fill the gap of her silence.

6

'My hands are warm enough,' Larry said, leering and reaching for the neck of her bathrobe.

Megan swatted him and side-stepped. Ruth's presence loomed darkly and her deepening frown couldn't, could it, be blamed on the rice cakes?

'Great body swerve,' Larry said appreciatively, reaching for the pot. He, too, burned his fingers on the handle. Using a napkin to hold it, he poured himself a cup and then bent down to retrieve Bill from under the table where he was humming to himself. He still had the banana skins in his hands but they were turning black from too many battles. 'What are you up to today, little soldier?' Larry asked him over-loudly, in his speaking-to-children voice.

Bill appealed to Ruth to save him. 'Going with Zoofie,' he said, squirming out of his father's arms.

'Good man,' Larry said, giving up the struggle and putting him down.

So much for male bonding, Megan thought, watching Bill crawl under the table again. The bare pink soles of his feet stuck out from under the cloth. What was he doing under there? She ducked under the table to find out. In the dark yellow tent of the cloth he looked up at her, surprised.

She felt like a gatecrasher. 'Oh, Bill, it's nice under here,' she said encouragingly, keeping her head low. 'Is it a tent?'

'No, it's a table,' he said, and after a moment's thought he gave her a banana skin.

'Thanks.' She looked at it for a moment and resisted the urge to fling it in the bin. It felt leathery and smelled nauseatingly ripe. Bill glanced at her and apparently deciding she could be ignored, began singing again. Megan felt her knees ache against the cold floor. It was getting late and her hair was still damp. She ought to go and dry it. On the other hand, this could be one of those quality-time moments that Bill would remember all his life. Should she sing to her banana skin, too?

She couldn't quite catch Bill's tune, so, compromising, she began to hum. It was quite soothing, really. What with the smell, and the colour of the tablecloth, it was like sitting in a banana milkshake. 'Hmmm . . .'

'Shh,' Bill said disapprovingly, clapping his hand over her mouth. 'Better give me that,' he added, taking the banana skin from her.

'Right.' Obviously she'd been singing the wrong tune. She looked at her banana-coated hands, sticky and dry at the same time, and held them out in front of her. 'I'll just go and dry my hair,' she said casually, trying to make out his expression in the bilious gloom.

'Okay,' he said, without looking up.

She backed out from under the table and straightened up, blinked and saw Ruth watching her with a superior smile on her face.

Megan fingered the fine gold chain around her neck, slightly self-conscious in the light of Ruth's scrutiny. 'I suppose it's natural, isn't it, for children to go under tables?' she asked diffidently. 'Not a sign of autism or anything?'

'He wants a Wendy house. You should get him a Wendy house,' Ruth said, all knowing. 'He wouldn't go under the table if he had a Wendy house to play in.'

Ah, thought Megan; not autism but deprivation.

She could see Ruth coming to life at the thought of shopping. Shopping was Ruth's hobby; in fact, shopping with their money was her whole mission in life.

Ruth was turning the packet of rice cakes on its end, acting casual. 'I could get him one today, if you like.' She looked up, staring Megan in the eye. 'By the way, you can get organic rice cakes, you know.'

'Really?' Megan said. 'At thirty-five I need all the additives and preservatives I can get.'

Ruth had a look that said weird better than words but she didn't use it.

'They sell very good Wendy houses at John Lewis,' Ruth went on.

'Maybe for his birthday. I'll leave it to you to check them out.' Megan glanced at Larry, who was leaning over the newspaper, drawing a moustache onto the prime minister. 'Hey, I haven't read that, you know,' she said, and tried to snatch it up, but Larry hid it protectively with his forearm.

'Won't be a minute,' he said. Larry took his daily newspaper seriously. He bent over it a little longer, and finally put his rollerball down. Politics meant a lot to him. He sat back for a moment and rubbed his freshly shaven jaw. 'What our prime minister needs . . .' there was a pause, 'is a monocle,' Larry said.

When Megan came back down, Ruth had disappeared and Larry was ready to leave for work. She gave him a quick kiss and snatched a piece of toast from the toaster. Bill was standing by the kitchen door, still in his pyjamas. Suddenly he turned and looked at her. 'Work?' he asked.

'Yes, 'fraid so.'

He ran at her suddenly and held her tightly around her legs. She felt herself knocked off balance by his passion and staggered backwards. 'Bill,' she said, alarmed, 'careful!' She grabbed the table, regained her balance and stuffed the dry toast in her mouth. She knew he was creasing her skirt, knew he probably had butter around his mouth . . . she looked down at him and saw she'd dropped toast crumbs on his fair hair. 'Whoops, sorry, Bill,' she said, brushing them off. 'Come here.' She lifted him to her, feeling him blissfully heavy and warm in his soft cotton night-clothes. His clutch was painful and she hugged him hard. 'You,' she said softly into his pale hair, 'what am I going to do with you?'

Ruth came back into the kitchen in a rush, her face pale with foundation. 'I didn't notice the time,' she muttered, an apology disguised as an excuse.

Megan kissed Bill's silky hair and rested her cheek against it. 'I'd better go,' she said regretfully, and looked over at Ruth. 'Has Bill had anything to eat apart from bananas?'

Ruth glanced at the toaster. 'Actually,' she said, 'you've just eaten the toast I'd put in for him.'

'Have I? Pop another one in. Can you take Bill?'

Ruth looked irritable. 'I haven't finished in the bathroom yet,' she said. Ruth had to be placated. She had an adolescent's moodiness that at twenty she hadn't yet grown out of. It was like permanent PMT. Some day it would become post-natal depression. And some time after that, the menopause; because there wasn't such a thing as a bad-tempered woman, was there? Of course not. But she'd looked after Bill since he was a baby and he loved her and that was what counted. 'Come on, Bill,' Ruth said softly, 'let's wave Mum goodbye and then you can come upstairs with me.'

Bill released his hold on her and stretched his arms out to Ruth to be comforted while his mother left.

Megan smoothed the creases out of her jacket and watched Ruth rock him out of the corner of her eye. See? she thought, Ruth might be strange about food but she did love Bill. And Bill loved her. He looked so small that morning, Megan thought. His fair hair was fanned out at the side of his head where he'd slept on it. His eyes had little pouches underneath them. He was looking very serious.

· He took after her, which was a shame, she thought; Larry's light-heartedness was by far the easier state to be in.

'I'll see you later,' she said, picking up her handbag, or humbug, as Bill called it. She kissed the top of his head.

10

Suddenly he seemed to fall out of Ruth's arms into hers and he held her tightly, burying his face in her shirt. She gently rocked him, and avoided glancing at the clock on the wall.

'Mummy's got to go,' Ruth said calmly; the voice of reason.

Megan got the feeling the message was for her, rather than Bill. 'Yes, I've got to go,' she said regretfully, 'I'll see you this evening, have a good day.' She handed him back and kissed him, feeling his forehead cool against her lips.

Bill raised his face to hers. He had his father's deep blue eyes. The pouches under them were more apparent than ever. She touched his cheek with her finger and kissed his little mouth. 'I love you. See you later.'

He nodded, resting his hand on Ruth's neck.

Megan could feel the small hand as though it was still resting on her. She went to the door. As she looked back his blue eyes were still on her, looking at her over Ruth's shoulder as by now Ruth had turned away to put bread in the toaster again.

Bill's hand lifted briefly and rested itself on Ruth's thin t-shirt.

As Megan closed the door she just heard, too late, his quiet goodbye.

2

In a large airy apartment which overlooked one of the Thames wharves Lisa Ashridge waited for her lover by staring at the collection of photographs on the marble mantelpiece. She felt as though she'd never seen them before, which was strange, as she knew this apartment almost as well as she knew her own.

She sat on the pewter-coloured scroll sofa and with a slightly unreal feeling looked at the framed collections of laughing people, their jollity frozen in time.

There was Chrissie laughing in the sea, Chrissie laughing with John, John laughing with Freddie, Freddie, toothless and naked in his nappy, laughing alone, Chrissie laughing AT John . . . now that was slightly safer ground, Chrissie laughing at John. She had seen that one before. Or had that been real life?

Whatever, there were now definitely more pictures of the laughing Chrissie on display, many more than there had been, she was willing to swear to that.

Lisa lifted her shoulder-length dark hair up in her arms and over the top of her head and raised her head up, sensuously. Then she let her hair fall for the just-been-to-bed look.

She picked up a photograph of the laughing John and stared at the broken tooth his wife disliked so much. She imagined his dental notes. King: John. Fitting for crown.

She wiped the glass and was gratified to see a pale grey layer of dust stick to her finger. She bent down and wiped it off on the Chinese rug on which she'd lain many a lazy evening, making love while the room darkened to inky blue and the trees outside turned black.

At first she'd been resentful at it having to be the rug, but marrieds were superstitious about doing it in the double bed and the ornate iron day bed by the window was too small for two. Anyway, John had bought the rug. Had Chrissie bought the bed? she wondered. She would have to find out.

She sat forward with her elbows on her knees and studied the laughing photographs again.

She realised that she was meant to.

What the photographs were saying was: look at us, we're a happy family, we have fun together, this marriage works! Whereas before, there had been pictures of Chrissie looking moody, and of John squinting at the camera in a *Die Hard* pose.

Lisa shivered and stood up, rubbing her arms through the silk of her skirt. What the pictures were also saying was, this is goodbye. I have chosen my colours and they're not yours, Lisa. I am staying where I feel safe, where I belong, where I am happy. (See – on the mantelpiece – there's the evidence!)

'Oh,' a voice from behind her, 'I'm sorry to have kept you waiting.'

Lisa got up, turned, smiled, shrugged good-naturedly whilst also staying cool. 'I've been looking at your photographs,' she said. As good an opening line as any.

Silence. Chrissie stood a short distance away from her as if one of them had something contagious. She was looking serious but not sorry, fiddling with an earring. The silence stretched, the photographs were unexcused. No, 'Oh, I've been sorting through the albums, fancied a bit of a change.' No, 'The others got ripped up in a jealous rage, had to fill the frames somehow.'

'A picture's worth a thousand words,' Lisa said, knowing she'd guessed right and taking no pleasure in the knowledge.

'You know why?'

'No.' There was no reason to make it easy. Let it be spelled out. She was done with letting people pass the buck, and especially when they wanted to pass the buck to her. Phone-calls, even – people couldn't end them, couldn't take the responsibility of saying, as she did, 'I've finished the call and I'm off.' The next person who told her they were sure she had things to do would find out just how right they were. She raised her head and stared at Chrissie. Explain yourself, she thought. 'No, I don't know why. I thought we were having fun.'

Chrissie looked at the floor, at the Chinese carpet, and briefly at Lisa again. 'We were, but – I can't see you any more.'

'Why not?' This was a multiple choice question, a trick question, if you like. If the answer was, in case X finds out, then she might make damned sure X did. It was not unknown for her to do it. This was where men and women differed. Women always wanted the partner to find out, men never did. Safer by far to have an affair with a man. She should tell Chrissie that.

'I don't love you any more,' came the answer, breathed rather than spoken, like a long sigh of regret.

So it was as simple as that, Lisa thought.

Ah, John, you lucky man.

What could she say in reply? Impossible to make someone love you, or even love you again, the 'any more' suggesting that she had once. 'You want to stay a Howard-and-Hilda,' she said, almost without thinking.

Silence. At the end of an affair, at the very end, not during one of those can't-stay-with-you, can't-leave-you periods, but at the end when weariness or worse, revulsion takes over, the end seems such a relief. That was how it was to Chrissie, now, she thought.

Careful not to look at the laughing photographs, she picked

14

her handbag up from the sofa and walked steadily across the room, not quickly as if she was afraid, not slowly as though she was waiting for a bid to stay.

She walked through a cloud of Chrissie's scent without looking at her, and she reached the door, opened it and headed out into the shade of Tooley Street.

Out of sight of the apartment she breathed deeply, getting Chrissie's scent out of her lungs.

It might be finished, she thought.

It might be finished, but when it hurt this much it wasn't over.

Not by any means.

3

James Wilder, naked, was eating his breakfast of Sharwood's vindaloo sauce and rice. Breakfast was a recent habit. He'd gone from lean to thin, and thin, he thought, didn't suit him. His tan was yellowing slightly but with his blond hair and the surfing shorts he'd taken to wearing he could pass for late twenties easily.

And that was something to hang on to.

He heard the letterbox clatter and put his curry down on the arm of the chair on his way to see what the postman had brought him this time.

He picked up the letter from the dusty pine floor and took in the fact that it was stamped as opposed to Official Paid and that it was from Lydia, his ex-wife.

He took the A5 envelope into the lounge and propped it up against the television screen before continuing with his breakfast.

His eyes were drawn back to the envelope as he ate.

She'd written the address with her fountain pen, all black ink and flourishes. Impressive. And an improvement. Promotion, even; towards the end of their marriage she'd graced him with witty crayon-scribbled notes which said: *Your dinner's in the Asda bag, mine's at Daphne's.* She'd made him live on dinners for one – and people said it wasn't possible!

So she didn't hate him, did she, he thought, scraping the bowl. She might have told him their marriage was at an end but despite the divorce he didn't for a moment believe it. Not even now, because at the weekends when he picked up their daughters she was always stunning for him, not a hair out of place. Last week she smiled him the brightest smile he'd ever seen. She'd had her amalgam fillings replaced with white ones, told him she thought the mercury might be rotting her brain, suggested it to him with a laugh. No comment, he'd said.

He put the bowl on top of another on the floor which was nicely textured inside. In warm weather it only took four days for a pale lining of mould to grow in a bowl. And only a week for discs of green fungi to float like pallid islands in his coffee mugs.

Hard to believe that in the concrete Venus era it had taken him weeks to get fungi to grow at all. Ah, all roads led to Lydia; all the roads of his thoughts.

The Venuses, or as she had called them, Veni, had been born of one rubber mould which they'd sent off for after seeing an advert in a paper. It was technical stuff. They'd filled the mould with cement and supported it, after much discussion, between two planks in a dustbin.

Wow, Lydia had been beautiful then, fawn hair flying in the wind as he'd mixed the cement, showing off to her. Her hair didn't fly around now. She'd had it cut to start work, come home one day looking like a field mushroom, her hair reaching the top of her ears, not a lover any more and all ready to leave him behind.

She'd been excited when the cement had dried.

So had he. But when he'd peeled back the rubber he saw the mould had become grossly misshapen with the weight of the concrete, and the slender neck had thickened and the body widened, and what they'd made was a flat-featured dwarf with a hump.

Lydia had cried.

17

Undaunted for once, he'd filled the dustbin with sand, which had acted as a bit of a support. It worked to the extent that the antenatal abnormalities weren't as severe again but the truth was, the concrete Venuses never captured the beauty of the original. Their features were, at best, surly. He had buried them in the garden to age them, and that had been an effort he didn't want to repeat, the burial of ten concrete statues with various disabilities. It was only through trial and error that they found the best way to encourage the weatherbeaten look was to cover them in yoghurt. The mould disguised their coarsened features.

He and Lydia had sold the statues at an auction. They'd failed to reach the reserve, and he'd had to let them go at a knockdown price to save having to carry them home again. The auctioneer, scraping the mould with his thumb, had told the buyer encouragingly that with a bit of a scrub and a lick of paint, they would look as good as new. It seemed, he thought, such a long time ago.

He was back to looking at the envelope.

Uneasily, he felt a longing for the long-haired Lydia.

She'd liked his ideas, once.

He'd once heard her refer to him as The Great Schemer, and had been pleased. Shouldn't have been; she'd meant it as an insult.

And now she wants me back, he thought, getting hold of his Zuma Jay surf shorts, pulling them on, keeping his eye on the envelope leaning against the TV screen, seeing his name upon it: Mr J. Wilder, written with flair in black ink.

Formal, that.

She wants me back, he thought again, not believing it, not for a moment.

They were years further on from the Venus days. They were two children further on. They were her job further on. They

18

were divorced, two trains side-by-side and he'd thought he was the one who was moving until the other train pulled out of sight and he'd found himself still at the station. He hadn't moved at all, not ever, not even now.

He leaned over, reached for the envelope and stuck his forefinger under the flap, tearing it open. He could see the gilt edge of a card inside, and he eased it out. More extravagant writing. Dum-dum, dum-dum, dum-dum; his heart began lolloping in his chest and he made himself look at the black writing carefully. He read:

> *We, Lydia Wilder and Charles Black,*
> *would like you to come to our wedding party.*
> *Do try, the girls want you to and Larry and Meg and*
> *your godson will be there.*
> *June 29th, 7.00 p.m., at home. Black tie.*

He propped the card carefully against the television set again and stared at it, waiting for the pain to knock the breath out of him like a kick in the ribs.

The malaise of grief crept up on him gradually, crushing him so tightly that he thought his ribs would crack. He felt his stomach contract, double him up, dum-dum, dum-dum, squeezing his heart into his ears.

His gaze faded from the card and returned again. June the twenty-ninth. A lifetime away, he thought, nothing to worry about. He hadn't lost her yet.

He waited, trying to chase the pain, trying to confront it like he would a bully, but it didn't go away.

His heart was beating louder; sure and very persistent.

He took a step backwards and clipped the spoon in the bowl on the floor. Curry splattered orange on his legs.

He sat down as though the armchair might not be safe and he shut his eyes to listen to his heart.

He would like it to stop. He had got the message.

19

The message was that Lydia was not coming back.
But it carried on mocking him.
Dumb-dumb. Dumb-dumb. Dumb-dumb.

4

Megan, on her way to work, stopped at the lights and used the time to put on her lipstick.

This was the point at which she forgot about banana skins and thought of work instead.

She flicked up her sun shield and moved off with the traffic. The lipstick was her version of Superman's phone box, it transformed her into She-Man.

Unlike Megan the Mother who crouched under tables, She-Man haggled, seduced people from their jobs, took men to lunch and drove as if it were a competitive sport.

All that from a lipstick? She smiled to herself.

Not for nothing were lipsticks phallic in design.

In the male-dominated industries of advertising agencies, advertisers and media owners, men did not want to get the impression that they were being interviewed by wives and mothers – that was something they got anyway after late nights and long lunches. They did not mind, however, being interviewed by She-Men wearing lipstick; woman in a man's world, plus.

In the eighties, to headhunters, looking after a client meant parties and sex. In the nineties it meant offering a long-term working partnership for their mutual benefit.

Megan parked her car behind the grimy building and went up to the second floor.

Despite the condition of the outside, the design of the inside gave the impression of stylish efficiency. The reception area looked cool with its polished pale floors. On the wall hung a clock with no digits, and adjacent to it, a set of paintings with a dot of ultramarine positioned in different areas of the canvas.

'Hi, Laura,' Megan said to the receptionist. 'Is Zelda in yet?'

'What do you think?' Zelda Colgin, wife of Gerry, who owned the company, was having sleepless nights. 'I've been here since the crack of dawn.' She was walking along the corridor from the kitchen, eight months pregnant and tired of it. Her short dark hair had a streak of premature grey down the front, like a flash. She held her hand-painted porcelain cup up over her bump. 'Who's been shortlisted for the ANI search?'

'David Elsworth, John Parrish and Steven Dyke. ANI said they'd let us know today.' In the background Megan could hear the phones start to ring. She walked into the office and reached for the nearest one. 'Hello?'

'Mrs Fitzgerald? It's Gary Barnes.'

Megan grinned. 'Mrs Fitzgerald is just coming.' Zelda's code names were never subtle. She put her hand over the receiver. 'Gary Barnes for you.'

'Thanks.' Zelda put the cup on her desk and took the phone, suddenly coming to life, all tiredness gone. 'Gary!' her tone was warm and effusive, almost seductive. 'Gary, Gary, I've got to tell you, you're ninety-nine percent what they're looking for. Will they find the hundred percent-er? Does anyone? I'll let you know as soon as I hear. Probably by the end of the week. 'Bye, Gary.' She put the phone down and dropped the smile, looking at Megan.

Megan returned her gaze. 'So how's Gary?' she asked.

'The truth is, he's not up to it, he's still a bit young, too much one of the lads. I'll ring him on Thursday, let him know diplomatically that it's not for him.' She grinned suddenly. 'Poor old Gary. He was doing quite well in his interview until

he said the person he most admired in the world was himself.'
She looked at the tea in her cup and flicked out some stray
tealeaves.

Nigel, who dealt with graduate recruitment, had finished his
three-way conversation and was stretching noisily at his desk
in the corner of the room. Graduates approached early retained
a loyalty to the company which became useful further along
the line in their careers. His phone started ringing and he
dropped his arm out of the stretch and grabbed it. 'Hel-lo?
Kensington Nannies? Right, one moment. Zelda, it's for
you.'

Megan watched Zelda hurry to the phone. She got through
more nannies than a rutting goat, Megan thought. She looked
at Nigel, and wondered whether it was his goatee beard that
had made her think of the metaphor.

Her phone rang and she picked it up. It was someone she'd
arranged to interview the following day and was keen on meeting. 'Simon! You can't make tomorrow lunchtime? How about
tomorrow evening? That's fine. Around six? You want it later,
all right, six-thirty, seven? Seven, I've got that down.' Shame,
she wouldn't see Bill. 'Is Mario's still convenient? Mario's at
seven. See you later.' She put the phone down, and almost
immediately it rang again.

It was a call confirming an appointment that afternoon.

Megan replaced the receiver and stretched her legs. 'Alistair
Hoe,' she said to Nigel. 'Remember him? We interviewed him
as a graduate and he's been at Myles Cunningham since 94.
I'm meeting him in Knightsbridge – he's got an hour to spare
and doesn't want to waste time getting here.'

'Are you thinking of him for sales at R&B?'

'He's a possible. He says he's quite happy where he is but
he didn't turn down the chance of an interview.'

'I remember Alistair,' Nigel said, and laughed. He raised his
arms over his head and flexed his hands until the bones cracked.

23

'He got a third, didn't he? I was the one who interviewed him originally. I liked him. To get a third implies spectacular indifference. Question is, is he a worker or a shirker?'

Megan, still bracing herself for the cracking bones, was only half-listening. She laughed. 'He's certainly not stupid. What did you get, Nigel?' she asked.

'Five "O" levels. Same as John Major.'

'Richard Branson got two.'

'Just think what he could have done if he'd got a degree!'

Megan laughed. 'Yeah, he could have become a head-hunter, couldn't he, Zelda.'

Zelda made a face and headed back to her office, rubbing her back.

'Anyway, I'm off out,' Nigel said, getting to his feet. 'I'm giving a talk to some graduates up north.'

Megan frowned and looked up at him. 'Up north?'

'Watford.'

Megan laughed and turned as Zelda came back in. 'I've just had Triton on the phone. They're looking for a broadcast director and if we can pull this one they'd be very useful financially to have as clients. They've briefed one other recruitment company. Can you work on the initial brief?' she asked, patting her rounded stomach as dispassionately as she would a beer belly.

'Sure,' Megan said.

'We've got a couple of researchers onto it,' Zelda said. 'I'll talk to you later about getting someone to fill in while I'm on maternity leave.'

The phone began to ring. Megan picked it up. 'Hello? Yes, it's Megan speaking. Hello, Don. John Parrish, yes, he was our front-runner. Yes, I'll let him know.' She put the phone down and swivelled round to look at Zelda with a grin. 'ANI are taking on John Parrish.'

'The drinks are on you with your nice fat fee,' Zelda said.

24

Megan gave a satisfied smile of agreement. 'The drinks are on me.'

She could feel the excitement of the job bubbling up inside her. It was going to be a good day.

5

Convertibles, Larry thought as he drove to Burgess McLane, were at their best in heavy traffic where there were people to see them.

More importantly, in heavy traffic he got the chance to see himself.

The warm wind skimmed his gelled hair as he saw the lights ahead of him turn from amber to red and he pressed his foot on the brake and came to a standstill. It was perfect timing. He was alongside the French Connection windows. In them he could see his reflection; he could see a cool man, a sexy car. He watched himself for a moment, then looked around. Sadly there were few pedestrians to see him but he checked the rear-view mirror and gave himself a grim, square-jawed, glance of approval. Yes, he was looking good.

The lights changed to green and the traffic began to move and he eased his foot smoothly off the brake and let his car begin the slow crawl towards the next set of lights. He watched them change to red and he eased on the brake.

Great Portland Street really was a great street, he thought. He could see himself so clearly it was like watching a film: David 'Larry' Lawrence, star of his own show.

He stared at his dark eyes in the mirror and rubbed his jaw. He adjusted the mirror again, checked the traffic behind him and returned his attention to the store window, but only briefly, as the lights had changed.

And he carried on along Great Portland Street to the offices of Burgess McLane, where he worked.

Larry approached the main door of Burgess McLane without having to buzz – another thing he approved of in his new job. It was opened for him by Peter, the security guard.

He strode into the pale grey lobby, all glass and marble, and felt he was where he belonged.

'Morning, Larry,' the security guard said.

'Morning, Peter,' he replied. After only two months at Burgess McLane he knew the names of everyone, not deliberately but instinctively; he had a head for names. His mind, though, wasn't on the security man – it was on his job. He loved it. He loved the smell of Burgess McLane; he loved the name and he loved the car they'd given him. He even loved the sound of the air conditioning; he liked to imagine it was the building breathing, calmly, mesmerically, like a god.

Larry was on the phone to a client that afternoon when the message came through from Deborah his secretary that his boss wanted to see him. Larry raised his eyebrows. Burgess only ever saw people over breakfast or lunch, on principle. He said eating made them better natured.

'Did he say what it was about?' Larry asked Deborah when he had finished his call.

'No. Just asked to have you sent in.'

Larry dampened a flare of excitement.

'Thanks, Deborah,' Larry said, looking at the receiver before putting it down. He smiled to himself. He'd already made an impression at Burgess McLane. As he leaned back in his chair, stretching easily, something touched the back of his neck and startled him, but it was only the billowing of the off-white bomb curtains that his predecessor had put up.

He'd heard the rumours but Deborah, his secretary, told

him the whole story, which was that this chap Mark Fletcher had had a bad feeling; he'd thought the IRA had him marked out. One by one all his favourite haunts, Regent's Park, Camden High Street, Harrods, Cavendish Square, had been hit in turn, which he took to be a pretty heavy hint, so he'd had the curtains put up and paid for them himself, although he'd probably got the money back by fiddling his expenses.

But the curtains didn't help. Even the ceasefire hadn't consoled him; he'd thought it was a trick and he'd spent months waiting for it all to go horribly wrong. It wasn't the kind of thing a man could keep to himself. It became a joke. One of his clients had taped cans of baked beans together to make a mortar, inserted a tennis ball into the tube and launched it before a presentation, using lighter fluid as fuel. The bang had nearly killed Fletcher. Eventually, tired of waiting for the worst, and tired of the dry-cleaning bills caused by having crisp packets burst behind his back, he'd left. Which had been lucky for Larry, who'd got his job.

Larry was afraid of nothing. 'I'm going to get rid of these things,' he said, giving the billowing net a punch.

Deborah nodded.

'I'll do it when I get back. Better find out what's worrying Burgess.' He stood up and took a gulp of coffee. He didn't want to appear too eager but he didn't want to keep him waiting, either. He put the cup on his desk and made for his boss's office, enjoying the bounce of the thick red and grey carpet under his feet.

He was greeted by Marcia, Burgess's secretary, who smiled at him tightly from the doorway where she stood hunched like a gargoyle.

'Looking good, Marcia,' he said, and tried his winning smile on her. The tight smile snapped off her face like released elastic. Two months, and she was still impervious to him.

'Go right in,' she said coldly, 'they're expecting you.'

28

They? Larry raised his eyebrows and wondered who 'they' were. He pushed open the door to Burgess's office. He was surprised to see John King in there too, sitting next to Burgess, facing him from the safety of the checkpoint barrier of Burgess's desk.

Larry paused, puzzled. He took a deep breath and found his nasal cavity filled with the smell of sweat and Paco Rabanne. It was a man's smell. One day he would be there in that line-up: Burgess, King and Lawrence. It was just a matter of time.

He looked placidly at Burgess, aiming to look him in the eye. It was like trying to catch a fish with his hands. He glanced at John King. John grinned back. It was about time he got his teeth fixed, Larry thought, repulsed. It was the ugliest smile he'd ever seen. He felt worried, as though he'd killed King's mother. He looked away uneasily, wondering what all this was about. He'd had a drink with King the previous week. Impressed him, he'd thought.

But Burgess was looking at him now. The Fat Boy's requisite healthy tan had gone from Burgess's face as if it had been bleached. His face was grey and tight and strained as though he'd been ill for some time.

'Sit down,' Burgess said.

Larry walked over to the empty chair meant for him and sat down, raising his eyebrows in a query.

'Look, Larry,' Burgess began, frowning at the desk as though Larry was in it, 'any time is a good time to give good news but there's no such thing as a good time to give bad news.'

The statement baffled Larry. He went over it in his head.

Burgess was still frowning at the desk. 'We're being bought out by Xylus Enterprises. I expect you've heard rumours.'

No, he hadn't. No rumours. The Power People had not checked the pulse on this one. He latched onto the words bad news and he was suddenly aware of his skin creeping, as though it was trying to sneak away without him. He suddenly felt he should say something. He had the idea that if he said something he could deflect the terrible thing that Burgess seemed to be able to see on the surface of his desk. He cleared his throat. 'Yes. I knew that there was some interest,' he lied.

Burgess looked momentarily nonplussed. 'You did?'

John King glanced at Burgess and leaned forward. It seemed that it was only the desk that was holding him back from Larry. 'We've got to let you go,' he said, enunciating it slowly so that there could be no mistake. 'By the end of the week. Nothing personal.'

Larry felt his body alert itself into a state of panic. Not me, he told himself, despite what John had said. He looked at his boss for verification. He could see the grey skin tighten on Burgess's head . . . he could see the shape of his skull shining through his thinning hair, catching the light.

He stared at him until Burgess was forced to respond, and when Burgess's eyes finally met his, all Larry could see were two dull glints flickering from the weathered skin of his face like dimming bulbs.

'I'm sorry, Larry,' Burgess said. 'You're surplus to requirements.'

Larry's head felt strange. He could hear white noise. He felt panic frothing up inside him in a physical surge which made him momentarily wonder if he was going to vomit on Burgess's red and grey carpet.

He stared at them, the demolition men, and wondered what he ought to do. Wondered in fact what was the done thing in this sort of situation. He'd been given the boot. He tried to muster up some credibility as though he could use it to fill in the cracks. 'Burgess McLane and Xylus will be an unbeatable combination,' he said and rubbed his jaw.

Burgess looked up. He took strength from these words. 'Yes,' he said, as though it was something he'd forgotten.

It seemed to bring him back into business mode.

'Unfortunately,' Burgess said, 'as you have only been with us for – what is it now –' he was stopped by Larry's upraised hand.

'Hey.' Larry knew what it meant, oh yes, he knew and he didn't want the insult of having it spelled out. He'd only been with the firm for two months. They could get rid of him for free. No redundancy, no golden handshake. 'I know all the implications,' he said, and he did. He saw his hopes flash by as smoothly as though they were on a conveyor belt, toppling off in the distance, out of reach.

It was all gone.

The film was over.

All the trappings, his office, his lovely car, everything had to be returned.

'I know all the implications,' he repeated. He stared at Burgess, unable to say another word.

Apparently reassured, Burgess smiled. He was looking healthier now. He rubbed his hands together. 'You'll be paid your notice,' he said encouragingly. 'Three months,' he added helpfully, as though it was something Larry didn't know. All his tension had gone. Larry realised it hadn't been because of his sympathy for Larry, but from fear of having to tell him.

Larry watched the colour coming back into Burgess's face; he looked like a Polaroid developing before Larry's eyes. Larry watched Burgess become himself again, and then more than himself – he was becoming expansive.

'Keep the car until the end of your contract,' Burgess said, and slapped shut the leather-bound desk diary with a whump. A fresh puff of Paco Rabanne wafted Larry's way. Sentence had been passed and the judge was now washing his hands of him. The atmosphere had lightened considerably. Even the air conditioning seemed to breathe more freely.

Larry got to his feet. Even though all he wanted to do was

get out of there, he couldn't bring himself to leave. He wanted to linger. If he stood there long enough they might say – joke!

But the Fat Boys were scuffling their feet, turning to each other, shutting him out of their line of vision as if he had already gone.

'You can have the car back tomorrow,' he heard himself say. Now where had that come from? That puny blow? His body was heavier than he'd ever noticed before, but his head, strangely, was light. The white noise inside it increased, pushing out his thoughts. He felt drunk. He concentrated on walking in a straight line to the door. He didn't bother to smile at Marcia and he didn't bother to close the door behind him.

By mid-morning the news of the takeover had suffocated the company like slurry. The smell of disaster hung over them. People examined the fabric of their lives and saw it burst open. They talked of 'what abouts': honeymoons, holidays, mortgages, babies, all nipped in the bud.

Larry sat at his desk, swivelled his chair and looked at the city beyond the bomb curtains. He tried to break through the white noise. He thought that he knew what the white noise was – it was his future. It was a blank. His diary was a travesty – there was nothing in it to bother him next week any more. Or next month.

He picked up the phone and tried Megan. She was out of the office. He didn't leave a message.

He turned his chair round and stared out through the open doorway at his bods. He was all right, he had Megan, but he knew they would not all get jobs. They would be like ants rushing about. In the Invertebrates House at London Zoo he and Bill had watched the leaf-cutting ants cross a branch across the water. For every ant with a piece of leaf there were thirty jobless, rushing back and forth doing nothing. Reminded him of his last agency, he'd told Megan at the time, but now it wasn't funny. The futility of it appalled him. He didn't want to be a jobless ant.

Nausea filled his mouth. He would be all right, he told himself. He always landed on his feet. He swallowed and wiped his mouth with the back of his hand as he heard a gentle tap on the door. Deborah, his secretary, came in, stood in the doorway and just looked at him.

Her pallor showed through her foundation and her lipstick had got chewed off along the way. 'What are we going to do?' she asked him.

He gestured towards a chair and she came in and sat down.

Larry shook his head. His thoughts settled. He looked her in the eye. 'I don't know,' he said. 'Look for something else.'

'Poor Burgess.'

'Don't worry about him, he'll make a packet from it,' Larry said, with a bitterness he'd never had cause to feel in his life before.

'Tom was going to take his PhD in October,' Deborah said.

Larry looked away from her. He didn't want to have to hear her problems, he had his own to contend with.

'If it had been any other time . . .' Deborah said, and her throat squeezed a tremble into her voice. 'What am I going to tell him?'

Larry stared speechlessly at the bomb-proof curtains. Oh, Mark Fletcher had been right not to trust them and to leave. The bomb had dropped and they had been no use at all.

Burgess's voice replayed in his head like a reprimand, so loudly that he thought his secretary was meant to hear it. He repeated it to her in a low voice. 'Any time is a good time to give good news but there is no such thing as a good time to give bad news,' he said.

In the car park after work, Larry got into the car and leaned his head back against the headrest and shut his eyes. The smell of leather mixed with the smell of tar; warm smells of early summer.

He started the engine and drove out of the car park and eased his way into the traffic leaving the city centre.

His body felt heavy as though his troubles were really weighing him down, crushing him. At the first set of lights a car horn sounded behind him. He looked up and saw with surprise that the road ahead of him was clear – the lights had changed to green and he hadn't even realised it. He put his foot down and the car surged forward a short way before it caught up with the trail of traffic waiting to crawl across Euston Road. Coming to a stop again Larry glanced out of habit at the window adjacent to the lights.

This window was empty. The darkness inside made it as reflective as a sheet of black ice.

But as he looked at the window, he saw to his horror that he wasn't there. His skin tightened with shock. He felt the hairs bristling on his head. He didn't exist any more. He'd disappeared. He believed it.

Then suddenly he laughed, and the wood panels covering the window came into focus, he could see the firm's name stamped on them in red, he could see the rough grain. The empty shop had been boarded up, that was all. He laughed again, louder, but it sounded false and flat. He caught a woman looking at him oddly as she waited to cross the road and he shut up, pretending to concentrate on the lights ahead.

Once again, he felt his stomach heave. He tried to ignore it, easing his foot off the brake as he moved with the traffic, heading for home. But the thought of that blankness, that sudden invisibility, stayed with him all the way.

The film had finished and he'd been left on the cutting room floor.

6

That evening, Bill tugged the shoulder strap on his Gap dunga-rees and looked up at the white clock on the kitchen wall. He knew that when both red hands pointed down at him, that was when Mummy would be home. Sometimes she came before he'd even looked at the clock. And sometimes she didn't come at all, not until he was sleeping, but this wasn't one of those days because Zoofie always told him if his mother would be late.

He gave his strap another tug. The red hands of the clock, because he knew they were called hands, not fingers even though they pointed, the hands weren't pointing straight down at him yet, not quite, but they were getting closer. If he looked really carefully he could see the big one move with a jerk, as though it had remembered suddenly what its job was.

'Bill?' Zoofie came into the kitchen and scooped him up. He pushed through the blonde tangle of her hair so that he could carry on watching the clock.

He could see it better now that he was higher up. He looped an arm around Zoofie's neck.

'Shall we watch Mr Bean?' she asked him, kissing him on his cheek.

He nodded. They both liked Mr Bean, and he mostly knew where to laugh even though sometimes he wasn't sure what was funny.

'Would you like an apple to eat while we watch it?'

But Bill caught the sound of a car outside in the street. It was his father's car. He listened as the engine noise got louder and the car reached their drive, and he heard the long crackling as it crushed the gravel.

Bill waited for his father to slam the car door and crunch, crunch, crunch to the kitchen door.

'Bill?'

He looked at Zoofie. 'Daddy's home.'

'Do you want me to cut you up an apple?'

He shook his head. He had to prepare himself for his father. Sometimes his father threw him up in the air and caught him, and sometimes he tickled him until he squealed. It wasn't the kind of thing he could do with an apple in his hand.

'No thank you,' Zoofie said, putting him down. 'I'm going to have one. These are English apples. Always eat fruit in season. The Queen Mother only ever eats fruit in season. Organic. From her own orchards.'

Bill still hadn't heard the car door slam. His father was still in the car, in the drive.

He looked at the clock and wondered if his father was waiting until both the red fingers, or hands, pointed straight down. As he wondered, he heard the car door close at last.

Crunch, crunch, crunch.

He felt a giggle in his throat, and the kitchen door opened and there was his father coming into the house and slamming down his case on the kitchen table with a bang.

'Hello, Bill.'

Bill braced himself, but his father just rested his hand on his head. His hand felt warm and heavy and large, like a flat cap.

'Hi, Larry. Tea?' Zoofie asked. 'I've just put the kettle on.'

Bill felt his father's hand leave his head.

'Something stronger,' his father said.

'Bad day?'

'Bad day. The worst.' He sounded tired.

Zoofie put the knife down. She put the plate of cut up apple on the table. The slices rocked like little green boats and Bill reached up for one. He knew his Daddy wasn't going to throw him in the air now.

He was on the last segment when he heard his mother's car pull up. He held the piece of apple in his hand. The gravel crunch-crunch-crunch-crunched very quickly and his mother came in all of a rush.

He could smell her perfume and he blinked as she kissed his face.

'Ooh, yum, you taste of apples,' she said and she picked him up, holding him tight.

He rested his head on her chest.

He liked this bit of the day. They were all together, Zoofie, Mummy, Daddy and Bill. He was so happy he couldn't think of anything to say. He wriggled himself back to the floor.

'What's this about the Xylus takeover?' his mother asked his father. 'Is it true that Burgess McLane are letting some people go?'

His father didn't say anything, and his mother suddenly stopped talking too.

Bill put the remains of the last piece of apple in his pocket and looked at his parents closely.

His mother was looking at his father, Larry, and it was as if they were talking to each other without using any words.

Zoofie was looking at them too.

His father was nodding his head slowly.

'What's up?' Zoofie asked sharply.

'I've been made redundant,' his father said. 'Got to give the car back.' He looked at Bill. 'Sorry, son.'

Bill didn't know what the r-word was, but he didn't much mind about the car. It wasn't half as comfortable as his mother's. When the roof was down and he and Zoofie were in the back, he could hardly breathe, the wind was so strong.

He didn't mind about the car, although he could see his father did. 'It's all right, Daddy,' he said.

His mother got off the table and put her arms around his father's, Larry's, neck. She rested her cheek on his father's dark hair. He wondered if it tickled her, but she didn't rub her face or move away.

'Mouths of babes,' she said. She glanced at the clock. 'Could you run the bath, Ruth? We'll talk about it later. Go with Ruth, Bill, I'll be up to bath you in a minute.'

Bill hurried to his father and kissed him on his knee. His father smiled but he still looked sad.

Bill knew how hard it was to cheer up. He thought about the car. He knew how his father felt. He'd felt it himself, lots of times. He knew it from playgroup. It was a sad feeling, when you liked a thing so much and then you had to give it back.

By the time supper was ready, Megan had put Bill to bed and the dining room was humming with quiet. Larry looked up from the trout on his plate which Megan had just put in front of him and watched her sit down, her red linen napkin bunched in her hand. She caught his eye just for a second and he could see that she looked troubled.

In the car, before he'd come into the house, Larry had had the wild and sudden surge of an idea, that he wouldn't tell her. He would carry on as before, leaving the house every morning – *with no car* . . .

He remembered a story from long ago, he should have forgotten it but here it was, returning to condemn him, a story – *which he'd laughed at* – of a man who had kept his redundancy secret and had spent his days in the public library, leaving and returning home at the usual times. And he now understood it. He understood it so wholeheartedly that he couldn't remember why it had seemed ludicrous before.

38

The white noise came rushing back.

He wished he hadn't told her, because now that he had it felt bad, really bad.

People said sometimes when things were bad that they can't get any worse, but it wasn't true, Larry thought. Larry, his hands cold on the polished table in his carmine dining room, found things were worse because of the trout.

The dead trout's skin was black and charred and peeling, revealing the pale pink flesh beneath. One opaque eye, appallingly dead, was nevertheless looking at him. The whole thing was lying beached on a bed of green herbs, and he was overcome by a wave of revulsion.

The nausea started up the white noise in his head again. He looked away from the fish. It was making him wish he was vegetarian.

Megan's voice drifted lightly through his nausea, distracting him. 'We'll be all right, Larry,' she said softly, brushing her fringe out of her eyes with the back of her hand.

Larry couldn't bear to have to face the trout's dead glare and he looked up instead at his wife's clear, blue eyes. We'll be all right? How could she think that? 'You shouldn't have cancelled *Harpers & Queen*,' he said. 'Losing your job is one of the biggest stress-factors on the Life Crises chart.' He tried to smile. He moved a withering strand of coriander that was dangling off the edge of the plate.

'I was thinking about our options,' she said, staring at her plate. He wondered if she was as repulsed by it as he was but she deftly pulled her trout's tail, backbone and ribs clean off its remaining flesh and put it on her side plate. It looked like a prop from *Top Cat*. She looked up at him, wiping her fingers on her napkin. 'We can carry on for three months. Your first step is to let people know you're available.'

He watched her put the napkin down on the table. She was silent for a moment. Thinking, he thought. She was always discreet about her job. He liked that quality in her. It meant she never brought her work home and there was no competition when he wanted to talk about his – which, he thought wearily, wasn't going to be a problem for a while. However, there was a time and a place for discretion and just at the moment what he needed most was hope. 'What?' he prompted her.

'And I'll do what I can at work. Keep a look out. You'll have to update your CV.'

Larry was looking at the head of Megan's trout and swallowed the rush of saliva to his mouth as he noticed the eye had dislodged from the socket. He hated meat that bore the slightest resemblance to the creature it had once been – although he'd only just realised it. On Saturday he'd eaten quail – he quailed at the thought of all those little bones. He picked up his fork to touch the trout's heat-blackened skin and went over Megan's last sentence in his head.

Suddenly he heard the dining room door whispering open across the red carpet and he turned his head to see Bill coming through with his arms outstretched like a sleep-walker.

For a worrying moment he thought the tension had disturbed him but a golden glint in the boy's hand made him realise that Bill was bringing something for him to see.

Larry tried to smile encouragingly but his face felt stiff. 'Hello, son.' He glanced at Megan who was looking restlessly towards the door for Ruth.

Meanwhile, Bill was standing still, hesitating between them.

'What have you got there?' Larry added, forcing a false heartiness into his voice. Bill, now, was wavering.

He sensed a distracted mother on the one hand and an oddly matey father on the other. Following his mother's gaze he, too, looked back at the door as if it was Ruth he wanted really. He looked at his parents again and made his choice.

His outstretched arms swung towards his father and

he walked up to the table and looked up at him.

Larry was reminded of Burgess in the earnestness of his expression, at the small pouches under the blue eyes.

'What have you got there, Bill?'

'Nobby's sleeping,' Bill said to him softly.

And for the first time since his son had entered the room, Larry looked properly at the object in his hands.

It was their goldfish, slim and shining, two-and-a-half inches long, lying still and damp on the small palms. For the second time that night, Larry found himself drawn to the sightless eye of a dead fish.

He managed, somehow, to avoid recoiling. Still hunched forward, he swallowed, looked at Bill and nodded briefly.

'Yes, he's asleep,' he said.

Bill looked down at the fish in his hands for a moment, and then looked back at his father with infinite compassion.

'Nobby's dead,' he said gently.

Larry felt a flash of shame come over him at having been caught out in a lie. And then he realised that his not quite four-year-old son had tried to protect him from the death of the fish. He had tried to break it to him gently.

Larry stared at the fish and wondered momentarily how it was that Bill knew about death. His thoughts went to the trout – and out of the corner of his eye he could see it stretched out on the plate in front of him.

What would Bill think? He saw himself through his son's eyes; not just a carnivore, he was far worse than that. He was a pet-eater.

He flung his napkin quickly over the corpse, knowing that if he missed he would only succeed in drawing Bill's attention to it, but willing to take a chance. Bill was looking at the napkin with interest and the altered expression on his face showed that the plan had not come off. Larry dared to look. The edge of the napkin had fallen short of the fish's head. On his comfortable bed of fragrant, wilted herbs he looked for all the world as if he'd just been tucked up for the night.

Larry suddenly felt himself come to life. He patted himself and found a white handkerchief and shook it out, holding each pair of corners between his thumb and forefinger so that the handkerchief was like a hammock.

'Put Nobby in the handkerchief,' he said.

Bill put the fish in carefully.

Larry tightened his grip on the cloth but it hardly weighed anything, this small orange carp; it hardly took the creases out of its pall.

Still holding the handkerchief up, he could look, at last, at his wife. But Megan wasn't looking at him, she was looking at Bill. She looked as though she was going to cry.

She got up suddenly. 'Come on,' she said, picking him up, 'let's get you back to bed. Oh, your sleeves are all wet, let's change these pyjamas while we're at it.' She pushed her chair away from the table and scooped Bill up into her arms. He rested his head in the hollow of her neck for a moment but then looked over her shoulder as she carried him to the door. Larry hoped his son wanted to say something more but his eyes were on the trout, still tucked up on the plate.

'Fish sleeping?' he asked.

'Yes,' said Megan softly, 'and so should you be.'

Larry sat down heavily and stared at the handkerchief dangling in his hand.

Wasn't Bill lucky?

He had every Fisher-Price toy ever made.

He had two good-looking, intelligent parents to look after him; one jobless, the other a liar.

7

The merger was old news by the end of that week. 'I hear
Burgess McLane have let Larry go,' Nigel said, sitting on the
edge of Megan's desk.

'Yes,' she said, pushing back her chair. 'It came absolutely
out of the blue. He'd had a drink with John King last week
and got the impression he was destined for greatness.'

Nigel rubbed his beard back and forth as though he was
testing bristles on a paintbrush. 'How's he taking it?'

'Optimistically.' Their eyes locked and she shrugged.

The phone began to ring. She reached out for it, and paused.
'Hello? Yes, Ryan O'Neal speaking.' She glanced at Nigel and
saw him wince. It was someone who had changed their mind
about seeing them. 'That's fine,' she said. 'Keep in touch.'

'Who was that, Farah Fawcett?' Nigel asked dryly.

'Yeah, I know. Sad, isn't it. Association of ideas. Megan,
Meg Ryan, Ryan O'Neal. If I heard someone in my office
asking to speak to Ryan O'Neal, I'd immediately know they
were on to a headhunter and sack them on the grounds of
lack of original thinking.'

She reached for the mail and sifted out the unsolicited CVs
that had come in. It wouldn't do any harm to see what Larry
was up against.

Megan then checked the computer database for Larry's
details. She'd interviewed him once, years earlier. He'd turned
down the job on offer and asked her out, declaring professional
ethics as his reason. The truth was, he'd leaked the meeting

to his boss and had been offered an incentive to stay where he was; something that she'd guessed at and forgotten long before he'd told her.

She glanced at his details and read her own comments at the bottom of his file. 'Relaxed good-looker, doesn't have to work hard to get places. Lacks drive? Born salesman.'

She sat back and wondered what she'd put now if she hadn't married him. Probably much the same. If he lacked drive it was because he'd never needed it. Larry attracted good fortune.

Nigel was putting down the phone. 'Guess what? That was Xylus and they're looking for a new TV group head. Seems to me they shouldn't have got rid of our boy Larry.'

Megan frowned and looked at the screen.

Larry wasn't looking quite so fortunate now.

By Friday, the atmosphere at Burgess McLane had turned nasty, bad with ill-feeling. To an outsider it would seem as industrious a place as ever but Larry, sitting at his desk, knew that the industriousness was totally self-centred.

He got up and went to the kitchen to get himself a coffee.

He hadn't slept well. He'd had a bad dream. He couldn't remember it but it was hovering in the background, slipping in and out of his mind.

Larry switched the kettle on and stared at his reflection which looked grotesque in the chrome. Suddenly he remembered his dream.

Bad? It was the worst. It was a relief, in a way, to remember, because that morning, for the first time in his life, he hadn't wanted to look in the mirror and he hadn't at the time been able to work out why. He'd dreamed that he was bald.

It all came back to him now. He'd dreamed that he was in the supermarket, standing by the fruit display. He remembered that in the dream he'd picked up a lemon and as he'd glanced upwards at the angled mirror to check his reflection he'd

44

noticed for the first time that he had a bald patch on the crown of his head. Not just thinning, which would have been bad enough, but properly bald, a circle so hairless that it was hard for him to believe it belonged to him. He could see the hair lifting up around the pink skin. Newly uncovered, it was as bright as scar tissue.

In the dream he had realised that that pink and hairless patch was not something recent. He'd realised that unbeknownst to him he had been going bald for months and hadn't noticed. Other people would have seen it, though; he knew that. His colleagues. Marcia. Burgess. He knew now that all those days that he'd been driving to and from work, smiling at himself in admiration in shop windows, his body had been betraying him behind his back and had begun the process of withholding the hairs on his head. It was getting old and shutting down. His body, like his boss, had started laying off.

In the dream he knew that he was squeezing the lemon very lightly. He could smell its oils seeping through the pores in the waxed skin. And he understood, too, that Megan had known; that Megan had known but hadn't told him – instead she had slowly accepted that he was no longer a man, no longer young . . . she was kind, and pitying, and hadn't told him. He didn't like the way that made him feel.

It wasn't true, of course. He only had to lift his hand to feel his hair was evenly distributed, but the dream felt true. And he did feel old.

The kettle switched itself off again. He made his coffee and went back to his office to listen to the intimate, furtive mumble of telephone conversations.

They were all doing the same kind of thing; they were all trying to find a way out of the pit.

Being in the pit together should have, he'd thought, made for some solidarity between him and his colleagues. Wrong. In the pit they were alone, frantic, fighting for themselves.

He gave a shudder behind his grey desk and raised his hands and looked at his nails, expecting to see new moons of earth clogging them.

'I'm taking my plants,' Deborah said, walking into the office briskly without looking at him.

Larry stared at her. Even Debbie had gone sullen on him. Collecting her pot plants from his window – her own small office was windowless – she kept her back to him, paddling in the bomb curtains which were still up and not his concern now.

'Debbie,' he said, lifting himself out of his seat, 'what have I done?'

She glanced at him over her shoulder and didn't answer.

Larry picked up his pen and circled a name on his pad. Reeve. Reeve was a chap he'd worked with a couple of years previously at Redson Mather. Reeve was going to let him use his office, his fax and his secretary for a couple of weeks or as long as it took to get something else.

He felt better because of Reeve. He felt he'd had a bit of a leg up, managed to peer out of the pit, get a glimpse of what was out there. Maybe it didn't look so bad.

He looked up at Debbie's stiff back. 'What have I said?' he asked her plaintively.

'It's all right for you,' she said.

He saw it was time to pay attention. Hell, he wasn't used to people disliking him. It didn't happen often, and when it did it always surprised him. 'What's up? What have I done?' he asked, palms open, innocent. 'I'm in the same boat as you are,' he said. 'I'm sinking at the same rate.'

'Except you've got a wife to haul you out,' she said, clutching her spider plants.

So now there were degrees of bad luck, he thought, and some people's bad luck was worse than others.

'I'm in this on my own,' he said sincerely as he watched

46

her walk out leaving an intermittent trail of soil on the red and grey carpet. 'Debs, your pots are leaking on the company carpet.'

'What are you going to do? Sack me?' she asked bitterly as she walked out of the door.

Larry took a deep breath. Hormones, he thought.

He transferred his computer files onto disk, just in case he could use them in the future, and switched the monitor off.

He stretched, and wandered to the door.

There were only a few people still at their desks – the ones who were staying.

He went into Debbie's office. There was a large cardboard box on her desk full of papers. The plants were blooming out of the top.

'Have you got anything to put your things in?' she asked him, looking up. She sounded calmer, he was pleased to hear. He noticed that she wasn't wearing lipstick, as though she didn't feel the need to keep up appearances any more.

He could feel the disks in his jacket pocket.

'They'll fit in my briefcase,' he said.

'Oh. Well, here's a Boots carrier bag, in case you need it.'

He felt rather touched. 'Thanks,' he said, taking it.

'Well.' She jerked her head. 'I'm off.'

'Are you going for a drink?'

She looked at him and shook her head. 'You?'

'No. Thought I'd go home and spend the rest of the day with Bill.' Make the most of it, he thought.

They stood awkwardly in silence.

Larry stuck out his hand and she took it and laughed suddenly.

'Look at us, all formal. Been nice working for you,' she said.

He was surprised. Pleased, too. 'And you.'

She seemed uncomfortable for a moment. She coughed slightly, clearing her throat. 'Look, if anything comes up – if

47

you hear of anything, don't forget me, will you?' she asked quickly.

Larry shook his head. 'I won't forget you, no,' he said, and meant it.

'It's the pits,' she said, and it brought back the image Larry had had of himself climbing up, seeing out.

He watched her pick up her cardboard box.

As she struggled he felt suddenly strong. Survival of the fittest, he thought with a sudden surge of self-interest. He took the box from her. 'I'll help you to the lift,' he said.

'Thanks, Larry,' she said wryly. Probably, he thought, regretting her harsh words to him earlier. As he carried the box, the last of his pessimism and the remains of his dream drifted away.

PART TWO

Two's Mirth

8

It was sunny and James Wilder was sitting by the edge of an isolated pond with his eleven-year-old daughters. He'd promised to take them somewhere different, somewhere special on their one day out together. The venue was the pond he used to fish in when he was a boy. He'd decided to take his daughters fishing.

As he watched the wind ruffling the water he thought the pond was smaller than he remembered.

There were certainly no fish in it. He wondered whether there ever had been. All those fish he'd caught as a boy . . . or had that been only in his dreams?

His daughters were being brave about their disappointment. They were sitting behind him on the damp grass, enveloped in a smell of decaying vegetation. The sun had gone behind a cloud again and they were shivering slightly in their summer clothes.

He wondered what he could do to make things better. Too late now to regret the build-up he'd given this – puddle. Lydia had been doubtful about him taking the girls such a distance, i.e. in the car, an old Rover 90. She disliked him taking them anywhere there wasn't a tube line, in case he decided to drink – yes, that old one – in case he decided to drink and tried to drive them home. She'd doubted that they would like fishing, and he had laughed at her. They were his daughters, too, fifty percent him. Like fishing? It was in their genes. They just hadn't done it before, that was all.

But he had to admit that they didn't look happy, huddled together staring at the pond. Again, Lydia had been right.

Lydia was always right. Like Mussolini.

James was dazzled by the brightness of his yellow shorts. He looked at his legs and the hairs were prickling as the muddy water on them dried. 'Just have a paddle,' he said to his daughters, trying to raise their enthusiasm levels. 'It's quite warm.'

They looked at him seriously, and shook their heads.

'There might be worms,' Karin explained, 'and we don't like worms, do we, Jen?'

'No.'

'Nor maggots.'

James rubbed his nose, aware of the reproach.

'That was gross, Daddy,' Karin said sadly. 'But I'm sorry you nearly crashed.'

'It was meant to be a surprise,' he said. 'I thought you'd like your own fishing box. It's got everything in it,' he said, warming to the memory of the pleasure he'd taken in choosing the hooks and the bait and arranging it in the Barbie lunch-box. The scream that Jen had given on opening the tin had damaged his hearing, probably permanently.

'I don't think you managed to find them all, Daddy. I think some went under the car seat.'

'You're not supposed to stop on the hard shoulder, except for emergencies,' he said. 'Flying maggots don't wash with traffic patrols.' He found himself staring at the pond, too. 'I just brought you here because I thought you'd like it.' He couldn't keep the frustration out of his voice and he felt his daughters move closer together in alarm. 'Oh, s . . .' He had been going to say, 'Sod it,' but didn't want them going back to Charles Black with vulgarities leaping like toads out of their little mouths. He couldn't think of another exclamation beginning with an s, and so he let the phrase hang as he grabbed his polo shirt and pulled it over his head. 'Do you want another sandwich?'

They shook their heads, two serious girls on a duty visit. His two little girls, who, it was pretty obvious, would rather have been somewhere else. They were getting less substantial, less part of him with every visit.

They're only yours if you live with them, he thought, and his mind jumped. Which meant they were now Charles Black's.

He looked at their serious faces. He would have given the world to have them be cheeky to him.

'We could try fishing,' he said, in a valiant last attempt. 'You could hold the maggots in tissues while you put them on the hooks . . .' Perhaps not. He plucked a blade of grass and sucked the pale green stem. Then he reached for his baseball boots. 'What would you really have liked to do?' he asked, pulling them on. Out of the corner of his eye he saw the two girls exchange a covert glance. He looked up, curiously. 'What? You can tell me.'

Jen was reviving visibly. She popped her finger in her mouth and put her head to one side. 'You really want to know? Really-really?' she asked, testing him.

He shrugged. 'Yes. Tell me.' Talk to me, he thought silently, and remembered it was something Lydia used to ask of him with some desperation.

The girls looked at each other. Jen looked him straight in the eye, not like a child but like an adult, person to person, her small smile crushing his heart. 'Daddy, we know what we'd really like. Can you take us to get our navels pierced?'

James got to his feet with alacrity, slipping on the grass and swallowing his gut-reaction: No. He lifted his head, glimpsing, with surprise, the Barbie lunch-box firmly shut and nestling in the clover just by the side of them. He felt as if he had just travelled swiftly through time. It made him feel slightly dazed.

He stared at the two hopeful faces. 'What does your mother say?'

The girls looked at each other again and back at him. 'Definitely not,' Jen said, bit her lip and added: 'Of course.' She tilted her head appealingly at him, her eyes wide.

'Oh. Then I suppose I should say no, shouldn't I.'

'Charles says no, too.' And her eyes added: but you're different.

'Yeah, he would,' he said, and knew he was playing into her hands. He looked at the ruffled pond and wondered why the idea of fishing had seemed so blissfully simple. 'I'll think about it. Would you like to go back now?' he asked them.

They looked at each other and it was like looking at a composite photograph, different views of the same face.

'No,' Jen said.

Karin sat down on the grass again. It shone silver where it bent in the wind. 'We're going to be bridesmaids,' she said diffidently. 'At Mummy's wedding.'

The wedding. Dum-dum. James felt his heart begin to get noisy. 'Yes, I know.'

'Are you coming to see us?'

'Probably. Yes.' Bridesmaids, he thought. There was no way – had been no way he was going to turn up at his wife's wedding to Charles Black, the man who was everything he wasn't – industrious, neat, sober, with a couple of pension schemes on the go and life assurance to die for.

Lydia was a woman of extremes, not the kind of person who would make the same mistake twice.

She'd had it with dreams. That's what she'd told him. She'd got tired of supporting him through his projects but he'd never got tired of her. Or her support. He loved her. When he'd gone with other women it had only made him love her more. They never lived up to her. He'd tried telling her that.

James's only real hope now was that in six months she would be bored to death with Charles's predictability. Charles looked old. Life with Charles might be safe but it would never be exciting.

'Charles has bought Mummy a diving watch as a wedding present,' Karin said, breaking through his thoughts as though she'd read his mind.

He felt his heart agitate some more. *Dum-dum.* A diving watch? Charles Black was taking Lydia diving? Was that going to be their honeymoon? 'A diving watch?' he asked, in case he'd got it wrong.

They nodded together. 'It's so that Mummy doesn't have to take it off when she does the dishes,' Jen said seriously.

James fell back on the grass limply and stared at the dappled sky. He closed his eyes and began to laugh gently with relief.

It seemed so ludicrous that he found he couldn't stop.

The tears were rolling out of his screwed-up eyes and he laughed louder, laughed until his ribs ached. And he opened his eyes and his girls were looking down at him, smiling uncertainly, and he stopped for a moment but he couldn't keep it up and he laughed again and they were suddenly laughing with him, delighted, delighted at the accidental joke, delighted to be the cause of it.

And they fell on him, giggling, and he hugged them hard and for a small part of a short day, because he didn't, any more, ask too much, he knew they were his again.

9

Lisa Ashridge felt very strongly that some people should suffer.

She'd singled out Chrissie's husband.

Some marriages were made to be broken. It proved the absurdity of the concept.

She signed herself into the East India club as a guest of John King and was given a skirt to wear instead of her trousers.

'Ladies are not allowed into the lounge wearing slacks. You may change in the ladies' powder room,' the porter said, holding it out to her.

Lisa stared at him in disbelief. 'I'm not taking my trousers off. These are Chanel,' she said coldly, her hands going protectively into the pale turquoise pockets.

'Sorry, madam, ladies are not allowed to wear, er, trousers,' the porter said firmly. 'Shall I have Mr King come down here to speak to you?'

'NO! No,' Lisa said quickly, 'that's all right.' She glanced at the garment that was draped over his arm. 'What label is the skirt?'

The porter looked inside the waistband. 'There is no label, madam.'

No label? Lisa chewed the inside of her cheek and pondered on the dilemma for a moment. 'Give it to me,' she said.

The porter obliged and she lifted the skirt up and looked at it. She stepped into it and fastened it at the side. Then she carefully rolled up her trousers so they were above her knees and just hidden by the hem. 'Happy now?' she asked coldly, and looked down at herself. There was a sort of hump down the front of the skirt which she tried to smooth out with her palms.

'The zip goes at the back, madam, and the seams are meant to sit at the sides.'

Giving him a look, she twisted the skirt around. She had to admit it did feel better. 'Where is John?'

'In the lounge, madam.'

'Which is where?'

'Ladies are not allowed in the lounge, madam.'

'Why not? I've got the bloody skirt on, haven't I?'

'Ladies are only allowed in the ladies' lounge.' He smiled pleasantly. 'They were only allowed through the main entrance a few years ago,' he said, to let her know things could be worse.

'Are men allowed in the ladies' lounge?'

'Oh, yes, madam. Men are allowed anywhere. This is a gentleman's club.'

'Okay. Tell him his wife is waiting for him in the ladies' lounge.' She hesitated. 'No, better not. Tell him a friend . . . no.'

The porter watched her patiently while she worked out who she wanted to be.

'I could give him your name,' he suggested.

She had wanted it to seem like an accident, their meeting, but she could hardly accidentally ask for him to meet her in the ladies' lounge. 'Lisa Ashridge,' she said.

'I'm sure he will be only too pleased to see you.'

'I wouldn't bet on it,' Lisa said.

She was on her second gin and tonic and first dish of cashews when John King came in, not with the porter but with someone else, who pointed her out to him. Rather unnecessarily, she thought, when the only other person in the room was the barman.

He looked at her curiously, and smiled. Lisa saw the chipped tooth, the bane of Chrissie's life, and saw also why John King refused to get it crowned. It made his otherwise conventional face look roguish; made him seem slightly bruised and Eastender-ish.

'Hello. You asked to see me.' He gave her the same easy smile she'd seen in the photographs.

'You make it sound an unusual request,' she said, 'women asking for you.'

She knew damn well it wasn't. Chrissie had regaled her with stories of people he'd coveted; neighbours, neighbours' wives, their handymen, their cleaning ladies, their cows, their donkeys . . . Amazing that doing all that only broke one commandment, as Chrissie had pointed out some drunken evening.

John King laughed and sat down and was brought a drink.

Lisa crossed her legs and saw that the trousers were showing under the skirt. As soon as the barman returned to the bar she reached round and undid the back of the skirt and slipped it off onto the floor and rolled down her trousers. They were hardly creased at all. 'The skirt doesn't go, really, does it?' she said.

She looked at John and waited for his reaction.

John didn't leap up in shock, or call the porter or do any of the things she would have expected from Chrissie's description of him. Instead, he picked the skirt up and hung it on the wing of the ladies' chair next to her.

'My wife's done that in her time,' he said.

Lisa picked up her glass and thought about the remark. Only two sorts of men mentioned their wives in front of a pretty woman who had sought them out: the husband in love and the obsessive womaniser, the one because he doesn't want to

58

play and the other because he wants to and is setting out the rules from the onset.

Still, even womanisers didn't want to be cheated on.

She looked up speculatively and John King was still looking at her. He looked as amused as if he was reading her mind and didn't care what was in it. He looked neither troubled nor curious.

For a split second Lisa caught a glimpse of why Chrissie was frustrated in her marriage – this was a man so in control that he would allow nothing to surprise him. He was a con-man who got away with it.

Well, she would see about that. 'I know your wife,' she said. 'I know her very well.'

He didn't reply, but just sat watching her with polite amusement.

'I know this is going to come as a shock, but we've been lovers for some time now,' she continued, watching him and waiting for the explosion. And waiting . . .

It was hard to ignore the impression that it hadn't, in fact, come as a shock at all. He was looking at her as benevolently as if she belonged to the Salvation Army. She suddenly found that from here she didn't know where to go. She felt slightly uneasy.

'And what do you want me to do about it?' he asked presently, pressing the ball of his thumb against his broken tooth.

Lisa felt a flicker of hope. Divorce her, she thought, but perhaps he could think of something better himself, some more personal horror. 'I just wanted you to know that she was making a fool of you,' she said.

And then the uneasiness returned as she wondered how she had come to make such a mistake. Despite him keeping his smile in place the temperature plummeted and she knew she would have to find a way to retract. But it was too late.

59

'Actually, Lisa,' he said softly, 'you're the one who is making a fool of me.'

'No, I don't think –'

'Coming here where I am known and my wife is known and breaking the rules of the club.' His eyes rested sadly on the skirt, hanging from the chair. 'And rules are so important, aren't they? Aren't they, Lisa?'

'Yes.'

'Now put on that skirt and get out of here.'

Lisa had never been afraid before, but something in his voice made her afraid, very afraid, now.

She reached for the skirt and pulled it up over her trousers, her face flaming with anger checked by fear. She hated being afraid. She stood up and glared at him.

He watched her impassively back, the coldness gone. He'd had his own way and was content.

She began to roll up the trousers again.

'Just get out,' he said, and she picked up her bag in a hurry and left the trousers alone.

'Take it from me,' he said calmly, 'you know nothing, you understand nothing, about my wife, or me.'

Yeah, she thought, leaving the table, interview over. She tried to push the trouser leg up again.

'Get out!'

She was going. She misjudged it. She'd seriously misjudged it.

But sooner or later it would be payback time for John King. She would see to that.

10

The weekend was spent helping Larry make lists.

He made lists of people to ring, lists of people he'd already rung, people he wouldn't touch with a bargepole, people to have drinks with.

By Monday morning, the ninth of June and the first day of Larry's unemployment, Megan was having breakfast in her green linen dress and wondering why Larry was working twice as hard now he was unemployed as he ever did before.

She'd just finished her toast when Larry came downstairs in his suit.

'Wow,' she said, looking up from the folded *Independent* in front of her, 'I thought you were going to have a lie-in?'

Larry sat at the table opposite her and picked up the packet of All-Bran that had fallen over on the yellow cloth and poured some into his bowl. He looked up at Megan and grinned. 'I'm all ready for Project Employment,' he said as Ruth came in from the hall and tossed a letter onto the table. Larry grabbed it and opened it carelessly.

'What is it?' Megan asked, reaching for her mug of coffee.

'Wedding invitation,' he said, passing it to her. 'Lydia's managed to get Charles to do the decent thing.'

'Hardly a challenge, is it,' Megan said. They'd heard all about Charles from James. She looked at the stiff white card and read Lydia's handwriting. 'She wants us there for James. Sort of minders. Six o'clock at the register office.' Although she'd said it flippantly, reading the invitation gave her a pang of nostalgia for the olden days. The truth was, she thought to herself, she didn't like change. She far preferred things to stay as they were.

'She's nuts to leave him,' Ruth said, coming up behind her and reading the invitation over her shoulder. 'James is so hunky. She's absolutely nuts.'

'Nuts,' Bill shouted from under the table.

'Yeah,' Megan said, but she knew that Lydia hadn't really been nuts at all. She'd done it simply out of a sense of self-preservation.

The truth was, James did things to excess. The fact that he'd got Lydia pregnant and that she'd had twins had been an example. He did everything to excess except work. Work was something he didn't bother with at all.

James and Larry had met at school around the age of eight and had, surprisingly, stayed friends. It was an attraction of opposites combined with mutual admiration. Larry envied James's general recklessness, and James admired Larry's easy-going nature, but the point was, neither of them had the slightest desire to change places.

The friendship had survived expulsion from school on James's side and university on Larry's. There had been a lull in the relationship when James had married Lydia and the twins were born, but Megan's presence in Larry's life had evened the score again and for a few years the two families had met frequently.

The friendship had changed down a gear when Lydia had left home, taking the girls with her.

James had been hurt, and then angry, and finally, disbelieving. He'd looked after the girls while Lydia had worked, mainly by default, it was true, but he couldn't believe that they'd gone for good.

Nor could Megan, at first.

Out of all their friends, this was the first separation. There was something alarming about it. It opened up possibilities.

Megan shivered and reached for her coffee. For a while she'd hoped Lydia and James could have got back together. James seemed to think they would, but James's mind worked on different lines from the rest of the world. It all seemed unfinished, Megan thought. She felt an ache inside her. The truth was that when Lydia left James she hadn't only deserted him, she'd deserted Larry and Megan, too.

For a long time afterwards Megan had waited anxiously, then sadly, for Lydia to call. Months later, when the call finally came, it was somehow too late. Lydia had quietly got on with things, found a flat for herself and the girls, met Charles and been promoted, like some government advice video made to give divorce a good name.

In Lydia's absence they'd found themselves allied with James. James would come round night after night with a bottle of Scotch and get drunk with Larry.

Bill had been just one, then. After one particularly drunken night Megan had confronted Larry and James and considered divorcing them both – Lydia, she'd thought, would have laughed at that.

Megan put the invitation on the table and read the last line again: *Please could you come to keep an eye on James? All love, Lydia.*

It was friendly enough. But it stirred up all sorts of emotions that she'd thought had gone away.

Ruth sat down, reached for the invitation and studied it carefully. 'Are you going to go?'

Megan looked at Larry across the table. 'Are we?'

'We don't know that James is going yet. If he isn't, we're probably not expected to. I'll give him a ring.'

Megan put on her green linen jacket. 'Give him my love.'

'And mine,' Ruth said.

63

Megan went round the table to kiss Larry. 'Hope it goes well today.'

'Yes. I'll be in Mike Reeve's office all morning,' Larry said, rubbing the palms of his hands together. He glanced at Ruth. 'Might take Bill out this afternoon, take him off your hands.'

'You can't,' Ruth said possessively, flicking her blonde hair away from her face, 'we've already got plans.'

'Got to go,' Megan said, seeing a storm brewing. She picked up her bag and looked under the tablecloth for Bill. 'Bye, Bill.'

Bill emerged from his hideout and hugged her legs, and he and Larry waved her off from the door.

From Reeve's office, when he'd run out of lists, Larry rang James to tell him the news, which was that he had temporarily joined the ranks of the unemployed.

'Signed on yet?' James asked.

'It's not worth it. I won't be entitled to anything for three months and I'll be employed again by then,' Larry said.

James laughed heartily at that. 'Sign on now, mate. In three months' time they'll just about have sorted out your claim.'

Larry wasn't in the mood for James's streetwise pessimism. 'Got a wedding invitation from Lydia,' he said, changing the subject.

James's chuckling faded instantly, like a radio being turned off. 'Oh. Well tell Meg not to buy a hat,' he said after a moment. 'It's not going to happen, Larry. She's doing it to worry me. Listen, Larry, let's have lunch. I know a little place off the A40.'

Larry had been planning to have lunch in a restaurant in which he would bump into people in the business. On the other hand he could leave high-profile lunching for another day. Then a thought occurred to him. 'I haven't got a car,' he said.

'I'll be in Soho later this morning. I'll pick you up. Give me the address.'

So he gave James the address of Reeve's office in Wardour Street and they planned to meet later. As he put the phone down, Mike Reeve came into the office, straightening his Hermès tie. 'Help yourself to the fax, copier and Janie. Just don't answer the phone,' he said. 'A week should do it. Good luck, mate.'

Larry waited until he'd gone and then he sat behind his desk. He rested his palms on it and imagined he'd got Reeve's job. A week should do it, he thought happily. He smoothed his palms over the cool wood grain. Next to Reeve's keyboard was a mouse mat with a crossword on it. The squares were all blank. Larry looked at it for a few minutes and resisted the urge to fill it in for him. He took out his ancient Filofax and turned to his business card holder to check whether he had missed anyone out.

Having put out the word that he was available, he then rang a headhunting firm who had been on to him in the past. Nice, he thought, rubbing his scarred eyebrow, if he could get a job without Megan's help.

At the end of the morning he was tired but hopeful. By lunchtime he was just tired, and more than ready for a pub lunch off the A40.

'Larry! You bastard,' James greeted him.

His mind full of job prospects, Larry shook his head to clear it and grinned. 'You know more than I do,' he said.

'Get in.' James pushed a newspaper off the passenger seat onto the floor and Larry got in and sat down on the black, cracked leather seats of the Rover 90. 'You'll like this pub. Hundred and three varieties of beer. I'm working my way through them.'

Larry leaned forward and rubbed the windscreen with his

hand before realising that the grey coating was not condensation but dirt.

'Wipers are out. Won't need them today – look at the weather.' James reached for a piece of newspaper and got out of the car. He cleaned the windscreen vigorously on Larry's side and got back in again.

It was a hot day, he was right. Larry thought that rain might do the car a bit of good, but he said nothing. He glanced at James. He looked as though he'd given up eating. His tan was yellowing slightly, but his hair was as blond as ever.

As they drove, Larry told him about the takeover. If Larry had been hoping for a sympathetic ear – and he had – he soon found that James didn't possess one as far as jobs went.

'Why tie yourself down, mate?' James said as he drove. 'I mean, look at me. What do you see?'

Larry looked. He looked at the shorts and the thin face and the tanned legs and the tangled fair hair, a little too long for a man in his thirties, and he thought: I see a waster.

'Go on, tell me what you see,' James said, glancing at him with his light eyes urging.

Larry dodged the question. 'It's all right for you,' he said. 'What you don't have you don't miss.'

'I've worked,' James said. 'I worked in a tax office once. It was years ago. Went to sign on and they gave me a job, it was bloody awful. Do this, do that. Get up early. Wear a suit.' He shook his head at the memory. 'The best thing I ever did was look after the twins. Best time of my life. I would have educated them at home, too, except Lydia put her foot down. School of life, Larry, school of life. It teaches you everything you need to know.'

'What's it taught you, James?'

'It's taught me not to work.'

Larry exhaled loudly. 'It's different for you,' he said after a moment. 'I like working. I know who I am when I work.'

'Sad,' James said, 'sad.' He changed gear. He was silent for a long time and Larry had begun pursuing thoughts of his own when he next spoke. 'So you bastards are going to the wedding,' he said.

Larry thought he detected a certain amount of animosity in the statement. 'Only to look after you,' he said. The sun was hot and he wanted to let some air in. He reached for the winder but couldn't shift it.

'It's jammed,' James said. 'I'll fix it tomorrow. And I don't need looking after.'

Larry grinned. 'That's okay. I think we've only been invited to keep you under control.'

James straightened his arms as they gripped the wheel and seemed pleased. 'That so? Think you'll manage it?'

The atmosphere in the car lifted. They were on the A40 now and picking up speed.

Larry pulled down the sun visor and saw his eyes framed in the rectangle of the mirror. It was very hot and he could feel the sweat breaking out on his forehead, but he reminded himself of the beer he would have in the pub. He could almost taste it in his throat. He could feel the froth popping gently on his lips.

Suddenly he was aware of a change, only very slight, in the sound of the car. It was like a metallic buzzing, a low grade interference on the radio. It seemed to be coming from under his seat.

'I want her back, Larry,' James said forcefully. 'I can give her more than Charles Black ever could. I can give her a life.'

Larry was hardly listening to what James was saying. He was concentrating on the noise. It was getting louder and it was like something vibrating in a box, that was the nearest he could get to it, something vibrating in an enclosed space. He glanced at James and saw that James could hear it now. James looked back at him, frowning, equally puzzled. He glanced at the back seat.

The noise slowly lifted up around them, intensifying, darkening the car like black smoke, and Larry found himself sitting in a cloud of flies.

He panicked and as he tried to swat them off he saw they were clustering on the windscreen, covering it, and James was sweeping his hand across it like a wiper but as soon as they lifted they settled straight back on it again, heading for daylight.

James slammed on the brakes, shouting, 'Bloody hell!' and the car skidded sideways for what seemed a long time.

There was a smell of burning rubber and Larry felt the seat belt cut into his neck. He braced himself for the impact, shielding his face in his hands.

When nothing hit them he undid his seat belt in a sudden panic and flung open the door, scrambling out onto the pavement, brushing himself frantically. He could feel the flies everywhere, all over him, under his clothes, in his hair. He tore off his shirt and stood by the curb, shaking his shirt, his heart pounding as the noise of car horns blasted around them.

James was still in the car. He was trying to shoo the flies out but was only managing to stir the busy mass momentarily.

'Got a paper on you?'

Larry pointed to the one that had been by his feet and James picked it up and began slapping round the interior of the car. Larry winced as purply-red stains smeared the passenger window.

A few flies drifted lazily out and flew away.

Larry gave his shirt another shake before pulling it on. He fastened it slowly. Two of the buttons were missing.

He stared at the car. Nothing would induce him to get back in until the flies had all gone. He had never experienced anything so disgusting, so repulsive in his life as the feel of those flies on him.

The traffic was bottlenecking behind them and he didn't care.

James finally got out of the car, shaking his head and sticking his fingers up at the cars behind.

'What the hell happened, James? Have you got something dead in there?'

James was scratching his head. He looked bemused. 'Dropped some maggots on the floor on Saturday,' he said. 'Hell of a thing. Didn't manage to get them all out. Felt quite nice though, didn't they? Cool and fuzzy. Would've thought flies were hot.' He shook his head again and looked at Larry with his pale eyes. 'Tell you something, mate, I need that drink.' He got back into the car.

Larry looked inside it.

He wasn't going to ask what James was doing sprinkling maggots on the floor of his car.

He got back in reluctantly and shut the door, trying not to look at the smears.

Need that drink? The understatement of the century.

Friend or not, he couldn't help but think it was probably the smartest move Lydia'd ever made, leaving James.

11

Megan was jumping the gun by checking the database against the Triton brief, but a couple of people had sprung to mind and she liked to see whether the researchers had been doing their job in providing an accurate list of candidates. She was jotting down notes when Zelda came in.

'I want a word,' Zelda said.

Megan swivelled her chair.

'It's about the cover for my maternity leave,' Zelda said. 'We agreed on what we wanted –'

'A consultant,' Megan confirmed, pushing her blonde hair away from her forehead and guessing what was to come. 'But you've found someone else, equally suitable.'

'You've been bugging my phone,' Zelda said in mock astonishment. 'Well, yes, it's Lisa Ashridge. Gerry suggested her, as a matter of fact. She worked at TVS for four years then went to Carlton when they lost the franchise – she knows the media back to front.'

'But she doesn't know anything about headhunting, does she?'

'She knows how it works. I've interviewed her in the past. She'd work *for* you, rather than replace me. It could work.'

'I've picked her brains myself a couple of times and you're right, she's got her finger on the pulse, but we'd be taking a flyer, wouldn't we? And why would she want to leave Carlton for a temporary job that she's never done before?'

70

'She wants more strings to her bow, never a bad idea. She's not going to be stuck for a job, is she? She's got an excellent reputation.' Zelda paused. She gave a little smile. 'And she's single.'

'No one to rush home to in the evenings, you mean,' Megan said. 'I wouldn't be too sure about that. There must be quite a few wives out there who have made Lisa models out of Ikea candles.'

'Rumours,' Zelda said dismissively. She rubbed her abdomen. 'You'd be in charge but Lisa would be an extra, and useful, pair of hands. She knows who to chat up.'

'She's had plenty of practice at that.'

'I want to see if we can arrange for her to come in this afternoon. If you don't think it will work, we'll carry on looking. Give her a chance, that's all I ask. By the way, how's Larry getting on?'

Megan rubbed her temple. He'd hijacked the postman, planted weeds, dug up bulbs, annoyed Ruth, tidied the attic and been circling the business pages every night when she'd got home. She assumed this wasn't what Zelda was asking. 'Fine. Still available.'

'Any idea why Xylus didn't keep him on?'

'No.'

Zelda glanced at her watch. 'If Kensington Nannies rings, tell them I'll get back to them, will you?'

'Sure,' she said, her mind on Larry. Larry was giving the impression that he was quietly confident about Project Employment but his anxiety was showing through in ways she didn't much like. She'd seen so much of his back in bed these past couple of weeks that she knew the exact position of every mole. Or mole-hill, as Bill called them. Zelda's words finally sank in and she looked up at her. 'I thought you already had a maternity nanny,' she said.

'I'm going to get someone else for Cyrill.' Zelda looked

pained. 'Mandy took Cyrill to Kidz Grub last week and gave her a burger.'

Megan waited for the punchline. She realised after a moment that that was it. 'A burger,' she said. 'Ooh, I think that's terrible. No wonder you want to sack her.'

'It's not a laughing matter. Cyrill's been brought up entirely on organic foods since she was weaned.'

'Four years of age and she's just had her first burger,' Megan said. 'Imagine all those chemicals pumping through her unsuspecting system.'

'There's no need to be malicious.'

'Come on – it's not that bad,' she said, but Zelda was not ready to be reassured.

'I'm sacking her,' Zelda said. 'She's a stand-in for me and that means she does what I say.' Her gaze had wandered to her computer screen but it snapped back to Megan. 'I mean it,' she said sharply.

'I know.'

'Then why are you sitting there with BUT hovering on your lips?'

Megan shrugged and raised her hands in surrender. 'No buts, I'm on your side entirely. I was just thinking that we ought to swap nannies. Mine's become organic, big-time.'

Zelda was shaking her head. 'She shouldn't have taken her. It's sheer laziness. She knows how I want Cyrill brought up. And when I told her –' Zelda sat down heavily and reached for her cup '– do you know what she said? She told me to try doing it myself.'

Megan leaned back in her chair and clasped her hands behind her head. There's the rub, she thought. 'It would soon wear off,' she said. 'You'd atrophy if you stayed at home all day. When I think of my mother being a career housewife all her life and working her way up the ladder to whiter whites, it makes work seem like a holiday.'

Zelda patted the white streak in her hair. 'It's not as simple as that.' She sighed heavily. 'You know what I felt when they said they'd been to Kidz Grub? I felt angry because Cyrill had actually enjoyed it. Cyrill thinks I'm this stranger who doesn't want her to do ordinary things.'

'Hardly a stranger,' Megan said quickly, because the feeling of being one to her child, actually, wasn't unfamiliar.

Zelda sounded tired. 'The only way to have a child brought up the way you want is to do it yourself.'

'Zelda, you only feel like this because you're pregnant, trust me,' Megan said, thinking of Bill and his Zoofie. Hand on heart, she was never jealous. Not often. 'It's the Invasion of the Body Snatchers.'

Zelda laughed. 'You're right. Want a coffee?'

'Please.' Megan watched her walk away. From the back she didn't look pregnant at all. Working mothers had to stick together . . . I'll miss her when she goes, Megan thought.

Lisa Ashridge came into the office right on time.

She was shown into the informal interview room, the one with the chat-show set.

Megan had already looked up her file. She checked her face in her mirror and walked through. Lisa stood up as she entered the room. Her dark hair was gelled and pinned up at the back and her dark suit made her look disconcertingly androgynous.

She gave the impression of being tall, but in fact was the same height as Megan. They shook hands and Megan sat on the adjacent sofa, allowing Lisa and Zelda to share the three-seater.

Megan looked at Lisa's outfit. She herself always wore bright colours – Ronit Zilkha, Escada, Jaeger; people remembered bright colours, whereas dark outfits always looked pretty much the same, so she'd thought.

'Ghost,' Lisa said, noticing the direction of her gaze.

Megan looked away, discomfited. Good trick, she thought,

instinctively compiling comments. Too self-assured. Inflexible. Doesn't believe herself capable of making mistakes. Doesn't fit the company profile.

'What made you think of us?' Zelda was asking.

'Gerry said you were looking for someone. I met him at Madame Jojo's. Clive's leaving do?' She raised her eyebrow and gave a small smile.

Deduct a point, Megan thought. She'd seen Zelda's lips tighten. Gerry obviously hadn't mentioned Madame Jojo's to Zelda.

'Truth is, I want out of the terrestrial channel umbrella,' Lisa said. 'All this She-Man stuff . . .' She shook her head. 'Crunch time came when Howard Styles described me as a man with everything but bollocks.'

And score one to her, Megan thought. Here it was; truth time. She was saying aloud everything that was said about her. And the woman's body language was amazing – she had mirroring down to a fine art. Hopefully Zelda would start stroking her abdomen so they could see how far Lisa would take it.

'Truth is,' Lisa added, looking at Megan with pale green eyes, 'I've got more balls than most.'

Their eyes locked. Megan forced herself not to look away. 'What's your notice period? We need somebody ASAP.'

'A week.'

Megan raised her eyebrows. 'That's unusual for someone in your position.'

'I negotiated it. I only ever do anything by choice. I don't like being bound by other people.'

'You know the job is temporary,' Megan said. 'What do you intend to do when it finishes?'

'I'm attracted to the idea of taking time out. I'm thirty-six and I have no ties, no dependants. Nothing.'

Megan looked at her curiously. What had she heard in the

74

'nothing'? It had been said a little too harshly, as though it wasn't a word Lisa Ashridge was comfortable with. Well, well. 'Let us tell you about the company –'

'That's not necessary. I've done my research,' Lisa said, turning to Zelda. 'You've got a database with over five thousand names, including graduates; Gerry's a sleeping partner; you've got an impressive list of clients including two television companies that pay you a retainer. Megan's been here for seven years having previously worked for Green Thompson. Your record speaks for itself. You don't have to sell yourself to me. Now, do you have any more questions for me?'

'We've done our research, too,' Zelda said coolly.

Lisa glanced at her watch and got to her feet. 'Then I won't keep you any longer. I'm not here to talk you into anything, I'm here so that you can have a look at me.' She smiled a small smile. 'What you see is what you get. I'll wait for your call.'

Megan stood up.

A handshake was the customary ending; that swift exchange of warmth – or coldness and stickiness, as the case may be, but Lisa didn't make the gesture and Megan didn't precipitate it.

Megan walked with her to the lift, faintly amused at the way the interview had gone. Who had been interviewing whom? Lisa Ashridge had been in control from start to finish, and was leaving them with the impression that she had done them a favour by managing to fit them into her schedule. She couldn't wait to hear what Zelda thought.

They waited in silence for the lift to arrive. When it did, Lisa stepped in and jabbed the button. No farewells for this woman. Megan felt herself held by that pale green gaze for a moment, and then the doors closed.

Zelda was standing by the window when she walked back into the office. She was looking at the fire-escape.

'Lovely view,' Megan commented.

75

Zelda turned. 'Well? What's your gut-feeling?'

'A definite no. Yours?'

'A definite no.'

'Cocky.'

'Unladylike.'

'Bloody self-assured.'

'Thorough.' Zelda looked out at the fire-escape again. 'The question is,' she said softly, 'could you work with her?'

Megan sat down and stretched out her legs. She and Zelda had much in common. Not least, husbands and offspring. Sure, when they were working, and often when they were not, work came first, but there was always time for a phonecall home, or a chance to nip out to get something for supper. That was the She part of She-Man. Their relationship was like a comfortable marriage; a bit of bickering, a few disagreements, some highs, the usual stuff. It wouldn't be that way with Lisa.

Why did that seem rather exciting?

She smiled at Zelda. 'Yes. I could work with her,' she said.

12

On Saturday morning they woke late, with Bill sandwiched between them in bed, holding a blue Power Ranger in his hand.

Since Ruth had gone to her parents' for the weekend they had the house to themselves, and they were always more aimless when Ruth wasn't there.

Megan went to make the coffee, bringing it upstairs with the papers, and put Larry's cup on his bedside cabinet. 'Xylus are looking for a group head,' she said. 'I thought you ought to know.'

Larry peered at her from under the duvet. 'What was that?' he asked, but she could tell by the sharpness of his voice that he'd heard her, got it in one.

Bill had woken up and gone down the end of the bed, driving cars down the hills of his knees.

Larry pushed himself up the bed. 'Are you saying they gave me the push?'

'Not necessarily.'

'No wonder Burgess looked shifty.' Larry looked at her. 'Are Xylus your clients?'

'Yes,' she said.

Larry slumped back and pulled a pillow over his face.

'If it comes up in interviews, it's better that you know. The official line is that you went because of the takeover, isn't it?'

'Yes.' A muffled reply.

'Do you think Burgess will give you a decent reference?'

He took the pillow away. 'Yes, I think he will. I don't know. Maybe he won't. I just don't know. I thought I was doing okay. Not just okay – I thought I was doing well.'

Megan reached for her coffee and tried to read her paper. 'Have you remembered we've got people coming round tonight?'

Larry made a muffled response, then lifted half of the pillow up. 'Cancel it,' he said, and hid again.

'Why? We've got plenty of time to get food in before then. I'll do something simple, and you can make your date, banana and cream thing for pud.'

Larry lifted the pillow up again. 'Who've you asked?'

'Rob and Sonia, Verity and Josh.'

'Cancel it,' he said again, and retreated.

Megan carried on looking at the paper for a moment. 'I can't cancel it,' she said suddenly, 'they'll have arranged baby-sitters by now. Anyway, you like Rob.'

Larry put the pillow behind him and sat up in bed. His morse code eyebrow was ruffled. He looked at her very seriously and the creases around his eyes showed white in his tanned face. 'Meg, I don't want to sit around the table in my own house listening to two men talking non-stop about their jobs. For that matter, I don't want to hear their wives talk non-stop about schools. And I don't want them looking at me sympathetically while they do it.'

Megan glanced at Bill, who was now poised with a car in his hand at the foot of the bed. He was watching them with his blue eyes huge.

'You're being silly,' she said lightly, for Bill's sake. 'The world doesn't stop just because you've lost your job.'

'Lost it?' He gave a short, contemptuous laugh. 'I was booted out.'

Megan watched Bill balance a red Ferrari on the lumps that

78

were Larry's feet. Larry moved his feet irritably and the red car fell on the floor.

'You kicked my car,' Bill said.

'Well leave my bloody feet alone,' Larry replied sharply.

'Larry –' Megan began, objecting.

'I'm not in the mood, Meg.' He shut his eyes. His thick, dark eyelashes gleamed, but even with his eyes shut he was frowning. 'Why didn't you mention it last night?'

Megan made a mountain out of her knees and felt the car slide down her shins. 'I don't suppose you've any specific idea why you weren't kept on?'

Larry continued to frown. Then he opened his eyes and stared for a while at the wall opposite. 'John King,' he said slowly. 'That Monday, in Burgess's office, he acted as though he couldn't wait to see the back of me.'

'Any idea why?'

Larry shook his head. 'Nah,' he said shortly.

It wasn't much help, Megan thought. Maybe John King had come to the same conclusion as she once had, that Larry lacked drive.

'Anyway, it's irrelevant. You can't go into hiding,' she said. 'It's Bill's birthday in a couple of weeks. Your parents, and mine, will be assuming it's business as usual. Are you going to cancel that, too?'

'I'll be four,' Bill said helpfully.

'Yes, I know. Big boy.'

Larry looked at Megan and put his hand on hers. 'I don't care what happens in a couple of weeks, I just don't want anyone here in my house, not tonight.' He pulled the sheet and rolled over.

Megan looked at him. He brought to mind a curled up hedgehog using its prickles as its defence. He shouldn't be curling up, she thought, he should be attacking. Lacks drive, she thought, and this weakness suddenly annoyed her. 'All right, we'll cancel, but you've got to ring them,' she said shortly, and got out of bed. 'I'm not doing it. I'm not lying for you.' She'd bet she had to in the end, though. 'Come on, Bill.'

It was too soon for him to be discouraged, she told herself as she followed Bill downstairs, and the thought depressed her.

On Sunday morning Megan was sitting at the kitchen table in a bright orange t-shirt with Bill, watching him draw Thomas the Tank Engine in a corner of a blank sheet of A4. Funny how he only used a small part of the sheet, she thought.

She was still irritable with Larry. She *had* had to cancel the dinner, pleading gastroenteritis, which was enough to put anyone off. And she wasn't forgiving him for it, either.

'Are you listening?' Larry said, walking around the kitchen.

Megan, startled, lifted her head. No, she hadn't been. 'Of course I am,' she said.

Bill raised his head and looked at them both, his small face troubled, radar alert. His hair was sticking up on one side of his head, fanning out from being slept on. 'What's the matter?' he asked, still clutching his crayon tightly.

'What's the matter? I haven't got a job, that's what's the matter.'

Bill looked at him with interest and put his crayon down. It rolled across the table. 'If you don't get one, won't you ever have to work again?'

'No.'

Bill looked pleased. 'Will Mummy?' he asked hopefully, turning to look at Megan.

Megan nodded. 'Yes, I still have to go,' she said.

Bill stood up and reached for his crayon and began to colour the paper vigorously. Then he stopped and looked up at her. 'Why?'

'Why? Because working's my job,' she said in a bad American accent.

'And who would keep us if Mummy didn't work?' Larry asked, rubbing his jaw, looking at her slyly, getting it in first.

I wasn't going to say that, she thought resentfully. She hated it when he tried to read her mind.

She snatched a look at him and he was staring at her intently.

Bill went back to his drawing and although she was looking at Bill with feigned interest she knew Larry was still watching her over his head.

'It could be any day, now, couldn't it,' he said.

She felt for the gold chain around her neck and pulled at the crucifix on it, sawing it slowly back and forth. 'Yes.' Sounding bored. 'It could be any day. You'll be the right man in the right place, and whoosh . . . a job.' She didn't much feel like playing this game right now: reassure the Larry. A variation on an old theme. The same conversation that they'd already had at least once a day since he'd got the news. Once more with feeling, she thought.

'What if I don't get a job for three months? How long can we carry on on one income, Megan?'

'We'll see when – if – the time comes. You can claim for benefits, then.'

'And just be unemployed?' He was as indignant as though she was forcing him into it.

'Well what do you suggest? You're the one with the dooms-day predictions.'

Bill got down from the table and gave his picture to Larry. Larry took the drawing and looked at it, puzzled, turning it first one way and then the other. He gave it back to Bill and put his hand on Bill's shoulder. Bill ducked from under this fatherly pat and put the picture by his face again, too close for Larry ever to be able to focus on it. '*Look*, Daddy.'

81

But Daddy was not to be stopped. 'Great, son,' he said, returning his intense gaze to his wife. 'What do we pay Ruth to look after Bill? Ten grand?'

He said it so seriously, so thoughtfully, that Megan suddenly laughed. 'You're not thinking of becoming a nanny, are you Larry?'

'It's that funny, is it? I'd do it for nothing.'

Ah; the implication hit her. The build-up, the hopelessness. 'Larry –' and she reached out for his hand across the table and was surprised to find it was like ice.

He gripped her tightly, squeezing the blood out of her fingers. 'There's one boy I know who could do with seeing more of his parents,' he said.

Megan had never approved of emotional blackmail, especially when it was applied against her. 'But you might get another job next week.'

'Do you think it's likely?'

Megan didn't answer and looked down. A stray piece of cotton stuck out from her orange t-shirt, and she pulled it with her free hand. It puckered up the fabric of the hem. The thought of Larry getting a job next week wasn't half as unlikely as the thought of him looking after Bill full-time.

It wasn't that he was a bad father . . . it was just that he wasn't the sort.

'Larry,' she said, 'it's not the worst idea in the world, but you need to be available if something comes up.'

He was still gripping her with his cold hand and he pulled her with a jerk to emphasise his words. 'Meg, James said the best time of his life was when he looked after the girls. I need something to do, I need a job. I can look after Bill – it makes more sense than being here all day with nothing to do except duck and dive to keep out of Ruth's way. I can take him to the playgroup, the same as Ruth does. There are other parents at the playgroup. I'd have a role.'

Megan stared at him. Bloody James, she thought, putting ideas into his head.

Larry looking after Bill? In business terms, let's face it, if she had to interview Larry for a job as nanny there was no way she would take him. He had no qualifications and no previous experience in the field of childcare. He was not overtly child-friendly. He spoke to all children as though they were deaf. He disregarded mealtimes and when they went out he usually ordered something inappropriate for a three-year-old and finished it off himself.

She tried to flatten the puckered hem, smoothing it with her finger. At best she would say that somewhere deep inside him there was some innate paternal instinct but the bottom line was that he didn't really know Bill. He'd never had a chance to. He'd seen more of Bill in the last few days than in the whole of the previous three years. Even then he'd been protected by the buffer of Ruth.

She freed her left hand from his and rubbed her forehead. 'I don't think it's a good idea,' she said at last.

'Meg, I'm his father.'

'What about Ruth?' she said.

Larry shook his head. 'Don't worry about that, I'll tell her. I'll tell her we can't afford to pay her while I'm at home.'

Megan felt the beginning of panic. 'But it's not true,' she said. It was too sudden for her, far too sudden. Bill loved Ruth. Ruth had been with them since she was seventeen and she was practically one of the family; she didn't want to lose her. Not until Bill was old enough not to need her, anyway.

Larry got up from the table. 'Not yet. But before long it might be.' He put the breakfast bowls into the sink and began to wash up.

She saw him hesitate, bring something out of the soapy water and clear the suds from it with his hand.

It was large knife. For a moment she wondered if he was

checking whether it was clean. Then she realised that he was looking at his reflection in it.

What had he said? I need a role.

He was seeing himself as a composite of all the role models that the cinema had come up with in recent years; he was living *Mrs Doubtfire*, *Sleepless in Seattle*, *Jack and Sarah*, all rolled into one. For Larry, she thought, looking after Bill was not a job, it was a new part.

She could understand it, put like that; but it didn't make her feel any easier about it.

She could see Bill's drawing on the table with Thomas squashed up in one corner and a large area of blue in the other. There was one boy Larry knew who could do with seeing more of his parents – oh yeah? Bill was just fine with things as they were.

Of course, Bill's welfare came first, and Bill's happiness was all tied up with theirs. But Larry as nanny?

There was suction and a gurgle from the sink as the plug was pulled out.

That was Larry, proving himself on the domestic front.

It was Bill who spoke next. 'Can I have some more paper?'

'Can I have some more, please,' Larry said over his shoulder.

Bill smiled benevolently.

He loved his father.

'Yes you can, Daddy,' he said.

Megan ignored the triumphant look on Larry's face. My son!

Ruth was staying, she told herself. Larry'd had it. For all their sakes, but mostly Bill's, she wasn't going to be talked into this one.

PART THREE

Three's a Wedding

13

The following weekend, Megan, Larry and Bill were waiting with the other wedding guests in their cocktail dresses and black ties outside the Chelsea register office for Lydia and Charles to reach their slot on the list of early-evening marriages.

'When all the parties to divorce and remarriage are being adult about it, what is wrong with the ex-husband turning up at his ex-wife's wedding?' a friend of theirs asked Megan. 'Well, what?'

Megan smiled. 'It's very civilised,' she agreed, although it was an adjective she'd never thought of using to describe James. 'And actually, he's only been invited to Charles's, afterwards.'

As they stood in the fading sun James Wilder's name seemed to be on everyone's lips. Strange, that, that the possibility of his coming could cause a stir. But if he were coming he should have been here by now, she thought. Yes, she'd checked, same as they all had; and felt, over and above the relief that there wouldn't be a scene, a vague disappointment at the thought he might have changed his mind.

Lydia and Charles were in with the registrar and after a few minutes of their absence there was movement in the direction of the area where the wedding ceremony was to take place.

As Megan went into the airless room and moved along the rows of chairs, she hit unexpected pockets of perfume from the yellow roses and white lilies which had been tastefully arranged in strategic positions, presumably, she guessed, by Lydia.

87

Should have offered to help, she thought as they sidled into their seats. It seemed a sad thing to have to do on one's own. However, the idea of Lydia arranging her wedding flowers alone did not sit right; she would have roped Charles in at the very least, and probably Charles's mother. Or more likely still, a florist.

I feel like this, Megan thought, shuffling down the row, because in a way I'm jealous. I would like to have left a layabout husband – not Larry, of course, but a husband in the abstract – and taken my child and found a rich young man who would have me, and not only have me but marry me. And despite the angst of a broken marriage and a still besotted ex-husband, Lydia was bound to look stunning.

Finally the three of them reached the end of the row and sat down. 'Have you got the camera?' Megan asked Larry, leaning over Bill.

Larry patted his pocket and didn't answer. He was looking towards the door, seeming distracted. Bill was wriggling on the seat next to him, trying to see past the people in front, who were still deciding on which seat to sit on. Every now and then he tugged at the brass buttons on his navy blazer and Megan put her hand out to stop him.

'James won't come,' she said, smoothing her blue satin dress further towards her knees in the interests of decency. Before they'd started out, Larry had done a double-take and said he could see the shape of her nipples through it. Once he would have said it without the least sign of disapproval.

'He'll come. He said he'd come and he will.'

'He might come drunk to show how upset he is. It won't go down well with Lydia but if he doesn't go too far it might get him the sympathy vote.'

Larry turned his head sharply towards her. 'Why do women always think like that? As if everything's always stage-managed?'

88

'It usually is, that's why. A man wouldn't attend his wife's wedding to someone else just to throw earth on the coffin of their marriage. If he didn't love her it would be different, he could come to enjoy himself.' She knew Larry seemed to think it was some last noble gesture. 'So unless he's going to look so unhappy that Lydia can't go through with it I can't see the point.'

'Can't you? It's called being civilised. It's what women decided they wanted in a man, remember?'

Megan laughed but stopped as the room went suddenly quiet. She raised her head and saw James Wilder in the doorway. 'Wow, he's here,' she whispered unnecessarily.

Even at a glance James looked more like the groom than a guest. They watched him walk his nonchalant walk to the centre of the room – a few yards at most, but far enough for them to see what they were dealing with. He looked like a man who had been liberated. He looked like a man who had lost everything and was exulting in the fact that he had nothing left to lose. He looked, above all, dangerous.

Larry made to raise his hand in greeting as James stood with his back to the mahogany desk, but James was surveying the gathering with unhurried attention and Megan felt Larry's hand drop back down again, leaving James unhailed.

She watched James's finger and thumb curve round his fourth finger, as though feeling for a ring that should be there, and she felt an unexpected rush of lust. His dinner jacket, black bow tie and white shirt contrasted with his tan and he looked, yes, he looked noble. He'd done it. He'd shaved, and his blond hair was brushed back from his lean face and no one looked less likely to get a sympathy vote than he.

Megan saw the woman in front of her wriggle discreetly in her seat and she grinned. Good old James, she thought. It was the best poke in the eye ever. As far as looks went, Charles Black could never hope to compete.

She wondered whom exactly he was looking for, standing there with such authority, and she dared to believe it might be her. Suddenly James's gaze locked with hers. She felt an uncomfortable jolt shoot through her and she looked away, as though she'd been caught out doing something she shouldn't. Almost immediately she looked up again and straightened in her seat, but his eyes had already left hers, and gone on along the row, searching and silencing with a look.

Something caused James to smile. His smile always seemed like something he chose to put on rather than a response to an emotion. But there was something about him which made her always want more of him. He made her think of the darker things of life; danger and decay.

Of course, that was why Lydia had divorced him. Lydia had divorced him on the grounds of unreasonable behaviour.

Surprising, that, as she'd married him on those grounds too.

The room around them rustled slightly and settled again into stillness, as though it was generally assumed that James was about to break all tradition and choose the pre-wedding interlude in which to make a scene.

In the deathly quiet they waited expectantly.

Finally he said just one word.

It was a brief word, spoken conversationally, which Megan, to her disappointment, didn't catch.

There was a general stir as those who hadn't heard tried to find out what he'd said from those who'd heard, and during this stir he walked down the centre parting of the chairs and took a seat somewhere behind them.

'What did he say?' Megan whispered to Larry.

Bill leaned towards her over Larry's knee helpfully. 'Chewits,' he said.

Megan looked at Larry. 'Chewits?'

'I think he said Judas.' Larry rubbed his jaw and looked at

90

her. 'I mean,' he said uncomfortably, his voice so low she could hardly hear it above the growing hubbub, 'look at us. We were all there when Lydia married him, and now we're here to watch her marry Charles. Interchangeable spouses.'

Megan was silent for a moment. 'It's called serial monogamy,' she said.

Larry shook his head and cupped his hands to her ear. 'Cereal monogamy's having All-Bran again,' he whispered.

Megan giggled and Larry grinned at her and she felt a weight lift from her shoulders.

Maybe he did say Chewits, she thought. It wasn't fair of James to try to make them uncomfortable; they were on his side, after all.

There was a small commotion in the corridor and Lydia and Charles made their entrance at last, but owing to the puzzle of James's brief speech it was some moments before they were generally noticed.

As they all settled down again Megan looked at Lydia's hair. It was so short and bulbous and yellow that it looked like a cycle helmet. Her dress was clingy and green, cut on the bias, and it swirled out around her knees, leaving just enough fabric for her embarrassed daughters to hide behind. Megan's allegiance was firmly with James. Karin and Jen, despite their long dark dresses, were startled to see so many people looking at them in the small room. As Lydia and Charles sat at the mahogany desk, their backs to the guests, the girls squeezed themselves with their bare arms.

The registrar suggested in a monotone that they shouldn't take these vows lightly. Megan wondered if it was because of the girls that he emphasised the word 'these'.

Megan looked at the dazzling yellow roses and the creamy, scented lilies and wondered what the sight of his mortified daughters was doing to James.

*   *   *

The reception was held at Charles's flat, now Lydia and Charles's flat, on the tenth floor of a penthouse overlooking Lord's cricket ground.

It was all very civilised, Megan thought, putting her bag on the windowsill.

The spare room was full of presents and Larry disappeared for a while and came back looking flushed.

'Where have you been?'

'He's got some hash brownies,' he said. 'He's handing them round now.'

'Before the vol-au-vents? Lydia'll go nuts.'

Megan was caught by the arm by another friend who was knitting anatomically correct dolls and could do hair on men's bodies with mohair. 'I do it from life,' she was saying, and when the waiter, or butler, came around with a tray of champagne Megan took two, telling the knitter that one was for Larry and then absent-mindedly sipping both.

By the time the speeches began, the brownies had done the rounds and there was a certain amount of heckling. A man appeared with a basket on his head and disappeared into another room.

Charles stood in front of the cake with a glass in his hand. 'I want to thank you all for coming to celebrate our marriage,' he began.

Lydia was standing slightly behind him, her green dress clinging to her slim body in the way only a great designer, or static, could achieve. Her cycling helmet of hair was flawless. Her eyes met Megan's and she gave her a swift, warm smile, which Megan was too late to return.

As Charles's speech continued, Lydia began to look slightly bored. She checked her watch.

Megan was getting bored, too. She looked round for Larry and James, who had disappeared once more. She was glad Larry was doing his duty so diligently. She could see Bill still tugging at his brass buttons, but the bridesmaids, Karin and Jen, were feeding him crisps, so he was all right.

The next moment, she spotted Larry. He was sitting down, his chair pulled closely to James's. Between them was a worn garden ornament.

She glanced at Charles, who was still going strong, and eased her way through the group of people to Larry. As she approached, she recognised the ornament as being one of James's malformed Venuses.

'But they haven't got a garden,' she said, her words drowned out by cheers, possibly of relief, as Charles's speech came to an end.

James ignored her, and stood up. 'I've got a present for you, Lydia,' he announced, and with a heave, lifted up the concrete statue.

The small group that stood between them parted.

Lydia stared.

'Remember when we made them? Remember how we felt?' James's strong voice hushed the general conversation.

'Yes,' Lydia said, smoothing her hair. She bit her lip. 'Young and stupid.'

'We're ready to cut the cake, darling,' Charles called to her cheerfully, waving the knife and working on the assumption that if you pretended not to notice anything was wrong, then it wasn't.

Lydia ignored him and kept her eyes on James. 'Behave yourself, James, and take that lump of concrete out of here,' she said. Her voice was low and deliberate.

James was beginning to show the strain of holding, as Lydia put it, a lump of concrete. Perspiration was breaking out on his upper lip and the veins in his temples were standing out like pieces of discarded string. It was obvious he couldn't last much longer. 'It's a reminder of the good times, Lydia,' he said, gritting his teeth.

'There weren't any good times, that was the problem.' She turned to her husband. 'Get him out of here, Charles! If he's going to crack up, let him do it in his own place.'

'Mummy!' one of the girls said, shocked.

The statue began to wobble violently in James's arms as though her words had taken the last of his strength away.

Charles made his way to Lydia's side, looking anxious and wondering what was expected of him.

Megan could see the statue begin to topple.

She wasn't the only one aware of the danger – there was a light, brief squeal from somewhere behind her. 'Larry –' she shouted quickly, and Larry suddenly sprang forwards and put his shoulder under the bottom of the statue, steadying it, taking the weight. More hands came forward to help and together they all lowered it onto the carpet.

'Out!' Charles shouted, coming to the conclusion that words spoke louder than actions.

Larry and James staggered towards the door with the Venus, got it out into the corridor and leaned on the wall, panting. After a moment, Larry pressed the button for the lift.

Megan, hovering in the doorway, looked over her shoulder towards Lydia. She wanted to say something, to tell her she'd missed her, to apologise, and to say she'd had no part in the Venus affair – but Lydia had turned away, presumably to cut the cake.

She went quickly back inside for Bill. Karin and Jen gave him some grapes to eat in the taxi, and kissed him goodbye.

'What are you going to do with Dad?' Karin asked Megan softly.

'Give him a ride home, I suppose. If it's left to them, they'll probably go for a curry afterwards.'

Karin nodded, and gave a sad, half-smile. 'He's not that bad, you know. He can't help being who he is.'

'I know. Most of the time, you admire him for it. Not many

people remain themselves against the odds.' Megan kissed them on their freckled cheeks and went back out with Bill.

James had the lift door wedged open with his foot. The sweat was shimmering on his lean face.

'Why did you do it?' Megan asked him, squeezing up to the statue in the small lift.

'I saw it in a garden a couple of streets up from me, just by accident. Someone must have liked it.'

'You bought it back off them?'

James hesitated. 'Sort of.'

Megan knew what that meant.

He looked at her hopefully. 'Do you think she appreciated the gesture?'

Megan looked at him. 'Do you?'

James didn't seem to know. He stared at the lift doors as though he could see through them. 'I wanted them to keep it. I don't know what to do without them. I want them back. I don't know how Charles can live with himself,' he said. 'A man like that, with all his so-called principles, harbouring stolen goods.'

'You're not thinking of taking the Venus back in there, are you?'

'No, not the Venus.' The lift doors opened and Larry, James and the statue staggered out. The tears were rolling down James's face as he turned to look at her. 'Not the Venus,' he said, 'not the Venus. I mean Lydia.'

14

Zelda and Megan finished Triton's initial brief late that evening after a busy day. When Megan finally got home from work she was tired and hungry and looking forward to some pampering.

She opened the kitchen door to find Larry sitting at the table painting plastic soldiers. He muttered a brief hello without looking up.

She took her jacket off, threw her keys onto the table and went into the sitting room where Ruth was curled up on the sofa watching a pop video, surrounded by empty mugs.

Megan reached for the television and turned down the sound and Ruth sat up indignantly, folding her arms. 'Actually, Megan, I was listening to that.'

'This place is a mess,' Megan said. 'How long would it have taken you to put these mugs into the dishwasher?'

Ruth stared at her for a moment, her full lips slack with sulkiness. 'They're not my mugs,' she said, 'they're Larry's. I don't see why I should have to clear up Larry's mess for him.' She grabbed a cushion and hugged it to her.

'Fine.' Megan rolled her eyes and went back into the kitchen. She heard the volume being turned up behind her, louder than before. Larry was painstakingly hunched over a figure no more than an inch long.

'Couldn't you have cleared up before you started that little hobby?' she asked, putting the mugs in the sink.

Larry looked up. 'Come and have a look at these – careful,

they're wet – look at this one, I've given him sidies. Who does he remind you of?'

'I give up.'

'No, go on, have a guess,' Larry said. 'What colour is his hair?'

'Black,' she said in a monotone.

'Right, now who do you know who has, or did have, black hair and sideburns?'

Megan felt a silent scream building up inside her. She'd had a long day. She didn't want to come home to a mess and the prospect of having to cook supper for two able-bodied adults who could easily do it themselves. Resentful? You bet. 'Larry, I'm not in the mood,' she warned.

'Elvis,' he said, holding it closer to her face. 'Take a look.'

She pushed his hand away and went to the wine rack, pulling out a few bottles to check the labels. Sparkling Shiraz. Twelve years old. That would do. She put it down on the worktop, took the foil out and undid the wire.

'What are you doing?' Larry asked, getting to his feet.

'What does it look like?' she asked, twisting the cork out. 'I'm getting myself a drink.'

'Don't open that – it's a good one,' Larry said querulously.

'Too late,' she said as the cork gasped out. She gave him a false smile. 'Sorry.'

Larry sat down again. 'That was a stupid thing to do,' he said. 'It's not even cold. You're just wasting it.'

Megan reached into the cupboard for a Victorian saucer-shaped champagne glass which they'd been given as a wedding present and she poured the churning pink foam into it. 'Do you want one?' she asked without turning her head.

'No, I don't.' He was annoyed now, and making a big thing of putting the lids back on the Humbrol tins.

Just like Bill, she thought. What was she saying? Worse than Bill. Larry was a man who wasn't playing any more.

'You deliberately chose that one, didn't you, because it was the dearest,' Larry said, putting his soldiers in a row.

Megan took a sip and considered. 'Probably.'

Larry got up to wash his brushes in the sink. 'Probably,' he repeated, shaking his head.

'What's the problem? I'll buy you another,' she said dismissively.

The wine was lovely, she could feel it relaxing her.

There was a sudden splashing and she turned to see that Larry had aimed the mixer tap at the draining board and the water was sprinkling freely onto the quarry tiles.

'Larry, what are you doing?' she asked, her voice rising angrily. Then she saw the expression on his face; a look of cold dislike. It was so unexpected that she stared at him with her mouth open, unable to move.

'Don't you ever say anything like that again,' he said furiously and walked out of the kitchen and up the stairs, bang bang bang, she could hear him thudding around over her head.

In the background Megan heard the thud of the pop video join in tandem for moment. She took a gulp of wine, and as she swallowed it she leaned over the sink to turn off the tap, getting her dress wet in the process. What the hell had that been about? She took another gulp of wine and put the glass down with deliberate carefulness.

She threw a couple of tea-towels onto the wet floor and went upstairs after him, torn between anger and annoyance. She tried the bedroom door but it was locked. 'Larry?'

No reply.

She waited for a moment, listening, and went to look in on Bill. His night light was on and the room was warm with a pink glow. He was sprawled in his bed, his legs on top of the covers, his arms outstretched. His mouth was slightly open. She kissed his cheek. He twitched at her touch and lifted his arm and it flopped down again.

She retreated from his room to the guest room which over-looked the garden, and she lay down on the bed. She wasn't going to apologise, no, no way.

She thought of all the times she'd been home before Larry, getting him a drink, maybe supper, bathing Bill, juggling like an idiot. Reverse the roles and she finds him painting little soldiers and expecting her to admire them.

The leaves on the tree outside were playing tricks with the late-evening sun on the ceiling. If she lay there long enough Larry would come and lie down next to her and ask whether she was going back down and what there was to eat. Maybe.

She thought again of the look on his face. It was the first time she'd ever seen him look ugly.

She rested her bare forearm over her eyes to block out the rippling reflection of the light.

Something would come up; good people always got jobs eventually. Eventually . . . that was the problem, that one word. Still, she thought, her heart hardening, he should have made supper and tidied up. And she objected to him telling her which wine to drink. It's not on, she thought.

There was a tap on the door and she sat up hurriedly and smoothed her hair.

'Can I come in?' Ruth asked, popping her head round the door.

Megan nodded and sat up on the edge of the bed. Ruth came to sit next to her. The bed undulated with their weight.

'Have you had an argument?' she asked, plaiting the ends of her long hair.

'Yes.'

'Was it about me?'

Megan looked at her. 'No, it wasn't. Why?'

'Larry and I had a row this morning. It's not the first time he's taken Bill to the park and not come back when he said he would. He did the same thing on Monday, too.' She pulled

99

the plait apart and started it again. 'We were going to Damien's for tea and he didn't get back until almost five.' She looked at Megan, her dark accusing eyes beginning to film with tears. 'I was really worried about them today,' she said, 'because he promised he'd be back. I didn't know what had happened. And when they got back, I yelled and Bill started crying.' She wiped her nose with the back of her hand. 'I mean, Bill's my job, isn't he?'

'Yeah,' Megan said slowly, wondering why she'd put it like that, Bill's my job, like plumbing or something. 'Yes, he is, you're right. Larry probably thought he was doing you a favour.'

Ruth sniffed. 'Well, he wasn't. What are we going to do?'

Megan liked the 'we'. 'I'll have a talk with him,' she said. 'If he's going to be at home more, he could help you look after Bill but it's not right that he should upset your plans, I agree. See how it goes.' She got up off the bed. 'It's not an easy time for any of us and we'll just have to make the best of it for a while.'

Ruth got off the bed. 'I'm not going to apologise to him,' she said. 'He's the one in the wrong.'

Megan nodded. She knew exactly how Ruth felt. She didn't much want to, either.

'Put the kettle on,' she said, 'I'll be down in a minute. I just want a word with Larry.'

Ruth nodded and Megan went to the bedroom door again. 'Larry?' She tried the handle and the door opened. She went inside. Larry wasn't lying on the bed, he was sitting in a chair with his head in his hands. The bedroom was darkening fast.

Megan leaned against the wardrobe. 'You and Ruth argued today,' she said.

'Yeah. She said I was stealing her job.'

'She was worried because you were late, that's all.' She hesitated. 'Larry, about the wine –'

100

'It's not about the wine. The wine's not the issue,' he said, cutting her off. 'I'm sorry, Meg, I know you weren't rubbing it in when you said you'd get another bottle. It's just – I feel so bloody useless.' He fell silent.

Megan couldn't think of anything to say.

The darkness in the bedroom had become oppressive. Megan felt for the light switch and pressed.

Larry looked up, blinded and stunned like a mole pained by the light. 'What am I going to do?'

Megan felt his frustration rub off. He was doing everything he could. The fact was that although most people did get other jobs, she'd seen people at the Colgin Partnership who never could find anything.

They'd get in touch and months later they'd drop her a line, to remind her of their existence, and she'd be shocked for a short time that they were still jobless and then she'd forget them again. The people who were in the groove generally stayed in; the people who'd been pushed out lost touch. Not Larry though. It was early days yet, she told herself.

Larry heaved himself out of the chair, stood in front of her and put his hands on her shoulders. It was funny, it suddenly seemed ages since she'd seen him standing up. She looked up at him and he pulled her to him and she stood rigidly against him. She could smell his skin, a sweet, familiar smell. His arms closed round her and she let herself soften and leant against him.

They rocked together in silence, thinking their own thoughts.

She felt his hands stroking her back gently.

She didn't respond; didn't want to get hopeful for nothing. His hands slid lower, cupping her bottom; she could feel the warmth of them through her dress. She felt an ache of longing for him so fierce it made her feel sick. Her emotions were tumbling around her head; resentment, anger, need.

101

He bent his head and kissed her, his lips warm. She felt drunk, drunker than she ever did on wine.

They took a step, together, like dancers, in the direction of the bed. He held her, lowering her onto it.

He pushed her dress up and lowered her pants and she saw his hand go to his belt, undo it with a jerk.

As he entered her, the astonishment of the sensation came back to her as it always did, new every time. Her body, all of it, felt alive, she was aware of the coldness of his belt on her hip, the rough teeth of the zip scraping her thigh. She held him tightly, slowly losing him and gaining herself, concentrating only on the wide blackness with the pinpoint of light that she had to make for, had to get to, and as she strived she could feel it coming closer, closer until all at once it was on her, in her and her life burst apart with a dazzle of colour and light.

She felt him fall on her, breathing hard, his hot breath roaring in her ear as she fought to get her own breathing under control. Her heart was pounding and she felt the sweat cool swiftly on the side of her face.

He clung on to her and raised his head and looked at her, surprised. 'I can never believe this is legitimate,' he said softly, wiping her temple with the ball of his thumb.

They moved apart slowly. He stood up, stretched, and quickly grabbed his trousers before they fell.

There was something furtive, shy, unfamiliar about the way they straightened themselves hurriedly. Megan went to the bathroom and looked at her flushed face in the mirror.

Ruth would be downstairs, waiting for them with a cup of tea. She'd probably be wearing her disapproving look. Hopefully, she'd just think they'd carried on arguing.

As she splashed water on her face, she felt weak with relief that they hadn't, but it wasn't always going to be this easy.

In her mind she could see the puddle of water still on the kitchen floor, and the gleam of the wine glass by the sink. She shivered, although the night was warm.

No, it wouldn't always be so.

15

It was a weekday again. Bill knew weekdays – they were when his mother went to work.

His father was still in bed and his door was closed. Bill had looked inside but the shape of his father under the blue duvet didn't move.

For his father, it was always the weekend now. He got up late every day and never threw him into the air any more.

Sometimes when he and Zoofie came back from playgroup, his father was still in his dressing gown. Once, he had a letter on the table which he squashed in his hands and threw at the wall.

And one day he had taken him to the boats in the park, and rowed round the island and laughed and the swans had pecked the oars. But when they'd got back Zoofie had been angry because they'd missed a party and because of that he could hardly remember his father laughing – he could mostly only remember the pecking swans and the noise.

'Bill?'

Zoofie's voice startled him and he looked out from under the yellow tablecloth.

'Where are your shoes? Hurry up. I want to get out before your dad gets up. He'd under my feet all the time.'

Bill looked, but he didn't expect to see his father there. His father was too big to trip over. It was something grown-ups just said, without meaning it, like, catch the waitress's eye.

'Look, do you want to go or not? We can stay here if you

like. Someone else will get the Cozy Coupe, you know.'

He got out from under the table. He could tell that Zoofie wanted to go.

Zoofie lifted him onto a chair and pushed his shoes on and fastened them tight.

'You like the playgroup, don't you, Bill?'

Bill nodded his head. He got off the chair and followed her to the door.

He knew he had to go, but he didn't want to.

He really didn't want to.

'Come on, we'll be late.'

He let his hand be taken. He wanted to stay in, as a sort of guard. He didn't like the thought of leaving his father.

He didn't like the thought of him being in the empty house, big and noiseless, getting under people's feet, all on his own in bed, having a weekend again.

16

That week, Megan was meeting Harvey Fields for lunch at
The Ivy, where they both always ordered the squid ink risotto.
Megan had a weakness for black food, from caviar to black
pudding, and The Ivy's risotto she could live on happily for
ever.

Harvey Fields's company used the Colgin Partnership for
their entire sales department. Instead of the partnership taking
a percentage of the salary, they were paid a retainer for their
services. Professionally, Megan had no choice but to like him.
Personally, he was one of her favourite people.

When they'd first met, he'd had neat, dark hair. A couple
of years later she hadn't recognised him – he had no hair at
all. As soon as it had started thinning, he'd shaved it off.

She'd liked his style then and she liked it now.

'Don't look now,' he said, 'but Trevor McDonald's sitting
behind you.'

Megan giggled. His stock phrase was: Hey, isn't that . . .
when the truth was, financially he was worth more than any
of them. 'Where?'

'Don't look. He's going to get up in a minute. They want
his table by one-thirty.'

The risotto came, and Megan knew she could enjoy it. Some
lunches were strictly duty, but this was just a keeping-in-touch
one and one she could enjoy. MDs often used headhunters as
sounding boards on anything from changes in office policies
to what time of year was best to go on holiday.

'I hear changes are in the air at your place,' Harvey said presently as he poured a second glass of wine.

Megan raised her glass and paused. 'Zelda, you mean? She's leaving as late as she can so as to have the time at home when the baby's born.'

'Unlike Sue Fisher. She left when she was six months pregnant and came back a week after the baby was born. Said she wanted to make the most of her leisure time while she had the chance.'

Megan laughed. She could feel her napkin slipping off her knee and caught it. 'But that wasn't what you meant, though, was it? You were thinking about something else.'

'Lisa Ashridge,' he confirmed. 'Zelda's replacement, in more ways than one.'

The clink of cutlery on china filled the gap in their conversation.

Realising what he was saying, Megan shook her head. 'You're way off target on that one, Harvey.'

Harvey kept looking at her, his eyes steady. He certainly believed it, but it didn't mean he was right.

Hell, Lisa had been open about it. What had she said about Gerry? That she'd met him at Madame Jojo's. She'd been frank, hadn't she, said that he'd mentioned Colgin was looking for someone. She wanted another string to her bow. It wasn't a secret. 'Gerry and Lisa?' she said aloud, and she knew what she was pushing for; she was pushing for Harvey to retract.

He didn't.

'Is it common knowledge?' she asked, still with that edge of disbelief.

'It's not a subject of gossip at all, if that's what you mean,' he said. 'Look, Megan, forget I mentioned it. It's none of my business, anyway.' He brightened suddenly. 'Have you seen Peter Mahoney recently? He's got a new receptionist, can't be more than seventeen.'

107

'She's on a work placement scheme,' Megan said, glad that she at least knew something. 'She was expelled from Westminster for selling cannabis. She sells it in the office instead.'

'She's stunning, isn't she?'

'Don't look now, but Pierce Brosnan's just walked in.' Forget Lisa; she could tell that that, more than anything, had made Harvey's day.

Zelda was in the interview room when Megan got back to the office. Nigel was at his desk. 'Oh, Megan,' he said, 'something's come in that might interest Larry. BNM are looking for a group head.'

'Really?' She brightened instantly. 'Does Zelda know?'

'Yes, she suggested Larry. It would have to go through the usual channels, of course.'

Megan gave him a reproving look. 'Nigel, I'm sad you even thought you had to say it.'

'And you're to give Trevellyan a ring. They've taken on Paul Salisbury and they've got a new assignment for you; looks like you've hooked us another client, Meg. Xylus don't need us any more – they've filled their group head position internally. And Triton have approved our initial brief.' He looked at her coyly. 'Guess who's joining our little team tomorrow to help out?' Nigel stroked his beard to a point. 'Aren't you pleased to know you'll have a dogsbody around?'

'I'm not sure Lisa Ashridge will settle for being a dogsbody, are you?'

'You could have a point.'

Zelda hurried in, looking pleased. 'That was Mick Baker, you remember, Nigel, we saw him as a graduate. I was just interviewing him to update his file when we had a call from Capital about a job that's tailor made for him! Oh, Megan, talking of which, Trevellyan rang. Well done.'

'Thanks. Nigel told me they'd been in touch. I was just

108

going to give them a call. I hear you might have something for Larry?'

'Yes – I'll arrange an appointment for him. When is he free? If push comes to shove, Nigel can work on the assignment, but if I could see Larry in the next couple of days, so much the better. Is he at home now?'

Not only at home, but probably in bed, Megan thought. 'Should be,' she said. 'Do you want me to try him?' And then, 'Zelda – before you leave – have you actually rung Lisa Ashridge yet?'

'Yes, I have as a matter of fact. She starts next week but she's popping in tomorrow to get the feel of the place. She'd already handed in her notice, that's confidence for you. She said the job felt good.'

'She's not so smart after all then, is she,' Megan said sourly.

'You love it really,' Zelda said.

Megan stared out of the window at the fire-escape. Thinking about it, there was absolutely no doubt about Lisa's high confidence rating. Still, she'd taken a risk, handing in her notice before she'd been formally offered a job.

She wished Harvey had kept his thoughts to himself. She was going to have to work with Lisa, like it or not. She should have known there was no smoke without fire.

And she couldn't get it out of her mind that there was, of course, substantially less of a risk in Lisa handing in her notice if someone in the know had already given her the nod.

17

The following day Megan was late getting in, mainly because she and Larry had been arguing, over breakfast, about exactly where the best place was to meet Zelda.

In her hurry she'd dropped the coffee and a few other things out of the cupboard. More haste, less speed and all that.

Megan had suggested he meet Zelda outside the office, but Larry was stubbornly opposed to the idea, on the grounds that if anyone saw him with Zelda they'd assume that Megan had fixed it up for him. Megan tried to convince him that it wasn't true and that one of their researchers would have picked up on him in any case, but Larry dug his heels in.

Still exasperated by his stubbornness, she got to work to find Lisa Ashridge not only in the office but already on the phone, sitting back in Nigel's chair, her legs crossed, her skirt riding high and her voice so softly seductive that Megan was utterly convinced she was making a personal call. Surely she wouldn't ring Gerry when Zelda was around?

'Any chance of you getting to a phone where you *can* talk?' she was asking. 'Sure . . . sure. I'll wait to hear from you.' She replaced the handset, saw Megan and instantly stood up.

'I'm not a schoolteacher,' Megan said, 'you don't have to keep doing that whenever I walk in. Where's Zelda?'

'In her office.'

'And she's let you loose in here on your own?'

Lisa tilted her head slightly. The light caught her cheekbones like mother of pearl. 'I suggested joining the researchers but she put me in here. Insisted on it.' She shrugged with one shoulder.

'Oh yeah?' Megan kept her jacket on and went into Zelda's office to yell some more.

Zelda was leaning heavily on her desk, wincing and rubbing the base of her back so hard that her fingers were white. 'Meg,' she said, looking pained. She edged to her chair and sat down slowly.

Megan felt her heart skip. The annoyance burst like a bubble and was replaced by concern. She hurried over and touched her arm. 'Zelda, are you all right?'

'No, not really,' Zelda said ruefully. 'My back feels as if it's breaking apart.' Her mouth went into an 'oh', and she blew out in short jerks as though she was lifting weights. Then she took a deep breath and sighed. 'There, it's gone now.'

'Zelda, this is not the place to be. Let me ring Gerry.'

'It's all right, I'm not going into labour yet.' She smiled at Megan ruefully. 'Too much to do.'

The phone rang, making Megan jump.

'See?' Zelda picked up the handset. 'Hello? Larry!' She gave Megan a 'wouldn't-you-know-it' look.

Megan raised her hand. 'I'm going,' she said quietly, and backed out into the corridor. 'Shit,' she said, and kicked the skirting. She might be lumbered with a man-eating novice and no one to complain to, but she sure as hell didn't have to like her.

She went back to her desk, avoiding Lisa's gaze, and looked up the candidate profile screen to check on Jeremy Squires, a possible candidate for the Triton assignment. She tapped out his number. 'Jeremy? Meg Lawrence, the Colgin Partnership. Just thought I'd give you a ring. We've got a client who is looking for a high flyer and I was wondering if we could meet and throw a few ideas up together. You would? Any particular time good for you? Friday . . .' She flicked through her desk

111

diary and checked her schedule. 'I can't make lunch. Tea? Yeah, tea's good. At the Savoy, three o'clock?' Satisfied, she replaced the phone. That was how it was done. Softly, softly . . .

'So what's wrong with just coming out and saying it?'

Meg swivelled her chair. 'Pardon me?' she said coldly.

Lisa loosened her shoe. It dangled on her toes, the heel stabbing back and forth with the movement of her foot. 'It's always the way with headhunters, isn't it? A little dance, and we're talking barn dance, not rave – one step forward, one to the left – and finally you get together and go for it. Whereas you could cut the bullshit and say, look mate, we want you – and get an instant answer.' She put her foot down and the shoe slipped back on. 'But no tea at the Savoy, of course.'

Megan breathed in carefully. Anyone else and she would have gone to great lengths to explain why it wasn't a good idea, as Lisa so elegantly put it, to cut the bullshit. But Lisa wasn't asking out of ignorance or even out of curiosity. It suddenly occurred to her with the kind of clarity you feel on touchdown when your ears pop that Lisa was having fun with her.

Megan looked at her steadily. 'Well, you've got the job. And you went to some lengths to get it. So now's your chance to do things your way. Find out if it works.'

There was no change of expression on Lisa's face. Her pale green eyes continued to hold Meg's steadily. 'I always do things my way. It's the only way I know,' she said softly.

Both their phones started ringing at once. Megan grabbed hers with a small sigh of relief. She was still on her call when Zelda came in. 'I've got an interview in half an hour which I think you should sit in on,' Megan heard her say to Lisa. The annoyance niggled back into her.

When she put down the phone, Zelda had gone back into her office and she went after her. 'Are you having Lisa sit in on your interview with Larry?' she asked abruptly.

Zelda smoothed back the white streak of hair and looked at her in surprise. 'Yes, I am.'

'I'd rather she didn't.'

Zelda looked at her as though she was standing there naked. 'What are you talking about? I want her to see how we do things, get a feel of the business.'

'But Larry's my husband.'

'And he's my candidate. What the hell's got into you? This is the second time you've stormed in here. You okayed her, remember? Said you could work with her? So what's your problem?'

Megan shut her eyes. 'Yes, you're right. I'm sorry.'

'You didn't answer me.'

She opened them again, blinked, trying to clear her head. 'No. There's no problem.'

'I know what you're thinking. You're supporting Larry, things are stressful at home and you can't even moan about him to me in case you jeopardise his chances as a candidate.'

Megan nodded ruefully. 'On the pimple-dot.'

Glad that she was getting somewhere, Zelda softened her voice confidentially. 'Lisa's a people person. My suggestion is that we let her do an interview or two and get her to use her knowledge of people in the industry to our best advantage while she's around. Don't abuse her. Use her. What you're feeling is transference. You can't kick Larry so you want to kick Lisa.'

She *could* kick Larry, actually. But she nodded anyway.

Zelda's mouth formed an 'ooo' that was nothing to do with the headhunting business.

'Zelda –'

'It's just a twinge,' Zelda said impatiently.

'Don't rely on Larry to cope,' Megan said.

The wave passed and her face smoothed. 'Men shouldn't be

there at the birth,' she said. 'Gerry will be where he belongs – in the corridor, pacing.'

'You old-fashioned thing, you.'

Zelda smiled suddenly. It was the warm smile of old friends. 'Get out of here, and get on with Lisa. Swallow your pride – you've got things going for you that she couldn't hold a candle to. You'll make a great team.'

Megan raised her eyebrows cynically. Then she smiled, too. She was going to miss her.

Megan had briefed Laura to let her know the minute Larry was out of there. Laura was true to her word. 'He's gone,' she said and Megan picked up a pen and went to join Zelda and Lisa in the interview room. She took the sofa while they shared the three-seater. Same as at the interview.

'Go on, Lisa,' Zelda was saying, adjusting a cushion behind her back. 'I'd like to hear your observations.'

Lisa hadn't taken notes. She lay back against the sofa, chin in the air, and shut her eyes. 'He was nervous,' she said. 'It showed.'

She looks like a medium waiting for a message, Megan thought cynically.

Lisa crossed her legs. 'You know, nervous people have tricks that they use to try to disguise it. Larry didn't even bother sitting on his hands, so I would think he is usually confident, easy-going. This interview made him anxious. Maybe he's really not that interested. Or maybe a lot rides on it.' She paused. 'There was good eye contact and he made sure we were both included when he was answering questions which means he would be good with people and wouldn't only suck up to the boss. His track record's decent enough, but he was a bit cagey about his last job. He only lasted two months at Burgess McLane.'

'Xylus didn't need him,' Zelda said.

114

'Xylus did need him,' Lisa corrected. 'They're one of your clients. You're doing a search for them to fill Larry's job.'

Megan felt the hairs on her arms prickle. Where had she got this from? She swallowed hard, slightly reassured by the fact that Lisa Ashridge didn't, after all, know everything. 'You're a bit out of date,' she said. 'They filled it internally.' She shifted her position on the sofa. 'Where did you get that information from?'

'It's on your computer,' Lisa said. Her wide, green eyes gave nothing away.

I'll check it, Meg thought. I don't give a damn if she sees me do it.

'So that's your only reservation?' Zelda asked.

'Yes. He's good-looking, presentable, a great guy. The scar on his eyebrow makes him look horny. He'd make an ideal husband.' She turned to Megan, a slow smile curving her lips. She looked like a woman who knew too much. 'Does he?'

The Xylus brief was still on the computer, so that was that. Megan took it off.

Shortly afterwards she took a hysterical phonecall from Ruth. There was a mouse in the house and Larry had returned from his interview with four metal and wood mousetraps, the traditional kind, instead of the humane ones Ruth had suggested which led the mouse into a small comfortable box to be let free. Presumably to exercise its prerogative to return.

Probably it was the idea of the mousetraps which had made Larry nervous at his interview, Megan thought, and asked Ruth to go and fetch him so that she could talk to him.

'Ruth's cordoned off the section of floor with the mouse droppings on it,' he said. 'It's like a crime scene in here. She's all for giving it a fair trial.'

'Never mind that, how did you feel about the interview? Was it all right for you?'

'The interview? Yeah, fine. You were right, I shouldn't have come to the office, I kept thinking of you just the other side of the wall. You live and learn.'

Megan forced herself not to come up with words of encouragement. She thought they would sound patronising. And premature. 'Larry, watch Bill with those mousetraps,' she said.

'He keeps setting them off with cheese.'

Megan suddenly heard Zelda call out to her in an uncharacteristically shrill voice.

'Better go,' she said. 'Speak to you later.' She glanced at Lisa, who was on a call but who had also heard Zelda cry out. Lisa widened her eyes and Megan nodded. She rushed into her office for the third time that day.

'My waters have broken,' Zelda said calmly. 'Fortunately I was sitting on my cushion. It's in that bag over there.'

'Don't worry about the cushion – have you rung Gerry?'

'He's on his way here with my case.'

'Have you rung the hospital?'

'Yes.' The end of the word was stretched out as she grimaced.

Megan held her hand. She found herself going through the story of the mouse and Ruth and the mousetraps.

The pain eased and Zelda laughed. 'I like the sound of Ruth,' she said. 'What does Bill call you, Megan?'

'Mummy. Sometimes Mum.'

'Not Moom?'

'Moom? No, not moom. Why would he?'

'I thought you mentioned that Ruth was from Yorkshire. Hasn't she got an accent?'

'Yes, she has actually. I suppose I'm used to it now.'

Zelda looked distant. Megan wondered whether she was anticipating another contraction, and whether she should be timing them.

'Anyway,' Zelda said at last, 'even if it was moom you

116

wouldn't have to worry. You could easily get it ironed out at pre-prep.'

The door opened and Gerry came in, breathing hard, his tie slightly askew as if he'd been tugging it.

Zelda shook off their helping hands. 'I'm not *ill*,' she said.

There was a gathering of staff in reception, with good wishes called out in the atmosphere of general excitement.

'Just get back to work,' Zelda said grumpily, leaning on Gerry's arm as the lift door closed.

Not that there was any option.

By the time Megan got home that evening, she'd forgotten about the mouse until she saw the taped-off area on the kitchen floor.

She bent down to have a look at the mouse droppings.

They were in the same spot as the one where she'd dropped some gravy granules that morning while getting the coffee out of the cupboard. The mouse must have been attracted by the meaty smell.

Ruth was watching from the door. 'Can you see him?'

Megan got down on her knees for a closer look. Hell, the droppings *were* gravy granules. She licked her finger, touched one and put it in her mouth. 'I despair,' she said.

Bill came rushing into the kitchen, happy to see her. He pointed at the tape on the floor. 'Look,' he said, 'Mickey Mouse lives here.'

Megan grinned and picked him up, cuddling him.

'You can say that again,' she said.

PART FOUR

Four's a Birth

18

'Yes, but seriously Gerry, where's your mobile?'

Gerry pressed his fingers against Lisa's lips. 'I've got a pager in my pocket.'

'Clever boy.'

'Yes. Zelda's a bit of a prude at heart.'

Lisa lay back on the bed and watched the circular reflections of the chandelier slither across the ceiling. She only had to tilt her head to see their reflection bounce from mirror to mirror into infinity, distorting into the diminished distance.

Men liked mirrors, as she knew; they liked them a great deal. Women didn't. 'Have you got mirrors in your bedroom at home?' she asked him curiously, turning her head to look at his face.

He lifted a strand of hair that was half shielding her eyes. 'Mirrors? We've got them in the dressing room.'

'Women liked to be watched, they're used to it, but they don't like watching. Especially themselves. Women are tactile, they like to shut their eyes and feel and be dreamy and close in the dark.' She knew. Oh yes, she knew.

'Not you, though,' he said.

'No, not me.'

Gerry let himself fall back on the pillow. 'You're right, though. Zelda would be worried about her cellulite,' he said. 'She hammers away at it every morning with one of those wooden mallets that looks like a meat tenderiser.'

'That's probably what it is,' Lisa said, and gave a short laugh.

Gerry rolled over on his front and folded his arms and rested his head on them to watch her. His eyes were steady, almost wary. 'I know what you're thinking,' he said, 'but I love Zelda.'

Lisa smiled and stared at the ceiling. The reflections of the crystals skidded and danced. They were like fairies. She used to pretend that was what reflections were, once, when she was small, after her brother was born. She used to make wishes to them that he would disappear and that she would have all the love for herself again.

She could still feel his baby flesh pinched between her fingers, his scream almost drowning out her mother's yell. 'I'm loving him,' she'd said, all of a panic.

She'd pinched people with the same excuse ever since.

He reached out to her, sliding his hand down her body. 'But that's grown-up stuff.' He grinned and she could see the wetness of his tongue between his teeth. 'And this is fun.'

She'd heard it, she thought as he lowered himself on top of her, called just about everything, all the bad words, all the good words.

'It's not fun, Gerry,' she corrected him. 'It's business.'

'Whatever,' he said without a pause.

She shut her eyes, arched her back, panted, gasped for him almost automatically, hardly having to think about it any more.

She could see herself in the mirror as objectively as if she was watching a film. A man for business and woman for pleasure, she thought. She was not a participant at all. Staring at her reflection she could see her own cellulite, even; probably every bit as good, as bad, as Zelda's.

Gerry's breath was hot in her ear, penetrative, and she moved her head away. Gerry slowed the pace. 'Am I going too fast for you?'

'No, of course not.' Ridiculous question. The quicker the better. She stared at herself in the mirror, her lipstick all worn off, and she thought of her brother, his little mouth like a leech, sucking his mother's love away. She shut her eyes.

Gerry came to his silent climax and held her tight and in the compressed circle of his arms she began to relax.

Suddenly his pager bleeped.

He sat up. 'Wouldn't you know it,' he said, 'wouldn't you know it. She had a thirty-six-hour labour last time.'

'Good timing, then,' she said as he jerked his trousers from the back of the chair. 'Gerry, you can ring her from here.'

'Where's the phone?'

She jerked her thumb.

'I can't ring without my jocks on. Where are my jocks?' He was on the floor, feeling under the bed, and she watched him calmly.

'Try down the leg of your trousers.'

He pulled them on and dialled the number. Zelda's not the only prude in the family, she thought, watching him.

'Gerry Colgin. My wife's just – oh, a girl? Yes – yes – yes. I'll be right there.' He put the phone down as though the news had come as a tremendous shock. 'A girl,' he said, looking at Lisa with shining eyes. 'And it's a smashing hospital, it's like a hotel in there. She's got her own mini-bar. They're stitching her up at the moment.' He hopped around in his trousers, one leg in, one leg out.

She watched him, and herself, in the mirror. He'd almost forgotten her. He hadn't even covered her with the duvet, he'd just left her lying there, cooling, chilling, abandoned on the bed while he got dressed. 'Shirt's on inside out,' she said as he pulled on his jacket.

He checked the front of it and looked at the buttons.

'Joke,' she said.

He gave a laugh. He didn't quite know how to leave.

'I don't usually do this kind of thing,' he said. 'If you'd gone to Zelda you probably would have got the job anyway.'

'Or maybe not.'

123

'No, maybe not. I'll ring you.' He hesitated, as though wondering if something else was expected of him.

She looked at him with her cool green eyes. 'There's no need.'

'I suppose not.' He sounded half sad, half proud. He pushed his hands into his jacket pockets, hesitated, changed his mind, hurried out and was gone.

After his excited activity the flat was very still and quiet.

Business is business, Lisa said to herself. I pay my debts.

She reached down for the duvet and pulled it up over herself, shivering.

She stared at the reflections, at the fairies on her ceiling.

Shouldn't have wished so hard when young, she thought ruefully; shouldn't have wished so hard.

Now they all disappeared, the people in her life.

The good ones and the bad.

The Gerrys and the Chrissies.

Whether she wanted them to or not.

19

The good news about Zelda's baby – named Taylor – was balanced by the bad news, later that week, that BNM had approved the shortlist drawn up by Zelda and Lisa and that Larry wasn't on it.

He'd said little about it the previous night, but waking too early on a dull and blustery morning, Meg had turned to him in bed and found him staring at the ceiling, his hands behind his head. 'What are you thinking?' she asked, putting her warm hand on the matt of hair on his chest.

'I'm old,' he said.

'Rubbish.'

'Old and scared.'

His tone of voice disturbed her and she surreptitiously glanced at the clock. It was ten to seven; nearly time to get up. Thankfully.

The window was open slightly and the curtains flicked and snapped in the breeze. She used it as an excuse to get out of bed. As she closed it she looked out at the heavy, grey sky. It was like a bad mood over the house.

It's just the weather, she thought, hugging her arms.

'My luck's changed,' Larry said matter-of-factly.

'Luck's nothing to do with it,' she said sharply. 'You make your own luck.'

More silence from Larry. Don't, she imagined him arguing inside his head. Do. Don't.

It was cold, for summer, standing there by the window, but

she didn't want to get back into bed and what did that say about her. She'd never gone out with lame ducks; she'd always looked for equals, able to stand on their own two feet. If she'd thought about it at all she'd seen it as a strength. But now she could feel Larry lean slowly but increasingly more heavily, weighing on her and weighing her down and she wanted to step away.

Selfish.

She'd like to tell him to pull himself together, to try another dose of the shotgun method, let people know he was still alive, kicking, going for it.

She glanced at him. He was still looking at the ceiling with his dark, incurious eyes.

There was a tap on the door.

They shot each other a look and she grabbed her dressing gown with sudden animation and put it on hurriedly. 'Come in,' she said as she fastened the belt.

Ruth was already dressed. She had her hands in the back pockets of her jeans and she looked purposeful. 'Can I have a word?'

Megan looked at the clock, confused. Seven a.m. 'That clock hasn't stopped, has it?' she asked, but of course, clocks didn't while away the last ten minutes if they'd stopped. 'Do you want to talk downstairs?'

'No, I'll do it here if you don't mind.'

'There's nothing wrong, is there?' Megan asked.

'I'm handing in my notice,' Ruth said. She tossed her head and her fair hair settled itself over her shoulder.

'You want to leave?' Megan asked, shocked.

'It's not because of Bill,' Ruth said hurriedly. 'I love Bill.'

Oh yeah, were the words that leapt into Megan's head. Try not to panic, she thought. She wants to leave. 'Can you tell us why?'

'It's not working out, is it? Larry's here all day and you

don't really need me any more. I've always had sole charge and it's difficult with Bill now. He wants to stay with Larry and Larry doesn't tell him I'm the boss, he just goes along with it. You know . . .'

Megan turned to look at Larry. The suspicion that he might have put her up to it hovered, only partly formed, in her mind.

Somewhere during the conversation, or perhaps when Ruth had first come in, Larry had propped himself up in bed. He had the blue covers pulled high under his chin as though protecting his modesty. His expression was blank. He looked at her suddenly and she looked away, back at Ruth.

'And what about Bill?'

Ruth didn't look at all abashed. 'He's got Larry,' she said, as though it was obvious. 'You don't need me.'

The partly formed suspicion was solidifying rapidly. 'Is this something you've worked out between you?'

Oops, wrong, indignation from both sides.

'But where are you going to go?' Megan asked, thinking out loud, really, but this cry of puzzled concern, funnily enough, was the one to hit the mark.

Ruth's slender hands came out of her back pockets to rush and comfort and contort against each other. 'I've been offered something else,' she said after a moment.

'Is it with that woman from *The Bill*?'

'Oh, what does it matter?' Ruth said, in sudden annoyance and frustration. 'It wasn't working out and you know it.' Her eyes flashed angrily, but her mouth twisted in disgust. 'You're trying to blame everyone else, but really it's you. You settled it.' The tears sprang angrily into her eyes. 'I don't want to carry on working for someone who eats mouse droppings!'

'You'll laugh about it one day,' Larry said at the door before she left for work.

'Don't put money on it,' Megan said moodily as she picked

Bill up and kissed him on his soft, warm cheek. 'You,' she said to him, hugging him tight, 'you're the only normal one here.'

Ruth was vacuuming the hall in an energy surge of indignation. And guilt. Ooah, ooah, roared the vacuum cleaner.

Megan listened to it for a moment.

Sod the mouse-dropping business, she felt sick at the thought of Ruth leaving. She imagined more upsets, more complications, the trouble of finding a new nanny they would all have to like and get used to. She'd have to do it soon. Larry would have to be free for interviews.

Worst of all was the thought of how Bill would cope without his Zoofie. That didn't bear thinking about.

She hugged him again and reluctantly handed him over to Larry and looked outside. The clouds were dark, gathering themselves for rain.

'We'll have the house to ourselves again,' Larry said quietly, looking at her meaningfully and raising his one and two halves of an eyebrow lasciviously.

It was like Noah looking out and saying it was nice weather for ducks.

She gave him a half-hearted smile. Truly an amazing recovery, she thought, for a man gripped with malaise at six-fifty that morning.

She turned her collar up and hurried to her car.

She bleeped the door open and sniffed. Larry didn't have much to worry about after all. Despite everything, it looked as if he was getting lucky again.

20

Larry had decided to use the occasion of Bill's birthday to tell their parents that for the time being he was looking after Bill.

He and Meg had settled on that.

Megan was all for finding someone else straight away, but he'd talked her into seeing that it made sense for him to do Ruth's job. He preferred having the house to himself, just he and Bill, with no one to answer to.

Megan's reluctance was understandable – she wasn't the kind to stay home herself.

He was, though. There was something noble about a man and his son, womanless, at least during the day. He could see them bonding. Men had to bond. Women, of course, did it at birth, but men had to fit it in when they could.

As he cleaned the light smear of grime from the green garden chairs he stopped to marvel at the fact that yet again Bill's birthday was a sunny one. Funny that after four years he could remember them all perfectly, a thread of sunny days going back as far as the day Bill was born.

He'd gone home in the early hours of that morning and after a few hours' sleep he'd taken a cab back to the hospital. What a trip that had been; he'd never noticed the city so bright, the sky so blue, his vision so clear. It was not Bill but he who was seeing the world for the first time.

Larry paused and looked at the dirty cloth in his hand. He rinsed it out in the white bucket, causing newly dead flies to

129

bob and toss in the grey water. He squeezed out the cloth and went over the chairs again. They needed painting; the green gloss was beginning to flake and peel away.

The cabbie, when he'd told him he'd just had a son, hadn't charged him. So he'd had a free ride as well.

He straightened up and rubbed the small of his back, which was beginning to ache. 'Megan?' he called towards the house. 'Do you want the table doing?'

'Yes, if it needs it,' she shouted from somewhere above him. He looked up, narrowing his eyes against the dazzle of the sun on the paintwork. Megan was leaning out of the window. Bill popped his head up next to her to look out of the window too.

Noticing the water in the bowl, he called down. 'Can I help you?'

'You can do the table if you hurry.'

Bill disappeared.

Larry dropped his shielding hand. He was hot. He pulled off his white t-shirt and draped it on the branch of the sycamore tree. He picked up the bucket and took it into the cool house to fetch fresh water and when he came back out, Bill was waiting for him in his blue t-shirt and shorts. He was playing with his birthday badge: '4 today'.

'Do you want to take those off to save getting them wet?' Larry asked, putting the bucket down on the grass.

Bill shook his head and crouched by the bowl, dabbling his hands in the water. 'It's cold,' he said.

'It doesn't matter. The table only needs a wipe.'

'How long is it until my party?'

'Not long. An hour.'

Bill got to his feet, held on to the edge of the bowl and jumped up and down with pleasure for a couple of seconds before the bowl tipped and flooded cold water over his feet. He gasped at Larry and Larry picked him up, holding him away from him as he felt the cold, wet feet dangling against his stomach. 'Come on, you,' he said.

He could do with a beer. For fortification.

He wasn't at all sure how Bill's two sets of grandparents were going to receive the news of his new job.

Larry's parents arrived first.

'Now where's that birthday boy of mine?' Larry's mother asked.

There was a giggle of excitement from the new Wendy house which had been put in the shade of the tree. 'Boo!' Bill popped his head out of the flap that was the door.

'Timing hasn't improved,' Megan said.

The doorbell rang and Larry went to answer it. James was standing in a pair of cut-offs, holding a bottle of champagne, a custom ever since Bill's birth, when Megan had been the only drunk mother on the maternity ward.

'Hello, James,' Larry said. 'How's it going?'

'Fine,' James said quickly. 'Where's Bill?'

'Out in the garden.'

James strolled through the house and out again.

'Little pig, little pig, let me in! Let me in!' he roared from the garden.

Larry could hear Bill's squeals as he took a bottle of champagne out of the fridge and took off the foil and wire and eased the cork out. It popped and smoked a little and he took it back out into the sun.

Megan's mother and father had arrived and come round the side of the house. Megan was distributing glasses from a silver tray as evidence that their parents' wedding presents were being used.

'Everyone got a glass?' He poured out six glasses and went inside for another bottle.

The sun was hotter, and the leaves of the pseudo-acacia

Robinia flickered bright green in the slight breeze.

This was the pre-party get-together, to catch up on news and get it out of the way before the children arrived. They were talking about a cousin of his when his father diffidently brought up the question of jobs. 'Jake said he'd put in a good word for you at his place if you're at all interested.'

'Oh, Jack – he doesn't want to work there, do you darling? In a furniture store? Of course he doesn't.'

'It's selling, all the same. It's a job.'

'Haven't you been able to find him anything?' his mother-in-law asked Megan.

Megan looked up at her and didn't answer at first. She glanced from her mother to Larry, looking into his eyes. He was dazzled by their blueness and looked away. 'No, not yet.'

'There's no hurry,' his mother said quickly. 'There's no point in rushing into things.'

Larry took a drink from his glass and smiled. 'I've got a job.' He waited for the surprise to die down. 'Yes,' he continued, 'I'm going to stay at home and look after Bill.'

In the background Bill was pulling the Wendy house towards the shade of the tree.

His mother bent forward. 'Why, darling?' She received a look from her husband, and sank back into her chair, looking suddenly tired. Larry felt his father's eyes on him.

'Is it necessary? Is that what you want, David?'

Larry picked up his glass again and looked at the champagne bubbles chasing upwards in fine strings. 'Yes,' he said, 'it is. It was my decision. I might be out of work for months – this makes sense.'

'And is it what you want, Meg?'

Larry watched her nod. She couldn't, he thought, meet his father's eyes. At work she was fine, but in private, damn her, she was an appalling liar.

132

'How long do you intend to carry on with this – new career?' her mother asked him.

'For as long as Bill needs me.'

'Until he goes to school, you mean? Won't it look bad on your CV when you eventually do go back? Will it, Meg?'

Larry studied them in turn. They were all parents. They should be able to understand. 'If Megan were to give up work to look after Bill you'd all be pleased,' he stated. 'What's the difference?' He looked up at them, waiting for the reply.

'What if Meg wants another child? What would happen then?'

'It's only temporary,' Megan said, 'just until Larry gets another job. It's nothing to make a fuss about.'

Megan's mother spoke quietly. 'And when might Larry get another job? It's not as simple as you think, looking after a small boy, Larry.'

'That's what I'm going to find out, isn't it? I've never had the opportunity to do it before. This is a marriage of equals. If Meg wanted to do it, I'd support her.'

'And how does Megan feel about supporting you?'

Larry glanced at his wife. She was looking at the grass, smoothing the base of her glass over it gently.

'It's just until Larry gets a job that he wants,' she said.

'If it's Ruth's wages that you're worried about,' her father began astutely, but Megan lifted her head. 'It's not that, Daddy. Ruth's already left. She's got another job.'

'What does Bill think of these new plans? Don't you think he'll take it badly, losing Ruth?'

'He's losing a nanny and gaining a father. We couldn't force Ruth to stay, not once she'd decided.'

Larry found himself at the centre of a group of unconvinced faces. He didn't think they would take it as negatively as they had. Even Meg was a bit short on the solidarity.

He turned to look at James for some sort of support.

133

James was lying on his back, holding his drink on his chest, strangely subdued. He looked at Larry and saw that something was required of him. He sat up slowly and raised his glass. An insect was walking slowly along the rim. He turned the glass in his hand and as the sun caught the crystal a streak of light bounced across his lean face.

'And one vote for,' he said. 'I'm behind you, Larry. If you're with him all day then as you said you'll get to know Bill. How many fathers can say that? And Bill will get to know you. You can take him out with you, do men's stuff. Model railway exhibitions, strip clubs. You can take him to his playgroup and chat up those itsy-bitsy bored mothers in their little skirts.' He pushed his fair hair away from his eyes. 'Do it. The day might come, mate, when it's all taken from you and you'll never get it back again.'

He lay back down on the lawn, speech over, holding his glass steady.

Larry couldn't help but feel he hadn't really improved his case.

Megan was frowning and he avoided her gaze.

He did the only thing possible in the circumstances.

He picked up the bottle and he poured them more champagne.

What is it about 'Happy Birthday'? Larry wondered later when the rest of the guests had arrived and they gathered round the cake. Take ten random people, he thought, and put them in front of a birthday cake and each one will sing it in a different key.

Even when they started well, by the time they reached the octave jump they all sounded rather strained.

He didn't take his eyes off Bill, who was staring at the candles with intense concentration as though by not looking at them he could pretend they weren't there.

134

Meg's mother even managed a bit of harmonising at the end, but Larry was looking at his blond, newly-four-year-old son who was twisting his hands with a mixture of pride and anguish.

He watched Bill take a deep breath and blow at the four jittering candles whose flames were hardly visible in the sunlight. His friend Jonathan blew too and oh! the concentration – the embarrassment – the pressure to get them all out with one puff! But Bill did, and having done so, amidst cheers, he covered his face with his forearm whilst Jonathan seized his chance and took something from the top of the cake – a small cylindrical piece.

Larry at last breathed out. He felt light-headed from having held his breath for so long. Someone was tapping his arm.

'He's taken the chimbly off,' Jonathan's brother Edward was saying to him urgently.

'Chimbly?'

'Off the train.'

'Ah.' Before he could work out what a chimbly was, Edward had run off.

Relieved that he didn't have to do anything, Larry picked another dripping bottle of champagne out of the ice-bucket and looked for a glass.

Bill and his guests were in the Wendy house with party squeakers and the four grandparents had found the whisky and were pulling sun loungers into the shade of the tree.

'Bill's a clone of you,' James said as Larry flopped down next to him. 'I nearly offered him a beer.'

'Yeah.' Larry felt something tickle his arm. He lifted his hand and swept it away and opened one eye.

It was a wasp. It had entered their exclusive circle, darting around like a tired child spoiling for a fight. There was nothing quite like a wasp for livening things up, he thought as Megan got to her knees, ready to run.

Larry flinched and James propped himself up on his elbow and took command of the situation.

'Go away,' he said loudly, startling the foursome of laughing grandparents under the tree into silence.

The wasp wavered for a moment before it shot off above their heads as silently as it had come. Larry tried to follow its flight path but lost it in the dots that danced in his eyes as they stared at the brilliant blue sky.

He blinked. 'Probably gone for reinforcements,' he said ruefully.

'You just have to be firm with them,' James replied.

Megan handed round the birthday cake and sat down next to Larry.

She didn't look at James. Larry could feel storm clouds ahead. He reached for a stray piece of icing and noticed the wasp was back, joined by two others all bobbing around the icing on the plate.

'Go on, Wilder,' Larry said, 'do your bit.'

'GO AWAY,' Wilder said loudly. The wasps bobbed and dodged around the chocolate and settled on the top slice, antennae bristling. 'Ouch!' He put his hand to the back of his neck. 'One of the buggers has bitten me.'

'Stung you,' Larry corrected, but Megan was on her feet again, looking at the back of Wilder's neck with great concern. 'There's a tiny red hole here,' she said. 'Oh, it's coming up into a lump. Are you allergic to wasps?'

'I don't know . . .'

'So what happened to your powers of wasp-taming?' Larry asked with interest.

Wilder shook his head slowly.

'It always works, I can't understand it . . .'

'It's getting bigger,' Megan said. 'You're not allergic to them, are you?' She sounded rather hopeful. 'I'll get something for it, vinegar for wasps, isn't it.' She stood up reluctantly, brushing away the blades of grass that had creased her knees.

Wilder groaned. 'It was a super-wasp,' he said, 'one of those French ones. Striped.'

'Obviously didn't understand you.'

'I can feel it getting worse.'

Larry watched James pull back the neck of his white polo-shirt. The hairs on his tanned neck glinted in the sun.

Suddenly James turned his anguished face towards him. For a moment he was startled but then the pained look cleared and with mischief in his pale eyes James winked at him.

Later, when the party was over and everyone had gone home, Larry went into the garden to look for Bill. It was cool and quiet again with only the trampled-in crisps on the grass to prove it had ever happened.

Bill was kneeling on a wooden chair looking at the remains of his birthday cake on the garden table. After a moment he picked up the four blue candles, still in their frilly plastic holders. He touched the burnt wicks and one broke off and stuck to his finger. He brushed his finger on his t-shirt.

'Can you light them again?' he asked, turning towards Larry with the candles.

'Of course I can.'

Bill nodded as though his belief had been confirmed and he pushed the candles back into the cake. The chocolate coating, hard again in the evening air, cracked into dark fissures. Larry went into the house for the matches and came back out striking one on the edge of the box. He shielded the match with his hand as he lit them, and stood back as the small flames took hold.

'Did you make a wish the first time?'

Bill shook his head. A crumb of chocolate sponge dropped from his hair.

'Well make one now.'

137

But Bill didn't blow the candles out straight away. Instead he leaned against the table and watched them burn down slowly, their flames jerking from side to side in the evening breeze.

Larry felt something twist inside him as he looked at his son's grave, illuminated face. The small pouches underneath his blue eyes were more pronounced after the busy day – or perhaps it was just the candles, catching angles with their light, pulling shadows up and down over the small face.

He watched the candles burn until all that was left of them were flaming wicks in little pools of wax in the blue holders.

Bill blew gently and the flames stuttered. He paused, then blew harder, and the flames died, leaving the wicks smouldering gently.

He shut his eyes tight.

Larry watched him for the long seconds until he opened them again. They were silent for a moment. After the brightness of the candles, the garden was dim. Then Larry couldn't bear it any longer – he felt he had to know.

'What did you wish?' he asked as the breeze whipped at his hair.

Bill looked away from Larry. 'If you tell, it doesn't work,' he said.

'Oh.' They were silent again.

Then Bill asked, 'Does it?'

Larry watched the pale wisps of smoke get torn apart by the wind, absorbed by the dusk. He considered, rubbing his thumb along the indentation in his cheek. 'It doesn't make any difference one way or the other,' he said after a moment, 'I'm sure of that.'

He said it with conviction.

They didn't have to deprive themselves – they didn't have to deprive Bill. Not yet. They were – dreaded word – comfortable. Why did he feel sad? Looking at his son through the dying smoke in the dimming light, he was pained by a sudden love for him. It took him unawares and for a moment he was afraid. He felt his heart jerk. He felt his chest hurt with the pressure of love and he vowed that whatever Bill had wished for, he would get it for him. I'll do it, I'll do it for Bill. It didn't matter that it had been his birthday and that he had all the things a four-year-old could ever want or need. This rush of painful love had him by the throat and was strangling him. Whatever he wants, he thought fiercely, whatever he wants he should have . . .

Bill was still leaning stiff-armed over the table, his pouched eyes holding his father's. Larry felt himself drowning in their trust.

At last Bill spoke. His voice was clear and firm. 'I'll tell you what I want,' he said. 'I want Zoofie to come home.'

21

Monday was the first day of Larry's new job, so he slept late.

Correction; he stayed in bed late. He stayed in bed late thinking about his new role in life, his role as mentor to his son and friend of pretty, bored mothers. He stared at the white ceiling with a smile on his face and his hand resting on the alarm clock.

Megan was already up – he had heard her shower and now he could hear her voice drifting up from the kitchen as she spoke to Bill.

She sounded very far away, in another world. She *was* in another world; the world of the gainfully employed. He, on the other hand, was entering the world of the primary caretaker and he was going to make a damned good job of it.

He took his hand off the alarm clock without looking at it, and stretched.

He knew he should get out of bed but he wasn't sure what to wear. Not a suit, sure. Casual, he thought. Smart casual. He didn't want to give out the wrong message: hey, look at me, I'm wearing jeans on a weekday! No, he was steering well clear of the unemployed look.

'Larry?' Megan called to him from the bottom of the stairs.

He pretended he hadn't heard, and didn't reply. Perks of the job.

He heard her coming up the stairs. He heard a cup rattle on a saucer and he shut his eyes and relaxed back into the pillows.

'Are you awake?' she asked gently.

He feigned a groan and sat up, blinking at her. 'Thanks, Megan. Did you bring the paper up?'

She jerked to attention. 'Don't push it, Larry,' she warned. 'Bill's watching Cartoon Network. I've told him you're looking after him, we've gone over it, and he seems quite happy.' She put the tray across Larry's knees.

'A saucer, too,' he said, staring at it. 'It's like being ill.' He sipped the coffee and looked at his wife over the rim of the cup. 'Do I get this every morning?'

Megan picked up her hair brush and looked at herself in the mirror. She began to brush her hair vigorously. 'From now on, Larry, the domestic arena is your job.' She looked over her shoulder and her blue eyes caught his. 'What are you doing today? Have you got any plans?'

Larry grinned at her. 'Plans? Meg, I'm going to give fatherhood a whole new meaning.'

She raised her eyebrows and turned back to the mirror. 'Give the strip clubs a miss for today, huh?'

He knew she'd bring it up.

'That was nothing to do with me,' he protested, 'I hadn't even spoken to James about looking after Bill.'

She gave him a disbelieving look. 'Anyway, can you make sure there's something for supper?'

'"Can I make sure there's something for supper," she says.' Larry chuckled gently, patiently even, at his wife of little faith. 'Of course I can, woman, it's my job. Anything particular you'd like? Roast chicken? Steak?'

She turned to look at him again. After a moment she said, 'Anything. Whatever you fancy.'

'Come here and I'll show you what I fancy.'

'Larry!' She checked her watch. 'I've got to go. Could you call Bill up here?'

'I was going to,' Larry said. 'BILL!'

After a two-second silence they heard him scurrying up the stairs on his hands and knees. He stood in the doorway, waiting for orders. 'What?' His pyjamas were fastened incorrectly so that one edge was lower than the other. He seemed dismayed at seeing his father still in bed.

'Now remember, Daddy's looking after you today,' Megan said, crouching down to his level. 'You'll be good, won't you?'

Bill's big eyes went from his mother to his father and back to his mother again. He didn't say a word.

Megan chewed her lip. She put her all's-well-with-the-world smile on and smoothed his hair. 'I'm off to work now. I'll see you both later.' She bent over Larry and kissed him first, on the lips. Then she bent over Bill and kissed him on his nose. 'Be good for Daddy,' she said again.

Flashing Larry a brief smile, she ran downstairs and moments later they heard the door slam so hard that his cup vibrated in the saucer. As the reverberations died away the house was left in utter silence.

Bill was the first to break it. 'Mummy's gone,' he said, and stood, still listening. After a moment, as though it was important, he added: 'And Zoofie's gone.'

Larry scratched his head. 'Yes, that's right. Except that Mummy's only gone to work. Er, Bill, do you think you could go downstairs and fetch Daddy's newspaper?'

Bill nodded decisively.

'Good boy. Off you go.'

Larry watched him as he padded out of the room. He heard him slither down the stairs. It occurred to him that it was rather a shame that he was too young to pour the coffee because another one would have been very nice. After a moment he heard Bill come back up the stairs again. As before, he stood in the doorway tugging at the mismatched edge of his jacket. There was no sign of a newspaper. 'Couldn't

142

you find it?' Larry asked urgently. 'Couldn't you find the newspaper?'

'No. It's gone.'

Larry put the tray on the bedside table and heaved himself up in bed, slightly disgruntled. 'Did you look on the kitchen table?'

A nod.

'And it wasn't there?'

'No.'

'It wasn't by Mummy's breakfast plate?'

'No.'

I'll train him, Larry thought as he got out of bed. He just needs guidance, a bit of encouragement and a firm hand. 'Okay!' he said heartily, picking Bill up. Carrying him downstairs he made for the kitchen. 'What shall we do today, little soldier?'

Bill looked at him silently.

'A list,' Larry proposed, thinking of the young mothers who might have to wait. 'We'll make a list. We'll write down all the things you would like to do. What would you like to do if you could do anything at all in the world?'

Bill rubbed his eye with his fist. 'When's Zoofie coming back?'

'Zoofie?' This question so soon? Hell, it was her first morning away, Larry thought; he can't be missing her yet. 'Look,' he said, 'sit somewhere I can see you. On the table. Come here.' He picked him up under the arms and put him on the table and looked at him. 'When's Ruth coming back? Well, she looked after you because Mum and I were working. Now that I'm not working, I can look after you. Do you remember that I already told you that?'

Bill's blue eyes washed him with their gaze and he received the words in silence.

It was, thought Larry, like throwing stones in a bottomless

143

pit. No splash. 'We'll have fun,' he said cheerfully. 'We'll enjoy it.' Even though he meant it, his words sounded suspiciously false, even to himself.

'But when's she coming back?'

'Ah. Well, if I got another job fairly soon, we could ask her back then,' he said.

'Fairly soon?' Bill asked, grasping the few words that could be taken as an answer.

'Well, maybe. But for now . . .' Larry shrugged. 'Look,' he said, 'I think the best idea for both of us would be to think of this as a sort of adventure. We can do what we like. We can go to the zoo again, or to the park – whatever.' He was warming to the theme now – it was something he could work on, this idea of him and Bill going off together, doing things he wouldn't normally do, going places Ruth couldn't afford. 'What would you like to do today, Bill?'

Bill wriggled on the table and sank his chin onto his chest. 'I want to go to the playgroup,' he said.

Larry nodded wisely. That was fine with him. The itsy-bitsy girls were back in play. In his mind he could see them in rows, like kebabed players on their metal rods in table football. 'There. We've made a decision, haven't we? That's what we'll do. We'll go to the playgroup. Look, I'll take my newspaper with me, here it is, on the table, like I said.' The better to watch the bored young housewives over. 'Now. Let's get dressed.'

Bill looked at him hopefully, shuffling to the edge of the table to get off and get dressed and go to the playgroup. 'Will Zoofie be there?' he asked.

When they were ready and finally out, Larry was pleased to find it was sunny, a perfect summer day, the kind of day that looked warm and beguiling from office windows even through the blur of bomb curtains; the kind of day, he told himself with satisfaction, that made you glad you didn't work.

144

Walking along the dusty pavements with the pushchair, to the accompaniment of the traffic, Larry discovered the strange phenomenon of invisibility. He'd never been invisible before. He had never blended into the background, ever. People always looked at him. He was good-looking, he smiled a lot, he expected it. So why were they getting under his feet? It was as if people couldn't see him. It didn't take him long to work out the cause. He was now A Person With A Pushchair.

Skirting a bus stop queue he suddenly remembered a boy he'd known at school who had turned up to their reunion in a wheelchair, suffering from MS. Sanderson, his name was. Drinking their beers in the pub they used to drink in under-age – poignant, that – they'd been wondering where Sanderson was and he was there all the time, in the midst of them, as it were, but the wheelchair had rendered him invisible. They'd registered the chair – it was hard to miss – but they hadn't registered the fact that Sanderson was the person in it.

Bumping the pushchair back onto the pavement Larry realised it echoed the premonition he'd had the day he'd driven home and had thought he'd disappeared.

His heart rebelled and he came to a decision. 'Okay, Bill,' he said, 'let's get seen.'

He manhandled the pushchair into a bicycle shop, a feat in itself. The shop smelled of rubber. The aisle was flanked by bicycle tyres and as he pushed him towards the counter Bill put his hand out to touch a wheel. It moved, ticking slowly on its axis.

'What shall we have, Mickey Mouse, Donald Duck?' Larry asked, looking at the bicycle bells. 'Or a horn? No, no, let's have a bell. Everyone knows the sound of a bicycle bell. Let's have Mickey Mouse,' he said, picking one out. 'Can I use your screwdriver, mate? It's for the pushchair.'

The thick-set proprietor grinned. 'It'll be too big for a pushchair. You need a smaller bracket.' He ducked under the

145

counter and came back up with a box and picked one out. 'This should do it. You left-handed or right?'

'Left.'

The man screwed it on tightly. 'Try that for size.'

Larry grinned, grabbed the pushchair and did a wheelie. See? he thought, you never get women doing that. He rang the bell smartly and in the confines of the shop it was satisfyingly loud.

'Great,' he said. 'What do you think, Bill?'

Bill looked at him and laughed.

'It's just what we need,' Larry said. 'Let's go.' He paid for the bell and at the door of the shop he hit the step with the wheels. Bill was jerked as far as the give in his straps. 'Sorry.'

'Will Zoofie be at the playgroup?'

'Well – no. But all the children will be. All your friends will be. You've got friends, haven't you?'

He reached a second bus stop and rang the bell. Accusing faces stared at him. See? He was no longer invisible.

'Smug bastard,' a man growled at him.

He speeded up, he could see the playgroup at the end of the street.

It looked like something out of Toy Town.

It was square, squat and basic and with its startling primary colours it looked as though the children had made it themselves.

It looked like a toy box surrounded by a fence.

And held, Larry thought as he got nearer, real-life Barbie dolls to play with.

He pushed his hair back, smoothing it as he looked at his reflection in the glass doors. And ready for action, he turned the handle. Nothing happened. The doors were locked. He pressed his face against the security glass and saw a grimy red carpet and no signs of life. 'It's locked,' he said to Bill.

'There's a bell, Daddy.'

'Ah, a bell.' He pressed his palm against it and heard its muffled ring inside. Suddenly behind the glass he saw the largest woman he'd ever seen, her smooth, black hair held back by the Alice band James had promised him.

Larry took an involuntary step back. The Alice band was in fact the only point of resemblance. He knew there was some mistake.

The woman stood like a guardian behind the door, disapproving and silent.

'Is this the playgroup?' Larry mouthed through the glass. His breath obscured her face. He wiped the glass and the woman made sweeping movements at him with her hands.

'Bill,' he said, 'let's go. We've cocked it.'

The woman lowered her gaze and for a moment she didn't move. Then she reached for the latch on the door and opened it.

'Hello, Bill,' she said matter-of-factly. And to Larry, disapprovingly, even coldly, 'Are you Bill's dad?'

Bill's dad. His new job title. 'Larry,' he corrected her, giving her his dental practitioner of the year smile and holding out his hand.

She ignored the hand, looked him in the eyes and her expression didn't alter. 'It's through there. Leave your buggy in here out of the way. I thought you'd grown out of a buggy, Bill.'

Bill was looking up at this mountain of a woman as though he was fearless. 'Daddy put me in it,' he said. 'I'm too slow to walk.'

Larry pushed his hands into his Chinos. 'Thanks, son,' he said, smiling to show it was a joke.

The woman gave him another cold look, the kind of look usually saved for something dead, that smells. She turned her back on him as she went along the corridor to the door of the playroom, with Bill following her close behind.

147

Larry folded the pushchair just as she opened the door – and the first thing he noticed was the noise. The noise shocked him – the incredible, high-pitched noise of children chirruped out so loudly that he winced. It was like an amplified aviary – a high-decibel budgie cage. Bill and the woman slipped inside the noise and the door closed slowly on them, leaving Larry standing in the renewed peace of the hall with the pushchair dangling on his arm.

He propped the pushchair against the wall of a doorway on the right and looked at the playroom door. He realised that the noise had made him hold his breath. He took a few deep gulps of air. Behind the door, somewhere, were the bored young mothers, ready to mother him. It was not all bad. He grinned, to stretch his mouth and limber up his gone-stiff face, and he walked to the door. He was a male in female territory. The star? Modestly, he wouldn't let himself think so just yet. Soon, though, he thought. Soon.

As he opened it the blackboard squeal of small voices drifted out again and he fought the impulse to close the door and run.

He stepped inside the noise and suddenly felt like Gulliver. All the occupants were knee-high, playing wildly in this tremendous din. Not together, though. They were either playing by themselves, or fighting. He looked for the bored young mothers and spotted them sitting at a round table: his harem, he thought, but was confused, as they too were unnaturally small.

He was aware of a smell – the smell of a dirty nappy. Now he had that and the noise. The noise!

He looked again at the bored young mothers. They were, he could see now, sitting on midget chairs. Instead of mini-skirts, they were wearing skirts and leggings, and they were talking with their heads together – smirking, it seemed, smirking at him!

The big one, the one who had opened the door to him, looked up, straight into his eyes, with open hostility! And he looked away.

To hell with the bicycle bell, he suddenly longed to be invisible. Their disapproval was obvious. It was like walking into a bar and having everything go quiet – it was as obvious as that, only it wasn't quiet at all, the noise continued unabated.

He couldn't go over to their table. It was unthinkable. It was also unthinkable to sit on one of those tiny chairs. What if it gave way beneath him? What if he fell backwards on the floor, an object not only of dislike, but derision also? Torn by indecision he glanced at the table again. They were ignoring him now, all except the big one. She continued to stare at him. She made a comment – how they heard it above the noise he didn't know – but a face here and there looked back at him, reappraising.

Larry forced himself to feel casual. He strolled over to a wall and leaned against it. Maybe his son would rescue him. He looked for him amongst the Lilliputians but all the small heads seemed identical, he couldn't see Bill there at all. He felt a wave of panic wash over him.

Then a small blue plastic pedal car stopped by his feet. Bill was looking up at him and he kneeled down, partly to hide himself from view. 'Good car,' he said.

'Where's Zoofie?'

'Son . . .' Larry looked round. 'Son, don't you remember?' He had to keep the conversation going and he racked his brains for something to say. 'Look, Bill, if you want anything, you can ask me. I'm doing Ruth's job now. Anything that Ruth did, you ask me and I'll do it the same way. I'm not just your father; I'm like Ruth as well.'

Bill climbed out of the car and looked doubtful.

'Do you want me to push you?' Larry asked.

Bill shook his head. He hurried across the room.

149

Larry was on his own again. He remained crouching for a moment or two. He checked his shoelace while he was down there. He checked the floor. And finally he forced himself to stand up. Towering up he was unmissable!

Sure enough, out of the corner of his eye he saw the women looking at him again.

At a table in front of him a small girl was hitting a lump of dough with a rolling pin. The dough was resting in a bank of flour and each blow sent small puffs up off the table. Larry watched her with a sense of envy. He would have given a lot to have been able to take the rolling pin from her so that he could do it himself.

Still towering, deserted by his son, he thought it was time to test a chair.

He chose an empty table, checked the women – who were ignoring him now – and quickly sat down. His knees were practically under his chin, but it was the best place for them – straighten his legs and these Lilliputians would have to design a bridge to negotiate them.

From quite close to him there was movement; a head raised and grew. It was not a child but a woman. Her hair was impossibly blonde – he could see now it was dazzling white, as white as her shirt. Rising up amongst the primary colours she looked ethereal, transparent. And she was, most definitely, pretty.

She walked towards him, dodging the children effortlessly. 'Can I get you a coffee?' she asked in a normal, earthly voice.

He made to get up. 'Yes – yes,' he said, appallingly grateful. He could think of nothing else to add. For a moment he looked into dark eyes fringed with thick dark eyelashes and then she was gone. He looked across at the group but they were involved in their own conversation.

He looked towards the kitchen and already she was coming back.

150

'Here you are,' she said, handing him a mug. 'It's hot.' She pulled up a chair next to him.

'You're Bill's father, aren't you? You look like him. Apart from the hair.'

Larry put the mug on the table.

'Keep hold of it. Emma's very careful where the children are concerned,' she said, and smiled, to show that the words had not been meant as a criticism. 'I'm – Lily's mother.' She laughed, and he realised it was a joke and that she was teasing him. 'Actually, my name's Helen,' she added. 'Mind if I join you?'

Larry glanced at the huddle of women near the door, the in-crowd. Mind? He was weak with relief. 'I'm Larry,' he said. 'Who is the big woman over there?'

'Emma's the play leader. Her grandson, Damon, is the boy on the slide, in the red t-shirt. Jean, the one who is just nipping out for a smoke, is a childminder, and so is Janet with the red hair. Becky, over there with the baby, is a nanny. She used to be Ruth's friend. There are others who come and go, but the regulars are all here.'

No pretty young mothers, Larry thought sadly. No itsy-bitsy Barbie dolls with their interchangeable wardrobes, lying around bored, waiting to be played with. Not that he would have, he thought, imagining Megan, but he was never averse to the possibility.

'They all thrive on maggots,' she said, and laughed at his reaction. 'Bits of gossip, that sort of thing,' she said. 'They live off it.' But the look she gave towards the table was one of longing.

Larry sat on his too-small chair and wanted, nevertheless, despite the maggots, to be on the table with the others. Despite the maggots he wanted to get up and join them, even if it meant hanging about on the outskirts, charming them slowly with his smile and his humour. He wanted to be on the inside.

151

That was what he wanted. That was where he belonged. 'Don't you want to sit with your friends?'

The whiter-than-white-haired Helen smiled at him. Through her tanned skin he could see lilac-coloured veins reaching from her eyes to her temples. Her dark eyes and eyelashes were at odds with her hair and she seemed as though she'd had a shock. Those staring eyes were that bit too wide. They reminded him of pictures he'd seen of soldiers in the trenches.

She too glanced at the round table. 'Yes,' she said wistfully, 'sometimes.'

Larry saw, too late, that the trap had sprung on him. He'd made things worse! He was the new boy at school! And on this, his first day, he had labelled himself an outcast! He'd allied himself with the kid that smelled, or was bullied, or was unusually thick! Those women, the inner circle, they would have accepted him in time – they would! But he'd joined the wrong side.

He tried, as he thought this, not to look at Helen, but when he did her shell-shocked stare had gone and she just looked gentle and faintly amused, as though any minute she expected something funny to happen.

Familiar though he was with being stared at, he knew that she had the upper hand and it irked him. She knew what he thought. He didn't like being controlled. He wanted to ask her why, if she wanted to sit with them, she didn't; but he didn't want the others to see them chatting. It didn't matter. It wasn't that important to him.

He cupped his hands around the mug. The coffee itself was instant but it was hot and strong and bitter and he rather liked it. He looked round for his son. It was easy this time – Bill was in the Cozy Coupe.

The yellow roof lent a jaundiced cast to his face and Larry, looking harder, thought he could see his lips move. Probably he was making car sounds as he stared into space. Bill turned

152

the car suddenly and Larry could see his face no more.

But his heart sank.

Even as he repeated the scene in his head he knew that the words his son was whispering were Zoofie, Zoofie, Zoofie.

22

On their way home from the playgroup Larry and Bill stopped off at Sainsbury's, mindful of Megan's instructions to get them something for supper. Bill was tired and fretful. Larry said, 'What shall we have for supper?' He was exhausted, resentful, and well into overtime now.

Bill didn't seem to care much what he ate.

'All right,' Larry said, putting Bill in the trolley, 'let's educate your palate while we've got the chance. Smoked salmon and scrambled eggs?' Then he remembered he was off fish and the flesh of smoked salmon seemed particularly goldfish-like.

Of course he hadn't only to think of himself and Bill, but Megan too. He had to get something for Megan. This was what a househusband's life was all about: the feeding of the breadwinner.

He looked at the rows of shelves, conscious of Bill's restlessness as he sat swinging his legs in the trolley. He began tugging at his sleeve.

'Don't do that, son.' The noise in the supermarket wasn't all that different from the noise in the playgroup. Larry blinked; the lights were so bright, he seemed assailed by a barrage of colour and noise. But no music, he noticed. He was thankful for that.

Bill grabbed at a can. It was standing in its cardboard pallet on the shelf, three cans left. They fell onto the floor with a clatter and Larry wheeled round, frowning.

'Bill,' he said sharply, 'I told you to stop it.' Bill's face seemed to collapse slowly in front of his eyes and yet he still wasn't able to stop. 'We'll just get something for tonight,' Larry said, 'and we won't worry about tomorrow.' He wasn't talking to Bill, really; he was talking to himself. What did Megan buy? He couldn't think. He tried to remember meals or menus – quail, trout – and felt he was getting there, just getting there, when Bill kicked out at the trolley next to theirs. It veered sharply, hitting Larry, causing him to bump into Bill. He felt his elbow catch Bill on the chest. Bill looked at him, shocked, and tears flooded his eyes.

'Sorry, Bill. I didn't mean to hurt you. Are you all right?'

But the indignity of it was too much for Bill. He started to wail. The volume of his cries grew louder and louder and he wouldn't be consoled by Larry's ineffectual pats. Larry could see people glance at them. Larry lifted him out of the trolley and tried to calm him by pressing him to his chest but Bill, angry and inconsolable, translated his small physical hurts to the larger hurts that he had suffered during his new change of fortune and started to kick.

'I want Zoofie!' he cried.

'Oh, shut up about Zoofie, bloody woman,' Larry said, holding his legs.

He was aware that people were stopping to look.

Abandoning the trolley, Larry pushed through the queues of people waiting at the checkout. He was nearly at the exit when a middle-aged woman confronted him.

'Is that your child?' she asked bravely.

Resisting his initial impulse, which was to shove her out of the way, Larry tried to smile. 'Why, do you want him?' He had to shout to be heard above Bill's rising scream. What lunatic, he wondered, would want to kidnap Bill?

'Zoofie!' Bill was screaming now. 'I want Zoofie!'

A small crowd gathered round Larry and his writhing son. It was all he could do to hold onto him. As he struggled with

155

Bill he could feel their eyes on him, the object of their hostile attention. They were disapproving but at the same time interested; here was a diversion from shopping. They wanted to see what would happen next. A security guard approached them and put his hand on Larry's shoulder. Larry's ears were ringing with Bill's screams and he shrugged the guard off. Larry had never had to deal with this aspect of Bill's behaviour before and couldn't think of any method to use other than brute force. He wouldn't have thought Bill could be so strong. The furious sweat on Bill's red face was soaking through his shirt.

'What's going on?' the security guard asked.

'I'm just – trying – to get him – home. He's had a – long day,' Larry shouted.

'This your dad?' the security guard asked Bill, trying to raise his voice above the screams.

Bill turned his head away and with flailing arms he hit Larry on the side of his head. Dazed, Larry put Bill down on the floor. Bill's pent-up frustration seemed to explode from him and he lay, kicking his feet on the cold floor while the crowd looked on.

To Larry, he looked like something from *The Exorcist*.

To the crowd, a toddler having a tantrum was fairly commonplace. They were getting bored now. Any kidnapper in his right mind would have run off. Therefore he was, as he'd said, the father.

A woman in her early sixties came up and looked at Bill and tutted. His fury was burning itself out on Sainsbury's floor. Dust balls were sticking to his damp hair. He was sitting up, no longer angry, but red-faced and confused and upset and frightened by his own fury as though it was something outside of him. He sat up, weeping, gulping in great sobs of air, but as Larry crouched next to him he flinched from his touch.

Larry could sense the displeasure of what was left of the

crowd. Even the security man was shaking his head, although this might have been a commiseration.

'I'd better get him home,' Larry said to the guard as Bill's sobs turned into gulps. His emotions had exhausted him. Larry held out his hand one last time and Bill stretched out to reach him and allowed himself to be picked up. He hung limp against Larry's shoulder.

'He's tired,' one of the stragglers said accusingly. 'Probably hungry, too.'

That's why I'm here, Larry thought angrily; shopping for food for supper. We're all hungry. He briefly imagined himself reclaiming the trolley but he strapped Bill into the pushchair instead.

As they left the store, Larry felt the dampness on the front of his shirt turning cold. He looked down at Bill who was quiet and flushed, and he felt how Bill looked. They pushed through the crowds and headed for home.

Bill was asleep by the time they got back.

Larry felt lonely and defeated as he lifted the pushchair into the house. The house was silent.

He looked at Bill. His face was clear, but black lines stained his cheeks and his mouth was open a little as if in dismay at the hand that life had suddenly dealt him.

Larry left the pushchair in the hall and got himself a drink. Tea, with brandy in it. The breakfast dishes remained unwashed on the table and a cloud of fruit flies hovered over an uneaten slice of apple. Larry sat at the table and sipped the alcoholic tea. The day was superimposed with nightmare qualities. Never would he have believed he could have made such a mess of things.

He went into the familiar, warm red sitting room and switched on the television. He watched it exhaustedly with little interest and no comprehension.

*　*　*

157

Megan was slipping her jacket on, ready to leave the office.

Lisa looked up from her compact mirror. 'Have you time for a drink?' she asked Megan.

Megan adjusted her collar. It was a long time since anyone had casually asked her that. She freed the bottom of her hair from her jacket collar. 'Better not,' she said. 'I ought to go and rescue Larry. Another time.'

Lisa had a direct way of looking at people when she talked that reminded Megan of James. 'All right,' she said.

Megan felt the momentary wash of her green eyes before Lisa turned, her bag swinging, and left without a goodbye.

As she passed reception, Megan heard Laura say something, and Lisa answer.

Megan felt in her pocket for her car keys. She realised that she would have liked to have gone for a drink, discussed a little about the business.

Still, at home she had two men waiting for her. And a meal. Larry would be waiting for her, taking her jacket in his new role as domestic man and chief caretaker. Proving to her that he'd made the right decision. And maybe he had.

She stopped at an off-licence on the way home and bought a bottle of champagne to celebrate the first day of Larry's new job.

Once home, she went to the back door and found it locked from the inside.

She walked back along the gravel to the front and let herself in and almost fell over Bill, asleep in the pushchair in the hall.

She hurried to the living room, relieved to hear the familiar strains of *Coronation Street*, and found Larry stretched out on the sofa, asleep. On the floor next to him was a bottle of brandy alongside a mug of tea. She went into the kitchen, which was a mess, and put the bottle on the table among the breakfast dishes. Not only had they been untouched since the morning, but the tray she'd taken up for Larry was still on the table too.

She took off her red jacket and slung it over a chair.

She went to the fridge and opened the door.

No food. Great.

She slammed it shut and went back into the living room. Larry was sitting up, woken by the noise and startled to see her.

'Hi,' she said, 'been busy?'

Larry looked at her with eyes that reminded her of pictures of seals waiting to be clubbed. Somehow he seemed to have missed the sarcasm because he flopped back on the sofa and shut his eyes. 'Hardest work I've ever done,' he said.

Megan picked up a deep pink cushion and hit him with it.

'Ouch! What was that for?' he asked indignantly.

'Hardest work you've ever done?' she asked in disbelief. 'Women have to do it every day of their lives. And what's for supper?'

'Pizza, Indian, Chinese; take your pick.'

'Larry!' Megan sat down in the armchair opposite him. 'A take-away, in other words.'

'Bill made a scene in Sainsbury's,' Larry said, raking his fingers through his hair. 'I got stopped by a security guard. People were looking at me. I couldn't do a thing with him. He was uncontrollable.' He undid the second button of his polo shirt as though the memory choked him.

Megan laughed. 'So? You're bigger than he is.'

Larry looked at her with darkening eyes. For a moment they were both silent.

She kicked off her shoes. 'Has he eaten?' she asked.

'He had something at playgroup.'

'What time was that? Larry – it's gone seven-thirty!'

'He's slept ever since we came in.'

'He won't sleep tonight, though, will he? And he must be

159

starving. You should have woken him up – no wonder he was upset.'

'Yeah,' Larry said. 'I thought of waking him up but I was glad of the peace.' He shut his eyes. 'I'm aching all over.' He struggled ineffectually to get to his feet.

'Oh, just stay there,' Megan said, her exasperation turning to the beginnings of anger, 'I'll do it myself.'

She went into the hall and unbuckled Bill from his pushchair. As she lifted him out and kissed his cool head, she noticed the bell on the handle.

Bill twisted his face at the unwelcome intrusion and opened his eyes and looked at her. His features relaxed again. 'Where's Larry?' he asked.

'Larry?' She smoothed the hair from his forehead. 'Daddy, to you,' she said. 'How about something to eat? Spaghetti hoops on toast?'

Bill nodded and kissed her blouse.

'You,' she said softly, hugging him, 'what am I going to do with you? My lovely boy.'

Bill smiled in her arms.

'Come on,' she said, carrying him into the kitchen. She popped her head round the door. 'Spaghetti hoops for three.' She looked at the dishes still to be done. She'd need that champagne. And as househusbands went, she thought grimly, looking for the can opener, she did so hope she wasn't going to find herself married to a slattern.

23

Megan was holding the phone with a tighter grip than was necessary for a call from her stay-at-home husband. Nigel was out of the office, the phones were going mad and Larry was taking up valuable call time. 'No,' she said again, 'I do not know what size shoes Bill takes. His feet couldn't have grown overnight, could they?' She looked up at Lisa who caught her eye and winked unexpectedly. Megan huddled over the phone, surprised by the gesture. 'Larry, have you checked that there's nothing inside them?' A sigh. 'Okay.' She put the phone down and said to Lisa, 'A Power Ranger.'

In Zelda's absence the relationship between Megan and Lisa had generally settled down to an amicable wariness. They were too different to be friends, and sometimes they knocked sparks off each other, but as far as the Colgin Partnership was concerned, it looked as if this dual energy was working.

Lisa was reading through Megan's notes and writing down her own comments on a large white pad in front of her. The window was open and she kept her hand on the pad to stop the pages from flicking up.

Megan watched her, sitting back in her chair, letting the breeze play over her face. Her fair hair fluttered. A Power Ranger, she thought, recalling Larry's phonecall with slight dismay.

Lisa had come to the end of her notes and had stopped writing. She was staring into space as though listening to some private conversation that only she could hear. Her dark hair,

Megan noticed, was untouched by the draught, but her skirt fluttered occasionally and fell still.

Lisa suddenly turned her attention to Megan. 'Why has Larry never been considered for the Triton job? Triton have a similar corporate structure to Burgess McLane, they use the same software systems and Larry is used to working on his own initiative.' She smiled a salesman's smile. 'He fits the briefing.'

'He was never on the board at Burgess McLane.'

'What sort of an answer is that? Tell him it's a goal stretch. Or are you happy being looked after?'

Megan laughed at the incongruity of the statement. 'Looked after?' she said. 'I wish.'

'Would he be interested, do you think?'

In promotion and another car and nah nah nah-nah nah to Burgess? In a leap from group head to broadcast director? Oh, he'd be interested, that was for sure. Whether he would be interested in setting himself up for another fall was a different matter altogether.

'I think we should add him to the list of preliminary candidates,' Lisa said. 'In fact, I think Larry's our man.'

Megan tilted her head to one side and regarded Lisa carefully. And Lisa stared back, as unaffected by Megan's gaze as she would be if she was looking in a mirror.

'Why?' Megan asked curiously. 'You virtually said you wouldn't have picked him for the BNM job. How can you think he's got a chance with Triton?'

Lisa uncrossed her legs, folded her arms and leaned forwards. 'Look at the guy,' she said emphatically, her voice reverting to the seductive undertones she used to persuade people by phone. 'He's lost some confidence, okay? But he's right for Triton, for the reasons I've already given. I can feel it. I can feel it here,' she said, touching the back of her neck and gliding her fingers back down slowly. 'If we put him up for it, it will bring back his confidence and what's more, when he sees the package he'll want it. Oh yes, he'll want it, make no mistake.'

Megan blew air slowly out of her mouth while she thought about it and tried to forget that this was her husband they were talking about and dissecting and planning on manipulating like an animated cartoon. 'Zelda's never considered Larry for Triton,' she said.

'But she wasn't working on it, was she? And she's not here, is she? It's our job now.'

Megan pushed her blonde hair back off her face. Forget he's your husband, he's another candidate, that's all, Megan told herself. What's important is his experience, his aptitudes, his character.

She felt warmer. Getting hot.

Lisa, it had to be said, had summed him up perfectly. Again. If he knew he was being considered, he'd want it, oh boy, yes. Fair play and loyalty didn't come into it. Objectively, objectively she could see that he fitted the brief, and a snug fit it was, too. She could see it so clearly that she wondered why she hadn't thought of it herself. She'd been too eager to push Jeremy Squires. And too modest to propose her husband, that was it. No. The truth was she never would have thought of him. It had taken Lisa to do that.

Lisa had a slight quirk at the corner of her mouth which meant she was smiling. Megan looked up and the quirk was there now.

Megan felt the hairs rise on the back of *her* neck, but for a different reason.

The woman was uncanny. She could read minds.

'I'll give him a call,' Lisa said.

That evening Larry told her all about his new method of topping and tailing beans. She picked Bill up and hoiked him onto her hip as she watched her husband patiently in the humid warmth of the steamy kitchen. It was so steamy she could hardly see him.

'Here are some I prepared earlier,' he said, indicating the row of French beans on the chopping board. 'One cleaver.' He brandished it, for her attention, and brought it down twice, with enormous blows that cleaved clean down the board. The pointed ends of beans, like pixie caps of various sizes, scattered around them with the force of the blow. A few fell onto the floor.

Larry grinned. 'What a time saver!' he said. 'I've seen you do each one in turn, taking you ages!'

'Can I have a try, Larry?' Bill asked, leaning forward out of her arms.

'No, son. This is man's work.'

Megan knew that Larry was waiting for his accolade. All she could see was beans a uniform five centimetres long. That was a lot of waste, whichever way she looked at it. 'Saves time,' she agreed. 'I suppose you did it to the sugar snap peas, too.'

Larry grinned. 'Nice try, Meg.' He picked up the saucepan from the hob to show her.

Megan looked at the handful of tiny peas scattered on the bottom of the pan. 'You shelled them?'

'I used to love doing that when we got them from the garden. They were bigger than this, too. Huge things.'

Bill put his hands on each side of her face and looked into her eyes. 'And, Mummy, we've been playing rolling the marble at the soldiers.'

'The Elvises,' Larry said.

'The elveses,' Bill said, correcting himself for her.

'You are clever,' Megan said, rubbing Bill's nose with her own. 'No playgroup today?'

'We went this morning. We came back for lunch.'

The itsy-bitsy mothers were losing their attraction, she thought cynically. Well; she'd heard about French beans, peas and toy soldiers. Either Larry was keeping the best till last, or the thought of a job was slipping into second place, behind the housework.

'What did you think of Lisa's approach?'

Larry was scooping up the beans and putting them into another pan. Some of them got mixed up with the tops and tails. More waste. The steam continued to billow out of the pans and roll across the kitchen ceiling.

'Did you put her up to it?'

'No! No, not at all. She had to talk me into it, in fact.'

Larry looked up from his pan and grinned ruefully. 'Thanks, wife. That bad, eh?'

'Oh, you know what I mean.'

'Yes, Meg, me old girl, I know what you mean.' He gave the beans a stir, frowned, and pulled out a pixie hat with his spoon.

'Well?'

He gave her a slow, lazy smile through the steam and gave the beans a slow, lazy stir. 'So? Bloody marvellous!' he said. 'I've got a good feeling about this one. It's like Christmas.'

She hit him hard on the arm.

'Ouch, what's that for?'

'Larry, you are a rotter,' she said. 'Why didn't you mention it when I came in?'

'I was saving it.'

'Saving it!' She hit him again.

Larry rolled up his sleeve and looked at his arm. 'Look at that mark! Behave yourself and go and give Bill his bath. By the time you've read him a story the meal will be ready.'

Megan grinned at him.

'Well go on then woman!'

'Yes, boss,' Megan said.

'You're not crying, are you?' Larry asked her in a mock-shocked voice. 'What an odd mother you've got, Bill.'

165

She fanned the steam with her hand and smiled at Bill. 'I'm not crying, honest,' she said, heading for the stairs. She shouted back the last bit. 'It's just my eyes misting up.'

24

The noise from the playgroup never seemed to get any quieter. It was raining, and the children were all indoors, as shrill and bright as a small cage full of budgerigars.

He went in and saw Helen. He thought she'd seen him but her upward-turning lips which always seemed to smile might have been acknowledging or might not. She was wearing a white, open-necked linen grandad shirt and looked like a healthy ghost.

Larry was going to get in with the in-crowd. A man had to have some ambition, didn't he?

And once he was in with the in-crowd, he would make friends with Helen.

Larry sat down and checked where Bill was. Then he rested back in the child's chair, not too far from the women, and tried to feign comfort. Emma came through from the kitchen and gave him a brief glance. 'Don't say you missed us,' she said to him before returning to her throne.

He winked. It was a good sign. He would take it as a good sign.

'It's a bugger,' he heard her say, continuing an old conversation, 'even in this weather I get cold feet at night.'

Larry grinned. He hadn't lived with Ruth for three years for nothing – this was something that he knew about. Cures for every occasion. He straightened, stood, picked up his chair and sauntered over.

Time to win their hearts, he thought.

A man was as good as a woman any day. Better. 'Ginkgo Biloba,' he said, setting his chair down right by them.

They looked at him, baffled, and he wondered for a moment whether it had come out right, so he said it again. 'Ginkgo Biloba.' He still wasn't sure it was right. 'For circulation,' he said.

Emma took her hairband off and put it back on and looked at him again through narrowed eyes as though her hairband helped her to see better. 'I've been using socks,' she said.

'Oh?' he replied politely.

It was only the raucous laughter that told him she wasn't, after all, talking about some sort of root. He joined in the amusement himself. Briefly.

'So . . .' Jean, Jean with the screwed-up face, legacy of years of peering through cigarette smoke, looked at him carefully. 'How's being a mother suiting you, Larry?'

The way she said Larry, lashing it off her tongue, made it sound like an insult.

'I like it. Shame I don't have all a mother's accessories, I could go to bed by myself.' This set line, this witty comment, this bit of repartee, was some old joke he'd read when he was about twelve. Where the hell had it come from after all this time?

Emma seemed to smirk. Perhaps she thought it funny. 'Are you going to join our aromatherapy massage class?' she asked.

For a moment he thought he was being rescued, but the laughter jerked around him again.

'How does that work, exactly?' he asked.

'How does that work, exactly? The council kindly pays for the unemployed to be occupied during their spare time. And to that end they send to this establishment a teacher of massage, who for a fiver gives us six aromatherapy lessons in the next room – there – the one we leave the pushchairs in, whilst

168

in this room, the children continue to be looked after by whomsoever does not want to do the course.'

Well, she had the accent all wrong, he thought. No one had laughed at Emma's little speech but there was that sort of relaxation about the table, a knowledge that if that wasn't so funny then at least the next thing might be. 'Is it five pounds a session?'

'Who could afford that? Five pounds the course. Interested?'

Larry shrugged.

Emma picked up the clipboard from the table in front of her. 'I'll put your name down,' she said.

Bill came hurrying up and the conversation went on without him for a moment, but as Bill left Jean was telling a story about someone she'd met in a pub, whom she'd liked, until she'd been given the tip-off ensuring she was never going to see him again.

'What was wrong with him?' Emma asked.

Jean narrowed her eyes at them, as though peering through cigarette smoke. 'What was wrong with him? If you found yourself fancying someone, and someone told you something about him, what's the worst thing you could think of to put you off him?'

'Him being a nonce,' Emma said without hesitation.

'Yeah, a nonce,' Becky said. 'They're bastards, they are.'

Larry nodded in agreement, wondering what the hell a nonce was, whether it was the same as a ponce.

'Wrong,' Jean said, with satisfaction. 'Worse than a bloody nonce. He was a copper.'

'Bloody hell. And you didn't know?'

'Couldn't tell, could I?' she said angrily and got up and went outside.

For a moment, Larry thought her feelings had been hurt but he saw through the glass her rising drift of cigarette smoke lift and tear in the wind.

169

He felt he'd been accepted. He was in. They might not be Barbie dolls, he thought, but at least he wouldn't be bored.

He looked over at Helen and thought about how different she was from these women, and from Megan too, come to that. With her almost colourless hair and her gentleness, she was what women used to be a long time ago when men had the upper hand. That was, he thought, why she didn't fit in. She was too gentle.

She was crouched down, talking to Bill, holding something out for him on the palm of her hand. He liked her for that, too.

Suddenly he was tired of the raucous women and wanted to be with her, to be in the presence of some of that gentleness.

He got up and walked over, negotiating the children and the little chairs. He'd thought of a good line. 'Are you doing the massage course?' he asked casually, patting Bill's head as though it was why he was there.

She was smiling her kind, perpetual smile. 'Are you?'

She'd obviously heard about it.

'Yes.'

'So am I. I usually try the courses out.'

Well now, that was something to report back to James. Not just pretty mothers but naked ones. Probably. You couldn't do a massage clothed. The thought of a naked Helen gave him the sensation of a feather stroking down his spine.

He wouldn't think about a naked Emma too hard just yet. Or even a naked Larry. He hesitated for a moment. 'Any idea what a nonce is?' he asked.

She gave him a strange look. 'It's a child molester. A paedophile.'

'Oh. Thanks.'

'That's all right.' She turned her back on him and went to the table where her daughter was sitting.

170

Larry felt she'd dismissed him. He couldn't think of anything else to say to bring her back. He was lost for words, somehow, when it came to Helen.

He went back to his little chair by the women.

'You fancy her, don't you?' Emma said on his return.

Larry laughed at the joke. But he wished she hadn't left him, all the same.

Later that morning it stopped raining and the doors to the playground were opened to let in some fresh air. Bill was outside in the Cozy Coupe.

Being in the Cozy Coupe was a bit of a scoop because he wasn't the type to pull anyone else out of it and he wasn't the type to cry to get in so mostly he didn't get to go in it, which was a shame because it was the car he liked best. He liked the Cozy Coupe best because it was the only car in the playgroup which had a roof which was a warm yellow colour, like being under the table at home. He'd been lucky to get it – wouldn't have, probably, if the previous occupant hadn't wetted on the seat and got out crying.

The damp seat had been cold at first, and uncomfortable, but now it had warmed up nicely.

Suddenly he felt something sprinkling in his hair and he turned round in the damp seat to find a girl putting woodchips on the shelf in the back.

'Stop it,' he said.

'Will you be my friend?' she asked him.

'No.' He pushed his feet against the ground and moved himself and the Cozy Coupe away. Then he tried to brush the woodchips off the shelf. He knew that the easiest way to do it would be to get out, but if he got out someone else who didn't care about the woodchips would jump in and that would be that. So he stayed in and picked some up and flung them out of the hole that was the back window.

'Bill, stop throwing things,' came an adult voice from nowhere.

He pushed his feet against the ground and moved away towards the fence.

Through the fence he could see the road that led home.

At home, something funny was happening.

He didn't like the feel of that. He turned the Cozy Coupe round and scuttled it towards the children gathered in the warmth of the doorway; aiming for where it was safe.

When they got home, Bill was restless. Larry had things to do but Bill wanted to be carried, and when Larry ignored him he hung onto his trouser leg.

Every time Larry prised him off, Bill's arms would reach for him again.

Larry was irritated, then angry. In the end he shouted, and Bill, to his shock, began to cry bitterly, the huge tears washing his reddening face. He put him down to get some tissues, but Bill's crying got louder and he picked him up again swiftly, not that it made any difference. The volume and intensity of Bill's tears amazed him.

'What can I do?' he asked, several times, not of Bill but of some unknown entity. He paced around, marvelling with horror at the length of the wails, and thought of ringing Megan. He imagined her coming home in a hurry to find Bill had cried himself to sleep. He imagined the look on her face that would say, 'Game's over, Larry. Let's get a proper nanny,' and he would be back to the degrading business of looking for a job again.

As for the Triton search – well, at first he'd thought he hadn't a hope in hell of getting that one, despite luscious Lisa's invitation to lunch at the Savoy Grill.

Megan had said that Lisa had talked her into it and he didn't doubt that. What Megan didn't know was that probably the only position Lisa had in mind for him was woman on top. He'd heard rumours about Lisa's reputation.

He would give it a go, not because of luscious Lisa, but because Megan would give him hell if he didn't. And he would go informed. He would go with as much as he could find on Triton, from corporate culture right down to the MD's zodiac sign and if he got it – if miracles happened – well, he would be a happy man. If he didn't, no one, especially not Megan, could say it was his fault. It was good to have been considered. It would help his credibility. He would make sure Reeve found out, for a start, Reeve and his odd look when he had not found himself a job after a week.

He absently mopped Bill's face with a pale pink tissue, and bits of it stuck to his cheeks.

Bill's long-breathed wails had subsided and he was gulping in sobs of air.

Larry sat down and jiggled Bill on his knee but Bill stiffened again, so he gave it up quickly.

Bill's small fingers reached for a button on Larry's polo shirt. Larry was relieved, even when he twisted it. 'Feeling better, little soldier?'

Bill looked up and gave another gulp. 'Oh, Larry,' he said sorrowfully to his father, clutching the twisted button, '*when is Zoofie coming back?*'

25

Lisa and Megan had decided to interview candidates for Triton together, where possible, at least on the initial approach, and if the potential candidate was able to come in.

One candidate, Steven Dean, was interviewed by Megan alone, as he'd told her he wouldn't be interested if Lisa was involved.

The other candidate to be interviewed alone was Larry.

Megan had raised her eyebrows at Lisa's choice of restaurant, but it never hurt to let people translate the choice of venue into a candidate's potential worth. And Lisa had her own reasons for making Larry feel pampered.

Lisa was already at the Savoy Grill when he showed up. Boy, he polishes up well, she thought, watching him walk to the table as though all eyes were on him.

He greeted her with a nod. Nothing ingratiating about Larry, she thought, waiting for him to sit down.

'What will you have to drink?' she asked him.

'Mineral water. Still.'

She'd been right in her analysis of him, and she felt her neck prickle with pleasure. This was not the nervous group head Larry, by any means. This Larry was senior executive material, not selling himself to her but seeing what she had to offer him.

Her particular interest, and problem, was in the real reason Burgess McLane had let him go when they initially had no one in mind to replace him. As a new client, Triton had to be impressed if they were to use Colgin again in the future. If there was a major weakness in Larry then she had to be aware of it and either not put him forward, or let Triton know of it and hope his strengths compensated for his weaknesses.

She had spoken to Burgess about Larry and Burgess had said that John King had suggested they let him go. She wondered what this good bloke Larry could possibly have done to upset him.

They were halfway through the main course when she mentioned what Burgess had said about John King, letting her knowledge of it drop like a hand-grenade in a supermarket. 'John King wanted you out even though it left him short of a group head,' she added.

She watched Larry stop with a forkful of food en route to his mouth, but the pause was momentary and then he carried on, not as if it was some great revelation, more as if she'd just told him something he'd already known but had forgotten.

'Well? Aren't you going to comment on that?' She almost smiled. 'Was it a personality clash?'

He did stop eating then. He looked at her and suddenly it was not business, not business at all. He was looking at her as though he was looking for something and wasn't sure whether he was seeing it or not.

'Is this to do with Triton?'

She felt her eyes narrow instinctively to keep him out. 'Make no mistake, Larry, it matters,' she said. 'Burgess will give you a good reference and your reputation is excellent, but Triton will want to know what went wrong there and I've got to be able to tell them. I've got to be able to prepare them.'

He was still looking at her. Into her. 'John King's done the same to you,' he said softly. 'He's pushed you out, hasn't he?'

It was an effort for Lisa not to respond. Bull's eye, Larry, she thought, and the pain of losing Chrissie returned momentarily, as sharp as it had ever been. She stared at her glass. 'I've

175

never worked for him,' she said abruptly, 'but he's a bastard, Larry.' She sucked in air between her teeth. 'And a headhunter is in a good position to destroy someone's reputation,' she added, lowering her voice.

Larry passed his finger along his morse code eyebrow and rubbed the scar. 'I don't think you ought to tell me any more,' he said. He looked tired. 'You've gone to a lot of trouble to find some dirt on John King when a phonecall would have done. Lunch really wasn't necessary. Neither was a bogus interview.'

Lisa whipped her napkin off her knee with such force that it cracked like a towel in a changing room. 'I'm not messing you around,' she said angrily, 'don't insult me. The Triton search is genuine. And so is my interest in you.'

'The Colgin Partnership is clean,' Larry said, 'and I'm thinking of Megan, not myself. If you muddy King's reputation without foundation, they'll know where the rumour began.'

'So you think John King is on the side of the angels, is that it? You must wonder why he didn't show you the same loyalty.'

'King owed me nothing and any company studying my CV will have to look at the overall picture. John King is not my problem any more. But he's obviously yours.'

She saw the speculation in his eyes. 'I have *not* slept with him,' she said sharply, and the force of her words seemed to come right up from her feet.

There was a silence.

'Shall I take your plates?' the waiter asked, and she waved him away.

'What did you think when you found out he'd let you go and there was no one to take your place?' Lisa asked, and she hardly recognised her own voice. Pleading wasn't her style. It was her last attempt at finding John King's weak spot and she had no real hope of getting an answer.

Larry rubbed the palm of his hand over his eyes as if to clear them.

Nothing, she thought, as Larry dropped his hand and looked at her, frowning.

'I remembered his look of relief,' he said.

Relief? She stared at him and saw the tiredness in his eyes. 'Thanks, Larry.' She didn't feel as disappointed as she ought. Larry shrugged and she bent down and reached for some papers from her bag, businesslike once more. 'These will tell you pretty well all you need to know about Triton,' she said, handing them over. Her voice was calm.

'I've done my homework,' he said, but took them anyway.

'We're giving our list to Triton later this week,' she said, 'and then I'll be in touch.' She placed her Mastercard on top of the bill.

Larry glanced at his watch. 'I've got to get back,' he said. 'Meg's mother's looking after Bill, but she's got a dental appointment at three.'

Lisa smiled, not at the fact of it, but at his telling her. 'I've heard of men like you,' she said, 'ones who care, but I've never met one before.'

This time he laughed. 'What an indictment,' he said, shaking his head, 'that we make sure it's so well hidden. Thanks for lunch.'

He held his hand out and she took it. His palm felt large and warm and dry against hers, like wood in the sun.

26

'Look at this place. It's all upside-down again,' Larry said, folding his arms and staring at the mess. 'Where's my Maglite? It was on the table. Bill?'

Bill was looking at the room. He raised his head to look at his father.

'Bill, we need a system. Newspapers can go in the bin; when it comes down to it I can't see myself reading old news. Dirty clothes can go straight in the washing machine. See if you can throw them in and get a goal, Bill. Cups and saucers and dirty plates go in the dishwasher.'

'Can we throw them in too?'

'No! Just the clothes. Don't mix them up. Clothes in the washing machine, dishes in the dishy. Then we'll go to the zoo.'

As he threw newspapers and clothes Larry wondered if he could write a book on Making Housework Fun. Women made too much of things, they really did. A bit of untidiness made a house into a home; he didn't know why Megan couldn't see that. He wished she would lighten up. Women liked to pretend cleaning was some big deal, like religion.

With his method, it was soon done.

He gave Bill a drink and patted him on the head. 'Can you remember how to put your shoes on? The one with the spot of paint goes on the leg with the scab on the knee. Good lad.'

It was another sunny day and the air was so warm that it

was like getting into a bath. The pavements shimmered in the heat. Larry could feel the sun on his skin as they walked down the steps to the still, green canal. Bill skipped alongside him for a couple of strides before losing the rhythm. Then he began to sing tonelessly. Easy to see when he was happy, Larry thought, taking his hand.

A few yards ahead of them was a shady tunnel where the Camden Road crossed the canal and Bill ran straight for it, disappearing into the shadows, his feet echoing under the bridge. 'Ha!' Larry heard him shout, and his amplified voice echoed close behind. Larry could see him now. He watched him jump up and down on the spot, feet together, and he watched him look up as the slap of his shoes on the path smacked above him. Something had caught his eye and when Larry got to him he was still staring at the underneath of the bridge.

'Look, Larry,' he said, his voice hushed as though noise would alarm the phenomenon, 'the water's making patterns on the roof.'

Larry looked up. 'Pretty, isn't it.' Dabs of light and shade interchanged with each other. He leaned against the railings that separated the towpath from the water and Bill climbed up beside him and looked down into the water.

'There's a fish,' Bill said.

Larry turned to look. Floating on its side in the still green water was a polystyrene cup. 'The canal is the polystyrene cup's natural habitat,' Larry said seriously and Bill laughed and swung on the railings, knowing from his father's solemn voice that it was a joke. 'Watch yourself,' Larry said. 'Don't want you falling in.' He held his arms out and Bill jumped into them. 'Oof,' he said and his voice echoed back and they walked hand-in-hand into the sunshine.

At Hampstead Road lock they lingered to watch the miracle of the gates holding back the wall of water. Nestled far down below them was a shoal of polystyrene cups, bobbing in the breeze. 'More fish,' Bill said.

'Tickle, for that,' Larry said, scooping him up in his arms. Bill giggled. They walked beneath an archway beyond which a narrowboat sat low in the water. 'That's the boat for the zoo,' Larry told him as they walked round to where it was moored.

As they got to it Bill crouched down to look through the windows. 'There are children in it,' he said.

'They're going to the zoo as well,' Larry said, helping him down the wooden steps into the boat and to a seat near an open window.

'Keep your arms inside,' the ticket collector said and shortly afterwards the boat pulled away, vibrating steadily as the engine laboured. Bill stared out of the window, kneeling on his seat and laughing to himself.

Larry suddenly felt a weight lift from him. They were enjoying themselves . . . it seemed to have crept up on them unexpectedly, a by-product of their decision to go to the zoo. They'd been left to their own devices and they were having fun. Bill laughed again and Larry looked through the window to see ducks paddling determinedly away from the boat. He found himself smiling too. He was enjoying the sun and the open air. He was having fun. But the biggest triumph of all so far was that he hadn't mentioned Zoofie once.

'Look at the people in their cages,' Bill said as they queued for a ticket.

Larry had never appreciated before just how convenient the zoo was for a child. No dog excrement, no traffic. He gave Bill his freedom as he would let a dog off a leash but Bill stayed close to him.

'Anything you particularly want to see?'

Bill shook his head.

'Okay. The lions are always good, and the monkeys.'

Bill looked up at his father with the expression of humouring him.

'Monkeys,' Larry repeated. 'Yeah, come on, we'll do that.' They stood at the chimpanzees' enclosure. One of the chimps was throwing mud at the onlookers – Larry hoped it was mud. The adults stepped back in alarm while the children made vomiting noises of delight.

Larry felt a certain amount of solidarity.

One of the females clambered round with a baby clutching her from underneath. Bonding.

The males swaggered and occasionally, violently, flung themselves at a branch.

Larry became aware that a man had come to stand next to him. He had a child, younger than Bill, by the looks of her, and the child was sitting on her father's shoulders. The man looked over his daughter's leg at Larry, and then from Larry to the chimps. Larry watched him out of the corner of his eye. The man looked from the chimps to Larry and back several times, as if comparing them. Then he seemed to come to a decision and started talking to his daughter, who was now resting her chin on his head. Larry tried to examine him on the periphery of his vision. He could see a tan suede jacket over his arm, and a denim shirt and denim jeans. The little girl was wearing denim too, and a tan jacket, similar to her father's, but not suede. To Larry it looked like some sort of thick cotton. Larry wondered why the man had chosen to dress his daughter in clothes so similar to his own. Perhaps it was for identification. The man looked his way again, as though he had suddenly been made aware of his gaze.

'Got custody?' he asked, but without a lift in his voice, as though the answer was a foregone conclusion.

For a moment Larry associated custody with the cages – some sort of imprisonment, and he didn't reply.

'I got custody,' the man said. 'Bummer, sometimes.'

Larry felt Bill twist around to look at the man; he was deeply interested in any words that could be classed by grown-ups as rude.

The man winked at Bill and looked at Larry again. 'What's your wife do?' he asked comfortably, as though this was a question he could predict the answer to.

'Er, executive search,' Larry said reluctantly.

'Thought so,' the man replied. 'Career woman. Climbing up the ladder to success. Too busy finding herself to find time for home. I didn't say that, the judge did,' he added. 'I was a painter and decorator myself. My ex-wife's a hypnotherapist.'

'Really,' Larry replied. 'A hypnotherapist. Well.'

'You're lucky you've got a little lad. Know what the worst thing about having a girl is? Toilets. I have to take her into the gents with me. Still, I'm glad I've got her.'

He jiggled her on his shoulders and one small, black patent shoe slipped off and he caught it deftly at waist level in a practised move. 'Probably see you around,' he said, pushing it back on her foot. 'We're off to Burger King.'

'See you around,' Larry said, turning to watch him go; a damp patch was darkening the denim between the man's shoulderblades as he walked off, clearly too hot in his long-sleeved shirt in the hot sun.

Larry was surprised to find he belonged to a club. He wasn't sure if he liked it. Got custody?

He looked at Bill. 'Where next?'

'Lions.'

They turned out to be a bit of a disappointment to Bill as they blinked and stretched in the sun as if they had nothing to be violent about. The tiger, however, came right up to the glass and watched them restlessly. Larry found himself staring into the tiger's eye, but the tiger merely looked back indifferently.

Bill began to get tired and restless, lagging behind Larry's legs with little interest in the animals. Generally he seemed miles away, yearning for something. Larry was not about to ask him what, he knew only too well what Bill was yearning for; he was yearning for the familiar, in the shape of Ruth.

They stopped by the fountains and Larry bought a coffee for himself and an ice-cream for Bill and they watched the plumes of water shiver like mirages in the sunlight.

'Shall we go to the playgroup now?' Bill asked him.

'If that's what you want,' Larry said. Resigned, he had agreed in a slightly martyrish way but when Bill's face lit up he put aside the games. I want what's best for him.

27

It was early evening and the office was quiet, so quiet that Megan turned suddenly from her computer to check whether Lisa was still there.

Catching the movement, Lisa looked from her VDU to Megan, her eyes blank for a moment. Then her expression changed and she smiled slowly, linking her fingers and stretching out her arms in front of her, her eyes half closed.

Despite her tiredness, Megan found herself smiling back.

Lisa sat back in her chair and glanced at her screen. 'Look at the time,' she said, still smiling. 'Haven't you got a home to go to?'

'Sometimes work seems more like home than home does,' Megan said. She immediately wished she hadn't. Played back, it sounded disloyal as well as unfair to Larry. She waited for Lisa to pounce on the statement as Zelda would have, but Lisa merely carried on watching her with the trace of a smile on her lips. It was a gentler smile now, less self-satisfied. 'It's not Larry's fault,' Megan added, 'it's just that when I'm feeling buzzy there's no one to buzz with any more. If I talk to Larry about work, it's like rubbing it in that he's jobless.'

'No one to buzz with. I like that,' Lisa said.

'Yeah?' Megan was smiling.

'Yeah. That's my problem, too. That's what I miss. No one to buzz with.'

They fell silent. The computers' fans hummed. Megan propped her elbow on the desk and rested her face against her hand. She could hear her watch tick. She was aware of the fact that she was waiting for Lisa to say something more, to add something, to consolidate this moment of intimacy between them.

'He may not be jobless for long,' Lisa said.

It was so different from her own train of thought that Megan felt momentarily disappointed. 'No,' she said. 'Hopefully not.'

'And then things will be back to normal,' Lisa added, keeping her voice light.

Megan had the impression she was being patted on the head. 'Just like that,' she said. She knew she sounded petulant and she laughed suddenly. 'Do you know what the problem is? It's that my husband doesn't understand me.'

Lisa's eyes seemed to sparkle for a moment as though they had filled with tears. 'That's what they all say.'

Megan laughed and, reaching for her mouse, she closed her document and switched off her computer. She glanced at her watch although she knew perfectly well what the time was. 'I've had it for today. Can you manage a drink?'

Lisa gave her a 'you have to ask?' look. 'Still buzzing, huh? Well, She-Man can always manage a drink.'

Megan got to her feet and picked her pen up off the desk.

Lisa was sitting motionless, her face speculative as she kept her eyes on Megan and Megan looked back, her eyes questioning.

'Do you want him employed at any price?' Lisa asked.

Megan was tempted to play for time by asking: 'Who?', but the knowledge that Lisa didn't suffer fools gladly stopped her. She put her jacket on. 'It's not that bad yet. Let's see what Triton thinks about him and then I'll let you know.'

Lisa shut down her computer. 'Come on,' she said. 'Let's get out of here.'

And they did.

* * *

185

It was dark by the time she reached the house.

She held her handbag tightly beneath her arm but as she tip-toed along the path a light strand of a spider's web caught across her face and she dashed her hand at it, shuddering as she felt it on her fingers. She wiped it on her dress and reached into her jacket pocket for her keys, clutching them to keep them from jangling. Her fingers found the one she wanted and gently she took the bunch out of her pocket, slipping the smallest key into the lock. Holding her breath she turned the key, pushing the door gently with one foot. It opened into the kitchen and she closed the door behind her and stood in the dark.

She could hear the television and from the inane brightness and high pitch of the voices she knew it was a children's programme. A single stray laugh came and went.

She walked over to the fridge and paused with her hand on the door. Inside the fridge was an unfinished bottle of red wine, left over from the night before. Dropping her hand, she went to the sink where a glass tumbler rested upside-down on the draining board. She picked it up and took it back to the fridge and opened the door. The fridge light illuminated the kitchen and she snatched up the bottle rather too quickly because it rang against the orange juice jar and the door closed with a pneumatic puff. She poured some wine into the tumbler in the dark and leaned against the work-top to drink it.

It tasted slightly bitter but she felt herself relax for the first time that day. It was lovely to stand in the kitchen in the dark. It felt peaceful; even the jabber of the children's programme wasn't disturbing her. It was someone else's jabber, not hers.

She bit her upper lip and wondered what it would be like not to work. What it would be like, in fact, to live with this sort of peace so that it became commonplace instead of something she had to steal. She rolled the glass between her palms to warm up the wine, although it would be drunk before she managed it, and thought of herself as a thief. A thief of time, stealing her son's time with her for herself. But she was human. She gulped down the glass, rinsed it at the sink, still in the dark, and opened the back door, slamming it hard and switching the light on. She was now officially home.

The scene in the sitting room was such a homely one that when she stepped into it she wondered why she'd bothered hiding at all.

Larry was lying on the sofa, talking on the phone. They looked at her, Larry smiling, Bill beckoning in his green pyjamas, reaching for the television remote control to turn the sound down. The small gold table lamps gleamed pools of light and Bill climbed off Larry's knee and onto hers and looked at her face.

'Hey, you're up late,' she said.

Then he whispered something. Bill, she noticed, had not got the hang of whispering at all; it was either too quiet to hear or too breathy to understand. 'What did you say?'

Bill put his face nearer hers and tried again. This time she caught it, and looked into Bill's blue eyes to repeat it. 'Daddy's done something terrible?' she asked, feeling her skin prickle tightly. She glanced over at Larry, who was nodding encouragingly at the unseeable caller. He caught her eye and winked.

Bill was trying to kneel on her lap and she winced as his heels struck her muscles. She held out her hands and he leaned on them with his palms down, pressed on hers. She tried to imagine that she found it impossible to believe Larry would do anything terrible. Wasn't that what loving wives thought? 'What did he do?' she asked, trying to make light of it.

Bill's face fell and huge, viscous tears filled his eyes and rolled over his lower lashes. 'Daddy put me in the bath with my slippers on.'

The impulse to laugh with relief was enormous but she hugged him hard, burying her face in the clean, newly ironed

187

smell of his pyjamas. 'Oh, Bill, I'm sorry,' she said, 'didn't you realise?'

Bill's mouth puckered again.

'We can dry them,' she said, 'they'll be back to normal by the morning.'

He looked at her, unconvinced, and she stood up, holding his warm body to her, her hands clasped under his bottom. 'Shall I take him up?' she mouthed to Larry, and he looked up and nodded, making winding-up motions at the phone.

The light was already on in Bill's room. His Thomas the Tank Engine covers were smooth and unwrinkled and she pulled them back and Bill climbed in and looked at her unwaveringly.

'What's up?' she asked him.

'You're the mummy and Daddy's the daddy,' Bill said carefully, watching her reaction.

'Mmm,' Megan said, pulling up a red wooden stool so that she could sit next to him.

'So, why doesn't Daddy go to work and you stay at home?'

'Oh. Some mummies like to work, if they're good at it.'

'In work you're a daddy and at home you're a mummy,' Bill suggested.

Megan stared at him and saw him not as her son but as a four-year-old boy trying to make sense of things that made no sense at all. 'I'm always your mother and Daddy's always your father,' she said, feeling as though she were about to tread in quicksand. 'That doesn't change. But some mothers work and some fathers stay at home. Sometimes both of them stay at home.' She saw a glimmer of hope in her son's eye and added swiftly, 'And sometimes neither of them does. Usually someone in the family needs to work to earn money to spend.'

Bill rubbed his eyes with his fists as though to clear them. 'I want you to stay at home and Daddy to go to work,' he said.

188

'Yes.' Megan nodded slowly, not taking her eyes off his face. 'I can see that.'

'Daddy put me in the bath with my slippers on,' he said, in a final effort to explain.

'I know. I'll dry them for you,' she said gently. 'Do you want a story?'

He nodded and closed his eyes. As she reached for a book from the shelf he opened them again sharply and seeing she was ready to settle down, he let his eyelids close once more.

'Once upon a time,' Megan began. Once upon a time, she thought, things were simple. Men were men and their wives and children were their possessions. Men would work away from the home and women would look after the children. The men's friends were the men they worked with and the women's friends were their neighbours. Why did Bill, who'd never known her not to work, have the idea that it was the woman who should stay at home?

She glanced at the bed. Bill was breathing heavily and deeply in his sleep. She bent down to kiss him and saw the tiny freckles on his nose.

She had supper still to make, and a pair of slippers that had to be dried out by morning.

PART FIVE

Five's a Christening

28

At the weekend Megan, Larry and Bill had been invited to Zelda's baby's christening.

Zelda invited Lisa, too, but Lisa didn't, she said, much care for churches, so she sent champagne instead.

The guests went into the cool, dark church out of the bright sunlight, bedecked in florals, like small shrubberies.

As Megan looked around she saw Zelda near the font, staring into it distractedly, her baby draped carefully over her shoulder.

As Megan went over, Zelda clutched her arm. 'What sort of water are they going to use?' she hissed into Megan's ear.

'Holy water's the general idea.'

Zelda looked troubled. 'I should have bought Evian, the vicar could have blessed it in the bottles and poured it straight in.' She looked at the baby. 'Because Taylor's never had nasty hard water on her head, have you, little thing?' The baby ignored her and looked into the distance, her fat cheeks resting on Zelda's cream dress.

'Cream, for the sick to blend in?' Megan asked, stroking the baby's hand.

'Posset.'

'Pardon me. See you later.' She and Larry and Bill sat near the back. Bill looked through the hymn book, a nice fat red book which banged satisfyingly when shut.

'Sh, Bill.'

Bill put the book down and unhooked the kneeler from the

back of the chair in front. He sat on it, stood on it and then unhooked another to make a tower.

The church was filling up. Taylor, from her mother's arms, let off a wail which echoed briefly in the vaulted ceiling.

'She sounds like her mother, doesn't she?' Larry said.

Bill liked the acoustic effect, and tried coughing loudly. Megan nudged him, the procession of clergy entered and they stood in a congregational Mexican wave.

'Come here, Bill,' Megan said, 'you'll be able to see better if you stand on this seat.'

The organ music began for the first hymn, encompassing them with its volume.

'Where's the baby?' he asked.

'There, in the front. The lady with the dark hair is holding her.'

'What's the baby's name?'

'Taylor. Look, this is the song we're going to sing. Do you want to hold the book?'

But something else had caught Bill's eye. He caught hold of Megan's hair and leaned forward, almost toppling off the seat.

'Look, Mummy, it's Zoofie!'

'Sh, it's not Zoofie. Come on, sing. You like singing.'

'It is Zoofie!'

Megan leaned over to look along Bill's line of sight.

In almost a mirror image, Ruth was holding Cyrill on a chair, sharing a hymn book. The little girl was swaying erratically to the music and Ruth glanced back at the people behind in an appeasing, half-embarrassed way.

Megan felt shocked. So that's who Ruth had left them for! Zelda, her so-called friend, had stolen Ruth!

She took Bill's hand and freed her hair from it.

'She's got someone else to look after, now,' Bill said loudly, his eyes wide. 'She's got some other kid.'

194

And not a mention of it, Megan thought. She looked at the family group rather resentfully. That could have been her and Larry, with another baby and Ruth to look after things.

The service distracted her from her thoughts, but it didn't distract Bill, who was craning his neck to see what was happening in the front. 'Can I talk to her?'

When they came to the back of the church, to the font, Ruth passed, looking bored, but saw Bill and smiled quickly. Her glance flickered towards Megan. Another shy smile, slightly apologetic, aiming for defiant. Megan smiled stiffly back.

By the flickering candlelight as they swore to forsake evil, Bill suddenly pulled his hand free of hers and ran to Ruth, his feet echoing on the flagstone floor. Ruth, holding Cyrill's hand, looked nonplussed as Bill lifted his arms to her, to be picked up.

She let Cyrill's hand go and crouched to hug him, love temporarily overcoming embarrassment. As she straightened, Bill sat down on her feet, making sure she didn't get away as Taylor was baptised.

Back outside in the sun, Megan glared at Zelda. 'You stole Ruth,' she said. 'Thanks a bunch.'

Zelda was brazen. 'I didn't steal her, I headhunted her. And you said she always complained because you bought the wrong food.'

Megan was still indignant. 'She said she was leaving because I ate mouse droppings.'

'There you are, then.'

The baby began to cry and Zelda looked around for Ruth, who was sitting on the springy grass outside the church, picking daisies.

Ruth took the baby and fussed her and she quietened quickly.

Zelda put her head close to Megan's, confidingly. 'You were right,' she said, 'she's great with children but bloody awful to live with. Had to buy her a new polyester-filled duvet. She said she couldn't sleep under the goose-down for imagining the agonies of all those dead fowl on her.'

'And is Cyrill saying "Moommy"?'

'It comes out now and again. Gerry thinks we could consider speech lessons when she's older.'

Megan laughed in spite of herself.

'I miss being in work,' Zelda said, 'but I can't bear the thought of leaving the baby. Don't tell Nigel I said that. How's Lisa getting on? Come back to the house, we can talk there. Ruth, we're going.'

Ruth gave her a belligerent look and dropped the daisy chain into Cyrill's hands. Megan felt a pang. It was strange to think you could miss someone's grumpiness.

'Come on, Bill,' Megan said, but Bill kept hold of Zoofie's hand.

'Look, Megan, don't see it as losing a nanny,' Zelda said, stroking the baby's pink forehead, 'see it as a way of keeping her in the family.'

Megan smiled ruefully. 'Thanks, Zelda,' she said.

29

Ever wanted to back out of something?

The aromatherapy class was about to begin and they were there in their loose clothes, Larry, not in shorts, but in jeans and a polo shirt, covered up for safety.

Larry was participating in equality at its finest and discovering that, speaking for himself, it wasn't equality that he wanted but the upper hand. He blamed it on his upbringing, *better than* being the key words that little boys were taught.

Jean, Emma, Janet and Becky were standing together. Helen, as usual, was hanging back. And Larry was trying his best to be cool.

'I'm Pat,' the masseuse said.

Pat! He waited for the laughter, but there was none.

They gathered around a collapsible massage bed with a hole in the top of it, and a pale blue blanket draped over the lower end. The blanket was darker in the centre than at the edges. It looked as if it needed washing.

The women were uncomfortable with each other in their skirts, edgy in their new personas.

'Who gets to sit on that?' Jean asked, to laughter.

'You're not getting me on it,' Emma said, with trepidation. 'It looks like a pasting table.'

It did, in fact, look to be a fragile thing. Larry put his weight on his other leg and watched the woman who'd come with the bed, a small, thin-lipped woman who was slipping into a white coat, with the attitude that the sooner this was over, the

197

better. 'Who is going to go first?' she asked. No volunteers.

Jean gave Larry a sideways look. 'Larry,' she suggested, nudging Janet. 'We've all wanted to get Larry on a bed, haven't we?' This was followed by raucous laughter that went on longer than it should have done.

Larry could feel his face tighten. Larry, my man, this is male heaven, a voice – his voice – reminded him. He was unconvinced.

'Go on, Larry, get them off.'

He turned to look at Helen for support. She was watching him with a distant look on her face and a slight smile and he couldn't tell whose side she was on.

'Take your shoes and socks off, then roll your jeans up and lie on your back,' Pat said.

'Woman on top, Larry. Just what you're used to.'

His face felt like a mask from the effort of not responding. He climbed onto the bed and listened to himself not say a word. This was equality, all right, sexual harassment at its best. He stared at the ceiling and thought of England. Thought of walking out.

'I'm here to show you the basic movements in massage. Sorry about the blanket, I do my regulars at night and their body hairs get stuck in the weave and don't wash out. Anyway, for an ordinary massage I use sweet almond oil which is easily absorbed by the skin. Warm it in your hands, first . . .'

Larry, lying on some other man's body hairs, could hear the sound of skin on skin. And suddenly the warm hands slid along his left foot, cupping it, sliding up as far as his ankle. And without wanting to, he grinned. It felt good, someone taking charge of his foot for him, yes, his own foot, one of those things that he stuffed into shoes and normally took no notice of. Sliding her hands, she began to straighten his toes, one by one, and he stifled a groan.

There was a murmur. 'Larry's enjoying it.'

'Wait until she gets a bit higher.'

Brought back to the unfortunate present, Larry turned his head. Helen was still standing apart in an isolation of her own making and she didn't meet his eyes.

He returned his gaze to the ceiling.

Pat was talking through the massage, rubbing along his tendons, kneading the balls of his feet, pressing around his ankle, explaining things that he wasn't listening to, talking about reflexology. The centre of Larry's being was now in his foot.

Presently, as Larry was wondering how long he could keep awake through these soporific ministrations, she clasped his foot tightly in both hands. 'You're done. Socks off, girls,' she said, 'and get into pairs. Take a mat each to rest on. Who's going to partner Larry?'

There were no volunteers. No one, for all the talk, seemed particularly keen for the honour.

Larry felt like the last one to be picked for a team.

The women were busy getting their mats and Helen stepped forward and looked down at him, shrugging ruefully. 'You seem to be stuck with me.' She took a hairband out of her pocket and pulled the impossibly blonde hair away from her face. For a moment he looked closely at her; the easy gesture reminded him of Megan.

She took one of the small sweet-almond-oil bottles, poured some in one hand and replaced the cap with the other. A careful gesture, he thought. He watched her smooth it in her palms and make to take his right foot.

She had the coldest hands he'd ever felt, and he flinched and pulled his foot back.

'Always warm the oil in your hands first,' Pat said.

He could hear Emma begin to laugh, and Pat's response was immediate. 'If it tickles, do it harder, with firmer strokes. There. There. To the ankle. Take your time, make it relaxing.'

'Warmer now?' Helen asked.

He nodded.

'What? Am I doing something wrong?'

'No,' said Larry, 'not at all. It's wonderful.' In the small room all that could be heard was the whispering of skin being stroked.

'Apology accepted.'

Then, to his disappointment, Pat called, 'All change!'

Larry got off the bed and minutes later found himself smoothing his hands on Helen's tanned and unshaven ankles. The hair on them was dark, like her eyelashes. Funny, he thought, how she'd looked like Megan for a moment. He felt as if he'd thought it before. A softer Megan, compliant.

He massaged the soles of her feet, pressing, kneading, pulling her toes, his hands slithering with the oil. She began to laugh and he stopped and looked at her. She had a lovely, thrilling laugh. He realised that despite her perpetual smile, he'd never heard it before.

'Oy, you two,' Emma called, 'less of that.'

Helen stopped as quickly as she'd begun.

Larry was sorry. He wanted to make her laugh again. 'You should laugh more,' he said, keeping his voice low. 'It suits you.'

'I don't deserve to laugh,' she said.

Larry looked at her, her foot still cradled in his hand.

He knew she believed it.

That night, Megan came in, late again.

Business was booming. The database was expanding, thanks to Lisa, but it meant more candidates to talk to, more clients to meet. She was more tired than she'd ever been in her life.

Larry, the ideal husband, was waiting for her with a glass of wine in his hand and she smiled gratefully and slightly guiltily, having had one with Lisa on the way home. She took the glass from him and had a sip before she kissed him so that he

200

wouldn't smell it on her breath. Just a drink with the lads after work, Larry, she thought. If she had to be a She-Man, then she'd better do it properly.

Larry led her by the hand into the sitting room, aglow with mellow light, and she sat down and thought, any minute now he will bring me my slippers and the evening paper.

'How's work?'

'Don't want to even think about it,' she said. 'Just before I left I got bawled out on the phone by someone who said headhunters were the leeches of the industry. I think he must have been approached before and turned down. For every person who's happy to talk, there's another who gets all precious.' She took another sip of wine. 'What did you do? Playgroup?'

'I've started a massage course,' he said. 'I'll give you a taster if you like.'

Megan looked at her wine and swirled it thoughtfully around the glass. You work late a few nights and your husband spins off in a totally new direction. Her heart was not rejoicing in the way Larry seemed to be expecting it to. 'A massage course? What about Bill?'

'It's at the playgroup,' Larry said. 'One of the mothers looks after the children while we do it.'

'The itsy-bitsy mothers,' Megan said, and she didn't fancy the idea at all, not one bit. Because if she was working her guts out, she didn't see why Larry should be having fun, especially not that kind. 'I thought the whole idea of not getting another nanny was because you wanted to be with Bill and now you're leaving him with some – mother – in a playgroup.'

'It's a one-hour session,' Larry said, 'and there are five of them over a five-week period. What difference is that going to make? If you're that worried about Bill you can try coming home earlier.'

She stared at him, and began to laugh incredulously. 'Larry

201

the nurturer speaks! Who are you, the Penelope Leach of househusbands? If I didn't work so damned hard, you wouldn't have the luxury of sitting back on your heels and waiting for jobs to come to you, you'd have to go out and find them like everybody else.'

'You're jealous.' Larry looked sick-makingly smug.

'WHAT?'

'But there's no need to be. There are no itsy-bitsy mothers there at all. The playgroup leader is a grandmother and the others are –' Lost for words, he waved his hands dismissively.

She looked at him with contempt. 'And that's supposed to make me feel better, is it?' she asked. 'I preferred Larry the nurturer to Larry the I'll-only-rate-them-if-they're-pretty.'

'I can't win, can I?'

Megan finished off the wine. 'No. Not tonight you can't,' she said. 'I'm tired. I'm going up to see Bill.' She saw an anxious expression cross his face and she frowned. 'I won't wake him.'

She put the glass down.

Upstairs, Bill was still sleeping. The glow of the night light gave her a deep shadow to accompany her to his bed.

What a day, she thought, looking at him. The phones had rung continually, and she'd missed Zelda desperately. A couple of researchers had come in to help and got high on the excitement. There was so much noise it had sounded like a non-stop party. Come to think of it, it was a good job Zelda wasn't there. She was a stickler for quietness, confidentiality, control.

The sleeping Bill made her long for sleep herself.

Where did he go to when he was asleep? What did he dream? She wanted to hold him.

Larry hadn't been far off when he'd said she was jealous. Maybe not of the itsy-bitsy mothers, but she was jealous nevertheless.

She was jealous of him.

202

30

It was only the rain that made the prospect of playgroup seem attractive, Larry thought as he listened to it beating on the window, the noise drowned occasionally by the sound of tyres swishing past. Bill wailed again as his Brio track failed to join up.

'You have to make sure it makes a circle,' Larry said with a sigh. 'Why didn't you leave it as it was?'

Bill didn't look at him, but carried on with his attempt to force the track to join up.

'You're going to break it,' Larry said impatiently, and wondered why he was trying to find an excuse to go there. Of course, there was no reason why he shouldn't. He and Bill couldn't be expected to get on all the time, any more than anyone else. Even children could have their off days.

He went to the speckled window again and watched the raindrops distort the view of the bright green grass outside. He thought of all the lonely mothers out there. There must be plenty of lonely fathers around, too, he thought, remembering the man at the zoo wearing the blue denim shirt on a boiling hot day, the sweat seeping through between his shoulderblades. 'Got custody?' Said more as a statement, not a question. He thought of all the fathers looking after their children and feeling second best when the child cries for its mother – knowing they were second best, or in his case, third best behind the nanny.

Behind him, Bill was saying, 'Ts, ts, ts,' and pushing the

Brio steam engine slowly along the track. He had given up trying to make it join and had put a buffer at the end instead.

Larry hunkered down beside him, going for jovial. 'Great track, son.'

Bill ignored him. 'Ts, ts, ts . . .'

'Okay, shall we go to playgroup?' No need for a verbal reply, son, he thought as Bill went to the hall to fetch his coat.

The rain which had attracted him to the playgroup seemed to have put others off. Only the stalwarts were there – the stalwarts, that is, and Helen. He thought she'd seen him but her upward-turning lips which always seemed to smile might have been acknowledging or might not. She was wearing her white, open-necked linen grandad shirt and looked like a healthy ghost.

Larry sat down and checked where Bill was. Then he rested back in the child's chair and tried to feign comfort.

Emma came through from the kitchen and gave him a brief glance before returning to her throne. She began laughing with Jean but the movement of his head caught her attention and their eyes met. For a moment she stared at him, unblinking, but her eyes flickered and she looked away. Larry wondered what it was about her that made her hate men.

Her loss, he thought.

He sat in Coventry a bit longer and didn't like it.

He got up, deciding to join Helen at the table where she was sitting with her dark-haired daughter who was threading shoelaces through card, her pink tongue lodged at the corner of her mouth. He slipped into a small chair opposite her and she looked up for a moment before going back to the threading.

'She's doing well,' he said as an opener.

Helen smiled, as though recognising the attempt for what it was. She curled her platinum hair around one ear.

204

'You weren't here yesterday,' Larry said. 'Didn't mean it as an accusation,' he added. 'I nearly didn't come myself.'

'Oh?'

He was aware of forcing the conversation, and wondered how to carry on. She obviously wasn't interested – funny how he'd misread her. Ironic, too, if now that he'd accepted his place as an outsider she'd decided she didn't want to be associated with him. 'Better see what Bill's doing,' he said, getting up.

'Bill's fine,' she said, reaching for him. Her hand stopped short of his sleeve and she pulled it back and picked up a yellow shoelace from the table. 'He's in the Cozy Coupe. He loves that car, doesn't he?'

'We should have got him one for his birthday. Only I didn't know he liked them, then.' He sat down slowly and her daughter looked up at him before popping her tongue back in her mouth. He smiled at her and she smiled shyly back and picked up her card once more.

'Maybe he wouldn't want one at home,' Helen suggested.

'Maybe not. He's got enough space at home. No brothers and sisters.' He realised Lily was looking at him again and he gave her another smile. 'How about you?' he asked Lily.

Lily looked at him uncertainly and wound her hair around her finger until it was curled right up to her head. She put her head to one side and looked at him out of the corners of her eyes, a picture of embarrassment.

Helen came to her daughter's rescue. 'No, Lily hasn't either. Not really.' She looked at him through dark eyes, uncannily like her daughter's, and pushed her hair behind her ear again.

Not really to a yes or no question? 'What did you do yesterday?' he asked, the only innocuous question he could come up with.

'I worked in the garden. Weeding, mostly; it's fairly low-maintenance apart from that. Have you got a garden?'

'Yes, we have. Ours is pretty low-maintenance too. And we add bulbs in the autumn and bedding plants in spring.'

'You're a "we", then.'

'I'm sorry?'

'You said ours. "Ours is pretty low-maintenance."' She put her head to one side, like her daughter had.

'My wife,' he said. 'Bill's mother. She works but I, er, my firm was taken over.' He nodded, then shrugged, as if it didn't matter. He was surprised to find it was true.

She nodded too and threaded the yellow shoelace through the fingers of her left hand, closing it on the loose ends so that it looked as though she was wearing two rings, one on her third finger, one on her index finger. She held her hand up, the better to see the effect. Then she unwound the lace and dropped it on the table again. 'I worked once,' she said and stopped. 'Oh, Lily, you've gone wrong, look, you've missed a hole. Shall I put it right for you?' She took the card and pulled out the thread. She did it with difficulty and Larry noticed for the first time that she had no nails; they were bitten almost to the quick.

'Go on,' Larry said, intrigued to find out what her job was.

'You really want to know?' She was laughing at him but somehow he didn't mind. 'I worked once,' she said again. 'I was a buyer for Needhams. I loved it.' Her smiled died away, leaving just a trace of it on her upturned lips. 'I was good at it, too.' She gave him a direct look, as though he might not believe her, but he nodded; go on, he thought.

She picked up the shoelace and pressed the hard end into the ball of her thumb. Larry watched as she pressed deeper and deeper. He could see the flesh around it bulge and redden and when it got to the point where he knew it must be hurting her she took it away and looked at the indentation in her flesh, watching it slowly fill again.

206

'We had it all,' she said, 'you know that feeling? When you know you're living the life you've always imagined for yourself? The peak of your success. You look down – and everything that happened before it looks small and insignificant. I liked that feeling. I enjoyed it – Larry . . .' Her dark eyes strayed restlessly over his and over his face, searching for something. Larry found himself hoping she would find it although he wasn't sure what it was.

She took a deep, shuddering breath and glanced at her daughter, whose head was bowed lower over the card and its coloured threads.

Somewhere, Larry could see, she had gone badly wrong. She'd lost the pattern, he noticed. The picture, in the shape of a flower, was criss-crossed indiscriminately with threads so that it looked as if it had been slashed. It looked as though the picture had been scribbled out.

Helen took a tub of babywipes out of her bag and dabbed her throat and neck with one. The atmosphere in the room was claustrophobic. He could see the sheen of perspiration on her face. 'Want one?'

Larry shook his head. A flash filled the room and the lights dimmed momentarily. He looked towards the window and saw sulphurous, yellow-grey clouds rolling in overhead. A rumble of thunder vibrated through the sky.

'I knew I was going to have to pay for that feeling of being on the peak,' she said when the rumble had died away. 'I knew it. I knew it and I didn't care.' She looked into her memory of it and smiled. 'It was worth it, it was worth anything, then. And it came to me that whatever happened I could look back on that time and know that I'd enjoyed it, that it was bliss. It was bliss,' she repeated, and looked towards the window. She was quiet for a long time.

The heat and the thunder seemed to have subdued the children. There was very little noise in the room. Even Emma was

207

quiet as she put out more biscuits and filled the cups with juice.

So what happened? He wasn't sure he wanted to know. But like a good psychiatrist he too kept quiet. He looked at Lily who was still working on the card. Some of the holes were so full that there was no room for another lace to be threaded through, but it didn't stop her from trying. Her tongue had sneaked back into the corner of her mouth, pink and moist and mobile. She appeared not to be listening but Larry guessed she was hearing every word.

'We belonged to a country club,' Helen said suddenly. She smiled at him. 'You know how it is? When you work hard you think that pleasure shouldn't come cheap, either. You want to pay for it. You feel you deserve it. We took up clay-pigeon shooting. We used the gym and swam with the children in the pool. Every weekend, almost, we went there – it had been so expensive to join but it was so lovely. It separated work from pleasure better than staying at home.'

Her restless hands reached for the yellow shoelace and she wound it round her index finger and bent it. Larry could see the tip of her finger slowly become pale and bloodless.

'They had a Jacuzzi in the room next to the pool. I got into it and I put her on the side, on a ledge that you sit on. She was chest-deep. She was happy. She liked the Jacuzzi, she'd been in it before, we always went in after a swim. I turned my back on her to read the notice on the wall. It said how you must have a shower before using the Jacuzzi and that under-fourteens were not allowed in unaccompanied and that smoking and drinking were not permitted in the pool. You see, it was nothing to do with me, really, that notice, but I read it in the splashing water from beginning to end and when I turned round she had gone under.'

Larry stared at her. Under her white linen shirt he saw her ribs heave as though to get rid of a weight on her chest.

'That's what the splashing had been. While I'd been reading the notice, she was drowning. It was that quick, that gentle, you wouldn't believe it. I think she'd tried to walk across, not realising she wasn't on the bottom, not realising it was just a ledge until she stepped off.'

Larry looked at Lily and then at Helen. 'Who –'

'Her name was Adele. She would have been six this year.'

Larry turned to look for Bill. He saw him climbing up the ladder of the plastic slide, his small hands gripping the rail. He turned back to Helen.

'I'd said I was prepared to pay,' she said, 'but I was wrong. It meant nothing afterwards, not compared with –' She turned to look through the window again, almost so that her back was to him. He could see, just beyond the platinum hair, the line of her forehead and her cheek.

When she turned back he could see the beads of perspiration on her upper lip.

'I don't think,' he said suddenly, 'that's how it works.' He knew he'd said the words too loudly. Lily looked up at him, her mouth slightly open, her lips gleaming from being licked. 'There's no payback,' he said to Helen. She nodded but he shook his head. 'You're wrong,' he said, 'because if you were right then it ought to be reversed and all those who have suffered would find at the end of their lives some glorious crescendo, the big reward, the Camelot.' He pulled a face. 'The lottery of life.' He glanced at her but she didn't respond one way or the other. 'But they don't, do they. Some people suffer all their lives and die suffering. There's no divine accounts system, debit and credit. Not in this life. Not here.'

He saw the tears flood her face and through them, like a cliff behind a waterfall, the upturned, slightly smiling mouth. It cursed him, he could see that now; imagining her coming back to the playgroup one child short and that smile to condemn her.

209

She wiped her face on her sleeve. Her eyes were puffy, her dark eyelashes divided into spikes.

'I'll get you a coffee,' he said. 'Lily, would you like a juice?' She twisted for a moment, then nodded. He got up, nearly colliding with Emma who had a broken doll in her hand. 'Can I get you one, too?'

Emma looked surprised, but nodded. 'You might as well do the lot,' she said, looking at her watch, 'we're due for one. They all take milk and if you put the sugar bowl on the tray they can help themselves.'

Larry climbed over the child-gate into the kitchen and filled the kettle. Through the window behind the sink he could see the darkness leave the sky. Something that had bugged him from the beginning about Helen all of a sudden became clear. He realised that her hair was not bleached.

It had turned white.

31

At the playgroup the following day, Larry made no pretence about where he wanted to sit. He took a seat right next to Helen and Lily and smiled at them in greeting. If she was feeling bad about what she'd told him then the sooner she saw he wasn't affected by it the sooner she'd feel all right. Behind her, by the door, he saw the main faction take note.

Helen did seem more reserved than she had the previous day. He also noticed that she was wearing a black cotton dress, and wondered whether the black was subconscious or deliberate.

Bill came up to him, trailing a pink toy pushchair behind him, a disgruntled look on his face. 'How do you do this?' he asked.

Lily raised her head, and her face came alive as she saw the pushchair. 'I know how to do it. I'll show you. You have to find a space, first,' she said and glanced at the play area. 'Come with me.'

Bill followed her, dragging the pushchair behind him.

Larry watched them, and blew a puff of air through closed lips. 'Like father, like son.'

Helen seemed confused for a moment, and then her face cleared. 'The woman taking the lead,' she said, and laughed, rather protectively. 'Is that so bad?'

'No. That wasn't what I meant.'

Helen looked at her knees and smoothed the black cotton flat over them. 'You were thinking of yourself, trailing behind

211

a woman. It's all right in theory but in practice you don't like it.'

Larry scratched his head, aware of her animosity and where it had come from. She wished, he knew, that she hadn't told him about Adele. 'The ideal is for people to do what they're best at,' he said mildly. 'If it's looking after their children, that's what they should do. It's not right for everyone.'

'And is it what you're best at?' she asked.

'I liked working. I like looking after Bill.'

'That's not an answer.'

'I'm hedging my bets.'

'It doesn't matter what you're good at, sometimes you have to make sacrifices,' Helen said, turning her face away from him.

'You shouldn't make ones that hurt the family,' he said, thinking of Megan and how initially he'd considered the Triton job mainly to please her.

Helen turned back to him, her eyes angry. She tilted her head to one side. 'You might as well get it from the horse's mouth,' she said, her voice low and urgent. 'I drove my husband away after Adele died. I supposed they told you that?' She paused and the pause seemed to stretch until she was lost in the grasping hands of the past. 'I didn't deserve him,' she whispered, 'and heaven knows, he didn't deserve me. I carried it around with me –' she held out her arms in front of her and looked at Larry '– like a millstone. I made life so unbearable that in the end he left. I didn't go back to my job. I devoted myself to Lily. I had to try to make up for things.' She lifted her head and looked around for her daughter.

Larry looked, too. He could see Bill sitting in the pink toy pushchair, being pushed around by Lily. They both looked pleased with themselves. He didn't know what he was meant to think. He knew what he did think, though. He glanced at Helen and saw that she had finished. End of sordid story.

212

Larry stretched out his legs. He could see the ridges of his veins on his tanned feet in his Timberland loafers. They reminded him, strangely, of carvings of Jesus's feet on crucifixes. He bent his knees, tucking his feet out of sight. 'Do you ever see your husband?' he asked.

She looked at him sharply and defensively, as though he had criticised her. 'Lily does, sometimes.'

Larry wondered what he looked like. Something like him, he supposed; with dark hair and skin that tanned easily, if Lily's colouring was anything to go by. He didn't want to guess what it felt like to have a child die, and to lose, also, a wife and daughter.

He got to his feet, suddenly tired.

'Where are you going?' Helen asked him sharply.

'I'm going out for a breath of fresh air,' he said. 'I'm sorry. Excuse me.'

The sky was cloudy and blessedly cool. He pushed his hands through his hair and was standing by the swings when Bill came running out to hug his legs and ran back in again.

Larry turned towards the building and could see Becky inside, talking to Emma by the big table, looking at him. Bill had disappeared out of sight.

He could still feel the sensation of Bill's arms around his legs. Thinking about it, Larry realised that since Ruth's appearance at the christening, Bill had stopped talking about her. It was as if it was her sudden disappearance from his life that had bothered him most, and that now he knew she was still around he had stopped worrying.

Larry leaned against the fence and his thoughts returned to Helen. He knew the conversation had angered him and he had taken sides, and not Helen's, but her unknown husband's. Men and women were a damn sight more alike than either of them cared to admit. This equality between the sexes was not

213

a myth, after all; both sides could be equally cruel, equally self-centred, equally blind.

He felt a hand on his shoulder and turned round. It was Becky. She looked happy and uncomplicated and young in a baggy white t-shirt and shorts.

'I want to talk to you,' she said.

He felt uncharacteristically tired. 'Shoot.'

'The council wants to close the playgroup and we want to keep it open,' she said in a rush. 'Will you help us?'

Larry turned and leaned his back against the fence. 'What did you have in mind?'

'Emma's husband thinks a petition to Downing Street might work,' she said. 'We could march there.'

All twenty of them, he thought. 'You'd do better marching to the town hall and making a fuss there,' he said. 'You won't be the only ones. Everyone in the borough's being affected by the council cutbacks.'

'Great!' Becky smiled happily. 'I'll tell Emma, shall I?'

'What?'

'That you'll organise a march to the town hall.'

'It was a joke, Becky,' he said, turning back to the swings.

She put her hand on his shoulder again. 'Is something wrong?'

'Probably not. Too much sun,' he said.

'Yeah.' She wound her hair around her hand. 'What shall I tell Emma?'

'I'll have a word with her. Do you want a coffee?'

'No, thanks, I've got a Diet Coke.'

As he followed her back inside he knew immediately that Helen had gone. The table was tidy, the toys returned to their basket.

'Hell,' he said, looking round. Bill was playing with Damon, Emma's grandson. He tapped Bill on the shoulder. 'Where's Lily?'

214

'Pshew,' Bill said. 'She's gone home. Damon's a fireman.' Damon had a Fireman Sam helmet on his head. 'And I'm Elvis,' Bill said.

'Where's your guitar?' Larry asked curiously. That was a conversation stopper, he thought, as the two boys ignored him and carried on with their 'pshewing' in the name of Fireman Sam.

He was in the kitchen making the coffee when Emma came in, stepping nimbly over the safety gate despite her size.

'Do you want one?' he asked.

She looked at him uncomfortably and took the band out of her hair. It was covered in navy and white polka dots, the same as her dress. Her dark hair fell forward, hiding her face for a moment, and Larry noticed for the first time the fine silver hairs among the dark. He took another mug out of the cupboard.

Emma replaced the band in her hair. 'You know about the playgroup?' she asked.

'Yes. Becky told me.'

'We usually get a grant from the council but they're going to give us less than half what we get now in the coming year.'

Larry nodded and spooned the coffee into the two mugs. He poured in the milk and then the water from the kettle. 'Here you are.'

'Thanks.' She leaned against the cooker. 'I don't suppose you'd know of anything we could do to make them rethink?'

'You need publicity,' he said. 'You should get in touch with the local press, that kind of thing. You could try a petition, bring it to people's awareness that way. This place should be kept open. It's not just for the children, it's for the people who look after them.'

As he said it, she looked at him. Her dark eyes seemed bloodshot, he noticed. He wondered how old she was – she looked older than he'd reckoned. She looked tired, too.

215

'Like childminders,' she said.

'Yes. And fathers.'

He watched her hand go to the polka dot band in her hair and then go back to her mug, as though it was a habit she was trying to break.

'We don't get many fathers here,' she said, raising her chin. 'There aren't that many fathers looking after their children. It's hard for them to fit in – lots of the women here are single parents and they want to moan about men, not have to be nice to them. And you know what men are like – always on the chat-up. Like you with Helen.'

'There's nothing –' he shook his head ruefully, thinking of James. Yeah, she came pretty close to the truth, he thought. 'Look, like you say, you're not going to be overrun with househusbands because there aren't that many of them. But it might be good for the children to have one or two men around.' He hesitated, wondering if he even cared.

She looked into her coffee mug, and then raised her head. 'So you'll think of something, you know, to try to keep this place open?'

'Yes.'

Emma nodded. A flicker of humour softened the edges of her face. 'A march, Becky said, to the town hall. You're not as useless as you look. And by the way, I take sugar,' she said. 'You'll remember next time.' And she winked.

32

Larry was on the phone to his mother, talking underwear. The dirty washing was climbing up the wall and Megan had pushed the booklet that came with the washing machine into his hands on the way out that morning.

He'd read it through from cover to cover but it hadn't mentioned pants.

His mother was pleased at having been asked. 'Just do the whites to start with. Have a look at the label, first, and see what they're made of,' she said.

Bill held up a pair of his own and Larry looked inside.

'One hundred per cent cotton.'

'Put all the white things in together, on a hot wash, that's fifty on your dial. Do you want me to come and help, darling?'

'I can manage,' he said, putting the phone down, armed with new knowledge. 'Whites in together, Bill. Hey, what do you want to be when you grow up?'

Bill looked at him stoutly. 'A man,' he said.

When Megan came home, the smell of burnt sausages was drifting inside the house and the sitting room was hazy with blue smoke.

She stepped out in the garden and found Larry and Bill crouched over the barbecue. As they heard her they both looked guiltily over their shoulders and Bill, she noticed, had the audacity to stand in front of it as though his slight body could hide it from view.

She could feel herself tightening up.

The men's club, she thought. If they didn't want her to see something, well then she wouldn't look.

Ignoring them, she brushed her hair out of her eyes with the back of her hand, and sat on the side of the sun lounger and peeled off her hold-ups so that her bare legs could get the fading rays of the evening sun.

She should have gone for a drink with Lisa. They could have chatted over a decent meal. She could have asked her exactly what it was she disliked about Stephen Dean and why she'd arranged to see Mark Howarth as well.

She lay back, wanting to be peaceful, but she could hear Larry and Bill whispering to each other. 'Having problems, chaps?' she asked.

'Larry put the sausages on too soon,' Bill said.

'Thanks, Bill,' his father retorted. 'And why did I put the sausages on too soon? Because we went to buy another goldfish and you took so long to choose it that I had to hurry up the cooking.'

She put her sunglasses on, the better to see him in the evening sun. 'You bought another fish?'

'To replace Nobby. His name's David,' Bill said. 'He's got a moustache.'

'A fish with a moustache,' Megan murmured, leaning back on the lounger and feeling peeved. 'You've been out in the sun too long.' She closed one eye. 'Why David? After Daddy?'

'After David Niven,' Larry said. 'Spitting image, I swear it.'

'How much was this hirsute pet?'

'Ninety pence,' Bill said, 'and Larry let me keep the change.'

'Which is now lost in the garden,' Larry said, straightening. He was holding a small pile of blackened shapes on a plate. 'With ketchup on they'll be marvellous. Carbon is awfully good for the digestion.'

'I can feel a take-away coming on,' Megan said, sitting up

218

and bending one knee to rub away the tickle of a fly.

'They'll be lovely, Mum,' Bill said, 'won't they, Larry?'

'Raw in the middle, cooked on the outside,' Megan said. 'We'll all get salmonella.'

Larry glanced at the plate in his hands and flicked away something from the edge of it before looking at Megan curiously. 'Yes, you're right. We'll have a take-away,' he said, going into the house. Bill followed him so closely that she saw Larry kick his knee accidentally as he climbed the step.

Megan flopped back onto the lounger and stared through her lenses at the brown-tinted sky. She took her sunglasses off and blinked at the bright blueness. With a sigh she got up off the lounger and followed them inside. They were in the kitchen. Bill was holding a tray with three glasses on it and Larry was pouring beer into two of them. She leaned on the doorframe and watched. The tray looked too heavy for Bill but obviously – obviously it wasn't. He was holding it steady, and, what was more, parallel.

'And Orangina for you,' Larry said and looked up at Megan. She felt rebuffed. His eyes were not hostile, but they were not friendly, either. It was the sort of look that people gave each other on the tube just before they looked away.

Megan bent and scratched her ankle awkwardly. 'The sausages will be great,' she said, straightening up. 'Sorry to be so –' she shrugged and rested her teeth on her lower lip.

Larry took the tray from Bill and offered it to her. She took a glass and it was refreshingly chilly and damp with condensation against her palm.

'Too late, I've put them in the bin,' he said, offering the tray to Bill. Bill stretched out his hand towards the beer. 'Oy!' Larry said and Bill giggled and took his Orangina and put the glass straight to his mouth.

Megan could hear the clink of his teeth against the rim as they went back out into the garden.

She looked at Larry, who saluted Bill briefly with his glass before drinking it. They had become close, those two.

She was glad.

She sipped her beer and looked at her husband over the glass. He wasn't smiling and she could see the fine white lines fanning from the outer corners of his eyes where his skin hadn't tanned. She imagined them both out all day in the sunshine, laughing. She sipped the beer again, smelling the yeast and feeling the fizz of the bubbles in her throat.

'What are you thinking?' Larry asked her and she felt herself blush, as though she'd been caught out.

'Oh,' she said, 'I was watching you and Bill.'

Larry smiled at her. It still made her heart go bump.

Larry came up to her and stroked a finger down her bare arm. She stifled a shiver.

'How's work?' he asked, so softly that she felt her hair stir with his breath.

'Fine,' she said. 'Lisa's exciting to have around. She sees things differently and it's made me wonder if Zelda and I aren't rather too much alike.'

'The Colgin Partnership is a success story. Don't worry about it.'

'I'm not worried. Just ringing the changes.'

'Do you think it's because Lisa's new to executive search?'

'More because she's Lisa, I think.' The words reminded her of something that Lisa had said: *I do things my way. It's the only way I know.*

He nodded. 'Keep an eye on her, Meg.'

'Yes, I will. She can be a little too unorthodox at times. How was playgroup?'

'It may have to close down. We're trying to fight it, of course.'

'We?' Megan asked, squinting at him. 'Don't use up too

220

much energy on it, Larry. You don't want them to start to rely on you.'

Bill came running up at that moment. 'Will you come and see David, now?'

'Who?' she asked, confused.

'The fish,' Larry said helpfully.

She'd already forgotten about the fish, but she put her glass down and followed them upstairs to Bill's room.

The fish was swimming lazily in the tank and she could see, just as they'd said, a straight black line following the shape of his upper lip. If fish had lips. Whatever, it really did look like a moustache. She looked at him closely. 'What a spiv. It's David Niven all right,' she said.

'It took the man ages to catch him,' Bill said and Larry nodded in agreement.

'He was very lively, wasn't he, Bill?'

'Yes. And he's for you, Mummy. Because something happened to your underwear.'

Megan looked at Larry, an is-it-true look.

Larry shrugged helplessly, like a sit-com husband. He went off and came back with a handful of shrivelled, grey undies that had once been white silk. It took Megan a few moments to recognise them as belonging to her.

She didn't feel able to speak.

She turned back to look at the moustachioed fish swimming idly around the tank. 'He's great,' she said flatly.

They had spoiled her undies and bought a fish without her. They could have waited until the weekend so that she could have joined them. They could have replaced the lingerie.

She stared at the fish with sudden resentment and what she was thinking was, Who has to clean him out? Who has to make sure he's fed?

She was aware of them looking at her.

Here she was, the mother who was hardly ever home and when she was she ruined everything.

'Let's go out and get a pizza,' she said, 'we'll feel better after we've eaten.'

She pretended not to notice the look they gave each other. She bet they loved the 'we'.

PART SIX

Six a Dearth

33

James was trying to clean the mould from his crockery. The pale green floaters were easy enough, but the grey fuzz was more resilient.

Hidden in his wardrobe were four dustbin liners containing things that he'd picked up off the floor: newspapers, clothes, magazines, biscuit wrappers, nothing important, and while he did the dishes he hoped she wouldn't decide to have a clean out and find them.

The point was, to act as if he could cope.

Well of course he could cope. It was just in a different way from Lydia.

The fact of her coming was quite unusual, as, since the wedding, Charles had taken to dropping the girls off. He did it ingratiatingly, as though he was a dog-hater who'd somehow got locked into a kennel, but even that didn't give James the satisfaction it might once have done.

He'd wondered about this visit of Lydia's. She'd been cagey on the phone, saying she would tell him when she saw him. It was hard to work out what would make her cagey like that.

He'd toyed around with a few ideas, just a few, something on the lines that her sex life was no good and would he oblige, but he couldn't, ha ha, come up with anything concrete on that score. The thought of Lydia and Charles doing anything as human as making love was ridiculous but then so was the idea of Lydia making love with him. She was as likely to start kissing frogs. Still, the idea of it whiled away a mossy bowl or two.

All the dishes de-fuzzed, he looked around for something to dry them with. In the end he had to use a shirt from one of the bin bags in the wardrobe. He was surprised to find it wasn't very absorbent but he persevered, and stacked the clean-ish dishes in the cupboard. He even had time for a quick shower.

Would have had time. He was still in the shower when the doorbell rang and he hurried down, afraid she wouldn't wait, and opened the door still fastening up the buttons on his jeans.

'Lydia,' he said, feeling the water from his hair trickle coldly between his shoulderblades.

'James,' she said with a small smile, inclining her head.

'Come in.' He made an extravagant gesture and bowed low.

'Your hair's wet,' she said. 'You ought to get a towel.'

'Yes.' But he had noticed, when he'd grabbed it, that the towel had taken on a strange smell, rather like hops. It had seemed to transfer itself to his skin and he felt it was better left where it was.

Lydia settled herself on the sofa, smoothing her beige dress, looking round, looking at him.

'Would you like a drink?' he asked her.

'Coffee, please.'

He went into the kitchen and picked up the tea-towel shirt and rubbed his head with it. He switched on the kettle and got out mugs, thought better of it and felt around for cups instead. And saucers.

'A mug will do,' she said in response to the sound of clattering china.

'No, a cup, I insist.' The saucer, he noticed, was dusty and he wiped it on the seat of his jeans. His hands were shaking as he put in the instant coffee. 'Still no sugar?'

'Still no sugar,' she confirmed.

226

He took the coffees through and his heart began to beat loudly again. He could hear his pulse beating in his ears and it had the same resonance as if he was listening through a shell.

'Shoot,' he said.

'The girls are going to board.' She said it like someone might have said, 'The girls have gone to seed,' and it took him a moment to make sense of it.

When he did, he found she'd shot him, sure enough. 'Why?' But it was clear why. 'This is old Charlie-boy's idea, isn't it,' he said, 'packing them off so that you can spend time alone. Not enough that he gets you to divorce me, he wants you to divorce the girls! I'll have them here. I'll look after them.'

She was rubbing her thumb over a chip on the rim of the cup. 'You can't look after yourself, James,' she said sadly. 'How could they stay here? Look at this place – you haven't even got a job, how could you look after them?' She shrugged wearily as though it was a subject she had considered and swiftly tired of. 'Anyway, James, it isn't a plot against you. They want to go.'

'When will I see them?'

'During the holidays, and there are plenty of those.'

'I don't want them to go,' he said again. 'I don't want to lose them.' It was, he knew, a little late for that sort of regret. 'All I want . . .' he put his coffee cup on the floor and walked over to the bookcase on which their school photograph stood, warped slightly in the cardboard mount.

'Go on,' Lydia said.

'All I want is for life to be as it was.'

'That's a stupid thing to say. It never will be as it was. If you want to change your life, get a job,' she said.

'I will. I'll open a surf shop –' he stopped as Lydia looked away.

'James, who buys surfing gear in London? Who wears it, for

227

that matter, apart from you? You're not suddenly going to get a business going, how the hell could you?'

She swung back to him and her voice rose to a shriek. 'What am I *talking* about? How the hell could you even imagine you could run a business? How could you?' And he had the sensation that every point was being hammered into him swiftly and cleanly, like tacks. He could feel the pain of them poking into him under his skin.

It seemed to show on his face, because all of a sudden she stopped and clasped her hand over her mouth as though a river of angry words might gush out if she took her hand away.

He saw her breath heave her rib cage up and down. He felt dizzy, as if he'd been tumbled about.

After a few moments she took her hand tentatively away from her mouth and nothing came out. No rivers, anyway. 'I only came to tell you what the girls wanted. They're going to start in the autumn.'

James knew he had one last chance to grab the rope that would save him. 'Lydia, you don't know how much I love you,' he said.

'But you love yourself more, don't you? You'll always do what *you* want. You'll never change.'

He'd missed the rope. Perhaps, yes, that was it, he'd only imagined it. He sat down again, defeated. 'Can you blame me for not being as good as you?'

'And can you blame me for giving the girls another father?' She got up hurriedly, shaking with anger. She put the cup down on the floor and hurried to the door. He thought she was going to run out but when she saw that he hadn't come after her, she hesitated. 'Marrying you was the worst thing I ever did, James. I'll regret it until I die.' She slammed the door behind her and he jumped at the force behind it.

He heard her feet on the path and knew she was running to her car. 'You don't mean that!' he shouted loudly.

He waited for his heart to boom in his ears.

He waited and waited until the silence was bursting in his head. But it was no use. It seemed not to be working at all.

34

Megan was on the phone to Paul Camberwell of Triton, who had approved the shortlist and wanted to arrange for the candidates to meet the Triton team.

After she put the phone down she turned to Lisa with a smile. 'That was Paul Camberwell. He wants our chaps there next Wednesday or Thursday, whichever's best. We'll arrange a briefing before then.' She paused. 'I'll do Larry.' She stretched with a nervous excitement at the thought that soon, Larry might be working again. Oh, please, she added to herself.

Lisa was looking at her in a concerned way that would have seemed patronising from anyone else. 'You look tired, Meg,' she said.

Bathed in the soothing wash of green eyes, Megan smiled again. 'I didn't sleep very well last night.'

Lisa got up and walked over to her. 'I'll give you a massage,' she said, coming up behind her and putting her hands on the thin cotton of Megan's shirt.

Megan shut her eyes and thought of Larry massaging mothers and grandmothers and letting the house fall apart without noticing it. She recalled fondly the days of Ruth who, by the end of the day, gave the impression of the chaos being kept in check, but only just. Lisa's fingers pressed deeply into her shoulder muscles, hurting and soothing at the same time, and her distinctive perfume settled around Megan. It was blissfully quiet in the office; it seemed ages, so long since they'd had a quiet day.

Lisa's fingers seemed to loosen her so well that she could feel herself dozing. She felt her head jerk up and her hair fall on her cheek. Brushing it away, she became awake and realised that it wasn't her hair – her hair wasn't long any more – and she turned, startled, to look at Lisa.

Lisa's pupils were so large that her eyes looked dark, as dark as Larry's, and her hair was hanging loosely around her face, heavy and glossy, but with stiff tracks around her face, from the gel that she used.

Meg's surprise turned to discomfort, and slight embarrassment. 'Thanks,' she said, 'I feel heaps better now.'

'Men just don't understand, do they,' Lisa said softly, her fingers still moving gently. 'They want you to be like them at work, and they want you to be a woman when they're ready to play.'

'Not that that's very often at the moment,' Megan said ruefully.

The phone began to ring and for an instant, neither of them moved. Megan reached for it on the third ring and in leaning forward she moved away from Lisa's soothing hands.

She saw Lisa turn away and gather her hair together and twist it into the silver ring that held it back from her face.

At the playgroup, Larry ended his hour of massage early so as to speak to the reporter from the *Journal*, while the photographer gathered the children together outside the building and asked them to look sad for the camera. The photographer asked for a pretty mother to go and stand with them and Larry, in the absence of Helen, suggested Becky, who wasn't a mother but was definitely pretty.

The playgroup was not the only potential victim of council cuts, as he had known. The library and the community centre were taking action too, and the local socialist party was organising a march in protest.

'We could join in from about halfway,' Larry said to Emma after the massage class had finished and the men from the *Journal* had left. 'The whole route is too long for the children, even if they're in pushchairs.'

Emma agreed.

'We ought to get some flyers made,' he said, 'so that we can hand them out on the way.'

An *Evening Standard* photographer came later on to take photographs of the wide-eyed children, with Damon and Bill and the children looking soulful in the playground and the childminders and the mothers looking glamorous in the kitchen.

Jean decided to start a petition and the photocopied forms were left in local shops to be signed as the mood took the customers.

If Larry, on dropping them off, recognised several names with the same signature, he didn't bring it up.

And although he kept looking out for her, Helen never came.

35

Larry went to Triton to be interviewed by Paul Camberwell and his team.

He interviewed well. Relaxed, with nothing to lose, his best qualities, which at the beginning of his job search had been masked by panic, were now evident. He was more himself than he had been since the day he'd stepped into Burgess's office vowing to take his bomb curtains down.

After leaving the Triton building, as his mother was looking after Bill for the day, he rang up James and asked him if he wanted to go for a drink.

They arranged to meet in a club in Beauchamp Square, near the Triton offices. Larry, a beer in his hand, hardly recognised James as he walked in. He looked gaunt, the skin pulled so tightly over his face that it made a ledge of his cheekbones.

For a while, James didn't talk, but the beer on an empty stomach brought the story out of him, how Lydia was sending the girls away. 'The myth of quality time,' he said. 'What children need is for you to always be there.'

'They're growing up,' Larry said. 'Maybe they feel it's time to go.'

James looked at him with the first flicker of feeling in his pale eyes. 'They're only eleven years old,' he said. 'They should be at home. They should be with me.'

Larry felt a hand on his shoulder and he looked up and found Lisa there.

'How did it go with Paul Camberwell?' she asked.

'They're a good team,' he said. 'What are you doing here?'

'An informal interview with a Triton executive who wants to get out. Don't let it put you off, Larry. And don't worry, he's gone now.' Her eyes kept returning to James, which was hardly surprising as he looked on the point of collapse.

'Lisa, this is James Wilder, an old friend. James, Lisa Ashridge. She works with Megan.'

Lisa held out her hand and for an awful moment Larry thought James was going to kiss it, but James just shook it briefly as though conserving energy. 'I don't usually look like this,' he said, 'but my wife has left me and she's sending my children away.'

Larry found himself grinning at Lisa in the vague hope that she would realise James was not himself and leave them to it.

Lisa raised her hand and ordered a drink. 'Will you have another?' When James nodded, she said coolly, 'You're well rid of her, I expect.'

'No,' he said. 'I love her.'

'Still?' Lisa said with a sneer. 'Most men can't wait to get rid of their little wives.'

James seemed to consider this statement very seriously before replying. 'No one would ever call Lydia that. She was the man of the house, wasn't she, Larry? I used to look after the girls for her.'

'You were a househusband?'

'I suppose you could say that. But I wasn't good enough for her. She got tired of having me at home. She's married to someone else, now.'

Lisa drew her fingers along the gelled strands of hair that led to the hoop at the back. 'You should get your hair cut. You'd have a better chance.'

James seemed to sink into a bubble of apathy at the thought.

'Can I have a quick word, Larry?' she asked when their drinks came.

'Sure. Will you excuse us, James?'

James nodded and wrapped his hand around a fresh glass and Larry and Lisa moved to the bottom of the bar.

'What do you know about Peter Dawlish?' she asked.

Larry grinned. 'You headhunters never give up, do you? Peter Dawlish.' He rubbed his chin slowly. 'He's worked at I&R for at least ten years – he used to do our sales promotion literature for us. When I say us, I mean Burgess McLane. Probably still does it for Xylus. John King used to deal with that side of things, it was one of the last things we talked about. I wondered whether or not it was time for a change.'

Lisa grinned and squeezed his hand. She put her drink on the counter. 'Nice to see you. I'll be in touch, Larry.'

Larry watched her go and turned his attention back to James.

He didn't know whether to be worried or frustrated about him. He told James that a lot of men went through it, and started again with new wives. There had to be many men out there going through it one way or another and coming out the other side so normal that you couldn't tell.

'Show me one,' James said.

The only thing that amused him was the fact that Bill called his father Larry.

'Demotion, mate.'

Reassured by the wry laughter, Larry told James he thought he ought to buck up. After all, it wasn't as if he hadn't been through a trauma himself. And got himself out of it, got himself through the white noise and out of the pit to where he was now.

'And where's that, Larry?' James said, his voice as flat and lifeless as dead fish eyes. 'Unemployed and pushing your son around, a rebel with a Mickey Mouse bell?'

235

36

Peter Dawlish was in Lisa's bath, a glass of brandy in his hand. The candles flickered and the Badedas foamed.

He'd never in a million years expected to find himself there, but something had happened, he'd done something, pressed the right buttons, he thought – yes, that was it, pressed the right buttons – and she'd come on to him like a hot potato.

And not just any hot potato – this one had brains.

Like to like, he thought, groaning as she soaped his foot, slipping her fingers between his toes. He'd never had anyone go *there* before, not since he was out of nappies. It was to have been such an ordinary night, too. A drink after work . . . he tried to concentrate on her voice.

It was amazing, he thought, what turned women on. He knew women who liked talking dirty but this one talked money. Non-stop money. She talked about rolling in it, sweating on it, licking it . . . never leaving his toes alone once.

'What do *you* do with money?' she asked in a soft-as-soapsuds voice.

'Roll in it,' he said. 'Spend it!'

Oh, he had the touch tonight, he had the touch. He felt her hands slither from his toes to his ankles; he'd never seen that in a book but his ankles were attached to parts of him he'd never have guessed.

He tried to think of the magic word that would send those soapy hands a little higher. What the hell else could you do with money? 'Throw it in the air!' he cried, but those fingers stayed right where they were.

And when he was almost sobbing with frustration, she asked in her smoothie voice, 'Have you ever fiddled money?'

'Oh yes, oh yes,' he said, and her fingers inched up and bubbles of lucidity popped in his brain and he thought – set-up!

'With John King?'

He groaned, not so much with pleasure, this time.

'Seriously,' she said. 'Or I pull the plug.'

His eyes widened and he looked at the chain in her hand and the smile on her face and got back into it *straight* away, shutting his eyes as her hands inched up his calf. 'Don't pull it! Don't pull it! I'll talk!'

Her hands were at the back of his knee, that soft crease of skin.

'He pays me ten grand to do his sales promotion literature,' he told her, and felt her hands move round.

The front of his knee! How could he ever have knelt on such a tender spot? 'I get Trappers to do it for eight grand.'

His thigh, and nearly there. Couldn't wait much longer.

'I invoice the company for ten grand and John King and I, we split the two k.'

'Is that all?'

'Over the months it mounts up. We've been doing it for years. Different sums, of course.' He opened his eyes briefly and could still see her smile.

He must be doing something right.

And then, so did she.

And as he sank into the bubbles he thought hey, drowning was the only way to die.

'What are you going to do?' he asked her afterwards. He wished he hadn't told her, but wouldn't have turned back the clock, not for the world.

'Nothing,' she said, finishing off her brandy. 'It's not my money.'

The word, he noticed, wasn't having much effect on her now.

'If John King goes down, I go down, you know that.'

'I wouldn't let you go down, Peter.'

And as she showed him the door, he had to be content with that.

37

On the day of the march the coach was full. Larry stood outside it, ticking off names as the women went up and found their seats. There was a general air of gaiety and not only that, there was also a sense of purpose.

Emma, in red, locked the doors of the building and came up to him. 'That's the lot,' she said. 'A good turnout. More than we expected.'

Larry took one last, hopeful look and saw Helen, hand in hand with Lily, walking towards them.

'Are we too late?' she asked softly.

'Never too late. Get in.'

Larry followed her up the steps onto the coach.

It suddenly seemed as if she was the person he'd done it for, and not the playgroup at all.

The doors shut with a hiss behind them and as he nodded to the driver he was aware that everyone was quietening down. He rested a hand on the fuzzy orange upholstery of the bus and faced them, sixty-four expectant people waiting for motivation.

'Right,' he said, clearing his throat, 'we are not going to be the only people outside the town hall because the cuts are not only going to affect us, they're going to affect everyone in the borough – those who use the library, those who use the sports centre, the elderly who go to the community hall. We're all going to suffer in our own way. But we've got a voice.' Rumblings of agreement, like the humming of bees, built up briefly, then subsided. 'And we'll make sure it's heard.'

The first smatterings of clapping were drowned out by the driver starting the engine.

Larry swung himself into his seat, next to Emma. He looked along the aisle and saw that Bill had gone to sit on Helen's knee. He gave Bill the thumbs-up sign (or was it really for Helen?) and sat back again in his seat and exhaled deeply, thinking of Megan and the Triton job.

Emma opened a packet of Polo mints and offered one to him. He put it in his mouth, sucking thoughtfully.

Emma was looking out of the window as the playgroup was left behind in the distance.

She turned to him and adjusted the band around her hair.

'Do you think we're going to make any difference?' she asked, and he was surprised at the futility in her voice.

He bit into the Polo and it split in half beneath his teeth with a crack.

'Every action causes a reaction,' he said. 'It can't make things any worse, can it?'

She looked at him again. He could see how the playgroup's problem had changed her. Her skin looked pale and fine over her plump cheeks and he noticed again the strands of white crinkling waywardly in her otherwise smooth, glossy hair.

'When you think things can't get any worse, they usually do,' she said.

'You sound tired,' he said, his head nearer hers so that he didn't have to raise his voice.

'I'm tired of struggling,' she said. 'The playgroup's the best thing that's ever happened to me, and I can't even keep it open.' She looked out of the window again at the hot, dirty streets, the grimy buildings, the cars driving alongside the bus pumping out carcinogenic, lead-free fumes. 'I used to think there was a purpose to things,' she said.

'And you don't any more?'

'No, I don't. I used to think things would get better, you

240

know, that you could achieve something . . .' she glanced at him again, swallowing her words as though they were threatening to choke her. Larry was surprised to see tears were blurring her creased eyes.

Larry too stared at the traffic, at the lights, the roadworks, the parked trucks with hazard lights on, winking audaciously as the traffic snaked erratically round them. He, too, had succumbed to the achievement idea. Perhaps that was the insidious side of it, the idea that you actually could reach some sort of pinnacle, and that once there a little voice in your ear would say: Look! This could all be yours. But it was what kept people going. It was what had kept him going.

When Emma next spoke, the tears had gone although he hadn't seen her wipe them away. 'I suppose I expected a reward for good behaviour,' she said, and laughed. 'I always was a silly cow.'

Larry rubbed his hand against the newly emerging stubble of his jaw and didn't reply.

She gave another short laugh. 'Do you know what I want? I want the playgroup to stay open.'

Larry laughed. 'It doesn't seem much to ask,' he said.

'It's all uphill, whatever, isn't it? What do you want? You don't want to spend the rest of your life taking Bill to school and dropping him off, do you?'

Larry rubbed the cleft of his cheek. 'I want a job and a car and money. And I know what I don't want. I don't want to only see Bill at weekends. I don't want watching my reflection in windows to be the highlight of my day. I don't want to hurt my wife.' He stopped suddenly.

Ahead he could see a police van and a small crowd of demonstrators. It was the beginning of the march. Police and demonstrators kept apart like two well-matched dogs who didn't feel confident about testing their strength just yet.

Larry stared at them. The talk with Emma had depressed

him. He looked out of the window at the two factions and it reminded him of his marriage.

As the coach pulled up he got to his feet. All faces were turned to him.

He checked his watch. 'It's three o'clock,' he said. 'We'll join the demo at the town hall. The coach will pick us up from Cleve Street at six-thirty. If anyone wants to go home sooner, let me know and I'll see you get transport.'

There was a buzz of conversation.

Larry had nothing more to say, but they still didn't move and he realised that he ought to end with something meaningful. He had become their leader. He looked down the aisle of the coach, his eyes checking from row to row, and in each face he looked at he saw expectation. 'We won't lose the playgroup,' he said. 'We'll find some way to fund it. That playgroup belongs to us.'

A couple of desultory cheers and the movement began, and children spilled from knees and purposefully the women picked up their bags and prepared themselves for the march.

Bill and Helen were the last to get off. Helen handed Bill over and Larry lifted him high over his head as he'd done when he was a small child.

Bill, thrilled with fright, giggled down at him.

'Let's get going,' Larry said.

People were gathering from nowhere, it seemed. They appeared to materialise instantaneously – young people in camouflage, wearing black, their faces pale.

Larry felt himself coming together in a concentration of energy. It was a familiar feeling, one he'd experienced in meetings and presentations and lunchtime lynchings; a feeling of readiness.

'We'll keep it peaceful,' he said.

The police were stringing along their side of the road.

As they started off there was the smattering of a cheer and

he suddenly caught a glimpse of the reality. For a moment, his old power had come back but he had almost missed the crucial difference. He had changed sides.

There were hundreds of people milling about outside the town hall.

There was a roar as someone emerged.

It was a man in his fifties, his hair rather long, wearing a mis-matched suit, as though he'd dressed in a hurry that morning. He stood on the top step and waited for the noise to die down.

He looked calm and unagitated. He looked superior.

'I can tell you this won't do you any good,' he said. 'We are not swayed by emotions, we are only swayed by budget.'

There was a roar of discontent.

'So I suggest you all go home,' he said.

'Yeah, you would, mate.'

A policeman joined him on the step.

'Get back in there, you faggot,' came a voice from the crowd.

The man in the suit seemed to find a good reason for going back in. 'We've nothing to hide,' he said, 'and you've nothing to gain by staying out here.'

Emma came up alongside Larry in the crowd.

'They want their supper,' she said with a laugh.

'You're probably right,' Larry said. He thought of her talk about pinnacles and he began to push his way through the crowd towards the bottom of the steps. When he was in earshot of the man, he called out, 'I'd like a word with you, if you don't mind.'

The man turned back from the door which the police officer was holding open and looked at him, surprised. 'How can I help?' he asked.

'Have your children got a garden?' Larry called.

The man's face hardened. 'You should know better,' he said.

'You sound an intelligent man. Why don't you act it?'

'Why does the council waste money on driving lessons for single parents who can't afford to buy a car? Let it go on the important things – a place to take their children where they can be outdoors and where their parents can make contact with others – it's a lonely business, bringing up a child.'

'And you'd know, would you?'

Larry could feel people pushing up behind him. There was a surge and he almost lost his footing. The noise had increased and so had the people. He stood on the next step up. He saw police helmets cut through the crowd like shark fins.

The crowd surged again. He turned, suddenly afraid for Bill.

Larry heard Jean's voice in his ear. 'You all right?'

He turned, crushed against her. 'What's going on?'

Jean grinned. 'Rent a mob,' she said. 'They're planning to march to Trafalgar Square.'

'We haven't got permission –'

'Bloody rabble,' the man in the suit shouted from the doorway and was swiftly escorted inside. The door slammed shut.

Thwarted, the crowd gave another surge. Larry felt the breath being squeezed out of his lungs. He found himself pushed towards the barriers and he braced himself against falling. Behind the barriers the police formed their own barricade. A young Asian boy was breathing heavily next to him, Larry could feel his breath on his face. He turned and could no longer see Jean – instead a small gang of Asian youths were surrounding him and the youngest, in a yellow sweatshirt, was screaming something at the impassive string of officers. He lunged forward at them, hitting the barrier.

Larry looked on in disbelief. The march, the peaceful march, had swelled into – what? Everybody's boiling pot. Where had these Asians come from with their anger and their hate? Everyone was fighting for themselves, he too, yes, he too.

244

'Don't do it,' he shouted to the boy, inches from him, above the noise, 'it's not worth it.'

The boy looked at him uncomprehendingly. For a moment he was distracted, his eyes unfocused as if he'd been pulled out of a dream. And he lunged again at the string of police. The barrier gave, sliding away, and Larry found himself poured through. There was a shout from the officers. They came undone like beads of a necklace and swarmed the boy neatly, packeting him up and taking him towards the waiting vans.

His friends looked at Larry. One took hold of his jacket. Larry found himself inches from half an eyebrow just like his own – the rest of it eaten up by a scar.

He raised his forearm with difficulty. They were pressed so close together; he had never before been so close to a human being that he did not know in all his life. He wrenched the arm away and from somewhere to the left of him came a shadow, briefly but noticeably enough to register on his consciousness, and a heavy blow hit him on the left hand side of his forehead. He felt as though he had slammed in to it. Through the blinding pain he felt the adrenaline rise in him and turn to rage. He blinked and threw a punch. He felt his arm being twisted behind his back. Hands were on him, bundling him up. He tried to heave himself free and turned and to his relief he found he was being held by a police officer.

'Thanks,' he said, still struggling, 'I'll be all right now.'

'In the van, sir.'

'Yes, but –' he strained to look around him at the seething crowd. He was no longer a law-abiding citizen, he was on the other side, an enemy of law and order, and it had happened so quickly. He was being pushed rapidly towards the van and he looked round, frightened for Bill and Helen and Lily and Emma. He was raging with frustration, being jostled – ahead he could see the van . . . and beyond it a television crew.

'DADDEEE!' One loud scream rose above the din. Larry

turned his head, frantically trying to find his son, but a spark inside him glittered for a second – he had called him daddy! He caught a glimpse of a pale face, riding high on Helen's shoulders, but someone pressed his head down as he entered the maw of the van and the doors were pushed closed behind him.

It was quiet inside, away from the noise. The darkness after the sun subdued them. Larry could feel his heart hammering and he looked at his watch.

There was an hour to go before the coach came and he wouldn't be on it. A wave of fear washed over him.

He wouldn't be on it now.

PART SEVEN

Seven's Heaven

38

As they spilled out of the meeting room, Megan checked her messages. 'Ring Paul Camberwell at Triton,' she said aloud, showing the message to Lisa.

Megan could feel the lift of adrenaline, the excitement, and the apprehension. If Larry doesn't get it, we'll be celebrating anyway, she thought. It's no disgrace to him when he's got this far.

Lisa was watching her, a small smile suggesting to Megan that she was reading her thoughts perfectly.

'Okay,' Megan said, clapping her hands, 'let's find out what's going on. And the winner of tonight's prize of one well-paid job in advertising is –' she tapped out Paul Camberwell's private line number '– it's Megan Lawrence. Yes, Paul Baker's got the experience. Yes, Larry. Right, I'll tell him. Thanks, thank you, Paul.' Her eyes were wide, and as she put the phone down Megan felt as though she'd bungee jumped off Tower Bridge.

'LARRY'S GOT IT! HE'S GOT THE JOB!'

Lisa's face seemed to mirror her own – eyes wide with astonishment, face split with an uncontrollable grin of sheer pleasure. She shook her head. 'I love this game,' she said, her eyes shining.

'You can ring him,' Megan said to Lisa, 'he was your man really. And your first big search. I'll get a bottle from the fridge.'

Wow! She'd hoped for it but hadn't dared believe it and

249

her heartrate seemed to be beating off the scale. She grabbed some paper cups and took a couple of bottles into research to break the good news and went back to Lisa, pouring out another two paper cups full and ready for a few words with Larry.

Lisa was still holding the phone. As Meg looked at her queryingly, Lisa looked at the receiver as though it had sorely let her down. 'It's the answerphone,' she said with a shrug.

Megan listened. 'That's funny,' she said, replacing the receiver. She checked her watch. 'It's ten past five,' she said. 'He's probably gone to Sainsbury's.' Her spirits took a slight dip, but only very slight. Just then, Nigel came in and saw the bottle on the desk. 'Ah!'

'What a shame, we'll have to open another bottle,' Megan said in a martyred tone.

'Larry got it, didn't he?' Nigel said.

'YES!' Megan said, punching the air. 'And it looks as though he's going to be the last to know! Who's for a drink? I'll just give Zelda a ring to let her know. We'll go to the club, shall we? I can try Larry from there and he can bring Bill with him – they've got a crèche there which is open until eight.'

She picked up the phone and dialled. 'Zelda?'

The Mannington Club was a short walk away. Although it had only been open for a couple of years, the atmosphere was one of faded comfort. The Colgin Partnership had taken out a corporate membership and they piled in while Megan headed for the bar to get the drinks.

The club tended to fill up after work and the noise inside was indescribable. In the corner opposite, the television was on, adding to the din.

Megan distributed the drinks and squeezed across to Lisa, handed her her glass.

'Here's to you, Lisa, for spotting Larry's potential,' she said.

'Sometimes it's easier when you don't know a person. There are no strings. It makes life simpler, somehow.'

Megan had the impression that she wasn't only talking about work.

A waiter came through, handsome and very young and virginal in his white jacket.

As he walked past, Lisa raised an eyebrow. 'Do you think he's gay?'

'I've no idea. Is he your type?' Megan asked in surprise, taking off her jacket. Lisa hardly ever spoke about men at all, and had certainly never rung anyone from the office.

Lisa smiled, and didn't reply.

'You've got something of a reputation with men,' Megan said, and someone pushed her from behind. She fell against Lisa and spilled some champagne down the front of her skirt. 'I'm so sorry,' she said, brushing at it.

'It's all right. Champagne doesn't stain. You were saying?'

It suddenly didn't seem such a good conversation to pursue. 'I just wondered,' she said, tailing off, remembering that once she'd thought her guilty of sleeping with Gerry.

Lisa was still smiling. 'The truth is that like most career women, it's not a man I need behind me, it's a wife.'

Megan agreed fervently. She raised her glass. 'Cheers.'

'Cheers.'

Megan thought she'd better try Larry again. Drinks on an empty stomach were never a great move, and at this rate she'd be wiped out by the time he got there. She gave her glass to Lisa to hold, and made her way to the stairwell.

The future was taking on something of a soft-focus gleam. She could see life getting back to normal with the Triton job. They'd be equals again, which was important.

She dialled the number and got the answer phone. Forget it, then, she thought, and checked the time. It was almost six.

She made her way back to Lisa, who had ordered another two glasses in the meantime. 'He's still not in,' she said.

'By the way, you know Dave Westacott?' Lisa asked. 'He took me to Langans last night to impress me. He'd booked a table downstairs. We were shown to our table on the ground floor and he said rather loudly that he'd specifically asked for a downstairs table. And the waiter said, "Sir, downstairs is the kitchens."'

Megan giggled. She knew Dave. 'I went there once with Ron Spry – you know how pompous he is. There were no side plates and when we took a roll, he broke it up in the ashtray. Worst thing was, I didn't want him to think I was doing the wrong thing by putting it on the cloth, so I used the ashtray too!'

Lisa started to giggle. 'Men, what can you do with them? You can't live with them and you can't shoot them.'

With a smile on her face, Megan leaned back against the oak-panelled wall. Her eyes drifted to the flickering television screen.

It was a scene in which a mob of people were chanting, led by a man in a dark blue jacket who looked as if he'd walked into the wrong shot. It looked like Larry. She nudged Lisa.

'Look,' she said. 'That guy looks like Larry.'

'Yeah. What's he shouting about?'

Megan leaned forward and squinted at the screen. 'I don't know. Can't make it out.'

It was impossible to tell, with the noise in the bar, whether the crowd was shouting at all. It could just as easily have been singing, or yawning. But suddenly the camera jerked. Now there was no mistaking the mood of the people. The yawns were snarls and the man in the blue jacket turned his head and looked straight at them.

'Megan?' Lisa said.

Megan had got to her feet. Larry had turned away from

252

them now and behind him, in the mêlée, in the pack of howling people, Megan could see Bill, his face pale and his eyes baggy and round with amazement. And he was on some blonde's shoulders. With an expression of glee she was looking at Larry, and Larry, turning back to the camera – to her, Megan – lunged, and Megan could see a police officer grabbing him, and the scene cut to a tanned, auburn-haired reporter, her hair waving in the breeze and her name printed beneath her in neat letters, and she was followed by a commercial for PG Tips.

Megan was looking open-mouthed at the screen.

She was not sure what her main emotion was – whether it was anger or astonishment.

'That *was* Larry,' she said.

The bar was so full that Lisa was pressed against her. Megan couldn't take her eyes off the screen, despite the fact that the news had ended and that Larry was very unlikely to turn up, now, in a tea advert.

'What was he doing?'

'He was with some blonde. She was holding Bill.' Megan put down her glass. 'It was a playgroup thing, he's mentioned it once or twice. I'd better get home.'

'They sure didn't play like that in my day. Do you want me to come with you?'

Megan felt for her handbag. 'Umm – no, it's all right. I'll get a taxi.' Whatever she was feeling – and she wasn't sure what it was at the moment, but whatever the emotion – it was on a slow burner.

Lisa was now crouching down, feeling for her own bag. Unfortunately she must have picked up the wrong end of it and there was a general clatter as lipsticks and loose change and a cylinder of Hermesetas fell out, all spilling and spin-ning and rolling around the floor.

Megan got on her knees again and scooped things up by the handful, getting trampled on in the process. She

253

straightened up, her blonde hair flopping in her eyes and her face flushed with the effort.

Lisa held the bag open and Megan dropped her finds in.

'But what was he doing?' Lisa asked. 'What was he demonstrating about?'

Megan shrugged. 'He's trying to stop the playgroup from being closed. I haven't really been listening, it didn't seem that important.'

'He's become a raving Leftie,' Lisa said, looking in her bag and sifting through the coins.

Megan looked at Lisa. 'Did it seem to you that he'd been arrested?'

'Kind of, yes. Yes, I should say so.'

'You can't live with them and you can't shoot them,' Megan said ruefully.

They pushed their way down the stairs and went outside to look for a taxi. The street was busy and they had to keep moving, just to stay in one place.

The orange glow on the roof of a cab caught her eye.

'You get this one,' Lisa said, and Megan bent at the passenger window and told the taxi where she was heading and she got into the back. She slid down the window and Lisa gave her a card. 'It's got my address on,' she said.

Megan took it and looked at the crowds on the pavement. Juxtaposed was the image of Larry with a megaphone in his hand, surrounded by people in camouflage. He'd looked as though he was starting a private war.

'Hey, Megan,' Lisa said through the window, 'this husband of yours, he's been having you on. He didn't look house-trained to me.'

Nor to me, Megan thought, nor to me.

39

'Name?'

'David Lawrence.'

'Occupation?'

Larry's gaze drifted to the walls in the room. They were blank, not even the smallest hole or indentation to show where a picture hook had ever been. They were blank so as to offer no distractions.

And so, undistracted, he returned his gaze to the officer.

'Occupation, sir?'

'Househusband.'

The officer gave a sigh. 'Do you have an employer?'

'My wife. Ha ha.'

'I'm glad you're amused, sir. Unemployed.' The officer wrote it down.

Larry laid his palms on the plastic table. The surface was cool and nobbly under his fingers and felt pleasant, very soothing. For some reason it seemed important that he let his hands feel relaxed on the table – to show that he, David Lawrence, househusband, had nothing whatsoever to fear.

The police officer was still writing on the sheet of paper. He looked up quickly, instinctively aware of Larry's gaze, and for a brief moment their eyes met with wry humour, like opponents in a card game who each knew the other was cheating. Then the officer looked at Larry's hands which were still resting heavily on the table.

He seemed fascinated by them. Larry was fascinated, too.

His hands were so relaxed that he could look at them there on the table and believe they weren't his. In a film the camera would zoom in on such hands and the viewer would stiffen in his comfy chair and feel the hairs bristle on the nape of his neck, knowing that those hands resting as benignly as warm tarantulas were killer hands.

Larry snatched them from the table and repossessed them again as though he had fleetingly slipped inside the policeman's brain. He, David Lawrence, had unconsciously used a gesture that he had seen in every two-bit cops and robbers film since time began.

He put his alien hands inside his pockets and looked at the form, trying to read it upside-down. 'Hold on,' he said suddenly, 'if I was a woman I'd be described as a housewife, right?'

'Possibly.'

'Well, I'm a househusband. During the day I have sole charge of our son. I am not in any way unemployed.'

There was a silence. The policeman's wry humour had been replaced by the weariness reserved for the know-it-all.

'Are you in receipt of benefits, sir?'

'No, I'm not. I'm not entitled to benefits yet. Wages in lieu. My wife keeps me.' Larry tried to quell the triumph in his voice even as he knew that it was not a fair fight, that the best man didn't win, that police officers were around to enforce the law – note that word ENFORCE – nothing gentle about that! And that to enforce the law they had to outnumber the baddies because there could be no doubt about the outcome. So that winning the appropriate answer to the question of employment didn't at all increase the odds of the police officer letting him out. In fact, it could make things worse. It could antagonise him.

The police officer was staring at him as though he had read the whole string of thoughts running through Larry's mind and was now digesting it.

'And where is your son now, sir?' he asked in a voice so lacking in curiosity that it was as if he already knew the answer.

Larry responded immediately, as though the lurch of his heart had kick-started him. 'Well he's with – I assume he's with – he was with a friend of mine.'

'You assume he's with a friend of yours but you don't know for sure.' The officer looked at him again, with those all seeing, all purpose, non-prying eyes. 'Was he with you at the town hall?'

'He was with me, yes.'

The officer scratched the side of his nose slowly with the bottom of his ball-point pen. He was grinning now in a way that said he was quite prepared to join in with the joke as long as it was explained to him one more time.

'You're a househusband with sole charge of your son who you take to demonstrations? Have I got it right?'

Larry folded his arms. It was for comfort, but even as he did it he thought – defiance! It's seeping out of me as if I can't help it! And he unfolded them again and put his hands back in his pockets where their absence might appear insolent but where the hands themselves couldn't incriminate him in any way. 'Perhaps I could ring my wife,' he said.

'Certainly, sir. Perhaps you should also make a check on the whereabouts of your child.'

No mistaking the message there. This was serious business. This was serious business, there was no doubt about that and there was no longer any space in the officer's mind for joking or humour of any kind.

He passed a phone over to Larry.

Larry took a deep breath.

He didn't know how to get in touch with Helen. So he called Megan, who, he was told, had just left.

'I'll try her at home,' he said.

257

He put the receiver back on the hook slowly and passed the phone over.

He glanced at his watch. The coach would be there and they would be filing back on it, the children, the women . . . He could imagine the coach, with its heater on, perhaps, as the day was becoming cool; and the children would be getting drowsy on the women's knees and the low thrill of a voice singing solo at the back – the courage of it, loud and clearly heard above the murmuring voices and the varying growl of the bus. Show me the way to go home. 'What would you have done?' he asked suddenly, wanting to know.

The police officer looked at him. For a moment Larry thought that he wouldn't respond but the wry humour was back again.

'I went on a march once,' he said. 'SPUC, you know what that is? Society for the Protection of the Unborn Child. I went with a Catholic girlfriend. At the end of it her friend said that I'd only gone because of her, not because I'd agreed with it, which was true. And she finished with me. What's your excuse?'

'The women need that playgroup.'

The officer looked at his wrist.

'And the other thing is . . .'

The officer looked up again. Bingo! It was like getting a question right in a quiz! Larry could see the beauty of confession – the lure of having someone hang onto every word, the approval! The initial approval, that is. Afterwards there was the very public disapproval, but at the time – hey, it was good! Like coming out with some juicy piece of gossip that you knew shouldn't be told, that you knew would have its comeback, but at the time of telling, people hanging onto every word, the thrill of knowledge . . .

'Women only like men in the right place,' Larry said as an opener. He would see how it went down, first.

258

The officer nodded.

'That's true. Ever seen women together on a night out?' He shook his head, to show his disbelief at the memory of his experience. And he looked at Larry again.

'This househusband business.' Larry frowned. 'There's nowhere for a man to go with a child; and at the playgroup – the one the council wants to close down – the women want to do women's talk. Diets, men. Secrets. Nothing big, just the usual subjects that belong to the women's club, the stuff they don't talk about –'

'Would have thought you'd be the first one to have the place closed down,' the officer said, eyebrows raised, waiting to be persuaded otherwise.

'That's when they found I had my uses,' Larry said. 'You know; letters to MPs, pictures in the *Journal*, petitions . . .'

'And the march.'

'And the march. Yes. It changed everything. Shouldn't have, of course, I didn't do anything they couldn't have done themselves, but it gave them somewhere to slot me.' He looked up suddenly from the nobbly table. 'What's going to happen to me?'

'You'll be cautioned. It means you have to keep out of trouble, but I guess you will anyway. You've got enough on your plate. Do you want to try your wife again?'

Larry nodded and picked up the phone. She wasn't at home. He tried to be sorry but he was glad, he was very glad.

'How's your wife going to take this?'

'We haven't been getting along too well lately. You know, the old home-making skills . . .'

The officer nodded. 'I'm divorced, myself,' he said. 'I've got used to it. Went through a stage of living in a dump and came out the other side. Now it's passable. You don't want to look too closely.' He sniffed thoughtfully. 'I'm letting you off with a caution. Keep the heroics for the playing fields, will you? You don't want to set your son a bad example. Want to try your wife again?'

'No, she won't be home yet.' I may not tell her, Larry thought, rubbing his cheek.

I don't want to bother her.

Ignorance was bliss.

40

He came out of the interview room and walked along the corridor rubbing his temple. He didn't know where Helen lived. And Helen didn't know where he lived.

An officer opened the door for him and he walked through to the waiting area, where he saw Helen sitting patiently, with Bill asleep on her knee and Lily swinging her legs next to her.

He took a deep breath of relief and crouched down to talk. 'They haven't charged me,' he said. 'Helen, thank you for looking after him.'

Bill woke up at the sound of his voice. He screwed up his face in the light, looked at his father and turned his face away immediately to bury it in Helen's hair.

'You're a little softie,' she said in his ear. 'You take him, Larry. I would have taken him home, but as you don't know my address it seemed easier to wait here.' Bill moved towards him and rested his hand on Larry's knee.

Larry wanted to hold him, wanted to apologise, but he let him be and moved his hand to rub his eyes. 'They just told me to keep out of trouble.'

'You're a hero,' Helen said, and she began to laugh. 'I don't think Emma and Jean even rate a man unless he's been locked up.'

'I felt like a hero,' Larry said, and smiled, and the moment flared up again in his memory: noise, adrenaline and pride.

He shut his eyes.

261

'You look happy,' she said, and touched the creases near his eye.

'I am.' Her attention was soothing. It made him want to lie down. He could still feel the cool line she'd traced, it felt like a kiss drying on the skin.

Someone was standing by him, taking up his space. He tried to stand up and didn't know if he could find the energy.

'Larry?'

Megan's voice, with a question mark in it, and he sure found the energy then. He got to his feet and the suddenness made him sway.

'Meg.'

'Have you been charged?'

'Cautioned.'

She breathed out slowly in relief. He could smell the alcohol on her breath and see a fever in her eyes. She looked from him to Bill, who had sunk back into sleep on Helen's knee. 'Shall I take him?' she asked Helen, her voice neutral.

Bill opened his eyes again and closed them and reached his arms out to her. She picked him up and he wrapped his arms and legs around her and rested his head on her shoulder.

Helen stood up, and Lily did, too.

'I'm Helen,' she said, 'and this is my daughter, Lily.' There was no trace of awkwardness about her, and holding onto Bill with one hand, Megan extended the other.

'Megan. Thanks for looking after Bill.'

Larry was relieved to hear that her voice was warmer now. 'How did you know I was here?' he asked her as she stood next to a poster for Operation Bumblebee.

'You were on *London Tonight*,' she said ruefully. ' "Triton's new broadcast director in brawl" .'

It took its time to sink in, the way she said it.

'Triton's new broadcast director,' he repeated, and it felt right. It felt very right.

262

'Congratulations,' Helen said.

Megan was smiling, now, the excitement back. 'We had to celebrate without you, Larry. Do you feel like catching up?'

'I do, and I'm ready now,' he said.

They stood outside the station and saw Helen into a taxi.

They got one themselves and went home and put Bill to bed.

The initial effervescent excitement had blown off and what was left was a deep thrill of anticipation.

They got out the Scotch and cuddled up on the sofa, switched on the television, and looked at each other.

Larry switched it off again.

They awkwardly undressed, lethargic with alcohol and the aftermath of tension. What was wanted was release, and warmth and love; the feeling of skin sliding smooth against skin.

Kissing with breath warm and pungent with Scotch, they created that old, familiar, unknowable tension, chasing its release along separate paths, silent except for their rhythmic accelerated breathing and the sweat slurping noisily between their bodies.

The curl of the carpet pressing their skin.

And all thought gone.

Sex, the great escape, the closest, the closest they could be . . . and the farthest they could go.

Holding each other tightly afterwards, sweat hot, but chilling on their backs where their skin didn't touch.

Cuddling into him, the smell of his armpits, the best smell in the world . . . 'I could live there,' Megan said lazily, smiling. 'My hero.' Thinking of Triton, and looking at him with darkening eyes.

Larry, thinking of the march, hooking his leg around hers, felt once more that strange, unlooked-for flare of pride, almost forgotten. It was the pride of belonging, of leading. He'd

263

belonged to a gang, once. What he remembered was the sound of running feet, he in the lead, flying past a bus stop and knocking into a woman as he ran and not saying sorry – not even thinking to say sorry, because he had been invincible.

He soared as he ran; their feet had sounded like war drums on the pavement and the faster they ran, the faster they had to run because their footsteps pursued them. And he ran with the feel of a woman's soft body giving way as he pushed her, and with her cry in his ears.

Hero.

41

The following morning, just after ten, the telephone rang.

'Give that here,' Larry said, reaching for the receiver, but Bill had it pressed to his ear. 'It's not your mother, is it?'

Bill shook his head and handed the receiver over. 'It's a funny man.' He frowned.

'Give it to me.' Larry took the phone. 'Hello?'

A hoarse voice creaked in his ear. Larry found himself wincing. 'What was that?' And inspiration struck. 'James, is that you? Hello, mate,' waiting for the joke, waiting for the laugh.

There followed a stringy sentence of half-finished words which Larry couldn't catch, but it was no joke, that was what was dawning on him fairly rapidly. James sounded as though he was talking with something stuffed in his mouth. Larry thought he could make out the name Karin. 'James, are they there with you?'

There was a choking, which tailed off into sobbing. Larry's instinct was to slam the phone down to cut the noise off. He felt himself grow cold. He steadied himself and waited for a lull. But as the sobbing continued he tried to speak over it. 'I'm coming round,' he said. 'Don't move.'

He put the phone down and looked at Bill.

'Who was that?'

Larry loosened his belt to a slacker notch. He felt as though he couldn't breathe. 'James, yes, it was James.'

'Are we going to see him?'

Larry pushed his fingers through his hair. What was he to

do with Bill? 'Listen, I'll drop you off with Mummy at her office and I'll go and check to see that he's all right.' He could feel his body rushing while he stood still, working everything out slowly like some old drunk. 'We'll get a taxi.'

He grabbed his keys and they went out into the street.

A string of traffic pulled past, and then he saw the orange glow of a vacant cab and they stopped it and piled in.

At Colgin's, they took the lift up to the third floor.

The receptionist looked surprised at a candidate turning up with his son and ushered him into an interview room. A couple of seconds later Megan came in, her face pale with alarm. 'What's the matter?' she asked, holding out her hand to Bill like a reflex.

'Meg, look, I need you to look after Bill,' he said. 'Something's happened to James and I've got to go round there.'

Megan frowned. 'What's happened to him? Is he all right?'

'I don't know. I don't think so. He could just be drunk,' he said hopefully.

Meg's expression didn't alter. His words didn't reassure her either. 'Go on,' she said, 'go now. Take the car. I'll get you the keys – stay here a minute, Bill.'

He looked up as Lisa walked in. 'Oh, Meg, Robert Baker rang . . .'

Megan turned. 'Larry's leaving Bill here for a while. A friend of ours – oh, Larry will tell you.'

And Larry did, briefly.

'I'll come with you,' Lisa said immediately. 'I've done a St John ambulance course. And if his daughters are there, they might prefer to see a woman.' She smiled at Meg, who tossed Larry the keys. 'Back soon.'

'Come on, Bill,' Meg said. 'Come and see where I spend my day when I'm not with you.'

Larry drove in silence, and Lisa, he was relieved to see, didn't attempt to keep the atmosphere light. He tried not to anticipate anything. James had sounded in a bad way, but on a good day he could sound in a bad way, it didn't mean anything. Karin and Jen, that was what worried him. Karin and Jen.

Every time he thought of them, there seemed to be a dark shadow over them. He thought of the flies in the car and felt ill.

When he finally pulled up, he jumped out and told Lisa to stay where she was. 'Wait here,' he said.

Lisa pulled a face and took a packet of cigarettes out of her bag.

Larry rang the bell, then tried the door; he didn't know why he bothered but amazingly it opened. 'James?' he called as he stepped inside. His voice rang back, as sounds did in an empty house. There was no one in the living room and he glanced into the kitchen and went upstairs. At first he didn't see James in the dark, he only noticed the smell; it was like a zoo.

'Uh.'

The sound wasn't a question or a groan. Larry went to the bed and looked between the bed and the wall. James was lying sideways in the gap. His head was back, and a white froth was around his mouth.

'Larry, have you found them?'

He was so glad to hear Lisa's voice. 'I've found James. Get an ambulance.'

Larry pulled the bed away and James fell to the floor with a light thump, as though he was almost weightless.

Larry crouched down by him. 'Sorry, mate.' He pushed the bed against the adjacent wall and crouched down. 'Are you all right? Are the girls here, James?'

James's pale eyes opened with effort and he looked painfully into Larry's. 'Goh.'

Larry wanted to wipe the froth away from his mouth, but couldn't. 'Gone? They've gone?'

267

He got up and snatched a pillow from the bed and put it under James's head, and began pulling the duvet off to put over him. Then he remembered the recovery position.

They'd done it once at Burgess McLane, during a first-aid course. They got the secretaries to do it too, so that in an emergency they could be revived by someone they fancied. He remembered Debbie saying that if she died and he touched her she'd get him for sexual harassment. 'Recovery position,' he said, pulling James's legs. James kept pulling them back into himself and Larry was getting desperate. 'Try to lie still, will you, mate?'

He abandoned it and ran back down the stairs and phoned for an ambulance and ran back up again. 'James?'

The froth was still around his mouth. He tried to wipe it with the corner of the duvet, but James began flailing at him and he gave up. 'What can I do for you, mate?' he asked in desperation.

'They goh.'

Larry jumped to his feet. The feeling came back to him that the girls were in the house and, suddenly convinced, he began to look for them; and everywhere he looked he prepared himself to find something worse than he'd ever imagined. He saw four bin bags in a wardrobe and thought his heart would stop. But they were light and opening them he found they were only stuffed with clothes and papers. Afraid, he returned to James.

The ambulance could be heard, getting nearer, stopping outside, flashing blue across the curtains.

Larry ran back down and opened the door. 'He's up here.' Three paramedics followed him, walked up steadily to the bedroom and in their calmness he found the panic leaving him.

When he came down, Lisa was in the lounge, smoking, scrutinising a photograph of Lydia which she'd taken off the wall.

They came back down with James on a stretcher.

'Where are you taking him? UCH? We'll follow.'

They were in for a long wait, but at the end of it they were allowed to see James briefly.

Larry was stunned at the sight of him.

The image came into his head of James as a battered bendy toy, shabby but indestructible.

He'd been wrong. James had tried to self-destruct. He had taken an overdose and written a letter saying he was depressed.

Larry was amazed at James knowing such a mundane word, but as he thought of depression, of James being depressed, he could see the black cloud of flies, and he wanted to cry.

The doctor took him into a room.

Larry tried to explain and the doctor sat down and put his hands in the pockets of his coat. 'The majority of divorced men lose touch with their children. The mothers move away, or make it difficult to visit, or find someone else. And the men start a new family . . .' he shrugged. 'It's not always easy.'

'What if a man doesn't want a new family? What if he wants the old one back?'

'I don't know about what if. I'm just telling you what I know.'

And Larry thought of Bill, and he began to talk, and he talked as though he was on his own, rambling, unable to find a place to stop.

He told the doctor about James, who didn't give a toss about his home or his wife or his children when he had them, but who couldn't bear it now they'd gone. He talked about the playgroup where they hadn't wanted him until he was useful, and about Helen's husband, whose name he didn't even know, who had lost everything he loved through no fault of his own. And he talked about the man at the zoo, with the sweat seeping through the thick blue denim shirt on a hot day, catching his daughter's patent shoe with a practised hand.

'Bummer, isn't it,' he said, and wiped his hand over his eyes and suddenly was wrenched by silent, wracking sobs.

They seemed to tear him apart for a long, long time, but when they finally stopped, and the extreme tiredness took over and he made one last effort to lift his head, the doctor was still there, a warm presence, waiting.

Larry's eyes met his and though he knew he wouldn't recognise his face five minutes from now, he knew also that he would never forget him.

The doctor got to his feet. 'Stay in here until you're ready,' he said. He was at the door when he stopped and turned. 'When you feel that strongly,' he said, 'my best advice is: do something about it.'

Lisa was waiting in the corridor when he came out.

Her hair was held back as immaculately as ever, but she seemed agitated where he'd only ever seen her calm. Her eyes kept returning to the door of the ward where James lay semi-conscious, his eyes flickering, a tube taped to the side of his mouth and a dark weight over him.

'He's needy,' she said. 'He ought to be looked after. I mean, I know he's in the right place, but afterwards, what's he going to do afterwards?'

Larry had never felt his head so heavy. 'I really don't know.'

42

'They're back. Larry's in the interview room,' Nigel said, popping his head around the door.

Megan looked up with relief. 'Thanks, Nigel.'

'He looks pretty grim.' Nigel glanced meaningfully at Bill who was drawing on laser paper on the floor. 'Want me to keep an eye on this one for you?'

Megan hurried into the interview room. Larry was sitting by the table, his hands resting flat on it. He looked up at her like a man who hadn't been allowed to sleep.

She put her arms around him. 'What happened? How's James?'

Larry kissed her forearm absently, leaving the prickle of his bristles on her skin. 'He's pretty bad. He took barbiturates that he'd bought from a man in a pub. He was serious. He'd written a letter to the girls . . .' Larry swallowed and she could feel the muscles working in his throat.

She felt a mixture of emotions rise to the surface like bubbles, and guilt seemed to appear more than anything else. We've done nothing wrong, she thought quickly, and rubbed her cheek against Larry's short, dark hair. 'Oh, Larry. Is Lydia with him?'

'I've just called her, but she said it was blackmail. She doesn't seem to think he's capable of real feelings at all.'

Larry got jerkily out of his chair and Megan let him go, her hands dropping to her side. She felt helpless, and it wasn't a state she was used to. 'Well at least you've done your bit,' she said, trying to comfort him.

'How? In getting there in time? I can't think he's going to see it as a favour. He'll get home and what will have changed?'

Megan felt a coil of fear heavy and tight inside her. 'He had his chance, Larry. Lydia put up with more than most women would. She held them together for years before getting out.'

'He was a good father,' Larry said.

'A good father?' She gave a short, incredulous laugh. 'A good father is one who supports his family, sees they don't have to go without. Those girls only went to state school because Lydia couldn't afford on her income to send them both privately.' She stopped awkwardly, but hell, it was true, wasn't it? It was no use Larry thinking of the hard-done-by James when James, let's face it, had brought it all upon himself.

Larry looked at her with the calmness of someone ready to pounce, and who knows he's got all the time in the world. 'And that's a good father, is it?' he asked softly.

She looked at him, surprised with herself. But yes, it *was* her idea of a good father; it was a description of her own.

'Megan,' Larry said, and stopped.

She was glad to hear that his voice was stronger now. It had been a shock, finding James like that, of course it had, but they'd got their own lives to think of. She'd written an advert to put in *The Lady* for a new nanny for Bill, and she wanted Larry to read it first; she could show him the advert now, yes, why not, then she could ring it through.

But she just stood looking at him. Then she said, 'What?'

Larry rubbed his eyebrow. His scar moved like a silver thread. 'I want you to get Lisa in here,' he said. 'I'm not taking the Triton job.'

It took a minute for it to register in words, but the coil of fear released immediately and she felt her stomach contract as she tried to contain it. 'No, Larry,' she said, and it wasn't denial, this was panic. 'You can't do that. You lost that option a long way back.'

'Megan, I don't want that life any more.'

She stared transfixed into his dark and once familiar eyes that weren't at all familiar any more. 'It's not negotiable.' She backed away, putting the table between them.

He leaned across it towards her. His eyes narrowed, the skin crinkling around them. 'I am tired of games,' he said slowly, enunciating the words as though they were new to him. 'Do you understand?'

'What games?' She was baffled now, she felt as though she'd come into a room halfway through an interview, couldn't mange to pick it up.

'This!' he said, flinging his arm out and knocking a vase. It fell with a crash and he looked at it, righting it swiftly. The water spread to the edge of the table and tapped slowly onto the carpet. 'This – fake – existence. Money. Products. Deals.'

She almost laughed at the absurdity. 'It's called work, Larry! Have you forgotten what that is? It's who you are, remember?'

'Was,' he said. 'Was. It was me.'

'Oh,' she said, mocking, 'it *was* you.' She pointed her finger at him. 'What do you want to be now, Larry? Leader of the young mothers? Is that your latest role? Grow up, because you know how it will be. You'll end up like James, with nothing.' She glanced at the door, afraid that someone would hear. Worse, afraid that Bill would hear them. But she was fighting for her life and she couldn't give up. 'Larry, you're just upset and I understand that –'

He smiled humourlessly. 'You want us to be in touch with our emotions and then you can't handle them! You see men as clowns until it suits you – a clown or a meal-ticket. Take your pick.'

Megan felt herself freeze. 'I wouldn't say too much about meal-tickets if I were you, Larry.'

273

'Yeah?'

'Or you might find yourself without one,' she added quietly.

Larry began to laugh. His tanned face creased into a rictus and Megan looked with alarm at the door. Suddenly he grabbed her arm and she pulled away from him but his fingers dug in deep. He jerked hard, pulling her round to face him. 'Look at me,' he said. 'Do you think you're so important to the family that you have to threaten me? We hardly ever see you. Why would we miss you?'

'I've been busy, you know I have. Now let me go.' She wrenched her arm from his grip. 'I'd rather you made a scene out of the office,' she said coldly.

'Aaargh!'

His roar deafened her.

'Tell me there's someone human in there,' he said through gritted teeth.

'Oh can't you just shut up,' she said angrily. 'If you want to get in touch with your feelings, do some primal therapy and have done with it.'

He looked at her, his eyes like those of a stranger encountering something new. Insulting eyes, their gaze ranging over her.

'We're talking feelings, are we,' he said, walking around her. 'Where are yours? You had some once, didn't you? What did you do, lock them away, tidy them up? This is this,' he said, putting his hands parallel, chopping the air, mimicking her again, 'this is this, this is this. A good father pays for his child's schooling and a good mother finds a good nanny. You're not a mother, you're a money machine. And I was a money machine. And I'm not one any more and I feel a damn sight better for it.'

She stared at him and felt a rush of pressure to her head, hurting her eyes, closing her throat: fear and injustice rolled into one. It was difficult to breathe. 'To see ourselves as others

274

see us,' she said bitterly. Her voice seemed to be tearing out of her. 'That's not how I saw you.'

He slammed his hand down on the table again. 'Yes! That's exactly how you saw me! And that's the way you like me. I've always been the dumb one, haven't I, Meg? Acting a part. Well I don't have to any more. This is the real me.'

The resonance of his slamming hand died away slowly. He hates me, she thought, and it struck her like a lightning flash, illuminating the block of their marriage, and she saw them stuttering along the years together as though in a strobe.

'And, Megan, from now on, this is my life.'

Each word hammered into her head. Megan tried to gather her thoughts but they were spinning away from her like un-nailed Catherine wheels. 'Larry –' she put her hand to her head, couldn't follow the thread of what she was saying. 'Larry –' tried to take a deep breath but found herself panting. Put her cold fingers over her mouth.

'So ask me what I want out of my life. Right, Meg, I want to set up a charity to listen to men like James, men who can't be the fathers they want to be. Does that surprise you? That original idea?'

Megan, shaking, fought to keep the tears away. 'Charity begins at home.'

The door opened and she turned and in walked Lisa, three glasses in her hands and a bottle of champagne under her arm. 'We haven't drunk to your future,' she said to Larry. 'Congratulations.'

Megan stared at her.

Lisa put the glasses down on the table and looked at Larry before turning to Megan. 'What's happening?'

Megan stared at the glasses, her mind a blank. Groping for something, the phones ringing in the background, trying to be She-Man, pulling on the ill-fitting costume. Finding it not so comfortable now.

'Get Paul Camberwell for me,' she said. 'Larry's changed his mind. We'll have to speak to Jeremy again.' She snatched the words out of the air and took a juddering breath. 'Larry's got himself a life.' Just getting the last word out in time before she saw the contempt on his face, before her voice gave out; leaving the room before the pressure in her head was too great, before the tears came.

43

When she got home that night the television was off and Larry was standing awkwardly in the doorway, having, she supposed, heard her car.

She went past him and Larry followed her into the living room and went over to the books in the bookcase, fingering a few spines.

'I'll pack some clothes for the next few days,' she said. 'I need time to think. I need some space.'

He kept his back to her, his hand on the books.

The pressure in her throat had returned and she went upstairs to their bedroom and opened the wardrobe. They kept their clothes together and she could smell his aftershave faintly mingled with her perfume.

She pulled a suitcase down and brushed the dust off it with her hand. Step by step, that was the way to do it.

She opened the case and put in dresses and a couple of jackets; opened her drawers, threw in undies, jewellery, t-shirts, shoes, make-up. She locked the case and went into Bill's room.

His night light was on and the room glowed. Bill was lying on top of the bedcovers, a piece of Lego in his hand, his face flushed.

She looked at him. He was still and peaceful. She picked up a white vest from the floor and put it in her pocket. 'It's not for long.' A promise.

She went back into the bedroom and fastened the case. It was heavier than she'd thought and she took it down the stairs, trying not to bump it. She was at the bottom of the stairs when Larry came through.

'Where are you going?' he asked.

'I'm going to Lisa's,' she said.

She hurried out of the house, half-carrying, half-pulling her cases out onto the path before closing the door. She bumped them as far as the car and hoisted them into the boot, slamming the lid down on them. Breathing heavily enough for sobs to catch at her throat, she stared at the house.

Turning, she checked behind her and started the engine. She began to reverse slowly out of the drive and now she was out of the drive and over the pavement, the car rolling onto the road at an angle; she would straighten up, she did straighten up, the car was parallel to the kerb and she could see the whole of the house – the light still on in their bedroom, and below it, the russet glow from the lounge, and in the hall, the light shimmering, welcoming. She felt a twist of surprise. It was a home, without her.

She changed gear and pulled away and as the car gained speed she knew that she had never seen things with such clarity. Approaching a puddle of light around a street lamp, a dog, plodding slowly, dragged his stretching shadow along the dusty path. Ahead the traffic light was a luminous blue-green permitting her to glide on along the road ahead, her lights shining cones of brightness on the tarmac, and she put her foot down harder. The windscreen wipers had cleared a fan shape in the opaque dust on the periphery of her vision.

At last she had reached Lisa's flat. She parked haphazardly and stopped the car and got out. Megan could actually see her leaning out of a window, smoking.

She got out of the car and a cigarette came flying down at her. Megan dodged. 'Lisa? It's Megan.'

'Oh, hello, didn't see you there. Saw the car, of course. Just a minute, I'll be right with you.'

278

Megan could see her outline through the door.

'Come in, Meg. What's up?'

When Megan didn't answer, she led the way to the sitting room and gestured at her to sit down. 'Just finished supper,' she said. And she went away for a moment. Megan wondered whether she was ringing Larry, as a delinquent's parents would. But of course she wasn't; she came back with two glasses of amber liquid in her hand.

'Here,' Lisa said, handing her one. 'Take it. Brandy.'

Megan did, gulping it, the antidote to reality. Which it is, she thought. The brandy tasted strange, unfamiliar, as was the room. As were the colours – white and blue – cold colours, iceberg colours. She suppressed a shiver.

'I've turned the heating on,' Lisa said, resting the glass on the arm of her chair.

Lisa looked at her. Megan could see that there was no surprise in her expression.

'You knew I would come here, didn't you?' she said.

Lisa didn't say anything. An old psychiatrist's trick, Megan thought; let the patient do the talking. It was something Larry had said. Just as suddenly, she wanted to leave.

Lisa got to her feet again and came back with another glass, a fresh glass, and as Megan let go of her old one Lisa placed it in her curled fingers where it wedged, cold.

And as Megan drank again the mellow drink, Lisa went and returned with a crocheted wool blanket, snowy white, spidery in its delicacy, and put it over her. Megan felt it rest gently on her body. She felt the heat trapped under, nowhere to go. Her head was still clear, clear enough to know there was time to finish the drink and go home.

'Stay the night if you like,' Lisa said, 'I'm going to bed. Stay where you are, you'll be comfortable enough and you'll be ready to leave if you want.' Lisa left the room.

Megan imagined herself going back, and then what?

She would lie here a little longer and think about it. Work things out. Come to some conclusion in the space she'd told Larry she wanted.

And then she would leave Lisa a note on the table . . .

Megan listened to Lisa switching off the lights, tick . . . tick . . . tick, leaving her in the centre of the iceberg, an island of dark in a room of light in a house that was dark.

PART EIGHT

Eight is Hell

44

Larry had watched her put her cases on the step, just as Bill had appeared on the stairs behind him.

They had heard the door closing quietly, as though by someone not wanting to disturb.

Larry picked him up. The weight and heat of Bill was like a hot water bottle. Larry hugged him. He sat on the stairs and he could feel a great pressure on his chest.

He looked down at Bill and wondered whether he was asleep, but below the wispy crescent of his eyelashes his son's eyes stared hard at the dark square of doorway as though he could, by concentration, bring her back again.

Larry slept fitfully that night in a chair beside Bill's bed.

In the blue and red room, dotted about with teddies and books and the accoutrements of childhood, Larry dozed, drifting in and out of sleep. 'I don't want to lose her, I don't want to lose her,' he said once, crying out, and next time he woke his eyes seemed to light on a fluffy lion and the travesty of the grubby white muzzle came to him time and time again, like the travesty of the room; a lie of sweetness and safety.

In his Thomas the Tank Engine bed, Bill's pale face lay still in the twisted sheets.

What have we done? Larry thought once, waking with a start. He felt he had cried out in his sleep but Bill slept on. We've broken him, Larry thought; and sank back into sleep and dreamt of his mother's precious china in ruins at his feet.

When dawn came he got up with a sense of release at no longer being prisoner of the dark. He went downstairs in the blue light of early morning and filled the sink with boiling water and stood with his hands in it, staring through the steam at the garden in which the colours were forming once again with the new day. The black leaves were turning pale as the sun began to rise and they glittered in the wind.

Carefully he washed the cups that they had used the previous morning, blinking in the steam and wiping them inside and out in the boiling water, over and over again, as though he couldn't get them clean. It was, in a sense, an act of faith for him to pursue such a trivial occupation so early and with Megan's absence like a gaping hole. But there was the possibility that she might come back and he wouldn't be ready.

When he finally dried his hands, his arms were red and tingling. Of that he was glad. The colour of the garden had changed again; the leaves had greened and the grass had solidified and separated from the black pool that had been the lawn.

He went to the front door. The two newspapers lay on the mat: her tabloid and his broadsheet wrapped up in each other. He picked them up and once more a wave of emptiness came over him through the mundane. He took them into the dining room and looked at hers first. The headlines had little meaning and as he spread the paper out across the table his own emptiness took precedence; he was not interested in others' tragedies; his own was too great.

He was heaping the third teaspoon of instant coffee into his mug when he became aware of Bill behind him.

'Daddy.'

'Morning.' Larry rasped the bristle on his chin. 'You're up early. How about some toast?'

Bill climbed onto the chair opposite his. After a moment's thought, he nodded.

'What will you have on it – jam, honey, marmalade?'

284

Another pause for thought. 'Jam.'

'Jam it is.' He put two slices of toast into the toaster and waited for it to pop up, busying himself in the meantime with skimming off the small clots of cream which had drifted to the surface of the coffee. It was very early, he knew; not yet six. Four hours until the playgroup opened. Two and a half until Sainsbury's. Please don't let him ask about Megan yet, he prayed silently; not until I'm ready.

It was the next question Bill asked.

They walked into the aviary at ten minutes past ten and Bill was fussed over like a little dog. Larry's immediate thought was that they knew that Megan had gone, but when the banter spread to him he realised it was because of the march. Hell, he'd almost forgotten it.

'They let you go, did they?' Emma said with a small smile. 'What happened?'

'I was told to behave.'

'We always had you down as a troublemaker, didn't we, girls?' She took her Alice band off and let her hair fall forward, then she scooped it with the sides of the band so that it was swept from her face again. 'We missed you on the coach.'

'Ah, you're just saying that.'

'I'm not just saying it. Anyway, come and sit down.' She pulled out a chair for him, a full-size one. The legs scraped along the floor with a screech. 'What next?'

Jean brought a tray of mugs over to the table and put them down.

What next? The end of the world had come, and they were making plans.

He looked up and Helen was taking one of the mugs. 'I think we should suggest a compromise,' she said. 'These courses, like the massage one – we can do without them, can't we? They're too short to be of much use, and they're hugely subsidised.

That will save the council money for their budget and they can keep their rent subsidy the same.' She looked at him queryingly. 'What do you think?'

My marriage has broken up, he thought. I should be with Megan, fixing that.

'Brilliant,' Emma said. 'We've got more stuffed toys in our house –'

Jean suddenly looked at her arm. She was reaching for the sugar and she stopped and stared, twisting her arm around. Just by the crease of her elbow there was a greenish-red mark. 'Look,' she said, looking up at them. 'What's that?'

Emma took Jean's arm and looked closely. 'How long has it been there?'

'I've never noticed it before.'

Emma touched it with her thumb nail and it sprang off, landing in the sugar bowl. She picked the bowl up and stared inside it. 'It's a tomato pip,' she said. 'Silly cow.'

Larry found himself laughing. Helen laughed too, but her eyes were not on Jean but on him.

Suddenly he found he couldn't look at her. He turned to look at Bill. He watched him climb into the Cozy Coupe and shut the door hard on a boy's fingers. The boy moved his hand to the top of the door and Bill hit it with his fist. The boy's mouth opened soundlessly for a moment before the high-pitched cry became audible: 'Aieeeeee . . .'

Larry jumped to his feet and watched the boy's mother hurry to attend to him.

Bill hurried away, his face impassive.

Megan might be back that night, Larry thought, watching him move the car to a corner. Might be. He ought to think of something, he, small master of the grand gesture, to get her to come back. But she wanted to think, she'd said.

He ought to have done some of that himself. If a charity was set up, it usually had at least one paid worker as well as volunteers. Megan was right, money was important, it was insane to think otherwise. If he could set up a support network for fathers alone he'd need money to start it off. He could have used the Triton money but it was too late for that now.

'It's not like Bill,' Helen said.

'Megan left last night.'

Helen turned to him in surprise. 'Why? For how long?'

'I don't really know,' he said.

'Where's Mummy?' Bill asked that evening as Larry finished reading him his bedtime story.

'She's working late. So what do you think of Chicken Licken, imagining that the sky is falling in?' Larry asked curiously as he closed the book.

'But it wasn't the sky, it was a haycorn.'

'Acorn. Yes. But to Chicken Licken, it felt as though the sky was falling in. Can you imagine that?' He could.

His sky had fallen, oh yes, right onto his unbalding head and he knew exactly what it felt like, it felt like the end of the world. And then Chicken Licken had been eaten. So he'd been right to worry, hadn't he? He'd had a premonition that something awful was going to happen and it had, by golly it had.

Larry pulled the sheets up to Bill's chin although he knew that as soon as he had gone out of the bedroom Bill would have freed one leg from them and stuck it on top of the blankets. And he remembered what had been niggling him.

'Bill,' he asked, 'who do you love best?'

Bill looked at him, his eyes big and dark in the dim light of his table lamp.

Larry knew that he was playing dirty, asking him like that just after the Chicken Licken question, but he really needed to know.

Bill squeezed the edge of his blanket.

287

'I love you best, Daddy.'

Guilty, beautiful relief.

'And I love Mummy best.' Squeezing the duvet as though he could feel his mummy in his arms. 'And I love Ruth best.'

'Okay, thanks, Bill. Goodnight and God bless.' He went to the door and turned out the light.

45

Even if his father had forgotten how men behave, Bill hadn't.

Bill was sitting in the yellow shade of the Cozy Coupe with the doors shutting him safely in, and safely away from the other children. He was thinking of his mother.

What he could remember was his father saying sometime in the night, 'I don't want to lose her,' but he suspected his father had lost her just the same and didn't have a clue where. Bill remembered when Ruth went and his father said the house was upside-down, although Bill knew that it was the right way up all along. At the time that his father thought the house was upside-down they had lost all sorts of things, and some things they never found, like the black Maglite torch.

They never found it although they looked everywhere, and his father had picked up the sofas just in case. Bill put his hand on the red plastic door and wondered if his mother and the torch were together somewhere, waiting to be found.

There was a jerk on the red door. Bill knew that always, when he sat in the car, someone would want to get in as well. He knew he had to *share*, but sharing meant giving a toy to someone and not being able to play with it yourself. He held the door tightly with both hands.

The boy who wanted to get in was Damon and he pulled the door so hard that the car moved round and Bill didn't want to move, he wanted to stay where he was. Who knows, he might get lost himself and then what would happen? He was only four. He let go of the door and picked up the block from the shelf at the back and hit Damon hard on the head.

Damon looked surprised and opened his mouth wide but he let go of the door and sat down.

Bill moved the Cozy Coupe over to the door. He guessed there was going to be trouble.

'Bill's just hit Damon with a wooden brick. He doesn't look too bright.'

Emma picked Damon up. He wasn't crying and he looked very pale.

'Did he cry?' Emma asked Jean.

She shook her head. 'It was a hell of a bang, though,' she said. Larry straightened and looked round for Bill. He was in the Cozy Coupe, looking over the door, his face impassive but his blue eyes perhaps just a little wider than usual.

Larry went over to him. 'Get out of there a moment,' he said, looking down at him.

'But someone will get in.'

'Get out, Bill.'

Reluctantly Bill got out and steadfastly avoided looking at the small group surrounding Damon.

Larry crouched down to Bill's level. 'What did you do?' he asked softly.

'He wanted to get in the car.'

'This car belongs to the playgroup. It's for everyone,' Larry said. 'It's not just for you.'

Bill looked at him defiantly. It was the defiance which led Larry to notice how much he had diminished. His heart went out to him.

'It's mine,' Bill said.

'You know it isn't yours. You hit Damon on the head and hurt him.'

Jean picked up the Cozy Coupe. 'I'm going to put this away

for the moment,' she said, 'seeing as you can't play with it properly.'

Bill looked at her and turned to watch her put it in the store room. When she came out and locked the door behind her, he looked at Larry.

'You'd better say you're sorry.'

Bill looked at him, his eyes huge and unrepentant. 'I'm not sorry,' he said.

Larry could see Emma lift Damon in her arms. He looked listless and Larry felt his own frustration build up inside. 'You can bloody well pretend, can't you?' he said. He caught Emma looking at him. 'Look, Bill, you can't go hitting people, you know. We all feel like doing it, but we stop ourselves, understand?'

'A man hit you, Daddy,' Bill said, his voice barely a whisper.

'Yeah.' Hell, Bill, he thought, what am I going to do with you? 'Come on.'

Bill turned to look at the Wendy house, and turned back to Larry with his hands in his pockets.

'I want to play with the Cozy Coupe,' he said.

'Don't mention that to me again,' Larry said through his teeth, biting each syllable as the frustration rose in him once more. He went over himself and crouched down by Damon, who was lying quietly in Emma's arms.

'Becky's going to drive me to the hospital,' she said apologetically. She put her warm hand on his, looking up at him. 'I think you should take Bill home,' she said gently.

Larry shook his head. 'I will. I'm so sorry. How is he?'

Emma passed her hand over her grandson's forehead. 'His eyes seem all right and he hasn't vomited.' She looked curiously at Larry. 'Are you all right?'

Larry shook his head to clear it, and stood up. He ran his hand through his hair. 'I'll survive,' he said.

Emma frowned. 'You have to do more than survive when

you've got a child,' she said. She looked for Bill and lowered her voice. 'What's the problem, Larry?'

'Meg's gone away for a few days.'

'Is there someone else?'

Larry was so surprised at the unexpected question that he almost laughed. 'No, of course not,' he said.

'Patch it up then,' she said. She glanced at Bill. 'And take him home. He needs you for himself.'

Larry looked around the room for Bill. Bill was the only one who was still. He seemed frozen.

Larry went over to him. 'Come here,' he said, and Bill looked surprised. When Larry picked him up, he rested his head on Larry's neck. Larry could feel his breath by his jugular. 'Would you like to go home?' he asked him gently.

'No,' said a small voice.

'Do you want to stay here?'

'No.'

'What would you like to do?'

'I want to go to the park,' Bill said.

Becky pulled up outside the playgroup and beeped her horn for Emma.

Larry watched them go and crossed Bill's name out of the lunch book. They walked slowly to Regent's Park in silence.

Bill went straight to the swings.

'Will you push me?' he asked Larry.

Larry was looking at a man who was leaning on the fence, looking into the playground. He was wearing a red t-shirt with a tear under the arm and could have been looking for someone, but he had the lassitude about him of one who'd given up hope of finding them. Larry hated him, and thought, they're not all alone, it's ridiculous, only one in three marriages – can't make fiction into facts . . .

Bill got onto the seat.

292

'I'm ready, Daddy,' he said.

Still half-concentrating on the man, Larry misjudged the push. Bill gave a swift, small cry and started to fall. Larry was near enough to grab his legs but his head gave a small whump against the red rubber matting and when Larry picked him up, Bill's tears came quick and profuse.

'I'm sorry, I'm sorry, I'm sorry,' Larry said, and carried him to a bench. He rocked him on his knee and felt his throat ache with sadness. 'I'm sorry, Bill.' Bill sobbed against his chest and Larry felt a wave of despair. 'Where does it hurt?' he asked. 'At the back of your head?'

'My headache's in my leg. You squeezed me.'

'I can see the marks. Shall I rub it better?'

'Can you kiss it?'

'You've always been stoical,' Larry said sadly.

Bill put his thumb in his mouth and took it out again as though he knew what being stoical was. 'How long is Mummy going to be lost for?' he asked in a small voice.

Larry felt it hit his stomach like a blow. 'She's not lost,' he said. He looked at the trees beyond the playground. One of them was dotted with starlings, they looked like large, dark leaves against the green. A couple and their dog walked beneath the tree and they flew up in a cloud, to land in the grass. 'I know where to find her.'

Bill seemed surprised to hear that. 'Is she at work?'

'She's staying with a friend of hers, just for a short while. You can go and see her if you like, see where she's staying. I'll ask her, shall I?'

'Yes.'

The starlings were back in the tree again. 'How are you feeling? How's your head?'

'It's all right, it doesn't hurt.'

'Good. Let's get something to eat.'

'Can we go to McDonalds?'

293

They walked back slowly, hand in hand, and Larry thought of the man looking over the fence. He'd hated him because he didn't want to be like him. But he was going down that path already, going of his own volition. The momentum of his argument was pushing him on.

'When will you ask her?'

'When we get back, I'll ring her. I'll ring her and see how she is.'

He was surprised at the way he felt, just saying that. He was glad of the excuse.

Out of every permutation he had thought of and practised and enlarged upon, when he spoke to her what he actually said to her was: 'How are you?'

'I'm fine,' she said. He could hear the office hum behind her. 'How's Bill?'

'Bill's fine. He's missing you.' We both are, he thought, but left it unsaid. 'He would like to see you. As it's the weekend, I wondered . . .'

He listened to the phone line humming and a telephone ringing in the background and his wife's thought waves hesitate.

'You don't want me –' she hesitated. 'I'll come home and see him tomorrow. Take him swimming. I'll come as early as I can.'

As she could? What did that mean? He wondered what might prevent her, what else she had on. 'Bill's here,' he said, 'have a word.'

'Mummy,' Bill said, sitting on the carpet to talk.

Larry heard her speak, but couldn't make out the words. He wanted to listen, but Bill's hand was clutched tightly around the receiver and he was nodding. Suddenly he kissed the mouthpiece, his eyes shut. Then wordlessly, he handed the receiver to his father.

Larry listened but got only the burr of the dialling tone. 'You don't want me . . .' To come home? Is that what she thought?

He replaced the handset. 'Tomorrow,' he said to Bill, 'is when you're going to see Mummy.'

'I know, she told me. I'll kiss her,' Bill said, as though that was what he'd decided was missing, that lack of kissing had sent his mother away.

PART NINE

And Nine's the Devil
His Ane Sel'

46

She picked him up and took him swimming.

On Saturday mornings the pool was quiet.

After they'd changed into their swimsuits, Bill and Megan left Lisa applying waterproof conditioner to her hair and walked to the pool, hand in hand.

The pool was full of echoes and empty of people.

Standing next to Bill on the cold, dry tiles, Megan stared at the blue, untroubled water.

She had a thirst for it. She savoured the thought of being first in; she wanted to dive and smash the glossy surface and be swallowed by the cool, refreshing blue closing slowly over her head, deafening her with its muffled silence.

She jumped in and held her arms out for Bill and he leapt into them with a squeal. She let him go, and they bobbed together like corks for a moment before he swam to her, flapping the water, holding his head high. His limbs were warm against hers and Megan put her arms around his small, narrow chest and lay back, smiling with the combined pleasure of water and Bill. The water sparkled so coldly it was like floating in spearmint.

'This is our pool, isn't it?' he asked. 'It's private.'

Megan dived and rose slowly in a cloud of silver bubbles. She broke the surface and swept her hair from her face with the palms of both hands. 'It's our private pool,' she said. 'No one is allowed in except for us.'

'And Daddy,' Bill said.

'And Daddy. Of course.' She floated on her back. 'Don't you call him Larry any more?'

'No. I call him Daddy now.'

Bill paddled over close to her. He ducked and swam up, water streaming down his face. 'Do you know where Daddy's black Maglite is?'

'No. Why?'

'I wondered, that's all.'

Lisa smiled at them and stood poised at the deep end in a fluorescent green swimsuit for a long moment, then dived sharply into the blue water. The few gentle ripples that she made lapped up against Megan and Bill. Suddenly she surfaced a few feet away from them, her hair as sleek as a seal's.

'Wow,' Megan said, impressed.

Lisa put her arms out behind her to hold the bar and kicked off again, surging along underneath the surface of the water before using firm, clean strokes to take her to the deep end. The fluorescent swimsuit took on a pallor in the water. From where Megan floated, she looked like some beautiful marine species.

'She's your friend,' Bill said.

'Yes.'

'You're a beautiful mummy,' he said.

Her sense of unworthiness brought sudden, desperate tears to her eyes at his generosity and his love. 'And you're the best boy anyone could have,' she said.

Their peace came to an end with the arrival of a group of teenagers, whose noise bounced off the water and under the vaulted roof. They jumped and dived like compact bombs, exploding into life on reaching the surface. They surrounded Bill and Megan in the shallow end. Megan watched their long pale limbs float and kick and looked at Bill, who was paddling with his hands on the outskirts of the fun.

I want to be with Bill, she thought. The idea seemed to open her up inside.

But I have to work.

She swam towards her son and realised for the first time that her love for her job couldn't begin to compare.

Lisa swam up to them, drawing attention and a couple of comments from the boys, who she disdainfully stuck a finger up to. 'Are you ready to get out?' she asked Megan.

'Sure.'

She helped Bill out of the pool and she went to her locker for the Radox shower gel and the towels.

She left one shower free between herself and Bill, and Bill stood with his hands stretched up over his head, his face lifted to the spray and his eyes closed tight.

She squeezed the Radox onto her palm and frothed it on his head and the shower floated the suds away. He stepped out straight into the towel she was holding for him and she wrapped it round him.

'Go and dry yourself while I rinse off,' she said, and slipped out of her swimsuit. She caught Lisa's eyes through the rushing water. It's just like gym at school, she thought, concentrating on the Radox, and when she looked up, Lisa had gone.

'Meg, take a look at Bill's leg,' Lisa said as she towelled herself dry, naked and unself-conscious in the changing room.

Megan was sitting on the slatted wooden bench with her cheek on Bill's damp hair. Through the Radox she could smell the smell of him. His arm was draped around her neck and his slender limbs dangled along hers. She ran her hand over his leg and looked at the bruises on his thigh. 'What have you been up to?' she said with a laugh. 'You are a sausage.'

Lisa came and stood next to her, her arm resting across Megan's shoulder.

Megan felt uncomfortable at her proximity. She and Larry

301

walked about naked – had walked – but Lisa's predatory prowl was not an unself-conscious one at all. There was something very conscious about it.

Bill didn't mind. Impressed at the attention the bruises were causing, he traced his finger from one mark to the other like an abstract join-the-dots. He looked up suddenly, his eyes dazzling in his slightly freckled face. 'They don't hurt.'

'Of course they don't,' Megan said briskly.

She stood up and took Bill's clothes out of the locker.

'Step into these,' she said, holding his pants out for him.

'I can dress by myself, now,' he said. 'You have to look at the label because that's the back.'

Lisa laughed. She was bending over and her heavy breasts fell into the cups of her bra.

Megan glanced at her, then back at Bill. 'Well, I am impressed.'

'But I'm not very good at buttons.'

'Buttons can be a nuisance, I know.'

'Daddy helps me with my shoes. I can fasten them myself.'

'But not unfasten them, eh,' Megan said, tearing open the Velcro flap. 'You're doing really well for someone who's four. You'll be ready for school before long.'

Bill did a little jump on the spot.

'Shall I help you with that button on your trousers?'

'I can do this one,' he said, his chin on his chest as he struggled with it.

Damn you, Larry, she thought, any excuse to be in contact with Bill and you make him self-sufficient.

They went for lunch and Bill could see as soon as they went inside that the restaurant was one you had to BEHAVE in.

It wasn't like Burger King where you could join two straws together, or blow the wrapper of the straw straight off it to try and hit someone you knew. In that sort of place you could

302

eat with your fingers – you had to, because there were no knives and forks. But places like this were different. The best thing about them (the only thing, he thought) was that sometimes you got a small umbrella in your drink.

The waiters were very nice to Lisa and his mummy and were making them laugh. He liked the sound of his mother laughing but he wasn't sure he wanted her to be so happy. She might, he thought, never want to come home. They didn't laugh so much at home any more.

'They think you're the nanny,' Lisa said, and she was smiling.

His mother smiled back. 'I wish,' she said. But she didn't say what she had wished for; if you told, it didn't come true. Bill knew that now.

Lisa was looking at her carefully. 'Do you?'

His mother was staring at her plate. She looked very sad, as though she'd seen a mark on it like his father left on plates. His father had given him a breakfast bowl one morning with yesterday's cornflakes stuck like glue to the edge and pretended they'd only just gone like that.

But he knew better.

'What will you have to drink, Meg?' Lisa asked.

'A Coke.'

'Me, too,' Bill said.

'Two Cokes and a kir.'

Another waiter came and asked what he wanted to eat and he said, 'Duck.'

Megan and Lisa laughed again, and they ordered duck, too. Then Megan said she was going to the cloakroom and did he want to come?

He shook his head.

'So,' Lisa said when his mother had gone, 'tell me all about the bruises on your leg.'

It wasn't often a grown-up asked him things like that. He rubbed his eye and tried to remember. 'Daddy did them,' he

303

said. He tried to remember. It wasn't always easy and he could only remember bits. 'I was naughty and we left the playgroup . . .' he looked at her warily, but she didn't seem to be cross. She nodded. 'And Daddy pushed me too hard and grabbed my legs and I hit my head on the floor.'

Lisa folded her arms and leaned nearer to him and repeated exactly what he'd said, all except the naughty bit. He was glad about that.

'Your daddy pushed you hard and grabbed your legs and hit your head on the floor,' she said.

Bill, if he tried hard, could still see the swing leaping about as it had when his father had picked him up. 'And Daddy said he was sorry lots of times.'

'Did he? He will be,' Lisa said, looking pleased, and Bill was glad he'd said that, about how sorry his father was.

He could see his mother coming back, looking happy.

Lisa was looking happy, too. 'Oh, yes, he will be,' she said.

47

Roles were reversing themselves everywhere, it seemed to Larry.

Having set up a date between his wife and his son, he rang James, to ask how he was, he told himself as he dialled, not to tell him anything about the rift with Megan. But it came stammering out and he felt ashamed. 'Shouldn't be burdening you with this,' he said, digging his bare toes into the carpet. 'I rang up to see how you were.' A lie. 'You've got your own problems.'

He heard James give a sudden, hollow laugh. 'Your trouble is, you've lost your identity, mate. Trick cyclist at the hospital told me that,' he said. 'When Lydia went, I didn't know who I was. "Be what you are, mate," he said, "it's your only chance of survival." I'm a lonely philandering boy, Larry. Who are you?'

Larry wondered. There had been a time when he'd known perfectly who he was, and he wished it was still that way.

'Who are you, Larry?'

James's lonely voice along the telephone lines made him want to thump someone. I DON'T KNOW! he shouted inside his head, and saw the irony of wanting to be a hero again; yes, like the day of the march, being a hero, heading a thin, unhappy line of lonely fathers while at the same time making himself into one, and *shit*, he thought, where was the heroism in that?

'Want a bit of fun, try and find out? Guys' day out. It'll

305

while away a few hours for you until Bill comes back. Bet he's having fun with Megan. All fussed over again.'

Larry smiled. 'Yeah, I bet he's having fun.' He hoped Bill was having fun; he really hoped he was having fun, that was the truth, but not too much fun. He could imagine what it was like to be all wrapped up in Meg's soft arms and forget; forget everything, especially him, Larry, and the – how did James put it? the man's stuff. Because he and Bill kissed goodnight, but apart from that there wasn't any softness any more. Meg had taken the softness out of the house with her – she was the softness, that was the truth. Without her they couldn't hug the same. They wrestled instead. He could imagine Bill relaxing into her soft arms and never wanting to leave them.

'And you?' James asked, slapping his face with aftershave. 'Who's fussing over you? Which of those itsy-bitsy ladies is looking after you now?'

Larry rubbed his cheek and paraded them slowly through his head. Emma, adjusting her Alice band; Jean, finding tomato-pip skin-cancers on her arm; Helen, writing the letters, fitting in. Itsy-bitsy ladies. Equals and opposites. He'd come full circle again.

'That silence sounds like a big fat no one.' James's voice was raised in his enthusiasm. 'Got something planned to cheer you up, Larry boy. You'll have to give me an hour or so to fix it up.'

'Where are we going?'

'Somewhere you're going to love, Larry my boy; somewhere you're going to love.'

James came round in a cab, which waited for Larry and went, Larry found, along Great Portland Street. He stared at the large, reflective windows in the street. He could see the pale blob of his face staring back at him and tried to identify himself but the truth was, it could have been anybody.

James was silent next to him; silent, but vibrating with expectation. Hyper.

Larry didn't even try to wonder what was in store for him. The sad truth was, he didn't care. He wanted to be with Bill again. Bill's temporary absence had left holes in his life, holes that he kept falling into unawares. 'Look, fire engine,' he said as they came out into Langham Place.

'Thank you for sharing that with me, Larry,' James said, laughing.

But Larry couldn't laugh back. What if Megan didn't bring Bill home? What if Bill didn't want to come?

The cab stopped in Brewer Street, outside a window with *Live Girls* neoned on it. James paid the cab and turned to Larry, who was still staring at the sign.

'Not for necrophiliacs,' he said, in a bleak attempt at sexual humour.

James jerked his head impatiently. 'Come on.'

What Larry wanted to say was, where? There? He wondered suspiciously if James was calling his bluff. It's daytime, he thought, looking round. He saw James disappear down the steps below.

A bored blonde in a tight pink dress was waiting at the bottom. Her hair was as short as Megan's. She gave two tickets to James and he walked through heavy red velvet curtains into a bar. A topless bar, Larry could see as his eyes got accustomed to the dark.

'Have a beer,' James said, 'everything else is through the roof.'

'Sure, a beer.'

'Two beers, please.'

The girl who served them was friendly and normal. What had he expected? She was so ordinary that she seemed to be unaware that she was topless. 'Two beers, ho-kay,' she said, ducked under the counter and reappeared with two bottles, which she opened in front of them.

Larry felt uneasy but there was always the possibility that this was as bad as it got. He expected James to chat the girl up, but James seemed unaware that she was topless, too.

It was so gloomy, he thought, and so seductive with its red velvet curtains and dim light. It was like night-time. They drank the beers from the bottles and Larry looked around at the other men in the dim shadows. Here and there a red tip of a cigarette momentarily glowed more brightly. The room seemed charged and it occurred to Larry that they were waiting for something. 'Now what?' he asked James.

James looked at him and put his bottle on the bar. 'We wait for the show to start,' he said.

'Two more beers, please,' Larry said to the topless girl.

She ducked under the bar, came up again and took the caps off. 'Ho-kay,' she said, pushing them towards him.

Well a show wasn't too bad. He could deal with a show. He could enjoy it, even. He didn't know what he was finding so difficult. The only problem he could come up with was that he didn't really want to be here, not with James, not at all, but seeing as he was here, he might as well relax into it.

He back-stepped to the girl at the door and turned to James curiously. 'Have you been here before?'

James seemed surprised that he should have asked. 'Ye-es,' he said. He put the beer bottle on the bar.

Larry could see that there was a general movement, a general stirring, an air of something about to happen. He finished his beer with a grimace, and realised that was what the stirring had been – people finishing their drinks.

James was moving towards another velvet curtain, and he was getting his wallet out again. There was another girl behind that curtain and she took the notes and jerked her head at Larry, who followed James through into the deeper dark.

In this thick, smoky murk that made the previous bar seem floodlit, Larry could make out a few tables, because some dark red light overhead was reflecting off their polished shine.

'Another beer?' James asked.

'Yes, thanks.' He could see the stage, they were practically on top of it. He looked around for another table, wary of possible audience participation, but already they were all taken. The room was warm and cigarette smoke swirled above their heads like dry ice.

James returned and put a bottle in front of Larry, just as the music started. A singer, wearing a tight, red rubber dress, came on singing about spring. The curtains opened and suddenly a line of girls danced on, their skin dazzling in the spotlights. They were almost naked – they seemed to be wearing green leotards on back-to-front, because their breasts were exposed and so was their pubic hair. They were wearing headdresses of yellow feathers. Spring, Larry thought, pleased, as though he was at Sadler's Wells and had just made sense of it. Two of the girls caught his attention; one of them had very short, bleached hair (reminding him, he thought, of Megan again) and she danced with her chin up and her head held high. She was so defiant, brazen, almost, in her dancing, that she seemed to be clothed. The other had dark hair, caught up in a pony tail behind the feathers. She had her head down as she danced, and looked up coyly; she seemed more naked than the others, although of course the outfits were the same.

He was suddenly aware that James was looking at him. 'Which do you go for?' he asked.

'The blonde with the short hair,' Larry said.

James grinned; Larry could see his teeth in the dark.

Spring gave way to summer: back-to-front swimsuits and beachballs thrown, bounced on, embraced; and summer gave way to autumn: brown see-through gowns and a great deal of swaying; and winter was lively again: white leotards and red

309

fur cuffs. And then the lady in rubber came back and sang once more and Larry felt himself relax with relief. It had been fine. Fine? He'd even enjoyed it. The point was, he hadn't shown himself up in front of James. They were men of the world together – and his reputation was intact. He would soon see Bill again. It was an amusing enough way of spending the time. Dearer, he decided, thinking of the notes that had come out of James's wallet, than Sadler's Wells. It was no wonder James couldn't afford to eat.

The stage lights went off and the dim lights went on. The clapping had been desultory and there was no encore.

Larry finished his drink and got up slowly, as though reluctantly, but James told him to sit down.

'Got a surprise for you,' he said. 'What would you like in the world right now? No, don't tell me. Stay there.' He went to the bar and came back with a bottle of champagne and four glasses.

More for something to do than out of curiosity, Larry tried to read the label in the dark. 'Hey, this is Sainsbury's champagne,' he said. 'How much did they charge you for it?'

James laughed as though Larry had made a joke.

Larry stared at the four glasses. Everyone knew that topless (and bottomless) dancers were only dancers after all.

He saw them emerge, pale figures, from the direction of the stage and come over – how they could make them out in the gloom, he didn't know. James solicitously arranged the chairs for them, then tucked them in under the table, as though they were grannies on a day out. He asked them if they wanted champagne or something else and they said they would have champagne. The blonde was on Larry's right and a redhead with long legs was sitting on James's left.

James smiled at the blonde. 'He likes you,' he said to her, as though Larry was an elderly dog who had briefly lifted his tail. 'You remind him of his wife.'

310

She laughed.

'This is Mandalie,' James said to Larry with the same exaggerated courtesy.

Larry nodded, and attempted a smile. 'Unusual name,' he said.

'My real name's Mandy but Mandalie sounds nicer, doesn't it? It's after one of the actresses in *Brideshead Revisited*.'

'Is it?'

'Or something. I heard someone say it once and I liked it.' She still had her head tilted up and she looked, as far as he could make out, as brazen fully clothed as she had naked.

'And mine is called Serena,' James said.

Larry nodded at her. Mine, he thought, registering the word. But he was safe for the moment. Mandalie – yes, he too liked it better than Mandy – was firmly tucked under the table still. Like Bill at mealtimes.

James poured the champagne carefully, filling each glass accurately each time. 'To us,' he said, raising his.

'To us,' they echoed. Even Larry said it. Then he looked at his watch in a panic, wondering how long they had been there, but it was only three o'clock. Three o'clock in the afternoon, he said to himself. Soon he would be stepping out into bright daylight, squinting in the sun, picking up Bill; what a beautiful excuse, what a reason to leave. He felt light-headed with the thought of a legitimate escape. He drank some champagne.

'What time do you have to leave, Larry?' James asked. Nothing escaped him.

'I'm picking Bill up at four,' he said, trying to make his voice apologetic but not too apologetic, not so that they would try to be helpful and start thinking up excuses for him.

'Better get going,' James said.

'What's the hurry?' He could afford to be generous. 'I've got a bit of time, yet.'

311

'That's what I mean. Time that could be better spent having fun,' said James. 'Come on.' With a scraping of chair legs they got up, both girls and James. James picked up the bottle. Larry looked up at them.

'They've got rooms upstairs,' James said.

The two girls started talking, heads together. They seemed happy, unruffled, cosy in the gloomy room.

Larry imagined stopping it now by not getting up. Or, getting up and going upstairs and stopping then. Getting undressed and stopping then. Getting into bed and stopping then. Not stopping at all. Or stopping now.

James was looking at him. And so were the girls.

Larry looked back at them. Flick, flick, flick, an image change, man in a convertible to man on a bus to a man in a fight. Businessman to father. Lecher to husband. He wanted to be the man in the convertible, the businessman, the lecher, he wanted to be that man; he wanted to be him so fiercely that he heard his will scream it out silently in the dim smoky room, but he watched the two girls and he knew he wasn't. He was just an ordinary man. A man with a wife.

'All the more for me,' James said softly, reading his thoughts. 'Be what you are. Goodbye, mate.'

The word was curiously wistful.

'No, don't say that.'

'For an hour I can be myself. I won't be lonely. I'm going to have fun. I'm going to live. I know what I am,' James said, his voice as soft and heavy as the velvet curtains. He looked towards the girls. They were waiting and he left Larry and walked up to them and they parted for him to walk between them. The redhead put her slender arm around his neck and the blonde put her left hand in his and Larry could feel them, the arm and the hand, could feel how it would have been. Still could be.

He stepped forward and then they were gone, behind some

musty red velvet curtain somewhere where some other woman stood, bored, waiting to take the money.

He felt alone, totally alone.

No matter what the cost, he wanted Meg back.

48

On Monday morning, awakening with the sun shining determinedly through a crack in the blush pink curtains, Larry put his hands behind his head and wondered, not for the first time, what Bill had made of the day-long outing with his mother.

He had volunteered nothing except that they'd eaten duck. There had been no mention of whether he'd been glad to see his mother or sad to leave her, but Larry had noticed that he'd been quiet all evening; tired perhaps. Tired at best.

Megan had seen Bill back and left straight away, giving him no time to do all the things he'd wanted to. She'd waved at them, smiling, before she'd got into the car.

Larry moved his head. The pure stream of sunlight was burning his brain and he moved to a cooler part of his pillow which was in shadow, and against the blood red of his eyelids, now maroon with yellow and red discs, he tried to remember Megan's smile. He thought of her smiling a brave smile, her chin trembling; and of her getting in quickly before they saw the tears. Bill had hugged him and bent and kissed his knee all of a sudden and put his hand in his. It had felt a very small hand, he thought, as he reacquainted himself with it again after a day's absence.

Thinking of her made him want her. He listened for signs of movement from Bill's bedroom and imagined her lying in the bed beside him as she'd always done, curled away from him, making it easy for him to get close to her, to put his arm around her and rest his palm on a small breast. He would hear

314

her make a quiet, satisfying noise in her throat, one of the noises of lovemaking. One of the noises of their lovemaking, anyway; theirs was always wordless, always had been, no yes-yes-yesses, no oh-nos, no crudity. Their bodies were their language during those times. He remembered when he'd first realised the intimacy of silence, soon after they'd first made love, and the variety of the aftermath, tears or laughter or more silence or quiet words, came, too, as a surprise. He remembered the revelation of the first 'I love you', and the newness of her in the light of it.

He felt sick, suddenly, in the sunny bedroom, from wanting her and he rolled over with a groan and rolled himself out of bed.

He went to the window and looked out. There was a day to be lived. They wouldn't go to the playgroup, they'd have a change. He might have to get used to missing Megan. His wife had not been gone long and she might be gone for ever.

He wouldn't think of that.

When he came out of the shower, making wet footprints on the carpet, he shouted, 'Bill? Where's the bath mat?' Bill was awake and the sound of Cartoon Network gibbered happily from the sitting room.

'It's a sheep,' Bill called back.

'Oh, right.' The carpet had, by now, dried his feet anyway. Bill was sitting on the floor watching *Popeye*. Larry sat on the sofa and watched him too. All those years of pipe-smoking, he thought, and he was still going strong. 'I thought we could go on a picnic today,' he said.

Bill didn't even look up from the screen. ''kay.' Suddenly the message appeared to have got through. 'Where to?' he asked, with a sudden flare of interest. 'To the seaside?'

'Well, we haven't a car, so no, not to the seaside, but to the

Heath. It will be nice to have a picnic there, won't it?'

Bill looked at him with the air of one waiting to be convinced. 'What will we take?'

'What will we take? Sandwiches. Crisps. Drinks.'

'And what else?'

'And what else?' It was things like this he used to find tricky. Not any more, though. 'What do you suggest?'

'Bread for the ducks.'

'Just what I was thinking. We'll take a picnic for them, too, what do you say?'

Bill looked at him and giggled. Then he looked at Popeye and giggled.

'I'll go and get dressed,' Larry said.

For a four-year-old, the Heath was a long way from the tube. It was very hot and Bill was grumpy even before they got to the outskirts. The green parkland seemed to steam in the heat. And they still had to walk, because of the promised ducks. Larry found himself carrying Bill in one arm and holding the picnic hamper with the other. His t-shirt began to stick to the sweat on his skin. He wondered what had possessed him to bring the hamper when a carrier bag would have done the job just as easily, and then he thought, I don't want him to think we've gone downhill since Megan left – which was a pretty deceitful sort of argument compared with the poverty of being without a mother and a wife.

There was so much food in the hamper that he could have set up a stall and sold most of it and still had enough for himself, Bill and the ducks. 'You'll have to walk for a bit, now,' he said, and put both Bill and the hamper down, wiping the sweat from his forehead.

'Are we nearly there?' Bill asked in a thin voice.

'Yes, I think so. There's a kind of bridge with arches which is built over the pond. You'll like it.'

316

'I'm hot.' A fly buzzed low around his head and he flinched. He was dusty and his face was already begrimed. The hair on his forehead was damp and his face was flushed.

'We can stay here if you like,' Larry said, 'we can sit in the shade.'

'I don't want to stay here.'

'I'll carry you a bit further,' Larry said. He picked Bill and the hamper up with an effort and began to walk. His muscles were screaming and the heat was beating on his head and the light began to dapple in his eyes. He stopped and blinked.

'Are we there?' Bill asked.

'No, not yet.' He took a few more steps and thought of heatstroke and of what would happen if he collapsed. What would Bill do? He considered asking him, but thought better of it. Don't want to frighten him. But this is some walk, up a bank, careful not to slip.

And there it was, like an undiscovered Monet, all blues and greens and reflections and ripples, and tiny flies lifting out of the grass in a cloud and the surface of the water dinting under insect legs and the arches bestowing a grey shade for fish of a more delicate disposition. He put Bill down and Bill flopped backwards into the grass, arms and legs outstretched. He shut his eyes and smiled. 'I'm never going to die,' he said.

Larry put the basket down and leaned against it and looked towards the water. 'Nor me.' He liked the arching of the red bricks on the bridge high over the water. People were walking across it, looking down, looking at themselves, seeing themselves being a part of it.

He moved the hamper away from his head and lay next to Bill. He could feel the dry seed heads of grass tickling his face in the breeze; oh where had that breeze been when he'd needed it? It ruffled the hairs on his arms like a ripple. A hum vibrated near him and faded. There was a small splash like a stone hitting the water. He felt himself drift. Never going to die.

The ducks ate very little of the picnic in the end. They weren't given much and what they had they nibbled reluctantly and without enthusiasm, having partaken of people's picnics all day.

The only thing that restored them to any sort of vitality was a black labrador with religious delusions, who amused Bill and Larry no end. He'd start off like some cartoon Muttley, reach the edge of the land and keep walking and when with alarm he found himself sink he'd swim with head up to the bank, study the water, and try again, eyes fixed on the bored common shovellers, and be shocked to his bones to find himself wet.

This, to Bill, was funny enough. And Larry had begun laughing at Bill's laughter, which was infectious.

But the dog was determined and undaunted. Once it realised that its legs didn't float, it leapt at the ducks with its legs splayed out as if intending to belly-flop on them. They swam out of reach with increasing alarm as the attempts got more frequent. And then to Bill's disappointment, the dog gave up and lay panting in the sun not far from them.

'Is there any more juice?' Bill asked.

'I think so. Could you pass me the flask, too, please?'

It wouldn't be so bad going home in the cooling afternoon, the basket empty of food and the flask empty of tea. Why was it he could never throw flask tea away, he wondered. Sometimes it stayed in there from one picnic-time to the next, to be rediscovered in the kitchen, reconstituted as a thin gruel of tea and a thick layer of cheese. And why was it that flask tea always turned grey? He would have asked Megan. It was the kind of thing they talked about on lazy days. They had talked of nothing, very happily, making each other laugh.

'Time to go home,' he said. 'Will you pass me that carton,

please, and is there anything else on your side to take?'

The walk back was easier; mostly downhill of course, and the breeze refreshed them.

The tube was busy but it was with a sense of weary contentment that they walked from the station to their home.

As they returned, Larry narrowed his eyes to look at a familiar figure loitering near the gate. The street was in shadow and he realised that it was Emma, dressed in her polka dots. 'She misses us,' he said to Bill with a laugh but he knew that she had seen them and now he could see that she wasn't laughing back. Her face bore the set mask of the bearer of bad news. Damon, he thought, and began to run towards her.

Bill couldn't keep up, and Larry swung him up into one arm, the picnic basket hitting his leg. He was breathing hard when he reached her and she gave him a lop-sided smile.

'You two been having fun?'

'Damon?'

She smiled. 'He's all right. Bit of a headache, that's all.' She crouched down to look at Bill. 'And how are you?'

'I've seen a dog.'

Emma was smiling as she looked up. 'Look at his freckles. You've had a good day,' she said.

'It's been beautiful, hasn't it?' He put the hamper down on the pavement, feeling in his pocket for his keys, and looked at her quizzically. 'Not that you're not welcome, but why the visit? It looks serious.'

'Yes, it is.'

'Come on in.' He went up the path and unlocked the door and pushed it open with his foot. Bill dashed in through his legs, pleased at the arrival of the unexpected guest.

Larry put the basket down in the hall. 'Will you have a coffee?' he asked her, going into the kitchen.

'Tea. I'll have a tea, if you don't mind,' she said.

319

'Come and have a seat in the kitchen,' he said. 'Bill can watch the television and cool off. Or would you prefer to go into the sitting room?'

'I'll talk to you in here,' she said, coming into the kitchen and taking a chair. She took her hairband off, captured her hair in it and replaced it.

Larry heard the *Looney Tunes* theme music in the background.

'What's the problem?' he asked, leaning against the cooker, getting the question in before her nervousness could become too contagious for him to want to know the source of it. Even as he asked, he went though the possibilities in his head. 'They haven't reviewed the budget?'

'Oh, the budget. Yes, they'll pay all the rent and if we have any courses they won't be subsidised, that's what we've agreed.' Emma took the band out of her hair again. 'Look, Larry,' she wiped her eyes with her hand and blinked at him, 'Social Services have been in touch about Bill.'

He almost laughed. 'And?'

'They're checking up on a report that he's suffered non-accidental injuries to his body. Seemed to think we were a nursery school and might be able to shed some light on your home circumstances.'

Larry squinted as the phrase non-accidental injuries dazzled in his mind's eye, highlighter yellow. 'I don't understand.'

'Apparently he said that you'd caused them,' Emma said, watching him.

'Bill said I'd caused them?' He turned and looked at the mugs and the teapot. 'He hasn't got any injuries,' he said. 'Are you sure they meant Bill?' And he realised that Emma wanted to be reassured. It was why she had come; not to help him but to find out.

He scratched the back of his neck. It felt sore. Too much sun, he thought as he poured the tea. Pouring the tea made

320

him seem guilty, he thought. He should be looking at her, straight at her, so she could see the truth. 'You've seen him,' he said, and his voice sounded frightened.

Emma was not looking at him, but a little to his left. 'They specified finger bruising on his legs.'

Specified, Larry thought.

He felt himself being squeezed very gradually in a vice of slowly growing terror. They were right, weren't they? The bruises were there, they were the shade of blue of a stormy sky, and his fingers had made them.

49

That evening, Megan was sitting in Lisa's drawing room, an untouched glass of rosé in her hand, staring again into the space that she had asked Larry for.

When it came down to it, there was nothing quite so empty as space.

That anger she'd felt – and even now she could feel the heat of it creeping back uneasily – that anger had been the anger of a thwarted search consultant and she wasn't proud of it. It happened; candidates changed their minds, or were offered better packages by their current employers.

The other feeling; well, that had much more to do with the marriage. It had been fear. In every marriage there were rules, unwritten but no less solid for that, and Larry had stepped out of the boundary, ready, kitted up, emotionally prepared to play a different game.

And she had thrown down the bat.

Given space, and a lonely thing it was, she'd found out that life was not a game, or at least, not one game, but a series of them, all different, in which there was a need for players and groundsmen and managers and supporters. And given the role of supporter, she'd suddenly refused to play.

Nothing was for ever. Bill would go to school. Zelda would come back to work. Lisa would leave. It was constant movement and change and to survive you couldn't stand there shouting at it to keep still, you had to go with the flow.

Lisa came in with a mirror and a pair of eyebrow tweezers

322

and sat by a table, plucking her eyebrows. 'Is your drink all right?' she asked, without taking her eyes off her reflection.

Megan watched her frown, and wipe the condensation of her breath off the mirror with a tissue.

'Meg?'

'Oh, sure, the drink's fine.' But she didn't want a drink. Over the last few, short days, they'd drunk a lot, it seemed; now she wanted reality. She didn't care if it was painful or easy, she wanted her emotions to be genuine. 'I think I'll make a coffee. Do you want one?'

Lisa was concentrating. Peck, pull. Peck, pull.

There was a tinny sound as she dropped the tweezers onto the table. 'You're restless,' she said, turning, green eyes holding Megan's, gaze drifting to the full glass. 'You miss Bill.'

'I'm grateful to you,' Megan said. 'You've been a real friend.'

'But.' Lisa dabbed her little finger into a small jar of cream. 'There's a but coming, isn't there?' She smoothed a thin film of cream along her eyebrow and turned to look at Megan, waiting.

'No. No buts.'

Lisa folded her mirror and came and sat on the floor by Megan's legs.

Megan looked at her glossy, dark hair, so silky without the gel, and Lisa looked up at her, sensing her attention.

'You've got incredible eyes,' Meg said.

Lisa got up and sat on the sofa next to her, a strange expression on her face.

'You're not plucking *my* eyebrows,' Megan said warily.

'No. They're perfect,' Lisa said, and hooked a strand of fine dark hair around her ear. 'You're beautiful,' Lisa said. 'I love you. I'm in love with you, you know that, don't you?

Megan watched her, the words sounding odd in Lisa's light, ironic voice. She had a feeling of unreality, as though she was watching it from outside. She felt Lisa's hand reach for her

323

face, smooth her blonde hair from her eyes. The gentleness of touch . . . briefly, Lisa leaned forward, touched her lips with hers, barely a touch, almost a breath.

Green, green eyes, like glacial rivers.

Her wine taken from her clutching hand and put aside.

Lisa back now, swift, passionate, her mouth on hers, slowly, wetly forcing it open, as shocking as the first French kiss to a twelve-year-old. Megan pushed her away, scrambling to her feet, wiping her mouth on her hand. Lisa was standing, too, and they were panting, facing each other like fighters.

'Just wait a minute –' Megan began. Lisa's lipstick was smudged and she wiped her mouth again. 'What the hell are you playing at?'

Lisa's eyes were bright and hard. She was smiling. 'Admit it, for a moment there you were game-on. You wanted to. There's nothing wrong with it, Megan. Tell me you wanted to.'

And yes; she had.

'Come on, Megan. A man for business, but a woman for pleasure.'

'I'm married.'

'But you don't love him, do you, after he humiliated you? Turned down Triton for some New Age Vegetarian Quiche Eating Man's Club?' Lisa grabbed her by the shoulders, and suddenly pushed her hard.

With Lisa's whole weight on her, Megan lost her balance and found herself falling, with Lisa on top of her. Megan, with a surge of strength, twisted around so that she was on her knees. She backed away and got to her feet, sobbing for breath.

She ran to the door and swung it open.

'Don't go,' Lisa said, and there were tears in her eyes.

'I have to,' Megan said. She couldn't stop her own tears, flowing freely down her cheeks. 'You shouldn't have done that. Using force is no different whether it's a man or a woman.'

'And you think Larry doesn't use force?'

'What do you mean?'

'Those bruises on Bill's leg. Larry did them because Bill had been naughty.' Lisa wiped her eyes angrily. 'Bill told me himself. I rang Social Services, you might as well know.'

Megan stared at her. She could see the arc of grey-blue bruises on Bill's slender thigh, feel his thin arms around her neck, his leg swinging. 'He told you?' she asked, incredulous and sickened and above all, afraid.

'You can't blame me for ringing them,' Lisa said. She was crying.

'I don't blame you. I blame myself,' Megan said. She was his mother. She was supposed to protect him from harm, not leave him vulnerable to it. 'Oh, Bill,' she said.

She gave Lisa one last look. There was nothing left to say. She ran out of the house and jumped in the car and headed for home.

50

The evening was settling in.

Larry heard Megan's car pull up and stop.

He'd been waiting for this.

She's come for Bill, he thought.

He went into the hallway and stood waiting for her to open the door. He heard her keys jingle loosely, the crunch of her heels on the gravel. Then she stopped. Changed her mind, he thought, and his heart was galloping out of control. The keys jingled again. Silence.

The shrill ring of the doorbell shocked him to his core. Bill came running to the hall and stopped as he saw his father. 'There's someone at the door,' he said.

'Go back in the living room,' Larry said, urgently, 'go on, go back in there. Put the television on.'

'It is on,' Bill said, and took his hand and kissed it. As Larry walked along the hall, he heard the door close between them. He opened the front door, his pulse thumping in his throat. Megan was biting her lip, looking away, but she turned suddenly as she heard the door open and she put her hand on her heart, startled by his sudden appearance.

'Oh, you frightened me,' she said.

He just looked at her, deafened by his drumming heart. 'Say it,' he said, seeing the tears gather in her eyes, 'say what you've got to say.'

And she did. He heard her intake of breath. 'Larry, Lisa rang Social Services about marks on Bill's legs.' She paused.

The wind was blowing her dress about and she held it down with her hands. 'She told them they might be non-accidental injuries.' She frowned.

He waited.

She kept her hand on her dress. An angry look on her face. 'The bloody fool.'

He got himself back in her arms.

He got himself back in her arms and stayed there while she told him everything she'd thought, step by step, since she'd left, apologising over and over although he knew she had more to forgive.

She told him about the game, and the supporters and the managers and what counted was being together, the three of them.

She was right.

He wanted to tell her things but the words wouldn't come.

She was back, that was all.

Bill sat on her feet, to pin her down and keep her there. He was taking no risks. He had his mother back and he wasn't going to lose her again.

'Who are you now?' he asked her, holding her legs, just so that he could get it right.

'I'm me, your mother. Mummy,' she said, looking at him with her blue eyes.

'Oh.' She sounded, to him, very sure about that. But he had been worried. 'I thought maybe you'd gone to look after some other kid, like Ruth.'

For a moment he thought he'd hurt her, because a pain came into her face which looked the same as when he'd hit Damon and had had to leave the playgroup without any lunch.

'I don't want any other kid,' she said. 'I just want you.'

*   *   *

That evening they ended up in bed at seven o'clock. Bill hadn't wanted to stay on his own. He wanted to lie between them, afraid to leave them or not trusting them to stay. So they lay either side of him with the bedside light on, which shone as red as a setting sun until he fell asleep.

'I'm afraid I'm not much good as a mother,' she said, after a long silence.

'Bill's not complaining.'

'Bill never complains.'

'He complained that time I put him in the bath with his slippers on.'

They began to laugh and Megan suddenly found herself crying, great, wrenching sobs. Larry jumped out of bed, picked Bill up and took him to his own room. Then he got in on her side, right next to her, and took her in his arms. She sniffed a few times and he kissed her, salty and wet, salty and wet and home.

51

Win some, lose some, Lisa thought, pouring herself a brandy.

She'd known she was taking a risk with Megan, but hell, it was a shame not to try.

With Megan it could have been love or business – and she could cross love off, now. The house felt very empty without her and she felt pretty empty herself, but it was not like losing Chrissie. There was no pain.

Lisa brightened up, finished her brandy and decided to take a shower. The evening was young and she had business to think about.

And this time she would wear a skirt.

John King came into the ladies' lounge with his drink in one hand and a fat cigar in the other. He came in smiling and he was still smiling when he sat down, heavily denting the fading chintz. 'Let you in, did they?' he asked.

'Did you ask them to stop me?'

'No, but I do wonder whether you qualify as a lady.'

Lisa smiled at that. 'Chrissie often wondered if you qualified as a man.'

The smile went. She saw his tongue probe his broken tooth thoughtfully. 'You're not here for fun,' he said after a moment.

Lisa put her glass down. 'I wouldn't assume that,' she said, a flicker of a smile returning. 'You know, of course, that I've changed jobs.'

John King didn't reply.

'You changed your mind about asking Colgin to find you a group head. Didn't want anything looked at too deeply, did you? No.'

John King sucked his cigar and sat in the effluent of blue smoke motionless, hearing her out.

'Better the devil you know, eh?' Lisa said. 'Apart from your wife on your Chinese rug, who have I slept with recently that you might know? Ah, yes, I have it.' She sat back and picked up her drink, as smug with satisfaction as a snake full of mouse. 'Peter Dawlish! Does that name ring a bell? Or does it merely ring a cash register, to the tune of a grand a time? Pillow talk, see, that's the secret, John.'

A sigh, that of the long-suffering male. 'How much?'

Lisa shook her head sadly. 'Oh, dear, money isn't everything, you know, it's about time you learned that. There's such a thing as dignity. You should have thought of mine when you made me walk out of here with my trousers rolling down.'

His look of astonishment was the first real emotion she'd ever seen him show. 'All this is because of that?'

'Hell hath no fury and all that, all these little sayings have a grain of truth in them, including the seven-year itch. Where are you taking Chrissie for your anniversary?'

'You're just playing with me,' he said, and put his cigar in his mouth.

'And it's a bit one-sided, isn't it. Never mind. The bottom line, John, is that I want you to resign from Xylus. And if you don't jump, you're going to get pushed.'

'Bitch.'

'Larry should have kept his job. Don't think I'm trying to influence you here, but your job might suit him even better.'

John King rubbed his thumb against his chipped tooth slowly. 'Just say I left Xylus, with other fish to fry, this pillow talk –' he jumped as a section of ash fell onto his knee and brushed it off quickly ' – I suppose, could be forgotten?'

'I haven't got a very good memory for that sort of thing,' she said. 'I hear too much of it.'

'And is that all you want? For Lawrence to get his job back? It's very altruistic of you.'

'It's my nature.'

'Burgess,' he said, 'has the killer instinct of a slug. He'd welcome Lawrence back with open arms at my recommendation.' He looked at her again, puzzled. 'We're two of a kind, Lisa. I can't help wondering – what's in it for you? Not after his wife, are you?'

'I'm after his wife's job,' she said. 'If he goes back to work, she might give it up. And I can take her place. It's a good place to ruin reputations from.' She finished off her drink. 'Besides, it's one place I fit in.'

She saw the flicker of hope in his face, the willingness to believe. He'd never know, would he, whether she would keep her word. Hope was all that he had; he knew a scam on that scale couldn't easily be overlooked. If it got found out it would finish him. She smiled. That was power for you.

She put down her glass and got to her feet, feeling suddenly tired in victory. She picked up her bag. 'I'll be seeing you,' she said. 'Oh, John?'

He looked up.

She thought of softness, of someone always waiting for her, someone always there, and the loneliness of her empty flat lay agape in front of her.

She'd loved his wife. Wanted one of her own.

She swallowed hard. 'Be nice to Chrissie,' she said.

52

The following morning, Monday, Megan got up early so as to be in work before Lisa arrived.

'Are you coming back?' Bill asked her as she put on her jacket.

'Yes, I am. I'll be home by five. Big red hand on the twelve, little red hand on the five.'

'But you're still like the daddy, aren't you?'

Megan smiled. There wasn't enough time to go into it, but yes, she supposed he was right. Nothing had changed for Bill. She was still like the daddy.

Before she left, the letter from Social Services arrived saying that they would like to pay a visit. She passed it to Larry. 'They want to come on Wednesday. I'll take the day off.'

She kissed them and left.

A confrontation with Lisa wasn't the kind of thing she could plan, but the thought of her malice in ringing the Social Services made a confrontation necessary.

She was in the kitchen when she heard the hum of the lift and the subsequent jolt and the doors slide open and the click of Lisa's heels on the pale wood floor.

Forgetting the coffee, she went into the office.

'Lisa –'

Lisa combed her fingers through the gelled ridges of her hair. 'Yeah, I know. Sorry. Stupid thing to do. I wanted you to stay. I thought you'd be more likely to if you had Bill with you.'

The simplicity of the explanation whammed the breath out of Megan. She's lonely, she thought suddenly, and wondered how she hadn't seen it before. Lisa lived her life by different rules from the rest of the world and that was lonely enough in itself. Lisa had tried to warn her. *I do things my way, it's the only way I know.*

You took her as she was, or you left her alone. There were a lot of people in the latter camp, Megan thought.

'I suppose I should do the decent thing,' Lisa said, her green eyes cool.

Startled, Megan looked up. 'What? Shoot yourself?'

Lisa grinned and Megan started to laugh.

She reshuffled her thoughts and raked her fingers through her hair. 'Without you – the funny thing is – it's looking all right again. More or less.' The phone rang and she shrugged and picked it up. 'Zelda? Yes, actually, if you want to ease back in gently how about Wednesday? I'm taking the day off. What do you mean, can you bring the baby in? No you can't, we're too busy.' She held the receiver away from her ear. 'Behave, Zelda. Bye.'

'That was Zelda?' The old joke.

'Yes . . . I'm not sure you can shoot yourself after all.' She gave a sigh. 'I don't think Zelda in her heart of hearts actually wants to come back,' she said. 'We're all after the ideal, aren't we, and never get any nearer to finding it.'

Lisa looked at the mail she'd picked up on the way in. 'What would your ideal be?' she asked curiously, putting a couple of envelopes aside.

'Not to ever have to work again,' Megan said, smiling dreamily, thinking of Bill. 'No, you see, that's not true. I like working. I suppose ideally I'd like to work for a couple of days a week. I couldn't afford to, of course.'

'What if Larry got a job? Like – if he went back to Xylus, for example?'

Megan raised her eyebrows. 'Or if I won the lottery,' she said.

At five o'clock, Bill was in her arms again and Larry had champagne waiting in a bucket on the floor.

'Burgess rang today.'

'Oh?' she said, nuzzling Bill's silky hair.

'John King has resigned. He told Burgess he was like a killer slug and should get me back on the team. Same car, more money and I'd be a director.'

'You don't want to take it, do you?' she asked, thinking of Triton, but she looked at the champagne all the same.

Bill got impatient and she put him down and looked at Larry.

His eyes were asking for understanding as he took her hands in his. They felt warm and familiar.

'Meg, I'm going to think about it. I know what I said about getting a job but the truth is, Meg, I have to be practical. And like it or not, there's no going back. Even working with Burgess I'm never going to be the Larry that I was. And this charity, For Fathers Alone – well, if I'm going ahead with it I need money to start it up.'

'Lisa's a witch,' she said, wonderingly, and was surprised at Larry's response.

'Yes, she forced his resignation, I'm sure of that. Even if she hadn't, it was only a matter of time. There's a limit to the amount of time you can keep taking back-handers. Someone was bound to wonder why he was so against going over to a new company for our sales literature.'

Megan didn't miss the 'our'. She squeezed his hands tightly. 'I love you,' she said, and she loved him for the one thing he hadn't mentioned. She knew by the way he was holding her what it was.

He's doing this for me.

53

James was eating a bowl of Sharwood's curry for his supper.

He had a baggy sweatshirt on, and jeans.

There was a letter propped up against the television and his eyes kept on going back to it, although he knew it word for word.

> Dear Daddy,
>
> We are NOT going to board as it is only because charles, (small c) has such DISGUSTING habits and shaves his CHEST and hates us laughing. We want to be WEEKLY boarders and stay with you at weekends. We don't mind the fishing. PLEASE TELL MUM and don't forget about the NAVEL PIERCING, we are nearly 12.
>
> HUGS and LOVE,
> Karin and Jen.
> LOVE YOU DADDY.
> PS Hope your appendix is better.

James licked his spoon and wondered – did Charles shave his chest?

And wondered something else, too; why Lydia had told them it was his appendix and not an overdose. Guilt, maybe. Love – not for him, though: that living nightmare had passed. Poor Lydia, gain a man and lose the girls. It was a high price to pay for a man who shaved his chest. Allegedly.

The doorbell rang and he put the bowl down and went and

opened it and felt, rather than saw, a wash of green gaze and a bunch of lilies and a bottle of brandy.

All his sensations came alive at once at the smell of her perfume, taking him back . . . he didn't know where.

'Who goes there, behind the shrubbery?' he asked.

'Me. This is the Lisa Ashridge Get Well Kit, patent pending.'

'You'd better bring it in, then.'

He got rid of the bowl of curry and came back to find her sitting on his carpet, her hair loose around her shoulders and the lilies on the floor. The brandy cork was in her hand, oh boy, a vision of loveliness, he thought.

'I won't mess about,' she said. 'I was with Larry when we found you that day.'

'Yes, he told me.' The perfume, he thought. He must have smelled it then.

She picked up a lily. The pollen exploded off it in a yellow cloud. 'I've got a proposition for you. I want a flatmate. I work bloody hard, James, and I want someone to come home to who'll be waiting with a drink and a warm pair of arms. I won't pay you but I'll feed you and buy you clothes. Good ones. And a haircut.' She put the lily down and danced her fingers up the brandy bottle. 'And the other thing is, sometimes I get lucky, so I want my weekends free.'

'A flatmate,' James said softly.

'Yes.'

'Sounds more as if you need a wife, to me.'

He was surprised to see the tears in her eyes.

'When do I start?' he asked.

54

Lisa was in the interview room, grilling someone in her enthusiastic way.

Megan came in at three. The man from Social Services had been understanding and professional, and had said that though they had an obligation to follow things up, they were more than happy to find out when nothing was amiss.

Zelda was on the phone, and her warm and seductive voice was as beguiling as ever, but when she hung up she looked less than enamoured with her brief return to work. She had been hoping to ease herself back into it gently, but they were too busy for that.

'How's Lisa? She seems to get things done.'

'She might have a garish personal life but she's damned good at the job,' Megan said. 'It would be a shame to lose her, really.'

Zelda was squinting at Megan's screen. 'But if I come back, we won't need her.'

Megan sat back in her chair. 'Well, I've been thinking about that. You want to spend more time with the children and ideally, I'd like to spend more time at home. If we did a job share, two and a half days a week each, we could keep Lisa on.'

Zelda looked interested for a moment. Then she made a face. 'Wouldn't work.'

'Why wouldn't it?'

'We'd only have half a salary each. I couldn't afford to keep Ruth on if I only worked two and a half days.'

It was time for Megan to play her ace. 'The idea is, we could share Ruth as well.' And rub it in. 'I'd have to have a part-time nanny for Bill because as well as working for Burgess, Larry's going to be busy with the Charities Commission. He's setting up a scheme, For Fathers Alone.' She was on the home straight. 'Just think, Zelda, you'd have the house to yourselves for three days a week.'

She saw a faraway look come into Zelda's eyes. 'We'd be able to have steaks again.'

'And eggs and toast soldiers.'

'And the children, by ourselves. We could sneak them to Kidz Grub. Organic food can be very boring.' She smiled. 'Whatever happened to She-Man?'

Megan smiled. 'She grew sensible.'

On Saturday, Bill was sitting under the table, hidden by the yellow cloth. He liked the yellow cloth. It was like being in the Cozy Coupe.

He knew what it meant when things were upside-down.

His house had been upside-down for ages, just like his father had said.

His mother had been his father and his father had been Ruth and Ruth had been someone else's Zoofie and that was as upside-down as it could get, he could see that now. It was when things were not quite as they were supposed to be.

But suddenly they'd been put almost the right way up.

His father had got a job again and was going back to work. He was glad about that.

His mother had got rid of half her job and was going to be a mummy for the rest of the time. He was happy about that, too.

And Ruth, whom he'd missed, was coming back to look after him some of the time when his mother was working, so he was looking forward to *that*.

338

It was almost the right way up, but he, he was going to be the one completely responsible person amongst them to put things straight.

He was going to school.

Divorcing Jack

Colin Bateman

'Richly paranoid and very funny' *Sunday Times*

Dan Starkey is a young journalist in Belfast, who shares with his wife Patricia a prodigious appetite for drinking and partying. Then Dan meets Margaret, a beautiful student, and things begin to get out of hand.

Terrifyingly, Margaret is murdered and Patricia kidnapped. Dan has no idea why, but before long he too is a target, running as fast as he can in a race against time to solve the mystery and to save his marriage.

'A joy from start to finish . . . Witty, fast-paced and throbbing with menace, *Divorcing Jack* reads like *The Thirty-Nine Steps* rewritten for the '90s by Roddy Doyle' *Time Out*

'Grabs you by the throat . . . a magnificent debut. Unlike any thriller you have ever read before . . . like *The Day of the Jackal* out of the Marx Brothers' *Sunday Press*

'Fresh, funny . . . an Ulster Carl Hiaasen' *Mail on Sunday*

ISBN 0 00 647903 0

Frank Delaney

A Stranger in Their Midst

INNOCENCE IS NO DEFENCE . . .

In village Ireland of the 1950s, Thomas and Ellen Kane's daughters, Helena and Grace, are gullible young women. Then, into their lives slinks Dennis Sykes, a brilliant and driven man, with a secret history of emotional mayhem and scandal. The Kane girls, lovingly close in fear of their disturbed father, have no defences against this sexual terrorist. As the decades roll forward, the outside world comes to Deanstown. Rural electrification, intended to illuminate the land, brings instead a tragedy as dark as Thomas Kane's moods.

Using great dramatic themes – the drowning of traditional houses in an ancient valley to build a dam, the destruction of a family's inner life – Delaney draws you in deep, into a time, and place, and family, in a novel that will keep you thinking long after you've finished reading.

'*A Stranger in Their Midst* is a dramatic novel. Written in clear, dry prose, it seldom loses its conviction.'   *The Times*

'Blast Frank Delaney. With his devious, seductive writing he keeps story addicts from their sleep.'   *OK!*

'Frank Delaney's *A Stranger in Their Midst* is excellent.'
Woman and Home

'A powerful story vividly told.'   *Choice*

'A good old-fashioned tale of simple Irish folk doing battle with the future.'   *Evening Standard*

ISBN: 0 00 649318 1
(Published in paperback in May 1996)

Memory and Desire
Lisa Appignanesi

Paris, Autumn 1934. Dr Jacob Jardine glimpses a figure from his deepest imaginings: Sylvie Kowalska, half temptress, half innocent child. Despite himself, he is drawn into a troubled, erotic world in which the past haunts the present. A world which casts Sylvie first as the darling of bohemian Paris and, when war erupts, as a fearless member of the Resistance.

New York, 1980. Katherine Jardine has cast off her European heritage, but is now forced to face a past – and a mother – she would rather forget. It appears she holds the key to a thirty-five-year-old mystery. But at its centre is Sylvie's enigmatic light, still burning bright. Her chaotic, ensnaring web of memory and desire still has the power to entangle lives across two continents and two generations . . .

'A superbly plotted saga of passion and heartbreak. Appignanesi will keep you guessing until the last full stop.'
                                        Kate Saunders, *Cosmopolitan*

'A darkly erotic novel, *Memory and Desire* lays bare the many faces of a modern Eve.'   Sally Beauman

ISBN 0 00 617982 7

Absolute Truths

Susan Howatch

Charles Ashworth is privileged, pampered and pleased with himself. As Bishop of Starbridge in 1965 he 'purrs along as effortlessly as a well-tuned Rolls Royce' while he proclaims his famous 'absolute truths' to a society which he sees - with rage and revulsion - as increasingly immoral and disordered. But then a catastrophe tears his life apart and confronts him with the real absolute truths, truths which strip him of his pride and leave him struggling for survival.

Grappling with the revelation that he has failed his wife and sons, Charles's guilt steadily drives him into the immoral and disordered life he has condemned so violently in others. Fighting the threat of a complete breakdown he then embarks on a quest to rebuild his life, a quest which leads him to a final battle with his old enemy Dean Aysgarth in the shadow of Starbridge Cathedral.

'Compelling... I could not put it down'   *Sunday Times*

ISBN 0 00 649688 1